THE RELUCTANT OPENING—MARCH 12, 2009

Finally broke open this fricking notebook. A gift from Maggie: For my brother Dexter—May this book help you through the days to come. Love, Maggie.

This journal calls to me like a weak child yearning to suckle. The pages parched, aching to be quenched with ink. Haven't touched it for two years. Leather spine and all. Pages like the ones on which Dr. Johnson would've written. Maggie keeps asking about it. Don't want to admit I've opened it and am now writing in it out of pure guilt, but that seems to be the case.

So. The beginning, then.

Nobody takes me seriously. My colleagues especially. I love it. I roll down the English floor: a strutting cripple, shoulders lifted, baseball cards rustling on my chair's wheels, driving Hilde, the secretary, berserk. Plickety-plickety-plickety. Tell your chair to shut up, Dexter! I would, but he's not tame yet. You want me to risk life and limb? I leave gum in the water fountains. Really rebellious.

I love teaching. I've no illusions, though; I'm not Rumpelstiltskin. My students' minds are not straw for me to magically turn into gold. I do my job and if they don't learn, no fault of mine. You, the one with the phone and the haircut like day-old spaghetti. Turn to "The Love Song of J. Alfred Prufrock" and explain why the speaker is so alienated. You, young woman with the botox. Have you found the passage between Constance and Oliver? Good, now I'd like you to read it from the beginning. Start with the phrase "And you talk so coldly about sex." How many complaints over the last year? Even students' parents come to the school to see me. How wonderful to meet you, Mr. Schultz. You've raised a fine daughter, but unfortunately she can't tell the difference between a plot summary and a play. I recommend vigorous re-education: a sledgehammer to the head and a job in a chicken factory. Enjoy your drive home.

McTavish will never do anything. My research reputation's too impeccable for dismissal. I do need to watch my mouth, though. The whole department's a fricking Green Party caucus. Politically correct bunch, they purport to be. But I catch them out. They cringe when I tell a joke like, What did the quadriplegic deaf boy get for Christmas? And it's not even out of outrage that they glare at me. I can tell. It's envy. Pure and simple. I know they've told such jokes before and laughed their asses off. I know our Aboriginal specialist has told handfuls of Indian jokes, although he won't admit it.

Nobody wants to be equal. People simply want to be recognized. They want to be known and they want the power associated with being known. Thankfully, my body and my temperament serve me well in this regard. At first I hated my disability. Who the hell gets peroneal muscular atrophy? I did and I hated it at first. My body's betrayed me. It's not like when a woman betrays you—you just toss her to the curb and be done with it. Disability's embedded in you. I flexed, I fought, I festered. Some days I swear I could feel the power slowly draining from my muscles. Like a vampire was feeding on me. I broke mirrors, drank whiskey, failed my students on their essays. Before the chair, I was a prick. I admit it. Not the loveable kind, either. But I grew into my disability. It became a lens, a salvation of sorts, a place for me to focus my anger. If Camus and Eliot, bless their afflicted souls, had a lovechild, I'd be the hissing mangled product of their union.

Though it's hardly good for my reputation as an academic, I spend my days professing and the rest of the time in the Armstrong Residence for People with Disabilities, getting Epsom-salt baths, receiving vigorous rubdowns to try and awaken my depleting muscles, and gripping for dear life the hips of a young nurse, even when I don't need help with the toilet. The irony's tasty only to me: an internationally renowned pioneer of the disability studies movement spends his nights in a home crammed with a motley detritus worthy of P.T. Barnum.

My reason is simple. Life is easier this way. Since I don't have a wife, why not settle for the next best thing?

Dinnertime. Chicken, roast potatoes, and Greek salad. I smirk because I doubt that my colleagues, scurrying to meet their grant application deadlines or carting their children to gymnastics and finger-painting lessons, eat half as well.

ADAM POTTLE

BACK FOR MORE—MARCH 13, 2009

Surprised myself by having fun while writing here yesterday. Thought I'd keep a good thing going so I'm not here out of guilt, but for my own amusement.

My penmanship may become sloppier over time. Symptomatic of my obscure and unpredictable disease.

Peroneal muscular atrophy is known by its more common name, Charcot-Marie-Tooth disease. It's apparently hereditary, although I've never heard of anyone in my family having it, and it usually shows up in the late teens, but it can sometimes present later in life. My feet look a little like Roman arches—like I've been gripping bars with them all my life. I've a Gumby spine now, thanks to the resulting scoliosis. My shoulders and arms sometimes jiggle as the result of tremors caused by wasted muscle. I use a wheelchair to save my feet the torture. I'm constantly in pain.

My doctor goes berserk whenever she sees me: with her dark eyes sliding to the floor, she says, Most people with Charcot-Marie-Tooth get treatment and don't need wheelchairs. Nobody lets it progress like you do, Dr. Ripley. She called my case unprecedented. I love that word. Before my diagnosis I'd been an expert in British literature; I still am, though with a more focused specialization. After a few years the brilliant honey haze of Jack Daniel's slid away, and I started to see new patterns in the literature I love, and when I began studying those patterns, I began seeing myself in a deliriously wonderful way. Like a yogi, my body is continually bent into new positions, from which I must work to see clearly. I love my life. I love the Residence. I love the university. My condition will worsen over time. I've accepted that. In fact I embrace it, because the way I see it, and as I mentioned earlier, my disability has given me the proper perspective. The more disabled I become, the clearer I'm able to see the world. The sheen, streamline

and harmony fall away and I see the fat, jagged, grimy gristle of the soul. I'm forty-six now; by the time I'm fifty or fifty-five I hope to have x-ray vision.

HOW TO STAND OUT AMIDST A CONFEDERACY OF DUNCES—MARCH 28, 2009

This little bit before I go to bed. Gertrude's watching my door waiting for the light to go out. Not to be mean. It's her job. The staff at the Armstrong Residence aren't pushy or rude. They love me. Probably because I'm the only resident with whom they can have a real conversation. The others do well enough to last a few minutes, but then they get bored and want to play cribbage or watch a *Chronicles of Narnia* DVD.

In my first entry I called my fellow residents "a motley detritus worthy of P.T. Barnum." That was unfair. From what I can discern, they're good people. It's hard to tell, though, with cripples. People often mistake simplicity or ignorance or impairment for innocence. Dicks come in all shapes and colours. For every Tiny Tim there's an Ahab; for every Forrest Gump, a Hannibal Lecter. Intelligence and ability do not dictate morals. They merely exacerbate them.

One or two of the residents, especially Old Scratch, sometimes look at me suspiciously. Like I shouldn't be here. It's understandable. I don't interact much with the other residents. I'm either working or talking with the staff. I call him Old Scratch because his face has satanic angles. He looks like he belongs in a Dickens novel: high cheekbones, V-shaped face, pointed chin, curls of scepticism around his mouth and eyes. He speaks very little. I don't know his real name. I forget his condition but I remember hearing it affects the central nervous system. Some days I can hear him breathing down the hall. Wet and skidding. As though oxygen is hydroplaning up and down his throat. I refuse to pity him, though. I don't pity anyone. It's useless.

SPATIAL CONCERNS—APRIL 8, 2009

End of semester flurry. Lots to catch up on; hence the sporadic entries. Sometimes when I try to make a check mark on a student's paper, it ends up being a scribble, because of my tremors. Going to do an experiment and see if they try to decipher the scribbles in the margins. Dr. Ripley, what does this mean? It's Greek for learn to read.

The Residence sits on the southern edge of Saskatoon. Mansion-sized. Jacuzzi and exercise room and lounge and cafeteria. Four grassy acres crosshatched with paved walking paths. My room's tucked into the Residence's corner. Smallest room in the Residence: shelves upon shelves of books, a floor-to-ceiling *Edward Scissorhands* movie poster, a desk, a dresser, and just enough floor space to twist my chair around.

Once I finish my marking I have to prepare for a conference in New York. I'm headlining a panel on how disability is portrayed in North American culture. Need to unfurl some expectations. Stick my claw under their skin and wriggle it a little. Then maybe go to a Yankees game and weasel my way down to field level and poke fun at the pinstripes. Rub my peter, Jeter. Where's your entourage, Rodriguez? I'm hardly a baseball fan but I follow it enough to be allowed to complain.

ROLLING ON AIR—APRIL 29, 2009

En route to NY. Kept giving the flight attendant instructions as he was carrying me from the jetway to my seat. Watch out for that stroller. If you drop me I'm gonna sue your ass. Ooh, that tickles. Storage limit one hundred and fifty pounds. I could fit up there, don't you think? Got a first-class seat. Extra leg room for my shrivelled limbs. People walk past wondering what the hell I'm doing here. He doesn't need all that room, they're thinking. Like putting a midget in a king-sized bed. I sip my gin and think, God bless grant foundations that favour minorities.

The attendant dotes on me. Pudgy yet cute. Her hip brushes tantalizingly against my elbow. Just doing her job, though. When her day's over I'm sure she unfurls her hair, grabs a beer, and says Thank god I'm off that goddamn plane. People who act considerately are either faking it to work in their favour or they're genuine, and usually dull. To my delight, more people fake it than are genuine. Fakery makes the world go round. It's entertaining because we're perpetually discovering one another. People who are genuinely considerate have no layers. That's all they are. This is why I can't attend the United Way fundraisers our department keeps sponsoring. Too much good for my taste.

Wow. Have I become a lightweight. Only one glass and I think I'm in my chair about to tip down the aisle. Must be the pain meds. Well, what better place to relearn how to drink than NY?

Might need to watch it, though. I won't have any of the care workers looking after me. Could use a massage right now. My feet feel like they're arching all the way up into my ankles.

BACK TO EARTH—MAY 4, 2009

Back at the Residence now. Left the conference yesterday. Gertrude picked me up at the airport. Didn't write anything here because, as I mentioned in my previous entry, I relearned how to drink, and was hardly in a patient enough state to write. I delivered my paper. I enjoyed the applause. I shot down the sharks who tried to undermine my ideas. I did the necessary networking and catching up with colleagues. I extolled my ambition to come up with a new word for "disability," something more uplifting and galvanizing. Returned home nursing a cracking headache and a boiling gut. On the plus side, my tremors have relaxed, allowing me to write.

One or two points of interest came up at the conference. At the banquet on the second evening a woman named Mildred Archer approached me. A tall, older brunette with rich round hips, she must've been something in the eighties. She brought me a rum and coke and began talking about a film studio operating out of Toronto. This particular studio, she said, produces films exclusively starring persons with disabilities. We're aiming to be the most progressive film studio in Canada. What's the name of the studio? It's called Freaky Productions. Freaky Productions? Yes. It's a pornographic studio. I smirked. It's a legitimate operation, she said, privately funded, with no tolerance of drugs or abuse. The result is surprisingly sexy. I chuckled. No drugs or abuse, eh? I thought you said this was legit porn. I sipped my drink and studied her crotch; though loose around the ankles, her black pants hugged her hips and tucked neatly into her lap, forming a tantalizing V. And do you want me to star in a film? I'm here as a promoter, she said, handing me a CD in a plastic case. In black felt pen someone had scrawled the title, *My Left Foot Job*. I laughed. I could see it: a woman with palsy masturbating her lover, his penis wedged between her toes. I know you're more of a risk-taker, Ms. Archer said, which is why I'm giving this to you. I held up the disc. You don't look

like a porn peddler. You're not a performer on here, are you? She shook her head. It's not just about porn. It's about a message. What message? Of freedom. Pleh. To make porn is not freedom. It is with this kind of porn. I huffed and tucked the CD into my bag. We separated and began talking to other people. I haven't watched the CD yet, though I wonder if it actually is sexy.

Old Scratch looks perkier than normal. On the way home from the airport Gertrude told me his family had to take away his chequebook. He'd been writing cheques to himself and then depositing them into his account. His family took it as a sign of dementia, so they seized the chequebook. I chortled when Gertrude told me. Old Scratch knows better. It's nothing more than an old-fashioned cry for attention. And now that he's received his attention, he's in higher spirits—still silent and brooding, but with visible buoyancy in his knurled limbs, the curls around his mouth smooth and relaxed.

Lurch in the gut. Like a child below the surface of the water grunting and straining to break through. Need to go.

Better now. Gertrude's a saint. She handles me like a champ. Having anticipated my tiredness, she was making me a pot of coffee. She was about to bring me a cup when I rolled through and she asked if I needed help. She got me onto the toilet and maintained a smile even in the face of my stink. Normally, on a day like today when my tremors are slackened, I can do everything myself. But the trip and the drinking taxed me. I did everything myself while in New York. I could've asked for an assistant, but I chose not to. In such a public setting, my reputation required padding.

The last time I visited her, the physiotherapist recommended daily exercise. Might begin that now, though I'm pretty sure the arches in my feet and the tremors in my shoulders are here to stay no matter what sort of stretches I perform or pills I ingest.

PRESSURE SORE—MAY 10, 2009

Had a gloriously unusual dream last night. I stood in the middle of a field just outside Saskatoon. I was naked. I looked at my feet but they didn't hurt. My feet and hands grew more and more rigid and hooked. My skin glowed green and hardened to the consistency of a clam shell. My elbows acquired spines, teeth. I giggled as I bent them. My spine curved and sprouted sharp green wings. I kept giggling. I started making spitting noises, which spurred me into spitting laughter. My body stretched upwards and outwards; my joints made crackling sounds. I grew a hundred feet tall and became a giant praying mantis. I crouched and then exploded upwards, leaping a kilometre in a single bound. The power thrilled me. I landed on the highway and, out of elation, kicked over a semi. I swiped a Hummer out of my way. I jaunted through downtown Saskatoon and with my astonishingly telescopic eyes could see all the way to Toronto, where it was equally sunny and boisterous. People clapped for me in the street, even as I stomped on them. I guffawed in my spitting mantis way. I loved their admiration.

Windy this morning. High-pitched and whiny. Like the third string of a girl's choir. When I woke up I rolled over and felt like I left a blotch of skin on the sheet. A pressure sore. Just above my keister. Stayed in the same spot for too long.

Not the first time I've had one in that spot. It hurts. I feel it as I brush against my chair: a dragging squeak, like when you rub your hand over plastic. Needed ointment rubbed into it. I have to keep adjusting in my chair throughout the day.

I loathe summers. They make me feel aimless. I have lots of work to do—papers to write, grants to apply for, classes to plan—but without the in-session bustle of the university, it's difficult to conjure motivation. It's easier to work when you're surrounded by others working, and none of the other residents work.

Maggie gives me shit for living here. Well, not shit; guilt. She says I don't have to. She was here the other day, a Timmy's cup in her hand, sitting on my bed. I don't like visiting out in the open, with the other residents watching.

Maggie. Fifty-three years old, divorced, works for the federal government. A year ago, she cropped her hair and dyed it red, and now it squats limply above her brow, like a rooster's wattle. She always looks uncomfortable, her eyes swinging to and fro, her neck muscles jammed. When she wears pantsuits, she appears too official; when she wears hoodies, she looks like she's forcing herself to be casual, like she hopes her clothes will dictate her mood. For her, self-consciousness seems to be a way of life, borne out of an insecurity that seems to have no source. She was confident and independent when we were younger; if I ever galled her, she harangued me with the rigid efficiency of a Chinese private school teacher. Now, our relationship floats on a wobbly current of guilt and antagonism. At best, we annoy each other; at worst, we privately nurse jagged outrages.

You're a smart man, Maggie said. Surely you feel you don't have to stay here. You're not like them. I frowned. She asked me if I want to try living with her for a month or two. She lives in a small house with her son, Randal, a fifteen-year-old boy who aspires to be a pharmacist. A pharmacist, for god's sakes. I told Maggie no. She dipped her head in that manner she has. Pouting without the lip. I don't understand, she said. Sorry, I said. She looked at my curved feet. Are you in pain? Not really. I lifted my leg and scratched my calf. Can you even stand anymore? No. It hurts like hell when I do.

Maggie tilted her head. I felt the conversation veering toward physiotherapy, so I said I had work to do and escorted her out. Old Scratch scrunched his V-shaped face into a vile grimace as we passed him in the living room. Maggie saw him and, as she went out the door, asked me to think about living with her and Randal. I closed the door after her and turned to Old Scratch. Never get collagen, I told him.

Your scowl is just perfect.

There are eleven residents in total; I hang around two or three of them. One of them is Old Scratch, and that's simply because he doesn't bullshit. I know he's suspicious because I'm an academic, a thinker, and therefore I don't belong in a home where people do little or nothing for themselves. It's possible he hates me, which is strangely comforting. When he plays horseshoes in the modified pit on the grounds, I wheel up and watch. Plickety-plickety-plickety. He clenches the shoe too tight and often throws wide of the peg. He's a competitive bastard and goes berserk when he misses. When he yells at me, his voice drags over some sort of mucousy concoction of phlegm, turpentine, and Fireball whiskey. Fuck off, he'll say to me, glaring at the baseball cards jammed in my wheels. I'm just watching. You're fuckin me up. Go home. This is my home, Old Scratch. Stop callin me that, you skinny twit. It's just a nickname, a term of endearment. Go the fuck home. He'll lift a horseshoe like he means to throw it at me. One of the staff will step in. Dr. Ripley, maybe it's best you go inside. I pout a little and turn my chair. We'll duel again, Old Scratch! Eeeeeegh! I glance back and he's wheezing. The staff member scolds us both. As I go back inside, I realize that he seldom sees his family and spends his precious breath yelling at me. It's an honour of sorts.

Reginald's another resident whose company I enjoy. I call him Jeeves, after the P.G. Wodehouse character. While most of the other residents have run-of-the-mill disabilities—dementia, M.S., Alzheimer's and the like—he has a unique condition, something called Korsakoff's syndrome. His memory's been permanently damaged by alcoholism. Nobody will tell me the exact cause, but his dense eyes and the constellations of gin blossoms on his face make it pretty obvious. To fill in the gaps, he makes up false memories. It's endlessly entertaining. When I feel like it, I help him create memories. I'll roll up to him and say, Jeeves, you remember you were telling me about when you worked for Trudeau? How many girls did he have while you

were there? You get any on the side? Or, Jeeves, how many lions did you kill when you went hunting in Africa? Gertrude gives me shit for this. Leave him alone, Doctor. He's using his imagination. It's better than just leaving him vacuous in front of the TV. He has an extraordinary imagination. He could tell me what it smelled like in Africa. The grass was so dry it rattled in the wind, he said, like plastic almost. We saw giraffes first thing in the morning, a mother and her calf. (I looked it up online and saw that a giraffe baby is indeed called a calf.) He told me about the guide who drove him through the terrain and what the lion looked like when he shot it. I saw his eyes, he said. Two big globes. It was hot outside. No global warming or nothing then. Just pure heat. I stood up from my spot on the ground and walked over. He was still alive and I wanted to get closer. I came over the grass and saw his mane. His mane was all fluffy, no blood on it. His flank was a mess. I saw his ribs. He was huge. Four hundred pounds. He kinda rolled his giant head and blinked at me. Jeeves mimicked the movements he described, tilting his head and staring into space. I'll never forget the sound he made, he said. Not as long as I live. I don't know how to describe it but I haven't heard a sound like that since. Jeeves shook his head. When was this. Nineteen-seventy-three. Before I got married. That lion's eyes, two dark globes. They looked as big as my fist. I wanted to cup them in my hand. Jeeves started to cry. I left him alone, awed by the power of his imagination. He'd make the perfect actor.

Pressure sore's acting up. Need to lie down.

Redfaced—May 20, 2009

The pain in my feet has turned sonic. It makes an alarming bending noise in my bones, arching all the way up to my brain stem, raising my hackles. A noise like when Christopher Reeve bent a steel pipe. I took Vicodin.

My tremors are worse than usual today, too. My penmanship will suffer. Ah well. At least I don't have to worry about someone reading this. Even if someone does, he won't be able to understand a damn thing.

Finally got around to watching that video. Late last night I put the CD into my laptop and put my headphones on. I was greeted by a cheap version of *My Left Foot*. Instead of Daniel Day-Lewis in a wheelchair, there's a blonde young woman in a wheelchair: pasty skin, overdone makeup, breasts tucked behind her crossed arms. A man with a limp pushes her down a hill and into the house. There, they act out a condensed, almost parodic montage of the original film. The discovery of her left foot's dexterity. Her first painting. Her first typing. And then, prompted by the man's line, I wonder what else you're capable of, my dear, her first foot job. It is wholly unsexy: a grunt here, a slip there. I spend the entire time wondering how she doesn't cut him with her toenails. It's only when the man stands and puts his penis in her mouth that I notice my unsteady hands undoing my zipper. She removes her clothes then. The man picks her up out of her chair and puts her on the bed. I discover three things: she actually has lovely, pert breasts; she is impressively adept in bed (as is custom in the porn industry, the title must've been used for parody purposes only), conveying an arousing aura of both vulnerability and aggression, her palsy-sharpened limbs alternately locking up the man and cradling him; and having a tremor in your shoulder can bring unexpected pleasure when masturbating. It adds a bit of uncertainty. One minute I control the amount of force with which I squeeze; the next minute I don't. It's a strange and wonderful sensation.

Just as another unexpected tremor flicked up and I finished into a dining room napkin, Gertrude opened the door. Ah! she said. Sorry! Sorry sorry sorry! She closed the door. I fumbled with my pants and slammed down my laptop's screen. I saw the light on, she said from the hallway. I pulled off my headphones. You're supposed to knock! I said. I'm sorry, I did knock, she said. When you didn't say anything I thought something was up. Go away! I said. I'm sorry, Dr. Ripley. Go! You're okay? Go away!

I pushed off from my desk and faced away from the door, still fumbling with my zipper. I sat there for a while. Picked up the napkin from the floor and put it in the wastebasket. Mourned the fact none of the residents are allowed locks on their doors. I blushed from my armpits upwards, thinking, Please god, Old Scratch didn't hear me.

I haven't left my room yet. Haven't had breakfast. It's nearly noon. Gertrude must've informed the other staff and they're avoiding me now. Letting me come out on my own terms. I'm hungry. I want them to bring me something. Going to call for some lunch to be delivered.

Finished lunch. Asked the worker, his name was Stefan, if anyone knew of what happened last night. He said he didn't know. I asked him if I could have a lock on my door. He said no. As I ate I heard people moving in the hallway. I listened for and eventually heard the telltale ragged breathing of Old Scratch. He chuckled. His voice boogie-boarded over puddles of battery acid: You know what I feel like eating? A good long slice of beef jerky. He emphasized jerky; the k had a curt, squishy quality, like cleaving a fish in two. When I get bored with being in my room, or when I have to go to the bathroom, I'm going to corner Gertrude and give her hell.

Feet hurt. My arches creak. As though about to collapse. Might have to switch to a computer before this is all over. My writing is so shaky and my back hurts. Need to cut it off for today.

Birthday Hats Look Like Dunce Hats—May 24, 2009

Today's my birthday. Spent the morning listening to Jeeves tell me about the time he went skydiving and accidentally landed in a rubber chicken factory. I supplied the setting; he supplied the details. Swear to god, even William Burroughs soaring on the wings of a heroin flight couldn't come up with the things Jeeves does.

Maggie and Randal took me to a restaurant on Twenty-first Street called Amarello's. Predictably, Maggie gave me a gift certificate to the bookstore and a memory stick with family pictures on it. Now you can use that picture frame on your desk, she said. I grunted. Last Christmas she gave me a digital picture frame, the kind into which you download photographs and they move in a kind of never-ending slideshow. It's parked beside my computer, empty as the Canadian literary canon. I tucked the stick into my bag and leaned into Randal, asking him questions. He surprised me, even impressed me. I hadn't seen him for a year at least. He'd been living with his dad for a while. A bit short for a fifteen-year-old. Observant, though. Alert. I asked him if he plans to start a grow-op when he finishes his pharmacy degree. He said it'd be a waste of money, that he could do it any time. Maggie scolded him. I chuckled. I motioned for him to come closer and told him my quadriplegic-deaf-kid joke. In reply he made a joke I didn't hear until my first year of university: What's the hardest part about cooking a vegetable? Putting the wheelchair in the pot. Maggie gasped and hissed his name. I laughed—hard, nearly bucking out of my chair. Not only because it was funny and surprising coming from him, but because as I studied him, I saw he truly understood the joke. I could tell from the steadiness of his eyes that, like me, he didn't think of it as merely a cheap laugh. He got the gravity of the situation, that it's something to be shared between an uncle and a nephew.

Two days after *My Left Foot Job* I was on my way through the living room and Old Scratch veered his chair in front of me. Big goddamn grin on his face. So how was the jerking? he said. I shook my head and tried to move past. He stayed in front of me. You're a weak boy, he said, being in a place like this. I scoffed. This isn't a place for you, he said. This is for other people. Not for you. Not your business, Old Scratch, I said. I gripped my wheels. A tremor buzzed through my shoulders. I hunched forward and tightened my grip. Shouldn't you be off writing bad cheques? He seized my wrist. I yanked it away from him. He pushed me. I pushed him back. He pushed me hard. I tilted over, half out of my chair. He pushed me all the way over. I collapsed against the wall. A resident in the living room called for the staff. Two staff members came and helped me up and took Old Scratch away. They reported us both, him more severely for antagonizing me. Since then he's retreated back into silence, though he still glares at me. I asked Gertrude about the lock again. Sorry, she said. Can't you discuss it with the board? I said. Can't I be granted exceptional status or something? I can talk to them myself. We'll keep an eye on Mr. Myrtle. At all times, Gertrude? He's nearly eighty, Doctor. Not that difficult to monitor. I sighed and rolled away. Slowed down when I went past his room. My baseball cards going plickety-plickety-plickety. I rolled back and forth and then down the hall when he opened his door.

MEMORY LANE IS NOT WHEELCHAIR ACCESSIBLE—
JUNE 2, 2009

Have heard little from Old Scratch lately. Gertrude told me he's been in his room for the past three days. Bedridden. Sucking from an oxygen tank. I guess hatred can be exhausting. Thought about putting a DO NOT DISTURB sign on his door but I don't want to be responsible for his having a heart attack.

Email from McTavish. Pegging me to teach a course on Canadian literature in the winter 2010 semester. The professor scheduled to teach it needs time off to look after his wife, who has cancer. I groaned when I read the email. I'm not even a Canadian literature specialist. I wrote one article on two Canadian novels, a very small sampling. From my limited experience, Mordecai Richler is probably the only Canadian worth reading. The others write like they're lost in traffic. McTavish said I owed him one. Which is true. He prevented me from being suspended two years ago. I told him I'll do it but that I'll lose some of my soul in the process.

Took the memory stick from Maggie and plugged it into the digital picture frame. Thought there'd be just one or two pictures. Discovered she'd scanned photos from our childhood into her computer and loaded them onto the stick. A picture of me wearing a Mickey Mouse t-shirt and short pants. One of Maggie with big seventies hair. Another of Randal holding a frog close to his face. Many more pictures of me from infancy to adolescence. In the slick frame they slide from one to the other. My youth always moving.

I try not to think too much about my childhood or about my life before Charcot-Marie-Tooth disease. Not that my childhood was terrible, although Maggie in her teens was a hellacious bitch. I just don't want to be discouraged by memories of able-bodied life. Such thoughts lodge a splinter into my mind, leaving it lousy with What ifs, preventing me from looking forward.

If I am to say something about my childhood, it's that I have two conclusions about it. One, Maggie dotes on me now because of how badly she treated me when we were younger. This one memory juts upwards from the rest. We'd been really angry with each other this one particular week, the way siblings sometimes are. Usually we were just annoyed with each other, but during this one week in the summer of 1970, the annoyances twisted into pure anger. I was no longer content with merely tattling on her. After she destroyed my small but hard-won collection of comic books, and tattling yielded few results, I sought revenge. So one night I invited my friend Emerson over. His father ran the general store in Warman, where we lived, and I'd asked him to swipe several bottles of black ink from the stockroom. Maggie had gone out with friends for the night. She kept her room locked but her window was just down from mine, and because it was summer the window was open a little. Emerson and I took the bottles of ink and filled a dozen water balloons. I held a red balloon up to my desk lamp. Tiny black bubbles slid up from the bottom. I squeezed it. The ink rose up to the end. The warm weight of it thrilled me. We tied the balloons, put them in a bag, and lifted my window. I stepped onto the roof of our farmhouse and carefully crossed over to Maggie's window. Tell me if someone's coming, I said to Emerson, who nodded and watched from my window. I dropped the balloons into Maggie's room and climbed in. Numerous posters covered her walls, all of them ordered by mail and paid for through her work at the greasy restaurant by the highway. Dustin Hoffman's dumbfounded face in *The Graduate*. Paul Newman's slick expression in *Cool Hand Luke*. Sean Connery's vacuous gaze in *From Russia with Love*. Above her bed was an autographed picture of Lee Marvin. For Maggie, it read. Thanks for your letter. All the best, love, Lee Marvin. I opened the bag of balloons and held one in each hand. Like Connery against his many foreign opponents, I coolly surveyed her room. Then I wound up and threw a balloon square into Lee Marvin's face. A shiny black splatter-

cloud exploded all over the wall and settled on her bed of fine flowery linen. I doused Dustin Hoffman and Paul Newman. I went into her closet and stuffed a balloon into each of her red high heels. Using a pen, I poked a hole in each; they collapsed like egg yolks, the ink spilling all over the floor. I began hurling balloons at random targets. Her desk. The ceiling. The teddy bear our grandmother had given her when she was a baby. This last target didn't yield an explosion; the balloon bounced off and burst on the floor. I came to the last balloon and, spotting Connery's face, whipped it in his direction. Plsssh. Taking a breath, I glanced around. The room looked like the aftermath of an octopus orgy: ink running in narrow tendrils down the walls, ink gathering in tiny pools in the knots of the floor planks, the faces of her idols dripping with black.

Dexter!

I spun. Emerson stood at the window. Your mom! I grabbed my bag and, wiping my black hands on Maggie's curtains, climbed out the window and scuttled back to my room with Emerson. Mom was knocking at my door. I opened it. She asked me if Emerson and I wanted milk. I said yes. She asked me what we were doing. I told her we were drawing. Drawing what? Dragonflies. Why are your hands covered in ink? It spilled. Not on the floor, Dexter. No, on the paper. I'll get you boys some milk. You'll have to show me your drawings when they're finished. She went downstairs and Emerson and I took a few sheets of paper and drew crude, scratchy dragonflies on them. Mom gave us our milk and looked quizzically at our drawings. I think these need some work, she said. Try some colour. Longer wings.

Soon after that we went to bed. I didn't sleep. I waited for Maggie to get home. I anticipated her shrieking, her sobbing. It had taken me months to amass my comic collection, in which I had spent countless hours happily ensconced in vast, detailed worlds that I understood to be far more serious than what Blondie and Archie Andrews had to offer. After I had tattled on her for the second time in a day, she had

gone into my room, opened my closet, taken my entire comic collection, which I'd organized alphabetically and stored on the upper shelf, and carried it downstairs and threw it into the fireplace. Dad was out of town for work—he was a farming equipment salesman and had to travel often—and Mom, although capable of extreme outrage, did not ground Maggie. She had a job, and if she was grounded, she'd go to our parents for money, something which, due to their thrifty natures, they wanted to avoid. In the end Mom merely forbade her from going to Saskatoon on the weekend to see the movies. I was appalled. To me, it was like having to pay a fine as punishment for murder. From that instant, despite Mom's warnings, I began planning my vengeance.

I kept looking at my bedside clock. Emerson was sound asleep on the floor. Maybe Maggie's screams'll wake him, I thought. Maybe he'll snap upwards and start screaming, too. I chuckled. The minutes lurched past. I listened for footsteps on the stairs. I listened to Mom listening to the radio. Finally I heard Maggie talking to Mom. Then the footsteps. I sat up in bed. I heard Maggie unlock and open her door. Then silence. I listened harder, leaning in her direction. More silence.

DEXTER!

She stomped to my door and began pounding. Dexter! Open! Open the door! Now! Open the damn door! Mom hustled up the stairs. What happened? Look! Oh my. I'm gonna kill him! Dexter! Maggie. Open the door! Maggie, move. Move! Maggie, stop it. Dexter! Dexter, you awake? Open the door right now.

Both Emerson and I stared at each other. Don't, he said. Don't tell them I gave you the ink.

Dexter? Mom said. I'm gonna rip his head off, Maggie said. Maggie, calm down. Maggie sobbed and growled in the same breath. He ruined my picture of Lee! And Dustin! Dexter, you have five seconds to open this door and then I'm going to open it, and if I have to open it it's not gonna be pleasant. You understand? One. Two. Three. Four.

Emerson covered his head with his blanket. I skipped over and opened the door. Just as the dim hallway light fell on me, Maggie lunged and seized the collar of my pyjama top. She jerked me forward; my head smacked against the wall. She clamped her hands around my throat and shook me and choked me. Mom pulled on her shoulders and tried to remove her hands. Maggie picked me up and slammed me into the corner. Mom saw her chance and wedged herself between Maggie and me. Stop it! She slapped Maggie on the cheek. Maggie huffed. Her face flushed with rage. Her shoulders rose and fell with each coarse breath. What're you gonna do about him? she said, staring at me. I want him locked in his room for a month. Okay, Mom said. Dexter, go downstairs and get the bucket and the sponge. You're going to clean up your sister's room until there's not one trace of that ink left. Look what he did! Maggie stood in her doorway, pointing into her room. She was crying now. He ruined all my posters! After you're done, Mom said to me, you go to bed. I'm going to call Emerson's mom to come and pick him up. Tomorrow morning I'm going to decide on further punishment for you. Now go. It's eleven o'clock.

As I walked past my room Emerson was still under his blanket. Maggie shoved me as I went past her. Little shit, she said. Mom told her to go downstairs and set up her bed on the couch and stay there until the morning. Then she called Emerson's mom and told Emerson to gather his things. As I carried a bucket full of hot soapy water up the stairs, he came down with his pillow and his backpack. I hung my head. You didn't tell? he said. No. Thanks. He cocked his head and continued down the stairs.

It was impossible to get all the ink out. It had mostly dried and I needed two more bucketfuls of water to get the walls and floor looking somewhat clean. Most of the ink on the wallpaper had to be scoured out. Maggie had taken her posters and rolled them up and stowed them away. She looked at me with equal parts hatred and bewilderment, like she was astonished that I could accomplish such

a sinister act, or that I thought she deserved such treatment. Once I got her room back to a close resemblance of its former neatness, I emptied the blackened water out of the bucket and went to bed at around two in the morning. I never slept.

The next morning at breakfast Mom divulged my punishment. No friends over for a month and no reading for two weeks. Since we lived in Warman, a small town half an hour outside Saskatoon, such a sentence meant numbing idleness for two weeks. Dad unplugged the TV during the summer so I had no means of entertainment. Yet I protested little. I hoped the enormity of such punishment would discourage Maggie from seeking reprisal of her own design, which, judging from her still-hardened expression, she badly wanted. Her flower-laden linen came out of the washing machine bedecked with ugly black splotches. She threw away her red high heels and, later that night, carried her ruined posters out into the pasture. An old metal barrel sat about a hundred yards from the barn, and one by one she lowered the posters into it and then set them on fire. I watched from my window. As the posters burned, several cows gathered around her. She stared into the barrel; her face was orange and indistinct.

The next day Mom had to go to Saskatoon early for a doctor's appointment. The night before she'd told Maggie not to lay a hand on me or the punishment would be swift. Maggie had sat upright at the dinner table, nodding grudgingly. Before I went to bed, I locked my door. When I awoke the morning of Mom's appointment, I bided my time. I listened to hear if Maggie stood out in the hall. I crept up and looked beneath the door. Then I opened it and glanced down the hall and quickly darted into the bathroom. When I came out, Maggie lunged forward, grabbed me, and hauled me down the stairs. I kicked and punched her. She gripped me around the waist and carried me outside. I shouted at her.

Just outside the barn, she had built a small fire. Tucked into the fire was the branding iron Dad had used to mark his cows.

I screamed. I clawed. Maggie, six years older and twice as strong as me, tightened her grip and shook me slack. She wrestled me to the ground and, planting her knees on my shoulders, reached for the iron. I shrieked that I was sorry. She lowered the smoking iron toward my forehead. The metal glowed orange and smelled toxic. I sobbed, shutting my eyes, trying to buck upwards. I twisted my head to avoid the iron's heat. The iron's design was a cow with wings. Maggie held it an inch from my forehead. I tried to push my head back into the ground. I drew narrow breaths. Stop, Maggie! Stop! Will you stop now? she said, leaning forward on her knees. Yes! Will you stop touching my things? Yes! Will you stop annoying me? Yes! Will you stop tattling? Yes! Do you promise? Yes! Yes!

Maggie held the iron closer for an instant, singeing a few strands of my hair. Then she withdrew it. She put it back in the fire and climbed off of me. Go inside, she said. I scrambled up and ran into the house in my bare feet, huddling my shoulders together, crying as I went. I ran up to my room, locked my door, and sat on the floor, sobbing. I felt miniscule, weak. I touched my hair and expected ashes to crumble between my fingers. When Mom got home later in the afternoon I told her nothing for fear of having the cow with wings permanently seared into my forehead.

That's why Maggie dotes on me today, with her guilt-tripping the last reminder of those warring days. That's the first conclusion about my childhood.

The second conclusion: I turned out to be stronger than the child I was. I was weak as a child and as an adult; there was little difference between the two. My disability interrupted that weakness and forced me together. It turned my backbone from a splintering fence post into a Grecian pillar. It gave me direction, turning me into a lovable asshole and an eminent researcher. Odd as it sounds, I will always be thankful for that.

I'm exhausted. I shut off the picture frame.

THE FOUR HOARSEMEN—JUNE 6, 2009

Old Scratch is back. Came out of my bath to find him wearing his oxygen mask. He wears it full-time now rather than taking a swig of air when he needs it. I didn't give him much of a hard time. Just a little grin. Welcome back to the program, I said. Nobody's touched your spot at the dinner table since you've been gone. That was enough, apparently. He growled at me, his mask fogging up.

He's rounding up a posse against me, spreading neurosis, spreading the word that I'm bad news, that I think I'm better than the others, that I shouldn't be here. He and a few other wheelchair-using residents, two old men and a younger man with his chin always touching his chest, watch me like I'm a leper. The little professor wants a lock on his door, Old Scratch says, so he can keep everyone out and do his work. The selfish prick, says one of the old men. I wouldn't mind a lock on my door, says the younger one. Shut up! says Old Scratch, leaning into his mask. I can't take a book out into the garden without two of them trailing me. What're you reading, professor? Some high and mighty book? They don't let me talk to Jeeves, either. Whenever I approach him and ask him questions, they interrupt and tell him not to listen to me. This upsets Jeeves; he seizes his hair and shakes his head. I look at Old Scratch and his minions. Stop following me, I say. Mind your own business, or I'll talk to the staff and tell them what you're doing. Old Scratch lifts his mask for a moment. Stop treating him like a child, he says. He takes a long breath. He's not here for your entertainment, he says. Not your business, I say. Besides, I'm just asking him questions. Nobody else here talks to him except me, and we get along well. Don't we, Jeeves? I pat Jeeves on the shoulder. He pants and looks at me. His name's Reggie, the younger man says, pointing at me while glancing at the floor. I know what his name is. Jeeves is just a nickname. Friends can give each other nicknames. And if you guys had any friends, you'd understand

that. All four of them stir. You watch your mouth, boy. I chuckle and hold up my hands. Look, gentlemen, I'm not doing him any harm. All right? All I'm doing is talking to him, and I'd appreciate it if the four of you would stop hounding me. We want you to stop talking to him, Old Scratch says. No. If I wanna talk to him, I'll talk to him. Besides, you guys don't speak for him. He can decide whether he wants me to talk to him. Right, Jeeves? That's right, he says. There you go, I say. Now if you four amigos would please leave me alone. Not until you stop talkin to im, says one of the old men. You're mistreatin im when you ask im those stupid questions. If you guys don't leave me alone, I'm gonna talk to the staff and ask them to keep you in your rooms, or even remove you from the residence. Hwa! says the old man. You don't own this place. We can report you, too, Old Scratch says. For what? For talking to him? I scoff. Now are you guys gonna leave me alone or not? Are you gonna stop talking to Reggie? The younger man stretches his neck out and rubs his chin with the back of his hand. No, I'm not. Then we aren't leavin you alone, says the first old man. Oh for Christ's sakes. Like disability, being an asshole transcends age, race, and all the other categories.

It's been an interesting past few days. I reported them, they reported me, and Old Scratch and I are now on probation, a loose word meaning life goes on until you stir up shit again. Then it's a serious review. Then the board meets. Then you either get kicked out or you don't. It takes a Herculean effort to get kicked out of this place. Basically, unless I kill someone, I'm safe. I figure I need to wait Old Scratch out so he'll eventually get so overcome with anger for me that his body won't be able to take it, and he'll collapse and die in his chair. A horrible thing, to be sure, dying in a knurled, bony, liver-spotted heap. But if it makes my life easier...

RAINY DAY—JUNE 8, 2009

Got the issue of the journal in which my newest article appears. "The Rhetoric of Sympathy: the One-Dimensionality of Dickens's Disabled Characters." They missed a few typos, with Tiny Tim being spelled Tinny Tim more than once, but other than that it looks good. The typo even seems poetic in one instance: "Far from being a fully realized character, Tinny Tim is quite hollow, a doll's face, an empty name merely meant to stir sympathy from the reader."

I want a beer. I wonder if it'd help with the tremors. I can see the bubbles rising through my blood and settling onto my nerves like massaging little sprites. But to my everlasting consternation, beer and pain meds don't mix, as I discovered in New York. There are times I wanna say screw it and have Gertrude drive me out to grab a six-pack. But I value my mind too much to risk it in such a way.

Spent most of the last few days in my room. Don't wanna deal with Old Scratch and his amigos. Out of boredom I flicked on the digital picture frame and saw myself in my teens: sagging hair, quick eyes, an aggressive thrust to my jaw. In another I'm holding a trophy for finishing first in high school debating, an award won more for my antagonism than for any sound intellectual argument.

I compare my flat feet of yesteryear to my mantis claws of today. A number of thoughts curl up and collide. From one perspective I see how I've grown, how my disability has allowed me to take the hatred I felt for my sister and my frustration with the world in general and turn those emotions in a progressive direction, propelling me into the centre of the coliseum of disability studies. From that perspective, I see myself as a crude monk, my doctrine made flesh, my mantis claws folded in my lap as I fiercely meditate. The decade-long shift from specializing in British literature to specializing in disability in British literature has not been a mere expansion of my academic interests; it's been part of my spiritual development.

On the other hand, I don't like revisiting scorched earth, the churned-up, arid ground of the past. I admit that I have some days when I want to drive a car again and fix my own meals and live in a place where I can come and go as I please and lock the door and not worry about satanic old men hacking and harrumphing in the hallway outside my room. There are days I long to go to the bar and dance and fondle women and sit on a stool and have a few beers, days I wish I could look over my classes from behind the podium rather than at eye level, days when I feel bitterly impatient and angry with myself and with others. On those days, I think that nobody ever fully accepts his disability because he's always surrounded by memories of what able-bodied life used to be like. Those moments, sharp in their clarity and blunt in their impact, lurk around every corner. On those days, I wonder if that's the real reason I've sequestered myself in the Residence: to avoid the memories, the signs.

But then I shake off such musings, because they might mean that I am weak. And I don't feel weak.

Small Worlds Can Shrink Even Further—June 12, 2009

Got a haircut today. Got it cropped short. With my dense beard I was starting to look like a hippie. Now I look like D.H. Lawrence.

Came back to the Residence to find a young woman on her way out. Straight blonde hair. No older than thirty. I smiled as she approached. She said hi. Hi, I said, slowing down. Don't tell me they've begun letting Generation X in here, I said. Those roast chicken dinners aren't just for anybody. She chuckled. You know somebody here? I said. My great-uncle, she said. Oh yeah? Who's that? Calvin Myrtle. Myrtle. Oh, Myrtle! Ah, Mr. Myrtle is your great-uncle, eh? Heh, that's interesting. Are you the professor? I smiled a little. She moved toward me. You're the one who calls him Old Scratch? Her face darkened. It's just a nickname, I said. Why do you call him that? Why do you bother him? He's old, he's taking air from a tank. He doesn't need someone like you bothering him. Can you please leave him alone? I blinked. I'm not doing anything to him, I said. If anything, he's the one. Did you interrupt his horseshoe game? Did you make fun of his oxygen tank? I interrupted nothing. I was just watching. Your uncle hates me. Why does he hate you? I don't know. Why don't you ask him? He doesn't hate you for no reason. I bet he didn't tell you about him and his little gang. What gang? The Old Guns. The Four Hoarsemen. Hell's Elders. She shook her head. Her face tightened and I saw Old Scratch's brusqueness in her expression, those same wrinkles of scepticism. Look, she said, just stay away from him. All right? I glanced around the front foyer, waving my arms. It's a small world here, I said. Gonna be pretty difficult.

She left in a huff. I went to my room. On my way I saw Old Scratch, hunched in his chair and taking heaving slugs from his oxygen mask. One of his compadres sat beside him. They didn't speak. They sat in the living room, facing away from the TV, which was turned off.

Even though the curtains were wide open and it was sunny outside, with their chairs they took up a large amount of space, shrinking the room, making it claustrophobic. After a minute my breathing became strained, as if I was on Mars. I rolled away to my room, shoving hard on my wheels so the sound of the spokes striking the baseball cards ricocheted off the hardwood floor.

This later in the evening:

Disability is not a small world. It's actually quite vast, a galaxy of sorts. Just as there are thousands of mammal species, there are thousands of disabling conditions, with even more waiting to be discovered. It's just that individual spaces become crowded: residences, group homes, care homes, non-profit agencies, support groups, and so on. They become crowded because persons with disabilities, either by their families or by their own choices, are crammed into those spaces rather than distributed throughout the world. All the grizzly bears aren't collected and dropped into the same forest. If they were, some of them would probably die from starvation or conflict with others.

Not that the Armstrong Residence is overly crowded. Except for three or four people, I like it fine. On some days, I admit I do feel the pinch. But then everyone feels the pinch in their own house, disabled or not. Maybe in the future I'll move and get my own space. We'll have to see. Depends on my health, which depends on my initiative.

Rolling With the Devil—June 15, 2009

I can't wait until school begins. Another two and a half months, for god's sake. I'm languishing. Sweltering. I tried engaging Jeeves in his memories as a visiting professor at Harvard, but his limited opinions of Dickens and Kipling left me parched, and no other resident has read anything beyond Louis L'Amour and Stephen King. Even though I've tons of work to do, and even though I criticize them for their inflated political correctness, I miss the company of my colleagues, and by contrast the vacuous nature of my fellow residents leaves me frustrated and raw. Like handing a dust mop to a man dying of thirst.

Two days ago, out of my vehement boredom, I registered in a bocce tournament the Residence staff organized. To my chagrin, Old Scratch registered too, hoping no doubt to face me and engage in a pissing contest decided by heavy fibreglass balls. Just before the names were drawn, Gertrude announced we'd be playing in teams of two, a fact of which I was unaware, as I was keeping my eye on Old Scratch and his posse. Jeeves and one of Old Scratch's older rogues were the first team put together, followed by an older woman and the youngest of Old Scratch's crew. I glanced at the remaining players. I had three possible partners left: a fifty-year-old man who used crutches instead of a chair, but who had a head like a squashed block of clay; the other old member of Old Scratch's band; and Old Scratch himself. Gertrude reached into the plastic bag and drew two names. Mr. Myrtle and Dr. Ripley. Old Scratch and I looked at each other. His body hooked, like he was going to vomit into his oxygen mask. He groaned in protest. He removed his mask and shouted, No fucking way! His enthusiasm surprised me. Trade, he said. Who wants to trade? His other posse members shook their heads, huddling closer to their partners. Goddammit! he said. Gertrude approached us. Mr. Myrtle, can you keep your voice down? He downed a great swig of air

and pointed at me. I don't wanna be with him! Gertrude looked at me. Well, she said, it appears that nobody wants to trade. So if you want to forfeit... Old Scratch jerked his mask away, and because he had not completed his inhalation he coughed and his words stumbled from his mouth. Forfeit! Bullshit! I'm not forfeiting anything! I pinched off a smile. Gertrude tilted her head. Then I guess you two are partners. You'll have to deal with it. Old Scratch arched his head backward as he shouted into his mask: Fuck's sakes! Keep it down, Gertrude said. Let's go outside. As we rolled out the sliding glass door down the ramp toward the grounds, Old Scratch muttered to himself. Fucking weakling professor. We better fucking win. So, I said, teammates, huh? Shut up. So who's Butch Cassidy and who's the Sundance Kid? Shut up. Oh, and don't worry about my shoulder tremors, they're just for decoration.

Actually, my shoulder tremors were a nuisance. Whenever it was my turn to roll, I had to time it so that I released the ball just before a tremor curled down to my wrist and disrupted the ball's course. At least twice per game I rolled the ball in a direction that puzzled our opponents and infuriated Old Scratch. But I usually recovered enough in subsequent shots to both regain lost points and allow Old Scratch to denigrate our opponents instead of me. Aided by his gravelly voice and physical frailty, his trash-talking assumed a surprising gravity: You play bocce like elephants drop turds! Are you gonna shoot, or are you waiting for the frickin apocalypse? I've seen four-legged ants ruffle grass harder than that. Are you mowing the goddamn lawn, or are you playing bocce? Despite his weakness—he's visibly lost weight in the last week or so—his fierce competitiveness allowed him to roll the ball with impressive accuracy. He drew air from his mask in between shots, saying little to me other than Those aren't sheep's testicles, professor. Don't be afraid to hurl the damn things.

We ended up winning the tournament, beating Jeeves and his partner, Mr. Scartoretti. We won not so much as the result of skill

as the mistakes of our opponents. I thought I'd be horrible, but to my delight the others were worse. In the final game I made the winning shot, rolling the ball just enough to park it within two inches of the jack or cue ball or whatever it's called. Old Scratch laughed and slapped my shoulder. Now you're learning, professor, he said. Mr. Scartoretti, one of Old Scratch's posse members, looked oddly at him. As a prize, Gertrude gave us each a twenty-dollar gift certificate to the McNally Robinson bookstore on Eighth Street. I was pleased; I'd expected a McDonald's coupon or something. Old Scratch looked his over front to back, and then gave it to me. I got no time to waste on books, he said. He pulled his mask down over his head, pulling tight the elastic straps. His forehead, taut and creased, gleamed with sweat. I studied him for a moment. The quick transition from hurling barbs at our vanquished opponents to slumping in his chair with fatigue caught me off-guard. It disconcerted me. Stefan started pushing him up the hill. As he passed me, Old Scratch looked at the ground. He nodded and muttered, Good game, his words sounding like they were spoken from inside a jar.

I had fun. It was sunny and the competition gave me some exercise, meaning I've followed my doctor's advice for once. I'm not sure if things have changed between Old Scratch and me. He and his posse still kept watch yesterday and earlier today, though not with the vigilance of before.

The bocce tournament was only a brief respite. I need constant interaction. Intelligent interaction. I can only read and write so much before I start to seek real people.

TOKEN ENTRY—JUNE 23, 2009

Been working. Sending lots of emails. Posting comments on scholarly and literary websites. Assuming fictional personae and making outrageous claims. If you look carefully in *The Handmaid's Tale* and take the first letter of the second paragraph on the first sixteen pages, it spells Me a hermaphrodite. If you listen to a recording of Dylan Thomas reading "Do not go gentle into that good night" and play it backward, you hear the opening verses of a satanic séance.

Was invited to be the keynote speaker at a conference in Glasgow in October but won't attend. Not in the middle of classes. Too much planning. Too much hassle.

That's about it. Boredom reigns, holding its grey sceptre over my heavy head.

THIS IS NO COUNTRY FOR YOUNG MEN—July 2, 2009

Raging hangover. I was bad last night. Maggie invited me to her place for Canada Day and out of boredom I accepted. She had about fifteen people over, mostly co-workers. Randal had a friend or two. We sat around in the backyard talking and visiting. I sat under the tree in the corner. Not many people approached me. Maggie was hosting so she was too busy to introduce me around. I had to call out to people. It didn't help. In fact, I think it alienated me even further.

I asked Randal to sneak me a few beers from the drinks table. I was buzzed after two, roaring after three, and grabbing Maggie's friend's ass after four. I happened to have bad tremors, too, so to an uninformed bystander, it didn't look like I was merely grabbing her ass. The woman spun and stared at me with rank indignation. She drew back her fist. Ooh! Wait! Don't you know it's against the law to hit a cripple? She huffed. Her eyes were so rigid and beautiful. She clocked me on the temple, leaving me laughing and slumped over the side of my chair. Maggie pulled me from the crowd, to whom I said, How dare you people look down to me! How dare I look up to you! Can someone flip me upside down so we can get things right here? Maggie tucked me into the corner of her kitchen and scolded me. That's my boss, she said. I told you not to do anything. You said not to say anything around her, I said. I said nothing. You sexually harassed her, Maggie said. I chortled. You see how she looks in those shorts? I said. Maggie glanced around the party and told me to stay where I was. I asked her for a glass of water. She told me to get it myself. I'm crippled and I'm drunk, I said. You can't possibly be serious. She shook her head and got me a glass of warm water. What is this, I said, giraffe spit? Shut up and drink it, she said. I have to get back outside. Stay there and don't say anything. She went out. Randal and his friends sat by me. Hey, I said to them. Have you heard the one about the retard and the electric fence? The few adults in the

kitchen glanced over at me. Randal and his friends groaned and told me similar jokes; all of them were meant for cheap laughs; I laughed cheaply. After Randal had told a particularly blistering joke, one of the women put her drink on the counter and came over to me. Are you Maggie's brother? she said. Indeed I am, I said. Can't you tell by my deep voice? You're the professor who won the prestigious prize? I certainly am. I studied her hair, which had been dyed a shimmering red. I wanted to rub my face in it. How can you tell jokes like that, and to young people? I looked at Randal and his friends. Well, how will the leaders of the future have any hope if they can't tell a good joke? She grimaced. You're being very offensive. You're a professor, for crying out loud. You're supposed to be cultured and accepting, not bigoted and ignorant. I laughed and shook my head. Enormous thoughts swelled through my brain. I wanted to tell her that she was bigoted in her view on professors, which was no doubt based on a romanticized, left-wing stereotype: the asshole with elbow patches and smooth voice who donated blood and held up signs protesting Big Business. I wanted to tell her that I refused to be fixed in my language and in my thoughts, that we are conditioned to be politically correct, that I saw the world much more clearly than she did and that I accepted people on my own terms, and that I was neither a bigot nor an ignoramus. But these thoughts popped and dissipated before reaching my mouth. Instead, I twisted my eyes up into hers, gave a little grin, and said, Have you heard the one about the quadriplegic deaf kid and what he got for Christmas? When she exhaled and stomped away, I said to Randal, I guess all redheads aren't sexy, eh?

Eventually I rested my head on the table and dozed off. I swatted Randal's hand away when it was time for the fireworks. Ended up missing them. As I snoozed I heard the pops and crackles in the distance. I opened an eye. The kitchen was empty. The walls were dry brown like leather. Fucking, I said. Then I dozed off again. Maggie drove me back to the Residence shortly after. Her admonitions—

something about her boss and her good friend Adele—drifted past me as I rested my head against the window. When we arrived at the Residence she came around to the passenger side and opened my door. I drew a long breath. The air, laced with the scent of clumped mown grass, swept some of the bubbles out of my head. It left me both woozy and giddy. Maggie held my chair for me. I looked at her and said, Thank you, Maggie. I really needed that tonight. She raised an eyebrow and moved the chair up so I could drop myself into it. I'm serious, I said. I really needed to get out. I'm really grateful. You know how difficult it'll be for me to deal with my boss now? she said. I was drunk, I said. She'll forgive me. She hit you, Dexter. Well, then we're even. She pushed me up to the entrance and stepped in front of me. It was after eleven at night. A single light, circular and white, dropped its beam upon us. As I sat beneath it, I stretched my arms. The light that singles out saints, I thought. I am Dexter, patron saint of cripples.

Maggie kneeled down and planted her hands on my armrests. What're you doing? I said. I know it's hard for you to open up and be civil, she said. I need to ask you this before you sober up, or you probably won't answer. Answer what? I said, glancing past her at the windows to ensure no one was watching. My shoulders shook, and in my drunken state I couldn't tell if it was a tremor or if I was anxious about what she might ask. I need to know, she said, do you still hate me? I scoffed and looked away. Dexter? Do you? No. I don't know. I hated you when we were younger. Now you've worked your way up to bearable. Maggie stood. Then can you tell me why the hell you act like this? Like what? Like you're unhappy, like you're a miserable old man. Why don't you get treatment for your disease? Most people with Charcot-Marie-Tooth get orthopedics. They can walk. Why do you think I'm unhappy? For god's sakes, Dexter. No, why do you think I'm unhappy? Nobody's happy who acts like you do. Nobody just tells horrific jokes to teenagers, or offends people just for the sake of it.

They liked the jokes. That's not the point. They were funny. That's not the point, Dexter. Maggie, Maggie, are you feeling guilty? No, I'm not feeling guilty. Then why're you doting on me like this? You keep coming after me and calling me and everything. Always checking up on me. Because you're family, Dexter. Oh yeah. You're family and I want you to be happy. I am happy. There's no way that you're happy. Don't presume anything about me. I'm happy. I like it here. I'm happy happy happy. You wouldn't act like this if you were happy. It's impossible. No, I act like this *because* I'm happy. You just don't see the difference. I don't believe you. Well, I'm sorry.

Maggie folded her arms and bit her lip. Tears flashed in the white light, sharply framing her eyes. I don't, she began, and then she said good night and walked back to her car. I sat there for a while muttering to myself. Then Stefan spotted me and brought me inside.

Slept late this morning. At breakfast there was little left but dried bagels and eggs like mouse turds. I decided to wait for lunch.

Old Scratch wasn't around. His posse was there but dispersed, playing cribbage and watching the morning news. I steered my chair down the hall. As I neared his door I heard a soft, wet *sshh-ka sshh-ka*. I asked Stefan what the problem was. He'd had to be intubated during the night. His lungs were like crumpled paper bags. I leaned closer to the door. *Sshh-ka sshh-ka.* Not sure if he'll last a week, Stefan said. We're trying to get him transferred to hospice, but they're all booked up so he'll have to stay here. There are many hospices in Saskatoon, I said. Has the city suddenly been seized by the plague? Stefan shrugged. As I listened to Old Scratch's breathing I conjured a disgusting picture: rats the size of Smart Cars galloping out of the city's many potholes and taking bites out of every unfortunate Saskatonian who happened to encounter them. In my hungover state, such a thing seemed plausible; it could easily happen to me. In my chair, I'd have as much chance of getting away as a fat kid on a treadmill trying to run from a serial murderer. I shook away the thought.

Whenever I thought about Saskatoon, I inevitably compared it to Toronto and Montreal, where I'd taken my degrees. Mordecai Richler (I think) dubbed Saskatoon "a good place to raise children," which, in his caustic eyes, made it boring. Montreal and Toronto may be the asshole capitals of Canada, but I can't deny their substance. Things happen in those cities. If a teaching position opened at McGill or U of T, I'd be there in an instant.

I looked at Old Scratch's door. Someone had hung a white dry eraser board on his door and had written C. Myrtle and a medication schedule on it. He was to receive medicine every four hours. *Sshh-ka sshh-ka.* I wheeled away, unsure of whether to go back to my room and work or go outside and read or go into the living room and watch a DVD. I passed the living room and saw Mr. Scartoretti laying down his cribbage hand. He looked at me and adjusted his prescription glasses. I kept wheeling, unsettled, because I didn't know if I was in a residence for persons with disabilities or in a home for old men.

DEATH GAINS DOMINION—JULY 5, 2009

Lung failure. His great-niece was with him. I watched last night as they rolled his body out of the Residence on a stretcher. I asked Gertrude how he looked. Prepared, she said.

When someone dies I usually wish them well. Rest in peace, may the wind be always on your face, that sort of thing. But I don't believe that Old Scratch is the kind of man to whom Rest in Peace applies. He might find that insulting. Like me, he'd probably associate peace with stagnancy, something which, as evidenced through his competitive attitude and his frequent quarrels with me, he obviously hated. So I wish that his spirit continues on with a rattling vigour, renewed now that he is no longer bound by his wasted body.

Death makes me uneasy. Not only because of the memories it conjures, but because of how it colours my disability. To the old and enfeebled, death is often a relief from suffering. I confess that sometimes I feel that my disability is a kind of suffering: Camus's absurdity made flesh. Sometimes I feel embarrassed and weak, staring at my curved feet, flexing against my tremors, grunting when they power through my muscles' rigidity. On certain occasions, when the embarrassment and weakness and isolation reach a feverish boil, I feel like filling my pockets with rocks and rolling down College Drive, down the bank into the river, or taking the elevator up to the tenth floor of the Arts building at the university and then tipping myself over the railing, falling through that narrow pit, bouncing off the stairs all the way down.

The idea of death paralyzes me. For how can I see my disability as something that strengthens my character and cleanses my perception while at the same time admitting that death would be a relief from it? Saying death would be a relief betrays weakness, and I'm not weak. I sometimes worry that I'm weak, but I'm not weak.

A VALEDICTION: BRIEFLY ALLOWING MOURNING—
JULY 6, 2009

That morning, Dad had left for a meeting in Regina. As I said, he was a farm equipment salesman. He left our house at seven-thirty. His meeting was scheduled for one in the afternoon.

I saw him at breakfast. He sat to my right, going over some papers. He was always going over papers as we ate, which I took as implicit permission to read at the table. I had *The Catcher in the Rye* open in front of me, sitting on top of *As For Me and My House*, on which we were to be quizzed at school later that day. Mom was in the kitchen cleaning up. Maggie was at the university in Saskatoon. Dad said he might stop and see her on his way back. I asked him if he could bring me a copy of *East of Eden*. He said he'd see. He was frugal with his affections, but not withdrawn. He looked like T.S. Eliot with sideburns.

He stood from the table, stacked his papers, and put them in his satchel. What time will you be home? Mom said. Shouldn't be in Regina more than an hour or so, he said. Probably around five or six I'll be home. You look tired, she said, stepping over and adjusting his coat. I'm all right, he said. Is the bookstore in Regina any good, Dad? I said. I don't know, Dex. Never been there before. Will you have time to stop there? I'll try. You know which book? *East of Eden*, written by John Steinbeck, published in 1952. I'll look for it if I have time. I nodded. You're not even finished that book you're reading, he said. I will by tomorrow. Is that book for school? No. He cocked his head and gave a little smile. Mom kissed him on the cheek. He checked his coat for his wallet and walked out the door to his blue and white Chevy Cheyenne. He started the truck and pulled out of the driveway. I returned to Holden Caulfield for a few minutes more before I had to go to school.

Because I had not read *As For Me and My House*—even at age eleven I had a strong sense of what was worth reading—I failed my

quiz, and had to stay late at school. I had spent the day imagining Dad coming through the door carrying a book in a brown paper bag, and being detained strengthened that anticipation. After staying late for half an hour, my teacher, Mrs. Becker, let me go, and I ran the mile back to our farm. Dad wasn't home yet, of course. I asked Mom if he'd called. She said no and asked me to go out and ensure the cows had enough hay. I went, warily cutting a path around the stone pit where the branding iron was kept.

Five o'clock came. Then six. Then seven. I couldn't do any homework. I kept looking at the clock. At eight Mom called Maggie. Dad hadn't gone to see her. I kept asking Mom where he was. Probably stopped in town for a drink, she said, or is caught in the Saskatoon traffic. I grimaced. Even though Saskatoon did get some heavy traffic, Dad would've stuck to Circle Drive, the road that sat like a frame around the city and fed into the main highways. At nine o'clock I tramped up and down the living room, telling myself, If he went to drink instead of buying me a book, I'm going to hate him. At ten Mom began calling around. She called Dad's boss, his co-workers, his friends, his brother who lived in Rosthern. His boss said he'd called to say his meeting went well and that they were nearing a deal with a distributor in Montana. Nobody else had heard from him. At eleven Mom sent me to bed. I protested. She said, Go to bed, Dexter, and try not to worry. I'll worry more if I go to bed, I said. Mom sighed. She sat down on the couch. The radio was on but played only music. When it reached midnight, Mom called the police. I stayed up until one in the morning, watching her talk to a constable. I fell asleep on the couch.

When I awoke at six-thirty the next morning Dad still wasn't there. Mom called the police again and they took Dad's description, a photo of him, his truck make and model, his licence plate number. Later that afternoon they officially declared Dad a missing person and began searching for him. They gave the information to detachments

across Saskatchewan. Only a matter of time, they said. Even though a truck like that's pretty common around here, we should be able to find it.

Two months later, after expanding into Alberta, Manitoba, and Montana, they called off the search.

At the memorial, held at the Warman Community Centre, I festered. The community centre's main hall was dusty and pedestrian, used for bake sales and floor hockey. A picture of Dad was mounted on a table and framed by flowers. The few dozen people who came shook Mom's hand and shook Maggie's hand and touched me on the shoulder. My dad's boss told Mom that the deal with the Montana group had gone through and that, because Dad had orchestrated it, Mom would receive his share of the bonus. I squirmed under their sympathy. I stared at Dad's portrait, taken while he was driving a combine in our field. I prickled. The whole process felt wrong. The flowers framing his picture were inappropriate; iron or steel would've sufficed. The community centre was too common for such an event; a blackboard hanging on the wall listed the score of a recent floor hockey game; a few white strings dangled from the rafters, the ragged remnants of red and blue balloons hanging at the ends. During the eulogy, delivered by Dad's brother, Mom turned to me and said she knew it was hard to say goodbye, that it was okay to cry if I needed to. I sat up straight. I refused to say goodbye. Mom put her arm around me and said I'd have to. I refused still, not out of naïve denial, which she no doubt thought I harboured, but out of logic. I didn't know what to say goodbye to. The gesture felt empty.

The time following Dad's disappearance marked a crucial stage in my development. I had always been an imaginative child, as demonstrated by my sister's ruined bedroom, but the fallout of Dad's disappearance drove into me a stout, unswayable logic. I would wonder what happened to him—robbery, trouble with the truck, murder, escape with a woman with whom he'd been having an affair, flight to

America because he couldn't stand to be with his family anymore—and then my newfound rational side would step in, putting such fantasies to rest. As a result, two things happened: I became paralyzed whenever I tried to think about Dad's disappearance, with a stony grey block shunting up from the floor of my mind; and in the years that followed, I grew stiflingly self-conscious. I employed callousness as a remedy to this self-consciousness, something which led to success in a few areas (school, debating) and alienation in all the other ones.

Three years after Dad vanished, we were living in a smaller house in Warman, having sold the farm to one of Dad's co-workers. It was March. Snow hugged the corners of our lawn. I was reading *The Old Man and the Sea* in the living room. Mom was in her room down the hall, lying on her bed. She had gallstones blistering up her gut and was scheduled for surgery in Saskatoon the next week. The radio was on in the hallway. I detested when Mom had the radio on while I was reading, but because of her sickness I chose not to argue.

The radio was tuned to the CBC and the local news had just begun. After updates on the weather and accidents on the highway, the anchor started in on the top story: "While out examining his ninety-acre spread, Coby Blight, a farmer just outside of Chamberlain, Saskatchewan, discovered the complete remains of a human being. The body, which police say was badly decomposed, appears to be that of a man, based on the remaining clothing and estimates of the body's height. The remains have been moved to the medical examiner's office in Regina, where a coroner will attempt to identify the deceased. Police say that due to the level of decomposition, the body has likely been sitting in the field for at least two years."

I sat there with my book open, staring past it. I heard crying down the hall. Just as I started to get up from my chair, the phone rang.

They'd identified Dad by his dental records. Since his truck was never found, someone had likely killed him, dropped him in the field by Chamberlain, stolen his truck, and changed his plates. Cause of

death: stabbing in the back and in the back of his head. Mom, already in considerable pain, was overwhelmed. I hugged her as she sank to her knees and hunched over, sobbing dryly, her forehead touching the floor. The sergeant, who as a constable had taken Dad's information three years prior, sat back in his chair, playing with his pen. As I held Mom, her wool coat prickling my chest, I sighed and let my tears come slowly. By slow degrees tension unfolded from my shoulders. I rubbed Mom's back. Mom winced and shook her head and cried harder. Her sobs sounded like hiccups. I looked at the sergeant and asked him if they would ever find who did it. He tilted his head and shrugged with his hands. It's been three years, he said.

We hastened through the burial. We didn't have a proper funeral, which angered me, but Mom said we couldn't afford it and that she couldn't go through another one. Maggie, then in the third year of her sociology degree, helped with preparations and attended the burial. Dad was placed in the Warman cemetery, a plot marked with a flat indistinct stone. After that, people came to our house and offered condolences. Their gestures felt even emptier than the first time because they had already parted ways; this time they were merely going through the motions.

I hardly had time to digest Dad's closed-casket burial. I'd wanted to see him. Mom said no. I asked what they dressed him in. Mom said she had kept one of his old suits. I asked Mom again if I could see him. She refused. I asked her if she saw him. She said, It doesn't look like your dad.

Two days later Mom's friend Lana drove her to Saskatoon for her surgery. Maggie and Lana tried to talk Mom out of it, saying she'd been through so much and that it might be a risk, but Mom's hardening gallbladder decided for her. She'd stayed with Maggie the night before her surgery and then Maggie dropped her off at the university hospital the next morning. I went to school and spent the day dragging my feet. Schoolmates, even those wary of my notorious

temper, tried to talk to me. Sorry about your dad, they said. We heard you buried him this last weekend, that's pretty shitty. I told them to piss off. Not even a discussion about Yeats's poetry could rouse me from my haze of confusion and mourning. It was as though the fact of Dad's murder had been trapped in daylight savings time, and the clocks had just then been wound back, disorienting me, loosening the ground on which I walked.

I went home early. Science was my final period that year and I had no interest in learning which plants were native to the Warman area. Walking home, I passed a number of lawns populated by figures made of wood and wire. Woody Woodpecker's legs spun as fast as the wind took them. An old woman with black sunglasses painted over her eyes held a watering can and a spade, looking bored. Given the patches of snow, gritty with gravel, sitting atop the soggy grass, the figures seemed premature, and as I kept walking they began to upset me. I sped past them.

When I opened the front door, the phone rang. The school, I thought, probably wanting to know why I'm not in science class. I left it, and went to my room and lay down on my bed. I stared at the white stucco ceiling. Usually when I stared at the ceiling I made out shapes and faces from the stucco's unique and pointed shadows. My favourite was the jester face in the corner. A particularly long piece of plaster hung from the ceiling, creating its cliff-like brow and bulbous nose; three surrounding points helped form its hat and mouth. But this time, as the phone rang again, it seemed pointless to imagine figures and faces. The shadows flattened; the points dulled.

I sighed. The phone rang again. Fuck off! I said. Just as it finished ringing, I remembered that Mom was still in the hospital and that she'd be calling to tell me how things went. I looked at the clock. School was still in session. She wouldn't call this early and the school wouldn't be so persistent about student absences. I sat up from my bed and waited for it to ring again. Then I lay back down. Half an

hour later it started again. I got up and went down the hall and answered it. Mom? I said. Dexter? Who's this? Maggie. A crumple in her voice. Maggie? Dexter? Why're you calling? Dexter? What? Mom's dead. Mom's dead, Dexter. Mom's dead. You're joking. No I'm not joking. You're fucking with me. For chrissakes, Dexter, I've been trying to call you and I'm in the hallway at the hospital and two people are waiting to use the fucking phone! I'm not fucking joking! Her voice had a feline snap to it. I could hear people in the background, the bustle of a hospital. Then I heard Maggie say, Fuck the hell off! presumably to the people behind her. I called Lana, she said. She's coming to get you and bring you here. All right? You be ready. Shut up, you fucking—be ready! Fuck—

She hung up. The doorbell rang. I stood in the kitchen with the phone in my hand. Lana opened the door. Dexter? She spotted me, staring at the floor. Oh dear, she said. She took the phone from me and put it back on its cradle. She then led me outside. Oh dear, you're in shock. Let's get you to the hospital.

I was bewildered beyond comprehension. Sitting in the front passenger seat of Lana's rickety Ford, I spent the drive to Saskatoon trying to figure out the logic, trying to pull tight a line from Mom's health to her death. By the time we arrived at the hospital I'd collapsed into sobs. The floor of Lana's truck was littered with used Dairy Queen napkins. Lana escorted me inside and Maggie and I ran to each other and embraced, the only time we did so unreservedly.

Maggie explained that the surgeon had accidentally nicked an artery. They'd stopped the bleeding at first, but then it started again once they began removing her gallbladder. She lost blood too quickly for the doctors to replace it, and eventually bled to death.

Maggie let me see her. She led me to the operating room and held open the door. Mom was still laid out on the operating table. Her body was covered with a blue sheet. Her face was a bluish grey. Her mouth was partway open. Her hair sagged around her face. I smelled

salt and alcohol. I stooped over and lay my head on Mom's chest, which felt rigid. I hugged her, gripping her arms, trying to pull her around me. Her arms were heavy. Her elbow knocked on the table and I left them alone. I buried my face in her collarbone and cried. Maggie joined me and put her hands on my shoulders. She let me stay as long as I wanted.

When we left the operating room, a lawyer for the hospital asked to speak to Maggie. She went to talk to him while I stayed with Lana. Lana and I sat in the hallway. She talked about how she'd help with arranging a funeral and how she'd do everything she could to ensure I would stay in Warman. I paid little attention. Because of the quick progression of events following the discovery of Dad's body, my subsequent leap from grief to practicality, and my bitter outrage at the doctor, I felt expeditious. The details bored me. Funeral arrangements and meeting my parents' friends seemed burdensome, even useless. I didn't want to listen to vacuous condolences again. I didn't want to hear what other people thought of Mom. I wanted peace, my own private peace.

Maggie came back to tell me that the lawyer had told her that we had two options. We could accept a settlement from the hospital, or we could take the surgeon to court. I wanted to take him to court. Maggie said we didn't have the money and that the surgeon already faced suspension from the hospital. I asked Lana if she could help us. Maggie said she had already told the lawyer we'd take the settlement. Something snapped behind my eyes. In front of a mother and her sick little girl who were walking down the corridor, I screamed, Maggie! What the fuck! She said the settlement would be generous. I didn't care. The principle mattered. The murderer of one parent had already gotten away and I wasn't going to let the other one off. Maggie said that since we were accepting a settlement, the surgeon responsible wanted to apologize to us in person. I said no. I've already signed the papers, Maggie said. We can't take him to court. You already signed—

jesus, you stupid bitch, I said. Maggie hung her head. So you don't wanna see him? He can go to hell. Why did you do that, Maggie? I had to. No you didn't. The guy killed Mom. He should be put in jail. We can't afford a lawyer, Dexter. I don't care. Can't we do something? Can't we sell the house? Maggie sighed and wiped her eyes. I've already signed it. I rubbed my forehead. Fucking stupid, Maggie.

Maggie met with the surgeon a few days later. She called me and said that he cried and he wouldn't stop apologizing. He's very angry with himself, she said. He said he did his best and that he wished he could see you, too. To tell you he's sorry. I started crying into the phone. I moved it away from my ear and looked around the living room. I inhaled and said to Maggie, What's gonna happen to me? I don't know, she said.

After the funeral, which in my view was poorly attended, we put the house up for sale. Maggie and Lana tried to find someone for me to stay with, but people either didn't have the room or they had kids who didn't like me. I also suspected they thought our family was bad luck. Lana had three boys herself and did not have space for me. Maggie struggled through her sociology papers and came back to Warman to help me find a place to live. I limped through the rest of the school year. The novelty value assigned to me through Dad's death had increased, so I was now considered a permanent exhibit in the hallways of Warman High School. My teachers pitied me. My schoolmates approached me cautiously. I snarled at them. I wanted none of their company. Any friendship started then would've been formed on the basis of sympathy, making it nebulous and unsteady. I retreated into our home in the summer, during which our house remained unsold.

Maggie worked out of Warman—a friend of Dad's gave her a summer job—and surprised me by staying in Warman through the fall. The settlement money was paying the mortgage but we had to be out soon, and she felt an obligation to take care of me and make sure the house sold. I resented her. She was everything I hated: passive,

simple, weak. I eschewed her so much that, in time, I had no refuge. School was a coliseum to which I was sent to fight every morning, and home was a suffocating den. I spent most of my time in my room, reading or festering. In time Maggie became offended, calling me ungrateful and telling me that she was sacrificing school to take care of me. I told her I didn't need her to be with me. I'm smarter than you are, I said. I can take care of myself. I'm a university student, she said. Yeah, I said, in sociology. Anyone can learn that shit by going to a bar and listening to some poor idiot's life story. Money well spent. She stared at me for a moment. Ungrateful little prick. Unyanna-yanna-yanna. She picked up a bowl from the kitchen sink and threw it. It hit me on the ear and dropped to the carpet. I ran at her and slammed her against the counter. I tackled her to the linoleum and punched her in the face. She began crying. I slapped her. I started crying too. I punched her once more, and then I punched the cupboard to my right. I got off and sat beside her, my back against the cupboard. She rolled onto her side, holding her face, sobbing. I stood up and left the kitchen.

Death silences many people by driving their voices further and further inward. But in the years following, I became more and more loquacious, an intellectual predator. I sought arguments with schoolmates out of petulance or simply for the sake of proving them wrong. In literature class I asked one of my fellows if she thought Shakespeare was racist for his treatment of Caliban, and then proceeded to pick apart her assertion. In history class I argued that, in the event of a nuclear war between America and the Soviet Union, Canada should be willing to open its borders and allow the States to stockpile nuclear weapons on Canadian soil. My fellow students were outraged. I smiled at them. They said that such a move would destroy Canada's reputation and lead to dangerous precedents. Yes, I said, it'd make things a little more exciting around here. Excitement in Canada— what a dangerous precedent that is.

Maggie eventually sold the house and we shared an apartment until my graduation. In those two and a half years, we spoke only of practical matters: groceries, vehicles, cleaning. Even these subjects yielded shouting matches. We both knew that we would attain peace separately, but we could not legally do that until I was eighteen and out on my own.

When I finished high school the University of Toronto offered me a full scholarship, and I left Warman in August 1980 equipped with one conviction: I needed to create my own logic, a system of aggressive intelligence that would allow me to be both noticed and, by all appearances, correct. I began developing this system in Toronto, and by the time I emerged from McGill with my PhD, I had acquired a national reputation for being callous yet brilliant. My future as an academic was set.

FUNERAL PROCESSION—JULY 12, 2009

Old Scratch's funeral was two days ago. All the residents went and all the staff except one. Someone had to stay behind with me.

I worked on an article and tried planning my Canadian literature class. Made great progress on the former. Zilch on the latter. Already anticipating complaints from students of that class. Dr. Ripley? Yes? While I agree with you that Atwood is discussing gendered power structures here, I'm not sure that she's engaging in misandry. Thank you, Mike Teevee. I admire your input. Now open your book and keep reading until you see it.

Scartoretti, one of Old Scratch's posse members, probably appreciated my absence from the funeral. At dinner the day before the funeral, Gertrude and I were talking. I'd finished massage therapy and she walked with me to the dining room. Did you know Mr. Myrtle was an ardent Catholic? she said. I looked up from my pork chops. He didn't talk like one. Gertrude chuckled. When he first got here, she said, he made us drive him to mass at six every morning. One day I was at the end of my shift—my shift ended at six—and he came over and told me to wake the hell up or he'd miss the service. I smiled. He's probably rolling up to the pearly gates, I said, tripping everyone else ahead of him in line. Scartoretti had been listening from the table next to ours. He turned to me. He's not in a wheelchair anymore, he said. He's walking now, like a man should. Okay, I said. He turned back to his meal. I looked at Gertrude. Over my shoulder I said, Narrow interpretation of a man, but okay. Scartoretti—I'll just call him Dante, I'm tired of writing his name—put down his fork and turned back to me. Fixed me in his eyes; looked me up and down with those dark rolling fig pits. You are a smart ass, he said. I'm a professor, I said. He pushed back from the table and pointed at me. No man wants to be in a chair, he said. No proper man, anyways. I chuckled. I guess I'm not a proper man, then, I said. His brows pinched down

59

upon his eyes. Then he took his dinner into his lap and rolled away.

Noticed something at breakfast this morning. The Residence has changed. It feels fragile, creaky. As though Old Scratch has splashed his rickety soul all over the walls. I try to ruffle the dust and stir up some trouble, but everyone wants quiet. The residents are like mice with their tails curled around them. Even Jeeves won't talk to me. Tried to ask him about his experiences with death. Thought I might record his words and sell them as a short story or something. With his imagination he would surely conjure up something outrageous. He shook his head and turned up the volume of the Harry Potter movie he was watching. Don't want to share stories, he said. From his contorted face I could see he had conjured something brutal. I leaned closer to him; he cowered, held the remote control in front of him. I left him alone. Finding no one else to talk to, I retired to my room.

Maybe Old Scratch's death has reminded everyone that they will die quicker than most other people. Reminding them of their vulnerability: what they endure and what's left to endure. Their disabilities make them more sensitive.

Seems my tremors have plateaued. At a high level, though. A constancy that makes me jab myself with a fork when eating. Stabbed the roof of my mouth this morning. Drew blood; grunted out onto a napkin. The blood unsettled some of my fellow residents. I refused Stefan's help and took another pill.

THE CIRCLES OF HELL ARE WHEELS—JULY 16, 2009

I've shifted from writing in my journal to making entries on my computer and then printing them off and sticking them into the book. Because of my tremors, writing with a pen slows me down. I've timed it: it takes two goddamn minutes to write one sentence that is barely legible. The concentration taxes me; my stream of consciousness is dammed. I'll reserve pen-writing for when I make comments on my students' papers. That sort of gleeful malevolence requires a touch to which only handwriting can do justice.

The residents remain mired in their depression. Dante especially. Yesterday at lunch he came up to me and just started talking. I hated being at that funeral, he said. His voice had a grunting drive to it, the voice a rhinoceros would have if it could talk. Not because I didn't like the guy, he said. Calvin was all right. Pain in the butt sometimes. He chuckled. Unlike most of the geriatric crowd at the Residence, he had kept all his teeth. Small and infant-like, they were the colour of bruises. I felt that if I flicked at them with my finger, they'd bend backward and drop. You know, he said, I was sitting there, just looking around while the priest said his bit, and all I see's wheels, wheels, wheels. People from here, people he knew, everyone with a front row seat. I made sure to stay well back and lock my brakes. Otherwise I would've fallen into the damn grave. And that's something else. He leaned toward me, putting his hand on my arm. His breath smelled like guts. I'm looking around at all these people, he said, and I started thinking of the movies. You know how people in chairs, they always gotta sit off to the side, where there's the one or two spots with those markings on the floor? Well, I'm looking around, grave's in front of me, and I'm thinking, why is it when we go to the theatre, we always gotta sit off to the side, and when it's a funeral we're always front and centre? He shook his head and settled back in his chair. I've been scared or, you know, creeped out before, but at that funeral, with all

those people standing behind me, I felt like I was about to be pushed in with him. He picked up his fork and pointed it at me. Because this is hell, he said. He patted a wheel. Hell in the flesh. Hell made with metal. No man should endure this. Why are you telling me this? I said. 'Cause you know what I'm talking about, he said. You're old, I said. That's why you felt like you were going to join him. He grunted, then sat silently for a minute, eating his corn. But one thing I don't get, he said, turning to me as though I'd just finished speaking, that lots of people here don't get, is you. You seem to like it. You seem to want to be in that chair. It drives us up the damn wall. It helps me, I said. Helps you what? It helps me put the world into perspective. You mean you do like being in that chair? Yes I do. Dante chuckled. Do you find that offensive? Not offensive, but... He chuckled again. It's just not proper. What is proper? Man's an upright being. Two legs, walking around, running around. If we were supposed to be in chairs, we wouldn't have legs. Now, what's not proper is that you're enjoying something that's, well, unnatural, something you're not supposed to enjoy. Have you ever heard of anal sex? I said. Oh boy, he said. Let's not get into that. Some of life's purest pleasures come from enjoying what's unnatural to us. Boy, boy. Dante shook his head. I think I'm done, he said. He wheeled away, leaving his lunch unfinished.

His diatribe makes me think of self-hating Jews: those who perpetuate the stereotypes and laugh at words like kike or heeb. I'm not saying disability is a religion, but for me, it's a system of thought, a philosophy, something by which the world can be ordered.

The only one close to normal around here is Jeeves. I asked him about the night he got in a bar fight with Burt Reynolds. He gave me a staccato account wherein he was left with a bleeding nose and Reynolds had to go to the hospital, having broken his arm by absorbing a swing from a baseball bat autographed by Willie Mays. Not Jeeves's best effort, but still entertaining.

I think I might go to Glasgow after all.

LIFE GOES GRIMLY ON—AUGUST 3, 2009

Nothing much to report in the last while. Been working and preparing for the school year. Submitted the syllabus for my Canadian literature class. Argued with McTavish on which authors to include. Dexter, he said, this is a survey class. You can't base the whole thing on just Mordecai Richler. Why not? I said. Just about everything these students need to know about Canada and Canadian literature is contained in *Barney's Version*. McTavish persisted, so I ended up listing that novel, an Atwood novel (god help us), and an anthology. I hate anthologies. They're big, clumsy tools. Out of fifty authors, you might study five or six. It's like using a Caterpillar to excavate a dog bone.

Had an unusual dream last night. I sat in my chair in the middle of a field, dressed in a brown suit. The field was very much like the one we had at our farm in Warman; even though neither the house nor the barn was nearby, the shapes of the grass patches and the slight swales in the earth felt familiar. It was windy; the grass stalks brushed against the spokes of my wheels. I glanced around. There was nobody else. Then my head started rising. Just my head. My body remained still. I didn't panic. Somehow it felt natural. My head was light. It swayed in the wind. I looked down at my body ten feet below. Like a helium balloon my head was tethered to my neck by a white string. I could see the barbed wire fence on the far side of the field; soon I could see beyond the field. Over the trees, up the highway, along the prairie, like a strange, ragged growth, Saskatoon poked up out of the horizon. My head kept rising and swaying. The city grew darker, clearer. My body kept dealing out the string, or the string grew longer. I got to about a hundred feet in the air. My body was small, a tiny brown beetle. The string disappeared with the distance and I couldn't tell if I was still attached. I cried out. The wind whipped me. My head, my cheeks made noises like slapping a punching bag. I couldn't see straight. I tried to focus on Saskatoon but the wind

played fits with my head. My ears hurt. The string loosened. Then it jerked and tightened. I was tugged back down. I watched my arms haul on the string. The wind relaxed. My arms kept pulling until my head was rejoined to my body. I exhaled at the reunion. Flexed my arms. I swallowed and looked around. The field was flatter than it was. Paler. I plucked a long stalk of grass and bent it and folded it up and threw it away. I couldn't see the fence anymore.

Visited with Maggie yesterday. We sat around and talked and drank juice. I asked her for a beer but she wouldn't give me one. Randal was off at his dad's. Too bad; I was looking forward to sharing more jokes with him. I feel something toward him, a sort of mentor's call. He's a kindred spirit of sorts—smart, but not as corrupt as me. I've never been close with any family member; if what Maggie and I share can be called a relationship, it's certainly not a close relationship. I've pretty much ignored Mom's and Dad's brothers and sisters. Never had any use for them. But Randal. I will gladly take him under my knurled wing.

Maggie's worried about him. We were walking downtown the other day, she said, cupping her glass of raspberry-watermelon juice, going clothes shopping for school, and we walked past that bust of Gandhi down on Second Avenue. He made a kind of confused expression and said to me, Mom, why do they have Gandhi right in the middle of downtown? And I told him that he was a great man. And Randal said to me, Well yeah, but he's not Canadian. What's he done for Canadians? He's done so much for the world, I said. Read the plaque, I said. Gandhi is a man who represents peace and reason. That's pretty Canadian, isn't it? Randal didn't answer. We walked down to McDonald's and had some lunch there. Randal kept looking out the window and eating, and then he looked at me and said, Mom, wouldn't it be funny if someone drew a swastika or something on Gandhi's forehead? It just floored me. It shocked me. I chuckled. Maybe that was why he said it, I said. Maggie cringed. I'm wonder-

ing if something's up with him, she said. Where would he get an idea like that? Why would that occur to him? Looking for thrills maybe, I said. Thrills? Maggie shook her head. He's not the kind of boy to go thrill-seeking. He told me himself he's not into drugs and he hates the taste of beer. Maybe that's the problem, I said. He's too smart for drugs and booze and all that, so he goes for something different. He goes for cultural shock. I don't want him arrested, she said. Well, I said, in my view it's better if he gets arrested for defacing statues than for running a meth lab. The kid's smart. He's got a strong idea of what's really rebellious. Maggie grimaced at me. I don't want you encouraging him, she said. His dad's little help, he hardly spends any time with Randal now. He hardly did when Randal was living with him. I don't want him to turn into Charles Manson or anything. He won't, I said. He's got a mother who flattens him with love and guilt. Don't say that. I was kidding. No you weren't. I drank my juice. Someone died at the Residence, I said. Oh really? Maggie stared at her glass and slid it back and forth. I could almost hear her mood collapsing. Who? This older guy. He'd been there for a while. How'd he die? Lung failure. Maggie leaned on the table. I don't understand that about the Residence. Why do they have so many old people? It's not all old people. There's a few young ones. Shouldn't the old ones be in a home? I asked them that too, but never got an answer. Maybe there's just no room in seniors' homes. Maggie tilted her head. Were you uncomfortable? she said. With what? With his death. No. It didn't bring up memories? Not really. I hardly knew the guy. Maggie stretched her arms. I don't understand why you stay in that place. I keep trying to wrap my head around it but I can't...you're independent, Dexter. You may not be able to walk, but you can move and live on your own. Haven't you talked to your doctor about treatment? No. Why not? Because it wouldn't change anything. Are you sure? I shook my head. Living at the Residence is easier on me, I said. You don't think it's having the wrong effect on you? What do you mean? You're depend-

ent on others. You don't think that it's making you… What, weaker? I wasn't gonna say weaker. I was gonna say softer. That's weaker. It's not making me weaker. It makes my life easier, so I can concentrate on my work without having to worry about the little things. What little things? Just domestic things. You mean chores? Cooking? Yeah. That's life, Dexter. I don't want that to be my life. It wouldn't be your whole life. In the chair it would be, Maggie. I'd be focusing on getting all the dust off the coffee table rather than teaching my students and publishing books. It'd be a waste of time. If you got treatment, then you wouldn't be in the chair, and then you wouldn't have to worry. I don't want treatment. Maggie sighed. Her mouth curved. She spoke in a grey voice. You're becoming vainer, she said. You treat that damn chair like it's a throne. Your life isn't worth more than others. I don't know why you insist on avoiding treatment; maybe you're torturing yourself or something. Oh, for god's sakes, Maggie. Maybe that's it, she said. You're punishing yourself. For what? Maggie shrugged. Her hands opened and closed. A tremor arched through my shoulders. I've nothing to feel guilty about, I said. Maggie raised her eyebrows and tilted her head. We sat like that for a few minutes. Then she stood from the table. She went down the hall and put on her jacket and got her keys. She pulled me away from the table and wheeled me out to her car. When she turned the ignition, she said, I know you don't want pity, Dexter, but I pity you. I pity you so much. I sighed and looked out the window and said nothing all the way back to the Residence.

The mood at the Residence has improved a little, though not much. Dante won't leave Old Scratch alone. He talks to anyone who'll listen, asking them how they feel about their disabilities. When was the last time you felt right? Aren't you in hell? I'm in hell. It'll happen to us too, sooner or later. None of us are strong enough anymore.

If things don't change in the next few months I may actually have to move out. I don't want to wait a year or five years for Dante to kick off. I don't want to look at the other residents as though I'm

studying a Brueghel painting. As much as I love the Residence, I can't live in a place that conflicts with my philosophy. I'm a mantis, not a fly.

My Heart Leaps up When I Behold the New Resident— August 10, 2009

Arrived three days ago. Thirty-something. Uses crutches. Moved into Old Scratch's room.

It's unclear what her condition is. She entered the Residence like she'd lost a verdict. Heavy fault line of a brow. Penciled eyebrows. Dark brown hair with traces of burgundy dye. Lips like two orange wedges pushed together. Shoulders coiled inwards. Narrow body and sleek narrow hips. An angular beauty that stands out in a place like this.

Approached her two days ago. She stood in the living room in front of the bookshelf scanning the paperbacks. She was obviously unused to crutches; she teetered and kept one hand on the shelf. I rolled up to her and introduced myself. Gertrude had told me her name. Your name's Audrey? I said. She pouted and nodded. You're into reading? She nodded. I've read all these, though, she said. She touched a book by Stephen King and frowned. Do you like poetry? I said. Mmm. Hey, can I ask a question? she said. Okay. The person who had my room before me—did they die? They didn't tell you? So someone did die? Was it an old man? Yeah. She made a sound like she'd swallowed a tarantula. I'm sure they changed the sheets, I said. I wouldn't worry about it. That was a while ago. That's sick, she said. Yeah. Do you like poetry? She planted her crutches and leaned and moved away from me and toward the office down the hall. Later that night I wheeled past her room and caught a hint of wind. She must've opened the window out of disgust.

At breakfast yesterday I brought *The Wild Swans at Coole* by Yeats. I arrived at nine and sat at the table for an hour, picking my hash browns, glancing toward the doorway every few seconds. She didn't emerge until I was on my way out. I met her at the doorway. She looked like the morning had come too fast for her. Her eyes were pinched, and the way she balanced on her crutches reminded me of

the rickety scaffolding my high school used for its dramatic productions. Morning, I said. I handed her the book. If you're still looking for something to read. She said, Oh, and made her way past me. I started to say something but her aloofness alerted me that it might not be worth it. I rolled back to my room wondering what her condition was and whether it predisposed her to coldness.

Although she is cold toward me, the other residents have been roused from their depression. They're curious. They gossip. One of the women, her name's Candice I think, says her name actually isn't Audrey. Dante says he saw her family bring her here and that she was yelling at them as they brought her things inside. Darnel, the youngest member of Old Scratch's former posse, says he heard her crying the first night. I asked Gertrude about her name. Legal name's Audrey, she said. I don't know if she's called something else. What's her condition? I said. A.L.S., she said. Steadily deteriorating, too. She was completely healthy six months ago, but now she's got problems with her memory, her balance. What about her family? They can't take care of her. Or they won't. From what I hear they brought her here thinking it would help her. And it might a little, because she won't be under as much stress, but I don't know. It might not. Is she married? No. But I'd leave her alone, Dr. Ripley. I really would. She hates being here.

Haven't seen Audrey since yesterday. She must be in her room, letting it all come to her, bracing for that crash in the heart when it finally sinks in that this is for real. I can only hope it's not too damaging.

TOKEN REPORT—AUGUST 12, 2009

Still no word from Audrey. Gertrude says that staff members have been taking food to her room. The transition has been really difficult for her. She feels embarrassed when she goes out among the other residents. I wonder if she's reading my Yeats.

Accepted the opportunity to speak in Glasgow. Will go in October, all expenses paid.

Lesson preparation. Reading. Articles. Pain. Tremors. The usual.

HER CRUTCHES HER SILVER BANGLES—AUGUST 15, 2009

Knock-knock. Yes? Audrey stood there at my door. Holding my book in both hands, leaning uneasily on her crutches. You're Dr. Ripley? Yes. She scanned my room, my bookshelves, like a child observing whales in an aquarium. You have so many books. You can come in. She waffled. How do I…? There's a chair right there. I backed away from my desk and pointed to the chair just beside the door. She entered. Put the Yeats on the desk. Took her time pulling out the chair and settling it so she could sit with comfort. Her face compact. Did you like it? I said, pointing at the book. Yes. Thank you for giving this to me. I don't read much poetry, but I did enjoy these. Good. She smiled a little. I didn't understand most of them, but they're very beautiful. Did you have a favourite? "The Wild Swans at Coole." Oh. Made me think of the geese at the Forestry Farm. I used to feed them. I see. So, you're a doctor? What kind of doctor? A professor. At the university? Yes. What do you teach? English literature. Do you teach this guy? She pointed at Yeats. Whenever I can. She looked around the room. Her expression changed. Do you like it here? I said. She looked at the floor. I don't know. Her brow sunk as she looked at my desk, my books, my papers. She shook her head. My memory, she said, lifting her hand to her temple. Can I ask you a question? I said. She lowered her hand. Let it rest on her crutches, which lay crossed over her lap. Is your name Audrey? It's my legal name. I ask people to call me Esmeralda. Esmeralda? Yeah. Why? I like that name better. She looked at my books again. As she looked, the name seemed to settle onto her like pixie dust. Her crutches acquired an odd, yet attractive glint. Her chin lifted. You're welcome to take another book, I said. I just don't want any of the others taking them and tearing them up and making paper airplanes out of them. She chuckled. Her brow uneven. Her lips made small movements. She sighed. Shut her eyes. Is something wrong? I said. I'm trying to remember. Remember what?

She tapped the cover of Yeats and recited.

> But now they drift on the still water,
> A mystery, beautiful;
> Among what bushes will they build,
> By what…pond's edge or pool
> Delight our eyes when I awake some day
> To find they've all flown away?

That's close, I said. She grunted. I spent three hours yesterday trying to memorize it, she said. I wanted to test myself and prove that I could keep it there. I shrugged with my hand, saying, I've had students read this poem for weeks without remembering how it goes. I wouldn't worry. She hung her head. My memory's going, she said. Memory's overrated, I said. She frowned. Stood and locked her arms into her crutches and walked out. Came back a minute later for Yeats, saying, Can I have this again? I nodded and she said Thanks and left again. I pondered her eccentricity and decided that she's trying to prove to her family that she doesn't belong in the Residence, so they'll take her back.

Later that night she came down the hall and lost her balance and fell sideways into a recliner. As she leaned on her crutch her arm quivered. Her knee bent like a stick of gum. She stumbled into the recliner and flopped onto the floor, landing on her side. I went to her and, along with Stefan, helped her up. You all right? I said, extending my hand. Stefan did most of the work. I put my hand on her shoulder. If it's comforting for you, I said, I bet there's money to be made as a human bowling ball. She scowled at me. Stefan asked her if she was okay. She grabbed her crutch from him and ambled away. I looked at Stefan. I don't think she appreciates your kind of humour, Dr. Ripley, he said. That's a shame, I said. I think she wants to be alone, he said. She's still adjusting. She came to my room yesterday, I said. All the same, Stefan said. Let her do things on her own.

Dante sneers at me. Like I'm a horny teenager who keeps getting stonewalled. I admit that I am horny. The way her ass stretches her jeans as she leans on her crutches thrills me. But I'm also fascinated by her. The name Esmeralda hugs her like silk, and her crutches are bangles, adding to rather than subtracting from her name's music; and the clapping of her crutches' rubber ends on the floor beats an idiosyncratic rhythm, to which her body naturally undulates.

Esmeralda, the Elusive Beast of Loch Armstrong— August 22, 2009

Only glimpses of Esmeralda these last few days. She pokes her head around corners and otherwise turtles into her room. It's a bit maddening. Not only because I'm fascinated by her, but also because she's got my book. That Yeats is a first edition. I'm sure she's not staining the pages with coffee or tears, or underlining phrases from "Ego Dominus Tuus" to mark out some esoteric code of grief, as I sometimes imagine she's doing. But still.

I haven't been in a relationship since before I began my master's degree, and I entered that one already knowing it was going to end. I was in Toronto living in a bachelor suite looking out onto a mangy hedge, with the CN Tower just visible if I leaned far enough over; the people above me hung their clothes on a line and they constantly blew off and onto my balcony. I'd finished my BA and Maggie asked me if I was coming home for the summer. I said no. I'd found a job working at the Engineering library on King's College Road—not my choice; all the library applications were bunched up and mine was selected at random. I'd also received a scholarship that would see me through my master's. I'd no reason or desire to go home.

While working at the library I met a girl named Sofia. Like me, she was an arts student stuck in the pedantry of engineering. She'd come to Toronto from Portugal to do her BA in art history and was planning on going back to Lisbon to continue her education. She'd be gone by August.

Since high school I've always been wary of women and their potential influence on me. Perhaps I've Maggie to thank for that. I try to establish my assertiveness from the get-go. I'd had brief closeted jounces during my undergrad, mostly with girls who envied my aggression. I kept them at arm's length. Sofia was different. Hard yet patient. To test her, I told her about the time when, during a question

and answer period the previous year, I'd embarrassed Margaret At-wood so much that she stared at me murderously and asked security to escort me out. Sofia laughed and said, Atwood just kicks up a lot of dust. You want a writer, read Saramago. His sentences blush.

We traipsed through the summer together, poking fun at the en-gineering students' vests and mocking the theses of a hydraulics text. She tolerated my cynicism admirably. My brothers are soldiers, she said. You can't get more cynical than them. When we had sex both my body and my synapses exhaled. We grappled and gripped each other. I hugged her generous hips. She grabbed me and pulled me further inward. The tension completely drained from my neck and shoulders.

I think one of the reasons I felt so much at ease, besides Sofia's sly charm and pugnacious intelligence, was that I knew she was leav-ing in August. The temporariness of the situation meant I didn't have to worry about consequences. But she ended up mistaking my non-chalance for a carefree disposition. When it came down to our last day together in the library, we finished our shift and held hands as we walked to the exit. I held the keys in my hand. We faced each other. She bowed her head. Do you wanna stay in touch, then? she said. Mm, I said. I don't know if it'll be worth it. Oh. I mean, I enjoyed this. Me too. But, for me I don't think we're gonna see each other again, so I don't know if it'll be worth it. She scowled. I knew you were gonna say that, too, she said. Are you mad? No, I'm not mad. You look mad. Well. What's the point, Sofia? I really like you, she said. I don't love you, but I really like you, and I know I have to go back but I just want to make sure you feel something too. Well yeah, I do. How could I not? You hate Atwood almost as much as I do. She chuckled. Do you wish I wouldn't go? she said. It's hard, I said. Your school's already paid for. Your family's expecting you back. Answer my question, she said. I can go either way, I said. Whichever one. Sofia sighed. I knew it, she said. What? I said. She shook her head and walked away.

Haven't been in a relationship since then. Haven't had sex in five years.

I don't even know if I want a relationship right now. When I look at my colleagues and their relationships, they seem content enough, but I always hear talk of If I wasn't married I'd be getting a lot more done, or The kids are a handful, we have to make a few sacrifices, you know how it goes. These phrases are spoken with flat resignation. Not quite regret, but a few degrees away. For this reason a number of my colleagues envy me. It's plain in their words and expressions. I'm able to wholly devote myself to my work, and in the process become eminent. As a result, I've nothing to regret.

WITHOUT CONTRARIES, THERE IS NO PROGRESSION—
AUGUST 24, 2009

This last night:

Knock-knock. Esmeralda standing in my doorway, her hair in a ponytail. Leaning on her crutches the way an able-bodied person might lean on the kitchen counter. Hi, she said. She held up my book. I'm sorry, she said. I didn't mean to hang on to this for so long. It's okay. Can I come in? I nodded and directed her to the open chair. She sat down and put the book on my desk and crossed the crutches over her legs. I don't mean to be difficult or inconsistent, she said. It's all right, I said. I'm still getting used to things, she said. I'm getting better. Here, listen. She recited "'The Wild Swans at Coole'" in its entirety. Her voice sometimes snagged on the ends of the lines, but her recitation was otherwise pleasant. Her voice sounded as if she strained to speak, even though she didn't, and it lent a soft gravity to the poetry. That's very good, I said. She smiled. I must've practised it a hundred times, she said. Didn't I say your memory's fine? Her brows undulated. I'm trying not to worry, she said. She looked over my desk and pointed at a university envelope. So, are you ready for school? I think so, but I doubt my students will be ready for me. Are you a hard professor? I've been known to deliver tongue lashings in class. She raised her brows. Are you a hard marker? Do you give out any As and Bs? That depends on how drunk I am. She chuckled. She glanced over her shoulder at my open door. Are we allowed to drink here? No. She chuckled again. You're a troublemaking professor. The only kind of professor worth learning from. Do you work? I said. I used to. Doing what? She nodded at the digital picture frame on my desk. Animation. Cartoons? Sort of. You know the show *Amos and Craig*? I've heard of it. I've worked on a few sketches for that show. That's pretty popular, isn't it? She nodded. It's stop-motion animation—claymation, basically. I see. Before I came here I had a children's

cable show in Regina, showing once a week. It took a week to do all the animation frame by frame. You know how stop-motion works? I know the gist of it. The show was called *Coyote's Trails*, and it was about a coyote who kept getting chased by farmers, 'cause he was always on their land and going after their chickens. Just a little show, but it was mine. She glanced at the floor. That was where I discovered my A.L.S. I was trying to put the coyote figure in its place and I started getting dizzy and it felt like Coyote was moving. I took a break for a while but it didn't go away. I tried to go back in and film again but it just wouldn't work. Six months later, I come back to Saskatoon, and my brother and my dad bring me here. She shook her head. My condition is related to A.L.S., I said. It was discovered by the same person, I think. She stared at me. So your family forced you to come here? I said. It was a coerced agreement, she said. The doctor said I was getting worse and that I would need care, and my brother and my dad run a business together so they can't watch out for me. So they brought me here. Is your mother dead? Yes. Esmeralda pursed her lips. Sometimes I think it was my idea, but other times I think it was them. It depends on how I feel. She coughed. I try not to think about it. Is that why you were in your room for so long? She exhaled curtly and shrugged. I don't know. She nodded at the frame. Why don't you have any pictures in that? I do, I said. It's just not turned on. Why don't you turn it on? Because I see enough of my sister in person and I'm not interested in seeing her in my room all the time. She nodded. Do you see your sister often? Once every few weeks. She chuckled. What's she like? She's like a mother who abandoned her child and is continually trying to make amends. Did she put you in here? No. Who did? I did. You did? Yes. Why? I like it here. Really? Mm-hmm. Well... what, you can't live on your own? Between you and me, I could if I wanted. But you don't want to? No. Why not? It'd distract me. Distract you from what? My work. What work? My articles, my writing. Esmeralda made a face. Well, what're you writing about? I'm working

on a philosophy of disability. A philosophy? Yes. What sort of philosophy? A philosophy that allows us to see disability not as a stigma or benign medical condition, but as a clear and charged lens through which to see humanity, a lens that allows us to see below surface and artifice and fill the space in ourselves that might otherwise be filled by faith in god. Ah. How far along are you? I'm at the beginning stages, but I think I'll get there, provided I don't die first. Die? My disease. What's your disease? It's called Charcot-Marie-Tooth disease. You see my feet? I think of them as mantis claws. You see how I sort of lean to the left? Scoliosis. Oh, I thought that was just a comfort thing. I have tremors too, because the disease attacks my muscles. How are you allowed to live here? I meet their criteria—barely, but I meet it. Don't you want treatment? I take drugs for the pain, and I could've had surgery, I *should've* had surgery, or at least orthopedic shoes, but I chose not to. Why not? Because. She frowned and looked me over. That's just stupid, she said. Why would you put yourself through that? Look at your feet. You know how angry I'd be if I had feet like that? Oh, I was angry in the beginning. I could never do that. It's how I choose to see things. She scowled. Her shoulders rolled. She looked at my feet again and shook her head. You see disability as a philosophy? she said. Like existentialism and all that? In a manner of speaking. You think my A.L.S. is a philosophy? That it helps me see the world better? It's a matter of perspective, seeing things properly. Her brow creased. Well, it's not, she said. In fact I think it's repugnant. It's not a philosophy. It's a disability. It's a disease. It's a horrible thing that nobody in their right mind wants. Only if you look at it like that, I said. There's no other way to look at it, she said. It's a negative thing and that's the end. She rubbed her temple. I just spent the last three days… She stopped and took her time. You know why I tie my hair in a ponytail? Because I can't be bothered anymore. I don't see the point of curling irons or putting more dye in my hair. I just let it all go. Because I'm stuck. I'm stuck here. She pointed at the floor. This

is a place where people are stuck. And you choose to stay here willingly. I adjusted in my chair. A tremor whipped down my arm. She exhaled slowly and looked over my room. I'm probably going to die within a year, she said. I won't be on crutches for much longer. I'll have to be in a chair. My mouth—sometimes I drool like, like a baby, because my lips sag. She sniffled and huffed. She clamped me in her field of vision, like she thought I might drift away. It's insulting to me to hear that you could be living on your own away from this place without having your body and your brain betray you every goddamn day. Tears slipped from her eyes. She hung her head.

Gertrude knocked on the door. Dr. Ripley? One or two other residents peeked in. Esmeralda wiped her eyes and got up and staggered into her crutches and left the room. What's wrong? Gertrude said. Just having a philosophical debate, I said. She lost.

Just remembered that Maggie turns fifty-four today. Will call her if I have time.

ATTACK OF THE GIANT MANTIS—SEPTEMBER 4, 2009

Had another mantis dream last night. It was the same as before: jumping, hissing, spitting, stomping. I still felt the strange, unbridled glee of being admired while mashing people into the ground, but toward the end I became angry. The people watching me weren't getting it. I advanced on University Bridge and, with one chop of my claw, cleaved the bridge in half. Until I lowered my claw the traffic and the people walking had kept on going. A few people nodded at me. I broke all the way through the concrete arch. Pedestrians and vehicles slipped and tumbled into the river. My giggling ratcheted up into a shriek that I sustained as I continued to decimate the bridge. I plucked trees near the riverbank and threw them. I swept vehicles off the bridge like dust, clipped off people's heads as though they were dandelions. They kept clapping and waving and honking their horns. I saw their smiles, their lopsided teeth, their softened eyes. I jumped one hundred feet into the air and, my shriek reaching the urgency of an embattled and frustrated child, swung both my arms down upon the bridge. The shock jarred the people and they fell over like mannequins. The bridge cracked and split and finally crumbled from one side to the other, the debris piling up in the river. I looked below me. The cold water rushed past my rigid green legs. I knocked on my skin and it made a sound like hollow armour.

The dream came after I had an appointment with the doctor. After we discussed my tremors, she said, Dr. Ripley, I know I'm sounding like a broken record, but I'm required to say this. If you don't change your work habits, and start working less each day and getting more physical activity, your disease will accelerate, and it could be fatal. Your muscles are continuing to disintegrate, and the tremors will get worse, and the disease could reach your lungs and shut them down. I nodded. Do you understand? Mm-hmm. Can I refill my prescription? She sighed. I've never seen someone so negligent about their health,

she said as she got out her prescription pad. Is everything all right personally? Yeah. Have you seen a counsellor at all since your diagnosis? No. I know a counsellor here in town who helps persons with disabilities. I can make a referral if you'd like. No thanks. She scoffed. Wrote on her pad with quick, sharp strokes. Usually when my patients are self-destructive, I call mental health. It's unprecedented. I'm not self-destructive. How would you describe your mindset, then? Clear as a bell. She tore off the scrip. When I reached for it she withheld it. Can you promise me something? she said. Can you at least try to take care of yourself? I chuckled. I'll try. You will? Mm-hmm. She stared at me for a moment and then gave me the scrip, which I folded into my pocket.

On a positive note, Randal's been suspended from school for a day, two days into the school year. It's not good news that he's suspended; it's how he got suspended. The first day of classes he'd been assigned the task of writing a quick humour section for the school newsletter. He wrote a joke comparing Gandhi to Charles Manson— something to do with the symbols in their foreheads. Because he and his friend were the only ones working on it, none of the staff saw it before it was sent to all the students and their parents at the end of the day. Maggie, of course, was irate. This is your fault, she told me on the phone. You and those stupid jokes. He's trying to be just like you. What can I say? I said. The kid's smart. I bet most kids his age don't even know who Charles Manson is. Dexter, stop. I want you to talk to Randal. I want you to tell him to stop doing these things. I don't want him to stop. The kid's on his way to being a revolutionary, and I sure as hell ain't gonna spoil his potential. He could be kicked out of school, Dexter. Gad. Will you talk to him? Can you bring him to the Residence? A few hours later Maggie and Randal came to my room and I asked Maggie to give us some time alone. I closed the door and told Randal not to stop what he was doing, but to do it privately. I didn't do anything wrong, he said. It wasn't racist or anything. I nodded.

Clever irreverence is never appreciated in its own time, I said, especially in Canada. But you need to be diligent about these things. The time'll come for your day in the muck, young mantis, but right now, you're young and you've got some things to go through—you know, high school and all that. I know it seems ridiculous at times, but it's something you have to endure. Just keep it quiet. Keep a journal or keep it between friends. It's just a few years. Then once you're in university, you can hurl the Molotov cocktails. You know what a Molotov cocktail is, right? He nodded. It's a homemade bomb made with a bottle of gas and a cloth fuse. I laughed and squeezed his shoulder. When he opened the door a few minutes later we were both smiling, and Maggie looked at me suspiciously.

Esmeralda's retreated into her room again. I hear she's become volatile, lashing out at the staff. When I roll past her room I hear her crying and screaming. Sometimes she throws things. I imagine her perched on her bed, loaded with painkillers and sedatives, sitting up straight, cringing in the eye of what she perceives as the vortex of her disease. I can't help but pity her. If she'd let me, I'd sit beside her and read to her. Like a priest, I'd attempt to deliver her from the rattling anguish brought on by her knotted, misled mind.

These computer pages are beginning to outnumber the handwritten pages. They give this journal a disorganized, lopsided look.

ELEGY TO INTELLECTUAL BEAUTY—SEPTEMBER 14, 2009

On the first day of classes, my first-year students expect me to stride into the classroom with a chivalric gait and a regal bearing. When I roll in, the stunned, vacuous looks on their faces never cease to fill me with the purple, swirling, velvety glee that comes from anticipating and executing the noisy and inevitable dismantling of their expectations. I roll to the table at the front of the class; I put my books and notes on the table, set my bag aside, and roll up to the centre. Good morning, boys and girls. Welcome to my class. At this time I'm going to ask that you switch off all your cell phones, pagers, and global positioning devices. I don't want to be interrupted by hearing the reasons why your boyfriend won't call you. Chances are the reasons are self-explanatory. Now, my expectations for the term are fairly simple. Show up on time, do the readings, hand in your assignments when I ask for them, and speak regularly in class. If you fail to live up to these expectations, I'm sure that there are many courses in refrigeration and basket weaving that aren't full yet. Because this is a survey course on British literature, we'll be moving fairly quickly. Starting in the Romantic period, working our way through Dickens and the Victorians before ending up in the Modernist period. Therefore it is imperative that you complete the readings on time. If there comes a time you have not done the readings, and I'm quite good at spotting those people, I will ask you to leave the classroom, because you are not only wasting your classmates' time, but you are also wasting my time. Another thing—if you happen to have a disability and you require certain accommodations, please feel free to email me so we can discuss them. You may also contact disability services on campus. They can help you as well. Are there any questions? No? All right. The class looked anxious. Staring at their laptops or playing with their pens. Now, I said, to begin the course, I have a little quiz for you. How many of you are familiar with T.S. Eliot's "The Hollow Men"?

The students seem to look younger every year. Twenty-year-olds

five years ago looked older than twenty-year-olds now. Their expressions carry less weight. Their brains are like tar pits. I can almost hear the goopy little sucking noise when I give them information: it lingers on the surface for a moment before sinking into that clenching black oblivion. The few who do understand the texts usually say little in class, letting their essays do the talking. And by the time they graduate they'll have forgotten all about Lady Chatterley and William Blake and the dubious morals of the Ancient Mariner. All they want is the piece of paper saying they graduated. Then it's a lifetime of mortgages, marriages, divorces, child support payments, stomach ulcers, and recreational hockey. Too many of them seek to be merely satisfied, letting the tar harden so that anything else they learn merely skates across the surface. It'd be heartbreaking if I didn't have my own reasons for teaching. Teaching for me is hardly a public service. I'm not Annie Sullivan. Rather, teaching is a means through which to enjoy my favourite books over and over again. And although they may say otherwise, I'm pretty sure many of my colleagues feel the same way. We all like the sound of our own voices as they hover over the heads of a few dozen pupils. If a student happens to be taken with the subject and decides to make a career out of it, that's wonderful, but it's more out of his own initiative than any direction I've given. I do not inspire people. I'm much too callous, much too grounded. I merely present ideas. My students can take them or leave them.

No complaints after the first week and a half. Three students dropped my British survey course and four dropped my third-year study on Eliot. I imagine the complaints will come when the students really begin to know me. Our discussion of Lawrence's frank language should fetch a call or two from McTavish.

They make me think of Randal, these students. They make me think of how far ahead he is intellectually speaking. They make me proud and grateful to have him as my nephew. He sends me emails sometimes. Jokes and musings. I look forward to them.

You Can't Fast-Forward Stop-motion—
September 22, 2009

At breakfast yesterday, Esmeralda sat alone. Everyone watched her; she ignored them. She took a few dozen toothpicks from the counter and used her hash browns to create figures. Her talent was obvious. She made one figure a full six inches in height that stood on its own. It was clearly a woman. She sheared two hash browns so that they were identically rounded, and put them on the figure's chest. A few residents smirked when they saw this. She then took the small wrinkled leaves from the strawberries on her plate and, breaking a toothpick in half, stuck them on its head, giving it a semblance of hair. She scarcely ate. She eventually abandoned her breakfast and mounted her crutches and swung out of the dining area, leaving behind a half-dozen animals and a tall, slouching woman, an effigy that, with its soft, pan-fried complexion, fully exemplified her frustration.

I imagine her mind is like a crocodile: rough, parched, cobble-skinned, dormant and floating most of the time, and most active when it's hungry. When she really wants to she goes and talks with other residents. They keep the conversation quiet. They don't want to upset her. She looks at me as if she'd like to approach me, but she doesn't. Sometimes she gives me a surprised or quizzical expression, like she's trying to remember me. I asked Gertrude about her memory and she said she has been missing a few things, but overall she's keeping her wits.

Preparing to go to Glasgow in a few weeks. Will be meeting a number of disability academics. Many of them do not have disabilities. Sometimes this irritates me. Writing fiction from the perspective of another race or a different ability is one thing, because the imagination is boundless, but criticism is another. There are two key differences: imagination has little place in criticism; and fiction writers don't have to stand behind what they write. They can hide behind pseudonyms or fictionalizations of real people. Scholars must constantly

defend themselves, often to people who seldom understand what they're talking about.

On the other hand, disability is transparent. Out of the blue my colleagues could be bitten by monkeys and have their legs amputated. Or a child might be curious to see how Daddy would react if he smacked Daddy in the back of the head with a golf club. Disability is open. It's welcoming. That's what I love most about it. It is the only category that is unequivocally open and in which thousands of different conditions or identities can fit. Race is rigid. Gender is looser nowadays, but still more or less fixed. Disability is open.

Randal had his sixteenth birthday two days ago. Maggie told me she'd bought a present for him that could be from me. What is it? I said. A gift certificate to McNally Robinson, she said. You don't need to get him anything, she said. The subtext beneath her voice suggested she was afraid of what I might get him. I went and bought him a copy of *The Communist Manifesto*. Gave it to him when I got to the Wheatery restaurant on Eighth Street. Just him, Maggie and myself at the table. Told him that any modern rebel needs to read it. Maggie sighed and drank her water. I glanced around the restaurant. Saskatchewan licence plates from the 1950s adorned the wall. Old-fashioned oil lamps stood in the spaces between tables. From the outside, the building was shaped like a grain elevator. I groaned and leaned into my whiskey. Randal! I said. People glanced over at us. Did I tell you about this guy who lives at the Residence? Dexter, Maggie began. He's one of the most interesting men I've ever met. For years he was so cosmically inebriated that he erased most of his experiential memories. Dexter! So what I do, you see, is I ask him questions. Questions like, what was it like hunting in Africa? How many escorts did you have your first night in Moscow? And by asking him these questions, I help him create memories. It's an astonishing thing. Randal stared at me. And he's never done these things? he said. None of them, I said. It's extraordinary. He could tell me what it was like

to kill a lion in Africa. He could tell me what the coffee smelled like in Africa. Ah, thank god, Maggie said, the food's here. I chortled as the waiter set our plates before us. When he left, Maggie said, I won't have you ruin his birthday. You're only here because he wanted you here. Mom! It's appalling, Dexter, the way you act in public. I giggled and said, You should see how I act in private. Randal released a spurt of laughter. I seldom get out, Maggie. Give me a break. The people at the booth behind us stirred. I said over my shoulder, How many cripples does it take to screw in a light bulb? Dexter! Thirteen. One to screw in the light bulb, and a dozen piled up to the ceiling. Randal grabbed his stomach, lurching forward with laughter, his breath stirring his napkin. Dexter, if you don't stop we're going to leave. Mom, it's okay. It's not okay. He's drunk. He's funny. He's horrible. People like me are the ones who make life interesting. We make life worth living. Yes, Dexter, she said, playing with her fork and knife, I can see that your life is worth living. Whoo, I said. I chuckled. I grinned. I grimaced. Her words worked their slow clamp on me and pinched me off. I said nothing through the rest of the meal, glancing at Maggie every few minutes with rigorous anger. I ordered another whiskey. Maggie advised me against it. The waiter stood there, smiling stupidly. He looked at Maggie. You don't have to bring him anything, she said. The waiter nodded. Hold on a minute. I cocked my head. You don't speak for me, I said to her. I stared up at the waiter and held up my glass. My chair was in the middle of the aisle. People had to squeeze past me. Give me another, I said, or I'll complain to the manager about the lack of accommodations in this restaurant. Yes, sir. He went away. Maggie locked her jaw, and in the restaurant's soft light she looked slightly masculine. I would've sniggered if not for my outrage. I saved it, though. Randal was thumbing through the *Manifesto* and I didn't want to interrupt his reverie.

When we left the restaurant we shared a truncated goodbye. Randal gave me a hug and Maggie put her arm around him and they

walked to their vehicle together. You can't stop him from being what he wants to be, I called. Maggie looked over her shoulder at me and told Randal to get in the car. She followed him and they drove off. I'd called the Residence to have someone pick me up; Stefan was on his way. As I waited outside the restaurant I saw a hobo in a wheelchair sitting outside the KFC across the parking lot. He had a sign in his lap that read PLEASE CHANGE. He hung his head. I could spot the greasy sheen in his hair from where I sat. In the evening's liquid orange lights he was an oily pocket of dark. I stared at him. The whiskey twisted in my stomach. My fury with Maggie swirled through my mind. Hey! I said. People going into the restaurant looked at me. Not you, I said. I started wheeling toward the man, slipping off the concrete lip onto the pavement. You have any idea what you're doing? I said. The man looked up and blinked. I stopped short of the sidewalk. I couldn't find a ramp to get up. I locked my chair's brakes and sat before him. You're a disgrace, I said. Do you have any idea what you're doing, sitting there in that chair, with that sign, and that broken-down face? What're you talkin about? You're undoing my work. He looked around. I don't wanna work. You got any change? I'm not giving you any change, I said. It's people like you that are ruining any progress made by people like me. He scoffed. Piss on that. Look at you, I said, sitting there like that. You know how angry that makes me? Angry? You gotta be kidding. Why don't you get a job? Fuck you. I sighed. Gimme that sign, I said. Fuck off, he said. I want your sign. No. Gimme the sign. You gotta work for your money instead of hanging your goddamn head. Oh are you my boss? Yes, I'm your boss and I'm telling you to give me that goddamn sign. He chuckled. Are you gonna take it? Look at your arms. I reached for the sign. A tremor arched through my elbow and I accidentally knuckled him on the chin. Hey! He held the sign away from me. I leaned forward and seized his coat. He punched me. People inside the KFC and around the parking lot watched us. I saw us in the KFC window. Two

cripples battling for a cardboard sign. I slapped him and shoved him. A man came out and told us to stop or he was calling the police. Dr. Ripley! Stefan appeared at my side. What are you doing? Let's go, I said. Oh. Oh! The hobo laughed. Look at you! Aren't you the boss! Aren't you the big fuckin boss! At least I earn a living! I said. You're droppin your baseball cards, boss! I looked at my wheels. The cards were gone. Stefan looked back. Leave them, I said. What were you doing, Doctor? He lowered the ramp at the back of the van. Candidly exchanging ideas, I said. The hobo guffawed. You forgot your change! he said, waving his sign, his voice a bony, disjointed chug.

When I got home that night, I snarled at my fellow residents. In my whiskey-fired mind, they were extensions of the hobo, borne out of the same dispirited sediment against which I'd spent a large chunk of my life fighting. I told Esmeralda that I bet she couldn't remember the last time she'd been poked. I told Dante that he was my version of hell, that everyone in the Residence was my hell. Stefan rolled me through to my room. You know what my sister did? I said to him. She tried to silence me in the restaurant. She tried to make me insignificant in the eyes of the waiter. But I'm significant. I slapped my chair's arm. I'm significant, goddammit! Yes, Dr. Ripley. Now, stay here. I'm gonna go get you some water. He closed the door. Don't apologize for me! I said. These people don't deserve an apology. They deserve a kick in the ass!

Ended up being reported for harassing the residents. My grace period's over. I'm now up for review with the Residence board. Thankfully the board meeting's been delayed until after I come back from Glasgow. By then the incident will slacken in their minds and I'll be allowed to stay.

PUPILS ARE NOT NECESSARILY SYNONYMOUS WITH VISION— SEPTEMBER 27, 2009

Nicknames are easier to remember than names. I give many of my students nicknames. Some students are flattered, taking this habit for a kind of affection. Royal Highness, Sailor, Cabaret. These students straighten eagerly when called upon. Others squirm or roll their eyes when I call on them: Puck, Benjy, Fagan. I do this to assume control in my classroom. Since I can't hover over them and speak from behind a podium, I must wriggle into their heads some other way. If a student insists on being addressed a certain way—it's happened once or twice—I seldom call on her again.

Yesterday we were discussing the theme of paralysis in *Lady Chatterley's Lover*. I was expounding on how the immobility of Mrs. Chatterley's husband symbolizes not only the rigidity of the English class structure but also his wife's lack of sexual satisfaction when, as I raised my book to recite a particular passage, a tremor rocked through my upper body, and I dropped my book. I looked at my hand, and chuckled. Another tremor shunted through. A spasm worked its odd tickle through my arm and out my hand. My students sat up straight. Are you okay? one of them said. Yes. One moment. I moved my chair forward and reached down to pick up the book. As I reached, a third tremor spiked down my shoulder, and I knocked an elbow against the metal rail of my chair. I groaned and sat back up, holding my elbow. Do you want some help? another student said as she began to get up. Sit back down. I'll get it. My face was hot. Blood flooded up into my head. I exhaled and leaned back down. I grunted and pried a finger under the back cover and gripped it with two fingers. I snapped it up and settled back into my chair. I exhaled again. Now, I said, holding the novel with both hands, let's talk about paralysis.

My tremors are worsening. They're more intense and more frequent. Medication isn't relaxing them. I can hardly write on the

blackboard anymore. I tried writing comments on a student's paper and the pen skipped off the page. I can imagine the response I'll receive when I go to Glasgow. My colleagues in the field of disability studies will see me in a far worse state than in New York. My god, they'll say. What's happened to him? He's gotten so much worse. Hasn't anyone said anything to him?

Let them say that. In the classroom yesterday, under the anxious scrutiny of my students, I felt my spirit, my soul, my inner mantis, whatever it is, hardening, crouching, coiling, as though preparing to leap. I saw something in my students that I wouldn't have seen otherwise. I felt empowered. So I'll continue in this vein, crouching deep, hissing and spitting, giggling gloriously.

KEYNOTE SPEAKER, KEYSTONE TEACHER—OCTOBER 7, 2009

Glasgow is a sombre but beautiful city. Rainy. Narrow lanes buoyed by rows of colourful leafy trees. Plenty of places to drink and eat. The university's a converted medieval castle. Iron gates. Looming towers. Stone the colour of William Wallace's bruised back.

Delivered my keynote speech last night. Over one hundred and fifty people. Well attended for an academic forum. I spoke about language. The tyranny of it. How we're offended. How we are not being as honest with each other as we could be. I told them about the jokes Randal and I share. How we laugh at them. How it's not just appropriate that we laugh, but how it's necessary. By laughing, I said, I felt liberated, because I experienced true freedom from the hierarchical tyranny of language that fixes us in, to borrow Eliot's choice of words, "a formulated phrase." To make and uninhibitedly laugh at jokes is to experience true freedom. Laughing at such things is a way of accepting honesty. Stand-up comedians constantly employ this tactic; why not the rest of us? To this end, political correctness is as much a clamp as right-wing or dictatorial censorship, and we must explore the possibilities inherent in lifting a politically correct agenda from academia and from daily discourse. Such habits would emancipate not just persons with disabilities, but those who occupy restricted categories of race, sexuality, and class. My body, I said toward the end, is knotted and warped, twisted and arched. It is a letter in a foreign language, part of an ever-expanding alphabet consisting of thousands of letters and infinite accents. To speak this language, the tongue must harden and curl, and the voice must growl and lurch. This language is open to all.

Several people were outraged by my tirade. At least three people walked out of the room. One young woman picked up a book, one that I wrote, and threw it, hitting me in the shoulder. The audience stirred when I told them Randal's vegetable joke. I had to hold up my

hand and pause for them to stop jittering so I could continue. During the question period, some of them accused me of being right-wing, saying that such a system would privilege white men. Others told me I was narrow-minded, that such liberty is little more than anarchy, which amounts not to freedom but to fear. I rebutted that connecting linguistic freedom with anarchy was a tenuous link at best, and that white men would be just as open to scrutiny as other races.

Afterwards a handful of us went to a place called the Buddha Bar. At a table perched beside a gigantic plaster Buddha, one of my colleagues, a disability scholar from Manchester named Baron Raymond, leaned over and said, I think you've struck a chord, Dexter, but you wanna be careful with how you play those notes. It's ideas, I said, glancing down the table to ensure the others heard me. It's about suggesting ideas, putting these things out there. These things should be talked about. I agree, but perhaps in a more tactful manner. I shook my head. Tactful won't cut it. You need the right language to discuss these notions. Practise what you preach. Otherwise they won't fly. Baron drank his gin. And what do the folks back in the flatlands think about all this? he said. As I recall, you're part of a very left-wing faculty. I chuckled. What can I say? I'm a fish out of water. I've fallen off the political spectrum. Hmm. Well, I hope it all goes well for you, Dexter, though I have to warn you that a fish out of water does not live very long, especially in a scholarly institution. I doubt they'll fire me. I'm a good teacher and I've the strongest, most progressive research portfolio in the department. Yes, good work, considering you haven't been in disability studies for long. I smirked at him. I rise fast, I said. Like a dead fish in the ocean. Jolly good, Baron. Did you learn that phrase at a Red Devils game? Baron scratched beside his mouth. You were in British literature before, correct? That's right. And then you came into disability studies after your diagnosis? I'd been tinkering with disability before my diagnosis. My condition just deepened my involvement. Hmm. So it's not true that you're simply exploiting

the field to attract recognition? I glanced around the table. Several students looked at me. I beg your pardon? I said. I'd heard that you hated your initial field, that you said it was overcrowded. The arena for British criticism *is* overcrowded. Yes, well there are some, and I'm not included in this group, who think that you switched to disability studies because it's a field ripe for sowing, so to speak, and that you, even though you scorn politics, you exploit disability as a sociopolitical position to attract funding and increase your academic profile. Is this true? I sipped my whiskey and shook my head. Look at me, I said. How can I exploit disability when I myself have a disability? If anyone's guilty of exploitation, it's you. I pointed at Baron's long, perfectly functional legs. He chuckled. You speak, Dexter, like you're immune to criticism. Nobody's immune to criticism, I said. I'm safe, though. They can't fire me for advocating what essentially amounts to free speech. People have been fired for worse, said a graduate student who, upon speaking, immediately lowered her gaze. I drank my whiskey and felt it swell through my head. Surely, I said, you understand that when I talk about free speech, I'm not talking about being deliberately hurtful. I'm just talking about using whatever words come to mind. There are so many guards in our heads that rise whenever we talk. If we could eliminate the guards in our minds, do you know how much potential that would unlock? How much more innovative and creative we'd become? Many of the students cocked their heads as they pondered. I lifted my glass. A tremor leapt and I spilled whiskey onto my lap. Two students leaned over to help; I told them to leave it alone. I wiped myself clumsily with a napkin.

I came back to the inn and logged on to my computer and found an email from Randal. Good luck on your trip, uncle, he wrote, and I came up with something last night. You remember when you talked to me about that guy in the residence, was it jeeves or reginald, the memory guy? I thought last night, what would happen if you tried to plant the idea of a crime in his head, you know ask him something like, do

you remember where the body is hidden? LOL. I thought you might like that. Have fun in scotland, peace, Randal. The boy gives me so much pride. If he keeps it up, he'll end up with a genuinely great mind.

THIS WHEELCHAIR BOWER HER PRISON—
OCTOBER 12, 2009

Returned to Saskatoon to find Esmeralda in a wheelchair and thoroughly despondent. Her expression is flat. Her arms lie limply crossed in her lap. She sits in her chair as though it's an open jaw, a yawning mouth of metal and fabric into which she sinks, allowing it to consume her. Not sure if she's retained her faculties. I'm not allowed to talk to her until we hear from the Residence Board. Stefan supervises me, watches where I go like I'm an ornery kindergartner.

Asked Gertrude about the meeting. I don't know the particulars, she said. What are the board members like? I said. I've only met one of them, and he seems nice enough. Who's that? Somebody from the university, I don't know. A professor? I think so. What did he look like? Tall, glasses, like a professor. Egh. What're my chances, Gertrude? She shrugged. You'd been warned how many times, Dr. Ripley. What does that mean? I wouldn't be too optimistic. I don't want to leave. I know you don't, and I don't want you to, either, because I like your company, but it's not up to me. Will the board listen to me? They might. They don't usually meet with residents, but they made an exception in your case, because of your...I guess you could say uniqueness. I glanced around my room. Up at Edward Scissorhands on my wall. His pointed fingers branching from the poster's edge. The dense scar across his cheek suddenly striking. Can you help me? I said. Can you give me a recommendation or something? If I can, I will, she said.

She left my room. Dante went past in the hall. He sneered and tapped the moulding of my doorway. I shut the door. Gripped the knob. Started to shake. I flexed my arms. They rattled against the arms of my chair. My spine felt like it tilted to the left. My legs jimmied. My feet clenched. Tremors rolled through the shaking like an undertow. Like my body was angry with me. I tried to concentrate on

being still but the awful thought of eviction wedged in, splintering my thoughts in multiple directions. How pathetic I'd look. How Dante would laugh. How Jeeves would be puzzled. How Gertrude would hug me when I left. How Maggie would stand over me with her arms folded and her lips pursed. How my colleagues wouldn't be surprised. How lonely Edward Scissorhands was. How hollow that digital picture frame looks.

Meeting's in two days. I'm trying not to be afraid. Trying to finish my lesson plans and focus on work. But it's impossible not to be afraid right now.

L'enfer, C'est Les Autres—October 13, 2009

Slept little. An ambulance was here last night. Saw the flashes on the wall. Thought it was for Dante. Went to class this morning and whiffed through it and came back to find out that Esmeralda tried to kill herself. Took a knife from the dining room and cut her wrists. Stefan heard sobbing in her room; found her on her knees, blood unspooling from her wrists. Seeing him, she lurched to the wall and tried to shove the knife into an electrical socket. Stefan skipped over and wrestled her away. Another staff worker called the ambulance. She's now under twenty-four-hour monitoring.

I feel horrible today. Unable to concentrate. Dante prancing like he knows I'm going to be evicted. His meaty grin full of cheek and mottled teeth. I came back to my room and felt the need to throw something away. I tossed the *My Left Foot Job* CD. Broke it into three pieces and wrapped it in paper so nobody would see. Took the memory stick Maggie gave me and erased all the pictures on it except the ones with Randal and myself, of which there are only three. Put them in the digital frame. Two of me with Randal before I was diagnosed, and one of us with me in my chair. The gravity seems to shift from the earlier images to the last. In the pictures from before I was diagnosed the look in my eyes is flatter. Ignorant. My posture carries little animation. I look as though my voice is tinny. My mouth is closed. I'm beardless. In the first picture I have my arm around Randal as if he is a lamppost I'm leaning against. In the second I grip his neck. I seem on the verge of hurting him. He smiles in both. In the third picture I'm loud. Both Randal and I smile. I have a beard. I point at the camera. I must've been just getting used to my pain meds. Probably joking about the loopiness I was experiencing. My voice has an edge to it. Not quite booming, but possessing a lively rake that hooks and nestles in the ear. The prairie behind us is an indistinct haze. The backgrounds of the first two pictures are from downtown Saskatoon and Maggie's backyard.

I look at the pictures, my books, Edward Scissorhands. I think of their weight. They're all I want to carry with me. In my chair I feel they're all I have room for. It's more room than what I had standing up. Everything slid off me then.

Tremors are bugging me. Keep having to delete words and start over again. Need to stop for now.

This later in the evening during a lull in the tremors:

Beginning to get angry now. None of the residents will talk to me. Dante follows me. Stefan watches me. Even gentle Gertrude keeps tabs on me. Jeeves looks away when I pass him. I wanted to get everyone into one room and really give it to them. Wanted to vomit my anger into their laps. Listen, you morons, you vacuous limpid insects. I know that I'm under fire here but you don't have to make it worse by hounding me. I'm harmless. I understand the consequences here. Okay? Can't we return to life as usual? But I did nothing.

It's times like this I wish I had a lock on my door. This is one thing I hate about the Residence. When you're angry, you don't have the privacy to scream and punch the wall and throw a garbage can across the room. Your emotions become everyone else's business. So you fold into yourself.

Expulsion from Paradise—October 14, 2009

The meeting lasted thirty minutes. I said my piece: I understand the gravity of the situation, I was drunk, I apologize, I won't drink again, I'll behave in the future. But they hardly listened to me. One of them, some fatass wearing khakis and a Rolex, texted on his cell phone all the way through my plea. The cowfuckers had decided before we even met. I've a month to find another place to live and get out of the Residence. I asked if I could appeal the decision. They said no. I hurled swears at them. None of them had a disability and I accused them of being presumptuous. None of you know what it's like, I said. You don't have a damn clue. How dare you put yourselves in a position to decide what's best for people like me? I said to the fat-ass that I hoped he'd have a heart attack while he was driving down the highway and that I would laugh at him because being fat was his own goddamn fault. I told another board member, a young nurse who said little during the meeting, that her eyes were too close together. They really weren't, but with her air of insecurity and impressionability, I knew she'd be studying herself in the mirror later on.

Not sure what to do. Haven't told Maggie yet. Gertrude said she'd help me find an apartment if that's what I want. I shook my head at her. I don't know what I want. I haven't lived regularly for a long time. The trick's escaped me.

It's night now. The Residence has calmed. After the meeting I went straight to my room. Avoided everyone. Tried to work and failed. I only saw Gertrude because she came to bring me some dinner and remind me about my medication. I put a chair in front of my door. Didn't want to see Dante or anyone.

All of this on top of planning lessons and grading papers. A whole pile of papers beside me right now, awaiting my pen. I don't know what to do. I don't think I can live alone while maintaining my workload. I don't want to live with Maggie. Being around Randal all

the time might be good, but Maggie would diminish that. She'd harp at me to leave him alone. And she wouldn't do what the Residence staff does for me. Cook for me. Help me bathe. Drive me around. She works across town from the university. And taxis are too expensive.

Need to quit for now. My frustration's getting the better of me. And my tremors are upsetting me.

TRUTH IS UGLINESS, UGLINESS TRUTH—OCTOBER 19, 2009

Still angry. Hardly made it through class this morning. Chewed up a student when she commented on Keats. She said something about the heifer mentioned in "Ode on a Grecian Urn" and suggested it might be Indian in origin. Don't East Indians worship cows? she said. I stared at her. Shook my head. Told her that the title is "Ode on a GRECIAN Urn." Not "Indian Urn." Oh, she said. I leaned forward in my chair. Asked her if she was illiterate. Her mouth fell open. God! I said, gripping my book and whipping my eyes up to the ceiling. If only old age would waste this generation right now! That drew tears from the student and frightened the others. None of them said anything after that. Expecting an email from McTavish any minute now.

Still haven't talked to Maggie. She's called, though. I've been dreading her pomposity. Her speeches. What did I say, Dexter? Didn't I say you'd get in trouble? I asked Gertrude if there were other residences in Saskatoon and she said there were a few but either they had protracted waiting lists or they were in poor condition. She's helping me to find an apartment. She seems guilty for some reason. Wondering if she said something to the board.

I sometimes browse the internet looking at apartment listings. Just skim them, though. I pay little attention. I focus on my work more than ever. An article due in December. The final exam for my survey course. I don't want to deal with moving right now. Not like it's urgent. I don't have many possessions. And I have money.

Dante came to me at dinner two days ago. So I hear you've been shucked, he said with a cheery crescendo. Piss off, I said. I bit my lip; my voice has been meagre of late. And you don't have any place to go? It's not your business. A tremor in my hand. My fork rattled on the tabletop. I hunched forward. He chuckled. You're a smartass, he said. All smartasses get their due. Makes me proud, gives me hope to know there's some kind of justice in the world. If there's any jus-

tice in the world, I said, you'll have a vicious stroke tonight and be paralyzed down one side, so every time you try to push yourself in your chair you just go in circles. He chuckled again. Anything you say doesn't mean nothing anymore, he said. You're already gone. I'm not gone yet. You will be soon. I still have time to make your life miserable. Like you did with Calvin? You know you helped to kill im. What horseshit. The man died of lung failure. If you didn't bug im all the time and make im yell and curse at you he might've lived a bit longer. Maybe it was you and your little posse that killed him. Always gabbing and watching after me like a bunch of idiot sheriffs. He liked being with us, boy. A bunch of old incontinent feebs. He said so himself, he liked it. Whatever. I glanced around the dining room. You're still a miserable lot, I said. None of you are doing anything good with yourselves. Dante shook his head. We're no more miserable than you are, boy. You're probably even more so, now that you gotta leave. I'd feel sorry for you if you weren't such a little bastard. Dante started to wheel away. I threw my fork at him thinking I'd miss. The fork hit him in the back of the head. He whirled around and grabbed me and started shaking me and hitting me. I hit him back and took my plate and whipped it sideways and smashed it over his head; beans and potatoes fouled his face. I slapped him and pushed my fingers into his eyes. He hollered, and Stefan and another male attendant came to separate us. Doctor Ripley! Shut up, Stefan. I'm already on my way out the goddamn door, so what does it matter? Dante picked beans out of his face and threw them at me. The other attendant steered him away, and Stefan took me away. On my way out of the cafeteria I saw Jeeves. Hey! I said. This is important. Remember where the body of Helen Samson is buried. The police are looking for it. Remember! He cringed and shook his head. I saw Esmeralda in the hallway. She stared at the floor; her wrists were still bandaged. You know, I said, cripple blood is considered a delicacy in some cultures. You might consider donating. Doctor Ripley! Stefan shook my chair. I laughed

and wildly flailed my arms. I babbled and tossed insults up and down the hall. I rapped the arms of my chair; the beat drove my words throughout the Residence. Let us go then! You and I! When the evening is spread out against the sky like a patient etherised upon a table! Ha! I am an Eliotic idiot! I leaned back and looked up at Stefan; his face was upside down. I grinned. Look, I'm gibbering. Booga-ma-looga-booga. Doesn't that count for something? My mouth slackened; I dribbled onto my beard and wiped it on my shirt. I laughed and rocked in my chair. Stefan put me in my room. His expression was flush with worry. I stared at him. Stefan. Yes, Doctor Ripley? Do you have a crush on me? What? Geh. What should I do now, Stefan? A tremor jolted and rolled through me. For fuck's sakes. I touched my new baseball cards jammed in the spokes of my chair. I adjusted them so they were all right-side up. Stefan, I'm so goddamn screwed, aren't I? I put my hands in my lap and bent over and began laughing, and soon the laughter slid into crying. Ah, Stefan. Yes? I wiped my eyes. You can go. You sure? Close the door behind you. Okay. He left the room. I sobbed and rocked in my chair, rocking against the tremors. Rocking into the tremors. Pinching my weakening mouth with both hands and slamming my curved feet into the floor. The pain spun up into my hips. I squeezed my hair and bit my lip. I heaved against everything. Cried against everything. Laughed against everything.

ADAM POTTLE

We Can Find No Scar but Internal Difference, Where the Meanings Are—October 24, 2009

My vocal cords are beginning to slacken. My voice warbles some-times. Like I'm reliving puberty.

Still haven't talked to Maggie yet. She's left at least four messages. Saying Randal misses me. Saying she'll stop by sometime soon.

Had a dream last night; not a mantis dream. I was in my chair sitting atop some building. Based on the view, I think it was the Bess-borough Hotel downtown. It was night. My chair was on the edge of the roof. I was looking away; my back was to the river below me. Downtown Saskatoon glowed. Wind rose in spurts, ruffling my pants. I sat there for a moment and then without any prompting or pushing tipped backward and fell off the roof. Only I fell in slow motion. I could move regularly, waving my hands and shouting and glancing around. I just fell in slow motion. Like I was being lowered gently to the ground. I saw the windows of the Bessborough on my way down, all of them darkly curtained. I stuck out my foot and let it brush the brick and knock on the windowsills. It took over a minute for me to reach the ground. I saw it six feet away. Then I landed. Smack. Unjustifiably hard. As though I'd fallen from the roof in real time. My head bounced on the concrete. I groaned and winced and whim-pered. My legs pitched backward. My body unfolded from my chair. My arched feet jerked over my head and thudded on the cement. My chair came apart. I shut my eyes against the dark heave of head pain. I whimpered and coiled into a foetal position. The charged, intense darkness in my head collapsed into a flatter darkness. I heard another spurt of wind. Then I woke up, my head dense.

McTavish has put me on probation and threatened me with sus-pension. He'll visit my survey class at least once a week until he's sure I can treat the students civilly. Then he asked me if I was having problems. Said I've been more irritable than usual. Which is saying a

lot, he said, unable to resist the barb. I said I'm fine and that I'll expect him in my class soon.

Whenever she has a spare moment Gertrude packs my books for me. She's filled two boxes so far, gingerly wrapping the first editions with white paper. I asked her why she's doing this. I thought you could use a hand, she said. That's it? I said. Nothing else? No. You didn't say anything to the board? I made a recommendation in your favour. That's all? Yes. I studied her. She took my first edition of *Ulysses* and wrapped it up.

After I came back from the school yesterday, Esmeralda came to my room. She sat in her chair, filling my doorway. Looking at the floor, the wall, the boxes of books. Entwining and untangling her hands. She wore a ball cap. The rich burgundy had evaporated from her hair, which was now the colour of gophers. She sat there for a long time. What is it? I said. She looked at me like she was withholding something. Are you angry with me? She shook her head. Are you here to tell me that you're glad I'm leaving? She shook her head again. What is it, then? She met eyes with me. I'm sorry for you, she said. I can't imagine how bitter you are. Gah. The last thing in this world that I need is pity, I said. No, see, that's it right there. Your manner. How you treat people. I hated you for a while after you told me your philosophy or whatever it is that you call it. I still think it's a load of shit. But I started thinking about why you would think that way. And I decided it's simple. You've nothing much to live for. I blinked. Yeah, she said. People don't come to places like this willingly. Nobody in their right mind. Your life can't be enjoyable. I chuckled. You're very presumptuous, I said. She straightened in her chair. You're a hypocritical wag. You slit your wrists. You have no grounds to judge me. Her head swayed to one side. Is your life enjoyable? she said. I'm doing very valuable work. I swept my hand across my desk. That's not what I asked. I enjoy it. You do? Yes. Then why do you treat people the way you do? Part of the philosophy. Stop with the goddamn philosophy.

It's just misery. You don't understand. No, I don't understand. Why don't you explain it to me? That'd take time. I'm not going anywhere. Some other time. Why not now? I'm busy. Doing what? Planning lessons and finding a place to live. You're stalling. You don't have a philosophy. Yes I do. Then explain it to me. I'll be your student for today. I've had enough students for today. I'll be one more, then. I sighed. Glanced over the lesson plan I'd laid out on my desk. Looked at Esmeralda. A tremor scurried around my shoulders and flitted out through my fingers. All right, I said. Let's go to the dining room. I need some water first.

We went to the dining room and we each got a glass of water and we rolled to a table in the corner. I spilled most of my water on the way. She studied me. Her eyes had hardened and quickened since she first came to the Residence but as we sat at the table that rigidity was softened by earnest curiosity. She was a willing, if sceptical pupil. I took a drink and put down my glass and wiped my mouth and leaned forward on the table. My philosophy centres around a different view of disability, I said. It basically states that disability is a means of dealing with the insignificance of human life. Now, all of our lives are meaningless. That's just a given. We try to act like we matter, but we're really nothing more than sophisticated insects. Now people with disabilities, their lives are seen as even more worthless, or at least as having diminished value. As a result, they get a unique window into the meaninglessness of life. Most people don't see how unimportant their lives are, or they ignore it. Disability allows us to see it, and…it's like the Alcoholics Anonymous credo. You can't fix your life until you see you have a problem. You follow me? Esmeralda nodded. So because we, as persons with disabilities, can see our insignificance, we can confront it, and work to create meaning. That meaning is always individual, because every person's disability is unique, and the Western world in general is founded on the concept and perception of the individual. You know, iPods and all that. For me, I generate meaning

by employing disability as a philosophy. It's my life's work, and I hope that my individual meaning becomes communal through my writings. I hope that what works for me will work for others. And that's how I wanna be remembered. I sighed. So, really, disability is a solution to life's absurdity. I chuckled. I secretly hope that someday, someone will discover my writings and create a sort of cult where people have to break their backs or have their legs chopped off to be initiated. Is that morbid? A little bit, Esmeralda said. She stared forward. You look despondent, I said. She raised her eyebrows. There are other aspects to it, too, I said. Disability gives us personal strength and a realistic perspective of the world—how people treat each other, why people are motivated to do what they do—and through that perspective we can understand humanity. As a whole, this philosophy promotes the development of identity and conscience. Esmeralda blinked. Look at the world, I said. The Western world. Look at America and Canada. People are not as strong as they used to be. People no longer have common sense or consciences. Esmeralda smirked. Okay, I said, despite my own callousness and my habitual irreverence, I mourn the decline of the human conscience. We've simply stopped admiring good people. The people we look up to now are those who laugh at and profit from the misfortune of others. Our inability to relate to one another, to use our imaginations to genuinely plant ourselves in another's situation, has brought about a strain of immorality and general weakness. We live in a wholly individualistic world. Everybody's worried. We have to wash our hands ten times a day. We have to wear bike helmets. We have to wear seat belts. We have to watch our calorie intake. All of these things, all of this vigilance and overscrutinizing, amounts to weak people. Most people today are weak. Look at the people here. Look at people at the mall. All those fat-asses and spoiled teenagers. You know why obesity is becoming epidemic? You know why we have STDs and alcoholics and drug abuse? Because we can't control ourselves anymore. We live in a culture of permissive addic-

tion. And that lack of control, that lack of strength makes us weak and selfish. Look at my sister. Since she was divorced she's had at least two mid-life crises. She's been in therapy, she's been on medication, she hardly knows what's good for herself, let alone what's good for her son. Now, because we're weak, we're immoral, and we're angry, and because there's such a clamp on everything there's no decent way to express that anger. We can't get into a decent bar fight because someone's always carrying a knife or a gun. We can't start a riot over a proper cause. We just turn over vehicles because we lose a goddamn hockey game. We can't even do a proper protest anymore. It's just a bunch of old hippies and impressionable stragglers. So what happens? All that weakness builds and builds and builds, and then people explode. This is why Columbine happened. This is why that boy shot all those women at the Polytechnique school in Montreal. They're reacting against their own weakness. They're looking for something to react against and they're not finding anything because the world, especially Canada, is too clean, too sacred, too weak, so they cast their problems onto others. Look at me, I said. I used to be angry, too. I used to be weak. I lolled about and didn't care much. And then I was diagnosed with Charcot-Marie-Tooth. Years later, look at me now. My back is bent. My muscles are slowly wasting away. I have tremors. I have pain. I have feet that look like insect claws. But I'm strong. And it's because I've found something to react against, and react with. With this disease, I don't feel like I'm being melted into a steaming puddle of bone and mush. I feel like I'm being distilled into my purest essence, like I'm being broken down to my most basic self. My twisted spine is a moral compass. Are you following me? Esmeralda frowned. People in wheelchairs do drugs, she said, and deaf people, and people with palsy. They get fat, they lose control. That's because they want to live in spite of their disability, instead of with it, I said. That's not it. It's just humans being humans. It's got nothing to do with disability. I cleared my throat. Let me ask you something, I said.

How did you feel when your family brought you here? Were you angry? Of course I was angry. I screamed and shouted at them. When my brother came to hug me I shoved him away. And did you maybe learn something about them that you didn't know before? Esmeralda looked at the table and pulled her teeth over her lip. I don't know, she said. She dragged one finger over the table. Her fingernail made a soft hiss on the varnished wood. I think I learned something about them. I didn't expect them to just cast me off like that. I thought they were more loyal than that. I nodded. They said that they'd visit me each day but I haven't seen them in almost a week, she said. See? I said. You see what disability does? It allows you a perspective you might not otherwise have. It makes you a better judge of character, and it makes you a stronger person, because you have to deal with that abandonment. Esmeralda made a face and scratched beside her mouth. All it did was allow me to see that my dad and brother are neglectful. Is that something worth learning? You wouldn't have known that otherwise. I didn't want to know that, she said. I wouldn't have known if I didn't have A.L.S. She sighed. I'm sorry, but this isn't a philosophy. It's inconsistent, and there's nothing virtuous or good about it. You're not understanding. Yes, I am. All I see is a desperate man trying to justify himself. Aren't all philosophers desperate? If they don't know how to live properly. Albert Camus wrote that the only serious philosophical problem is suicide. Well, I disagree. Disability is another. We will all experience disability. All of us. Everyone could use this perspective. Even people with Alzheimer's and Down syndrome and such. Disability allows us to see our humanity, and inhumanity. In the process, it becomes a redemptive quality. She chortled. That's another problem with it. What? You. Me? How can you promote something so positive when you yourself are such an asshole? I don't think I've ever met someone as callous as you. I have to be callous. Why? Because nobody will take me seriously if I'm not. We associate antagonism with judgement, and negativity with realism. If I'm positive all the time, in

this wheelchair, I'll just be a poster cripple—one of those inspirational deals that always gives me diabetes. And I won't be taken seriously. That's a really narrow view. And it obviously doesn't help you. Yes it does. Then why are you getting kicked out? Because I was drunk. Her brows arched. She shook her head. You're a hypocrite. I shrugged. We all are.

She shook her head again and pushed away from the table and rolled off and out of the dining room. The tremors came on hard in those last few minutes. I got another drink of water, which I spilled again, and then came back to my room and sat in the middle of my boxes of books, feeling drained and dull. At that moment I didn't know if I believed myself. I looked up at Edward Scissorhands. Tremors stuttered through my muscles. My bones jarred and sharpened. Today I'm a little surer. But that's not enough.

TOSSING AWAY AN ALBATROSS IS MORE DIFFICULT THAN YOU THINK—OCTOBER 28, 2009

McTavish at my class today. He sat at the back with his notebook balanced on his lap. Although I hated it, the students seemed more relaxed with him in the room. I played nice with them. Even went so far as to praise the one I'd belittled last week. Well done! I said after she described the rhyme scheme for a Shakespearean sonnet. You'll be prepared for graduate school by the end of this term. Now, if you can identify the type of rhythm Shakespeare utilizes, I'll give you a cherry lollipop. McTavish grimaced. He didn't appreciate my sarcasm. "Shall I compare thee to a summer's day?" I said. This is a specific kind of question that Shakespeare asks. It's a strategy that authors use when the answer is obvious. Now, what kind of question is it? The class blanked. To myself I said, Apparently the answer's not so obvious in this room. McTavish straightened and wrote in his notebook. I sighed. Okay, I said to the class. When you ask someone a question to which you already know the answer, what kind of question is it? A student put up her hand and, in the voice of a child looking over the edge of the high diving board, said, Interrogation? I gritted my teeth. Nice try, I said, but this isn't CSI. McTavish: scritch-scritch-scritch. I imagined he was playing Hangman, filling in SUSPENSION letter by letter, a stick man in a wheelchair dangling from a gallows. Another student put up his hand. Manipulation? he said. It starts with an R, I said. Do you give up? No, McTavish said, holding out his hand. They can get it. Give them a bit more time. I'm trying to move the lesson along, I said. They can get it. There's time. I exhaled. Okay, I said. Does anybody have an idea? It starts with an R? That's right. What's the second letter? An H. H…rhombus? That's not it. Rheumy? That's not spelt with an H, is it? I looked at McTavish. Raised my eyebrows desperately. What's the third letter? Through my clenched teeth: An E. So it's not rhombus. What other words start with RHE? Hang on, let me get my dictionary.

It's rhetorical! I said. McTavish pursed his lips. A rhetorical question! That is the kind of question Shakespeare is asking! "Shall I compare thee to a summer's day?" It's a rhetorical question! A question to which the answer is obvious! The students looked at their books. Many of them puzzled. One of them put up his hand. How is it obvious? he said. I shut my eyes and said, Read the next line. Oh. Oh yeah! I looked at McTavish. His notebook was closed. I'm expecting a report from him soon.

Maggie came here yesterday. Asked me why I hadn't called. Asked me why my bookshelves were empty and why there were boxes all over the floor. Are you moving? she said. In a manner of speaking, I said. Where are you moving? I don't know. I haven't found a place yet. Then why are your books all packed up? I have only two weeks left. Two weeks left to what? To get out. Her jaw straightened. They're kicking you out? I shrugged. Are you surprised? I said. She exhaled. Shook her head and looked at me with her mouth open and her brow uneven. Jesus, Dexter! Why didn't you call me? I could've come over and helped, I could've brought your things over to my house. Come on, Maggie. You don't want me living there. I've asked you how many times if you wanted to live with us. You said no. That's not the impression I got last time we spoke. Well, this is different now. Why's it different? You're being kicked out, you need a place to live. It doesn't alarm you that I'm being kicked out? She blinked. I imagine you were just being yourself and these people don't know how to handle you. And you do? She hesitated. Look, if you need a place to live, you can come and live with Randal and me. I don't know. Where else are you gonna go, Dexter? You can't live by yourself. How do you know? You told me yourself. Look at your hands, look at your shoulders. You're just shaking. If you tried to cook you'd probably burn yourself. Thanks. Well, it's true, isn't it? How am I going to get around? Maybe you can call a taxi or something, or one of those Handi-Dart buses can take you to the school. Those are for grade school kids. I'm

sure there's some way of getting around. I licked my lips. Gripped the arms of my chair and adjusted myself. If I come to live with you, I said, are we gonna be able to stand each other? We'll find out, she said. You're okay with me being around Randal? We'll talk about that. When do you have to be moved out? By the fourteenth. Okay. I'll be back on the weekend and we'll move the boxes out of here. Well, we don't have to do it so quickly. I'd like to stay here a little longer. Well, the weekend's the only time I have to help you move. This upcoming weekend's best, because I have to go to Regina the weekend after. Well, can we just take my books and things to your house, and I can stay here until the fourteenth? Why do you wanna stay here, Dexter? I like it here. You're being kicked out. Yeah? Maggie groaned. Do you think Randal will like that I'm moving in with you? I said. Maggie rolled her eyes. He never stops talking about you, she said. He'll probably be ecstatic.

I rolled with Maggie to the Residence entrance. She suggested that because of my tremors I get a motorized wheelchair. I said I probably will someday. After she left I saw Esmeralda in the hallway. That's your sister? she said. The one that's had two mid-life crises? Yep, I said, and she's about to have a third.

NINETY-FIVE DOMESTIC THESES—NOVEMBER 3, 2009

Both my mouth and my vocal cords continue to loosen. Drooled a little during class. Wish we had been reading something sexy at the time. The effect would've gone over well. Thankfully McTavish wasn't there this time. So for one day I could resume calling the students Hee-haw and Cabaret.

Haven't even left the Residence yet and Maggie's already giving me rules. No drinking. No telling Randal those awful jokes. Prescription drugs only. Make my own meals. Give a monthly rent of five hundred dollars. Arrange my own transportation. Take care of my own hygiene. Do my exercises. I don't know how she thinks I live while I'm at the Residence. With all the time I spend wheeling around, how do I have time for anything else but work? A good professor works fifty to sixty hours a week. A great professor, seventy to eighty. I've no time for the smaller things. Well, Maggie said, then you're going to get very dirty very quickly, because I simply don't have the time to do everything for you. I can help you once in a while, if you need it, but that's all. Maybe once you're settled in we can look for a caregiver to help you out during the day. I groaned. After living around such wonderful people as Gertrude and Stefan for so long, the idea of having someone else is almost automatically a disappointment.

Tremors increasing still. Ramping up up up. Beginning to worry me, actually. Might have to start shortening my entries here.

By inserting these printed pages, this journal grows more lopsided by the day. Takes on an awkward weight. I'm glad.

DECISIONS AND REVISIONS WHICH A MINUTE WILL REVERSE—NOVEMBER 5, 2009

This afternoon, in the midst of packing away the last of my books, Gertrude stood up straight and faced me. Dr. Ripley? She put her hands on her hips. I did say something to the board. I stared at her. I couldn't help it, she said. I was the one who'd recorded the earlier incidents with Mr. Myrtle and a few of the others, so they came to me and asked me questions confirming the reports. I'm sorry. I didn't have—I tried to downplay it as much as I could, I tried to make it sound like you were just misunderstood and that you needed an outlet that the Residence couldn't provide, but it didn't work. My shoulders sagged. A tremor scurried through, irritating me, galling me. I looked at her. I wanted to appear grave. My tremors undermined that. She bit her lip. Waffled. Her eyes penitent blue bulbs. Her face and hair seemed to soften before me. Sorry, she whispered. I kept staring. Resisted blinking. Stared through my tremors. To her I must've looked unsettling. I wanted that. Her shoulders shrunk inwards. I'll go, she said. She closed up the box of books and left my room.

I didn't realize how close I felt to her until she left. I expect to be disappointed by many people: my students, my colleagues, my sister, my fellow residents. But not Gertrude. She hasn't slipped once in the years I've known her. I closed my door and sat at my desk, doing nothing, staring. I'll miss her the most.

Et Tu, Brutus?—November 7, 2009

Met with McTavish today. His office, like all my colleagues' offices, was crammed with books and smelled dry and sweet. Reminded me of a martini I had in New York. When I rolled in I was instantly thirsty. Dexter, he said. There's something we need to discuss. I sighed. So I am being suspended? I wasn't sanitized enough in the classroom? No no no. It's not about your teaching. I was speaking with a student in your British survey course. It's another complaint, then? Not a complaint. I was surprised, too. McTavish's lips, normally hidden beneath his whitish-red beard, curled a little at the corner. Not a complaint, but a concern. The student said you were drooling in class and having difficulty articulating yourself. I rolled my eyes. Just for a moment, I said. My mouth was a little looser than usual. McTavish nodded slightly. You're not drinking again, are you? I'm not allowed to drink. That hasn't stopped you in the past. I'm not drinking. Are you having problems with your condition? Not really. He pointed at my shoulders. You didn't have those convulsions before, or at least not like that. Have you seen a doctor? Yes, I saw one just before the school year started. What did they say? My disease is on course. What does that mean? It's degenerative, so it'll continue to get worse. Is there any treatment you can get? I'm on meds for the pain and the tremors, but you can see how effective they are. There's nothing else you can do? I'm too far along. There won't be any improvement? I shook my head. Does that mean you're going to…leave us soon? I hated his choice of words. Even though most English professors have a decent command of the language, they choose euphemisms over direct phrasing. I don't think I'll die anytime soon, I said. I'll just get worse. You knew that when I disclosed my condition to the department. McTavish pursed his lips; it looked like his beard was folding inwards. Have you had any problems outside of work? Anything with your family? Not really. Anything at the Residence? No. He nodded.

Stared at his desk for a moment. Dexter, as you probably know, during the last few weeks I've been faced with a difficult choice. Even though you are a prominent researcher in the department and you bring a strong amount of exposure to the school, you're also something of a risk. A risk? And I'm not talking about your disability, or just your disability. It's your attitude toward teaching. How you treat your students. I have a file of student complaints in my desk drawer. Out of thirty-two complaints in the last two years, twenty-nine of them belong to you. Really? Who has the other three? McTavish shook his head. I've overlooked many of your mistreatments before, he said, but because of your declining condition and your increasingly vehement diatribes toward your students, I just can't look away anymore. I don't know if your condition and your mistreatment are related, and frankly, at this point I don't really care. So what I'm going to do is, I'm going to recommend to the faculty committee that you be placed on sabbatical beginning next term. Sabbatical? Just so we're clear, this is not a suspension. You've long been due for a sabbatical anyways. I know how hard you've worked over the last five years and I think it's time you took a break. We apply for sabbaticals. They're not just handed to us. In this case we're going to make an exception. Try to think of it as a vacation, a time to relax. Who are you to decide for me? I don't want to relax. I want to keep working. He leaned forward, elbows on his desk. You don't have to be ungrateful, Dexter. Most people in the department would kill for a surprise sabbatical. It doesn't mean you have to stop working; you can keep working. You can't do this. You're superseding university regulations. This is a special circumstance. I slammed my fist on his desk. I don't want a sabbatical. Don't be childish, Dexter. I'm not be—don't even. Don't use words like childish around me. Then stop behaving like one. The committee's meeting in a few days. We'll give you the official notice when it's over. Is all this a segue into dismissal? Am I gonna be fired after all this? No, you're not going to be fired. Who'll teach my classes? We're going to ask one

or two of the sessional instructors, and then a few grad students will take over the sessional courses. You're asking a sessional to teach my courses? What've you been smoking? They couldn't teach the way to the bathroom, for chrissakes. Dexter, calm down. It's not that big a deal. It's my work! What if you could pick the person to teach your course? I don't want to pick someone. I want to teach the goddamn course! You're not teaching the course. You're going on sabbatical. I'm coming to that meeting. I'm going to fight your recommendation. It won't do any good. What do you mean? McTavish raised his irritatingly bushy brows. You've already decided, I said. You assholing cretin. Dexter. My tremors flared. I felt like I was seizing from the waist up. I leaned forward and dropped my flexed fists on the desk. You Scottish prick. Dexter, stop. I've been manipulated in my time, but you...yeah, to be undermined by you, that's something else. Are you going to embarrass yourself? How could I? You've already done it for me. My voice twanged unexpectedly. He lowered his eyes. I exhaled. It sounded like a hiss.

I thought about threatening the department with legal action, but my past behaviour would undoubtedly be taken into account, so I held off. After that meeting I didn't want to come back to the Residence. It was belittling to go from one place I wasn't wanted to another. Gertrude asked me how I was. I said nothing to her. I went to my room and closed the door and propped the spare chair in front of it. I glanced at my books. My piled clothes. My Edward Scissorhands poster, now rolled up and standing on its side in the corner. An immense load, metallic and sharp-edged, tumbled inside me. I hunched over, trying to flex against my supreme fear of being rendered useless. Beat my arms against my chair. Punched my legs. Hit myself in the head. Stomped on the floor. The pain came hot and hard and soothing.

My anger didn't subside until later at night. The darkness softened the edges of the boxes of books and clothes so it felt like they weren't

as present as in the daytime. My tremors took a long time to calm down to a level where I could eat without spilling or missing too much. I missed dinner, so I had leftovers. Stefan warmed a plate for me.

I cried. For the first time since Mom's death, I dread what lies ahead of me.

A STUFFED MAN, LEANING ALONE, HEADPIECE FILLED WITH PAPER—NOVEMBER 9, 2009

Had another mantis dream last night. Except I wasn't wholly a mantis. I sat in my chair in the field and had my foot in my lap and my foot gleamed green and hardened in parts, but not all the way. A toe sharpened, then softened. The arch turned rigid and then relaxed. As though the circuitry inside my body that had previously allowed me to be the mantis was shorting out. I rocked in my chair, trying to will out the green armour, the glorious towering height. The gleaming green faded. I pinched my foot trying to coax it out. I wrapped my fist around my hardened toe, which then softened in my palm. Soon the green and the density evaporated completely, and I was left soft, bendable, and small.

Maggie's taken my books and my poster to her house. She's had two steel bars installed in the bathroom, one by the toilet and one in the tub. She said that one of Randal's friends asked what they were for. Randal answered, For those times when the going's tough and you need something to grab onto. And the kid wants to be a pharmacist. God.

I'm going to have Randal's old room on the ground floor and he's going to sleep down in the basement. Randal is so excited, Maggie said. He's already anticipating dinner table conversations with you. Oh yeah? Does he know what you and I were like when we were younger? For the most part, Maggie said. What doesn't he know about you? Nothing. Ha, you're lying. A few things, maybe. Like what?

Although I love my nephew, I can't say I'm equally excited. In fact, I'm depressed that living with Maggie and Randal is my only viable choice. My increasing tremors have become an aggravating reminder of that fact. I imagine Maggie is apprehensive as well. Wary of the apparent influence I have on Randal. Shaken by my condition and the accommodations I require. I imagine she's telling herself she's stupid for doing it. I can't blame her.

Esmeralda and I ate together at dinner earlier tonight. I can't get over her inconsistency, her moodiness. I don't know what she wants when she's around me. Entertainment? Simple conversation? A respite from the clattering in her head? Her condition seems to be holding for the time being. She still wears her cap. Her limbs have begun to take a sharpened, fixed look. As though someone's been jamming her joints with toothpicks and glue. The staff members remain vigilant. I try to be civil.

My brother came to see me today, she said. Lip service, basically. Hi Audrey, how're you, just checking in, dadda-dadda-dadda. I can tell he doesn't wanna see me, he comes only out of obligation. I told him, if you don't wanna see me, then don't come. No, I wanna see you, he said, but it was…yeah. I could tell. Esmeralda stirred her spaghetti, dragging the noodles around her plate like a wig splattered with sauce. Do you get along with your sister? she said. Depends what you mean, I said. We get on each other's nerves really easily. She can't handle my moods, she gets impatient, and then I get impatient with her impatience, and it just blows up and we're angry at each other for a week. Have you always been like that? For the most part. What was it like when you were young? She once held a searing hot branding iron to my forehead, if that's any indication. A branding iron? Yeah, like what you brand cattle with. She burnt you with that? Esmeralda searched my forehead. You can't really see it now, I said. Did it hurt? What do you think? Why did she do that? Beats me. Are you still angry with her? Some days. Why're you going to live with her, then? I don't have a choice. You don't have anyone else to stay with? No friends? I don't actually have many friends. Or any. How long have you been here? Just over three years. Did you live alone before that? Yeah. Then my condition started getting worse and I converted to a wheelchair and eventually came here. Did you have to come here? Honestly, I could've lived alone longer, but my quality of life would've diminished considerably. How's that? I wasn't taking very good care

of myself when I lived alone. I was angry when I first got diagnosed. I broke my arm because I kept beating the railing on my apartment balcony. I was drinking way too much and almost got suspended at the school. So of course all that aggravated my condition, or at least I think it did. The arches in my feet grew. My spine tilted sideways, and I started getting the tremors. I've gotten used to them, but sometimes they sneak up on me. And what really pisses me off is that I'm being kicked out of the Residence when my need to be here is the most urgent. When I got here I was more manageable but still had a case for being here. Now it's a no-brainer. Anyone else with my condition, they'd bring them in. But they're kicking me out. Whose fault is that? Esmeralda said. I know it's my fault, I said, but still, it's against the health care system. The Hippocratic Oath and all that. Well, when one person is hurting others who are just as fragile as he is... Hold on, I said, I'm not fragile, and neither are you. Yes I am, she said. And you are. We all are. I'm not fragile. Esmeralda raised her fork. If human life is insignificant, doesn't that mean we're fragile? Your half-baked philosophy doesn't change the fact that you can hardly put your food in your mouth. I stared out the window across the cafeteria. The sky was grey and two-dimensional, like the backdrop of an old film set. That's not the point, I said. You created that philosophy so you wouldn't feel weak. Right? It's only a justification. A band-aid in writing. I grimaced, hissed through my teeth. That's a harsh way of summarizing my life's work, I said. When were you diagnosed? she said. Five years ago? Ten years ago? And you're what, forty-five, forty-six years old? That's not your life's work. That's just a reaction to what's happening to you. No, it's a direction, a redirection. A re-direction of what? Of where my life was going. While other people become born-again Christians, I'm a born-again Cripple. Esmeralda laughed. I huffed. If you don't agree with the philosophy, ignore it, I said. Just don't come rolling up to me the next time you take a knife to your wrists. Esmeralda straightened in her chair. Making fun of me

like that…at least I'm making my life worth something. You're trying to make your life worthless. She inhaled sharply. That's none of your business, she said. I leaned over. It is my business when an ambulance shows up and wakes me up in the middle of the night. How can I get my beauty sleep then? Esmeralda took up her plate and mashed the spaghetti into the side of my head. Cocksucker, she said. She rolled out of the room. I chuckled and spit.

I don't burn bridges. I rig them with nitroglycerine, picking my spots to ensure maximum devastation; then I wait until the perfect moment to push down on the plunger and blow the whole damn thing to hell.

Everyone in the Residence seems so eager for me to leave. Dante especially. I don't see him as often because I'm usually in my room mourning or working but when I do see him he carries himself with the self-assuredness of a man whose problems are all about to be solved. Even Gertrude seems to want me gone. Not out of spite, but out of guilt. I'm a reminder of her disloyalty.

In five days I will slip from heaven into purgatory, which, depending on how Maggie and I handle each other, could very soon become hell.

ONE-MAN EXODUS—NOVEMBER 14, 2009

Tears from Gertrude. Grins from Dante. Esmeralda nowhere to be seen. Shook hands with Jeeves. He said, Goodbye, Doctor, we'll see you soon. Stefan led me outside. I had my laptop and my journal in my backpack, hanging off the back of my chair. My baseball cards sounded like a frustrated child turning the handle of a jack-in-the-box. Maggie waited for me at the entrance. Her passenger-side door open. I sighed. Stayed silent. Let myself be helped into the car. After they put my chair into the trunk, Stefan said, Take care of him. Maggie said, I'll do my best. The tires groaned over the snow-packed pavement as we left. I stared back at the glinting glassy face of the Residence. I caught my distant reflection: that of an adopted child who wanted to stay at the orphanage.

In Saskatoon Did Kubla Khan a Crappy Torture Home Decree—November 16, 2009

Brief entry. Long day.

You never realize what someone else's home is like until you live there, until you enter it with a mind to inhabit it rather than just visit. I'm two days in and I'm already sick of it. Banged both elbows on the narrow hallway walls. Knocked my wrist against the moulding of the door leading into my room. Slipped off the toilet twice, my arm too wobbly to grip the bar, which I found to be two or three inches too far away. Took half an hour to get out of the tub this morning. Decided I'd only bathe every few days. But the effort of getting around and doing things for myself amounts to a shit-ton of sweat and frustration, which inevitably leads to more sweat and frustration, which leads to more baths. I'm chafing in my chair as I write.

My room is too small. I can hardly manoeuvre. Keep hitting my feet on the bed or the desk. Bed's too narrow. Have to keep the chair right beside it; otherwise I might roll off. Bed's too soft. The wallpaper's the colour of bile. It shrinks the room. There's a crack in the ceiling. The ceiling leans down toward me like the hard palate of some crusty beast. Found some discarded Golden Books and a used Old Spice deodorant stick in the closet—not to mention balls of dust that swarmed around me when I dropped my books inside (no room for a shelf). Randal's a smart kid, but unfortunately he's still a kid.

Maggie made me write up my schedule and tape it to the fridge. Beside that she put the numbers of three different cab companies that have vans for wheelchairs. She'd called all three to check their average response time. Her organization irritates me. Even though she's doing all she can to help, or at least appearing as if she is, it's clear she wants me to know this is her house, her schedule, her rules. Meantime I put myself on the wait-list of another residence across

town. Wait-list is five years. Hoping for a plague or a mass shooting.

When I first arrived Maggie gave me a welcoming gift: software that converts voice into type. For your diary or your work or whatever you need it for, she said. I put the software under the desk, out of sight. Although my tremors are bad and she probably paid good money for that software, I don't want her to hear what I have to say.

PITY IS AN ABOMINATION—NOVEMBER 21, 2009

A number of colleagues have emailed asking how I'm doing. I heard about your sabbatical. I hope you're doing okay. McTavish told us about your condition. If you need anything, please let me know. They don't mean it. It's out of some obligatory need to pity that they send these notes.

Yesterday when the cab driver came to pick me up, I asked him if he picked up many people like me. He said, Every day I pick up people like you. His face was mottled with grey and black stubble. He wore a Saskatoon Blades hat. None of em know when to shut up, he said. Always blathering about this or that, always complaining. Oh I didn't get my disability pension so I have to go down to the government office. Oh I need to go to the doctor, I'm not feeling well. Just blah blah blah. And then I get em down there and, surprise surprise, they can't pay for the fucking cab ride. Well, I didn't get my pension, they say. How can I pay? And I stare at em and they look at me like they're little children, sad, like they're about to be punished, eh? And what do I say then? What're you supposed to say to people like that? There's people walking past in the street. What'm I supposed to do? Do I yell at em? Do I waste more time taking em back? He shook his head. He raised the van's platform and got in through the side door and secured me in the back using straps embedded in the floor and in the ceiling. Put your brakes on, eh? he said. I keep close track of these things. Ninety percent of the time, I swear to god they're doing it on purpose. Taking advantage of me and the company. They know I won't yell at em or make em pay or anything, so they keep calling me to pick em up. It's frustrating as hell. I keep losing money like this. How can I make a living? If it keeps up I might have to quit or drive a regular cab. He finished strapping me in and went up to the front seat and started the van. By the way, he said, you've got money with you, don't you? Yes, I do, I said, patting my coat pocket. Where we going?

The university. University, eh? Any particular spot? The arts building. Why you going there? I'm a professor of English and I have a class to teach. He looked at me in the mirror and smirked.

Semester is winding down. Students are doing review for their exams or are preparing their final papers. At the beginning of the semester my British survey students were given an eight-page essay assignment to be completed by December second. Two days ago I reduced it to four pages. Depression tends to bring out my small generous side. Also, I don't want too much marking.

I seem to sink when I'm in Maggie's house. Sink into the floor. Become a piece of furniture. Enfolded into the smells. I don't enjoy the privacy when I have the house to myself. I feel anonymous. Like a fugitive hunkered down in someone else's house.

This place is too small for me. I think about leaving the house and exploring the neighbourhood, but snow's a bitch on wheels. I'd get stuck every few seconds, or I'd slide on the ice and into an incoming car.

Randal provides a bit of relief. When he got home from school a few days ago we sat together in the living room and I asked him what he'd done during the day. He said he'd had an appointment with a career counsellor at the school. You still wanna be a pharmacist? I said. I don't know, he said. I think I just said that to please Mom. She keeps asking me what I wanna do when I finish school, even though I'm two years from graduating. I nodded. You don't look the type to wear a white coat, I said. I think you're well suited for the arts. He chuckled. What makes you say that? You're creative, and you have a bit of your uncle's mean streak in you as well. Trust me on this. The sciences wouldn't have you. The stock market wouldn't have you. You're too smart for those areas. I don't know about that. Trust me. I adjusted in my chair and grinned at him. Got a riddle for you, I said. He straightened on the couch. What animal has four legs in the morning, two in the afternoon and three at night? He chuckled. Raised

his brows. I don't know. Think about it. Morning, afternoon, night. Three stages of the day, right? Early, middle, end. Okay. Now those stages don't have to be taken literally. We can think of them as metaphors for larger periods. What is the earliest stage of an animal's life? Embryo. No, I mean after it's born. As a baby. That's right, infancy. What is the last stage of an animal's life? Death. Not quite that far. Um...I don't know. You can do it. When they're old? Old age, that's right. Now what animal has four legs when in infancy, and then two when it gets into the middle of its life? A gorilla? I sighed. What does an animal do when it's on four legs? It crawls. Right. What does it do when it's on two legs? It walks. Okay, so what animal begins life by crawling, then learns to stand and walk on two legs, and ends life on three legs? Randal considered. Then his face lengthened. A human? That's right, well done. He made a face. Wait a minute, he said. How does a human life end on three legs? It's meant to be a cane, I said. Oh. He pursed his lips. Looked at me and my chair. I cocked my head. The riddle's not perfect, I said.

Even on a maximum dose of anti-convulsants, my tremors persist. Maybe I should wean myself off of medicine and take up heavy drinking again. I don't remember shaking when I drank.

But I'm also proud that my body's idiosyncrasies are too powerful to be overwhelmed by medicine.

Better to Serve in Heaven than Reign in Hell—
November 24, 2009

I'm beginning to see that, where disability's concerned, there's more than one kind of independence. There's physical independence, where you do everything yourself: chores, transportation, cooking, and so on. And there's intellectual independence. Thinking for yourself. Thinking about and discussing deeper, more important issues while others handle the domestic duties. The independence of Camus and Eliot and Hemingway, who sequestered themselves in their work rooms while their wives took care of their households. No wonder they married so often. These two types of independence are not co-existent. You don't have to be physically independent to be intellectually so. But the former can definitely interfere with the latter, as I'm experiencing now.

The smell of this place is getting to me. The bristle of the carpets. The weight of the walls. Wondering if I'll ever get a decent day's work done again. At the Residence I worked fourteen hours a day; here I'm lucky to get in seven. Everything's slowed, jamming my mind with delay and twisting me into anger and anxiety. I can no longer do things my way. And if you can't do things your way, what's the point of doing them?

Yesterday Maggie and I had an argument. Randal was at a friend's; we'd just finished dinner and she stood at the kitchen sink wearing blue rubber gloves. She asked me to bring her my dinner plate. I was on my way down the hall. I have work to do, I said. It'll just take you a second, she said. I'm on my way down the hall, I said. Dexter, you're two metres from the table. This is what I mean, Maggie. About how things add up, how time adds up and slows me down. Maggie scoffed. Instead of wasting your time arguing, she said, you can just pass me your plate. Well, if all it takes is a second, then why don't you step over and get it? You're quicker than I am. I'm

busy. You're not busy. You're washing dishes. You can get it yourself. Maggie strode over and picked up my plate and dropped it in the sink. Water and suds puffed up. You're like a goddamn child. Are you finished? I started to wheel away. I know you'd rather be at the Residence, but you got expelled, so if you're living here, can't you try to be civil? I haven't done anything to you, not since we were young, and I've apologized how many times for that. Yeah, and that's why you've taken me in, isn't it? Because you're still feeling guilty. I have nothing to be guilty about. Then why did you bring me here, Maggie? She stepped forward. Put her sudsy hands on a chair. You're family, she said. Despite everything we've put each other through, I still feel obligated to look after you. I groaned. I also—I confess I wanted to see if things could change. I don't want to have this anger around us all the time. I don't want to look at you and be hesitant or be anxious or angry. I don't want to worry about what you're gonna say next or do next. And I really don't want to worry about Randal idolizing you. That keeps me up at night. It scares me, Dexter, how seriously he looks up to you, because I don't want him to become cold and bitter and self-destructive. I want his future to be bright and open. I want us to be open. I exhaled. Pondered, then let my tremors carry me. First of all, I said, don't think of me as a charity case. And don't think of yourself as a benevolent provider. Because you're not. You've forced me into— Forced you? Forced me into this situation. What planet are you living on, Dexter? You got yourself into this. I have given you a room, a place to stay, which you know I didn't have to do. Yeah, and you think that glosses over everything. What're you...ah, Dexter. Maggie shook her head and turned back to her dishes. I rolled a little ways into the kitchen. And I'm insulted that you don't want Randal idolizing me, I said. Do you know what I've accomplished in my life? Do you know how hard I've worked to get what I've received? That's all great, but it doesn't matter, Dexter. Doesn't matter? I huffed. The hell with you, Maggie. She brandished a soapy fork at me. All that

matters is your personality, she said. How you treat people. Right, I said, because you know everything, Maggie. I glanced down the hall. Randal's school pictures hung from the walls in consecutive years. That's why you got yourself pregnant at thirty-eight, isn't it, to get yourself out of some trumped-up mid-life crisis. Maggie stiffened. That's why you had Randal, isn't it? Because you're weak and you needed something to give you strength, but you couldn't stand being alone and you couldn't maintain a relationship, so you needed a blood connection to give you someone else to focus on. Maggie turned. And now that Randal is taking after me, it's become another crisis for you. You're fifty-four years old, Maggie, and you're still lost. You're still weak. And that's why you want me here. Because even though you hate me, you think I might give you some kind of direction, some kind of strength. Because you know that I'm strong. I could hear the clockwork grind of Maggie's anger. She slowly fixed her hands back on the chair. You, she said, licking her mouth, are not strong. You only think you are. And I am not letting myself be sucked into your anger. If you enjoy being angry, be angry. But if you do anything to hurt Randal, I'm kicking you out. I don't care if you have to live on the street. I'm not putting up with that. You understand? I pursed my lips. Can I go work now? Maggie sighed and went back to the sink and hunched over it. I backed out of the kitchen and went down the hall to my bedroom, minding the walls. Shit! when a tremor forced my elbow into the wall.

How Frugal Is the Chariot that Bears the Human Soul—December 4, 2009

Early Christmas. Bought a new chair a few days ago. A cheap motorized model. Has a joystick. Manoeuvres like a dream. Only one previous owner who used it to go to the denturist. Owner died two weeks ago. Massive stroke while cruising past a high school. Misfortune breeds discounts.

Maggie doesn't talk to me. She watches Randal and me when we talk. Her eyes both anxious and accusatory.

Doing all my marking by computer. Key by effing key. As much as I want to use my red pen to bloody up the margins of my students' papers, my writing has become too illegible. I wouldn't normally care, but I don't want all my students emailing me asking what I was saying on page three.

Randal and I had a fantastic conversation yesterday. We talked about his father, whom he hardly sees and whom he won't be seeing for Christmas. We talked about how he likes living with his mother. He loves his mother, but sometimes doesn't understand her moods. As he spoke I noticed his voice has a natural depth to it. Most teenaged boys, the depth in their voices feels forced. Like they're trying to plough their way through puberty. Randal's voice is smooth and planed and he possesses profound delivery. The voice of a prophet, if I ever heard one. Yeah, I said. It was like that when we were younger. She was up and down and all over the place. Oh yeah? Randal put down the Pepsi he was drinking. That boy drinks at least three Pepsis a day and doesn't twitch. Not even a little bit. In light of my tremors, it seems a small miracle. What was she like when you were a kid? he said. Ah, I said. What has she told you? I don't know. You guys argued once in a while. Your parents died when you were teenagers, and she went back to Warman and took care of you when they died. I smirked. She told me to be wary of you, he said, not to believe

135

everything you say. Randal shook his head. Why did she say that? Your mother doesn't like me very much, I said. Why? Because she's afraid of me. Why's she afraid of you? Because of what I am. Randal looked me over. Because of your disability? Partly. Mostly it's because she doesn't agree with how I feel about my disability, or how I live my life, rather. Randal grimaced. That's pretty shitty, he said. I know, I said. She told me you mistreat people, he said, that that's why you got kicked out of that home. Your mother doesn't understand. Do you treat people badly? Well let me ask you. Do I treat you badly, Randal? No. Do you feel that you can trust me? Yeah. But Mom doesn't like that. I know she doesn't. So what do we do? Well, you're smart enough to make your own decisions now. You've reached the age of consent. The way I see it, you can decide whether you want to spend time with me. Your mother doesn't have to make that decision for you. Randal nodded. Your mother and I had a talk a week or so ago. She said that she wants things to be more open. Therefore, shouldn't you and I be talking then, if that's what she wants? She said that to you? Yeah, she did. And one thing we can't forget—I'm living here now, so I think it behooves us to talk to each other. Yeah, I thought that was weird, too, how Mom doesn't want me to talk to you even though you live here. Did you ask her about that? Yeah. And what did she say? Well, I said Mom, how can we do that? Uncle Dexter's living with us and you don't want me to talk to him? You can talk to him, she said, just be wary of him. What does that mean? Just be careful, she said. Randal cocked his head. Like she thinks you're trying to manipulate me or something, he said. I'm not trying to manipulate you, I said. Far from it. I want you to think for yourself and express those thoughts. Your mother said she thought you're a lot like me when I was your age, except maybe not as angry. You were…why were you angry? I cleared my throat. Wiped my mouth. My vocal cords felt like they sagged. My voice felt weak. I arched back my neck in an effort to tighten the cords. Well, I said with a twang. The way your mother de-

scribed our youth was really just the tip of the iceberg. There's much more to it than that. Oh. Randal adjusted on the couch. Get cozy, young mantis, while I tell you all about your mother.

I told him about how we fought. About the water balloons filled with ink. The branding iron. The time I got my foot caught in a rat trap and she took her sweet time going back to the house to call Dad to tell him I'd broken my foot. The fight we had in the kitchen shortly after Mom died. How I read one of her university essays and corrected her spelling and received a kick for writing on it in ink. How I went to Toronto and then to Montreal for school. Randal listened to it all without commenting. It was only after I finished with my return to Saskatoon that he sat back, pondered for a moment, and said, So why did you come back here? I mean, you won all those awards in school. You got your doctorate from McGill and everything. I bet you could've gone to any other school in the world to work, like Harvard or something. But you came back here. There was a job open here, I said. There wasn't much else for me. Randal studied me. And you didn't wanna see Mom? he said. She didn't have anything to do with it? I looked at him. I don't know, I said. I doubt it. Randal hung his head. Mom said you're angry all the time, and she doesn't know why. Is it just because you two see each other? I pursed my lips. I was like this in Toronto and Montreal. So you're always angry? I'm not angry. I'm antagonistic. I like to pick fights. Why? Conflict strengthens the mind. Randal nodded and frowned. Did you ever feel happy? Did you ever, you know, feel love? I was happy when I lived at the Residence. But you're not happy now? Not entirely. But I do feel love. I feel love toward you, Randal. I never pick fights with you, and that's because I don't have to, because you already think like me. Randal squinted. I don't know about that, he said. You're a smart kid, I said. I'm proud to call you my nephew. He smiled. The living room, airtight during my narrative, seemed to decompress around us.

The Crippled Broadcasting Corporation—
December 7, 2009

Writing this in the afternoon. Watching the snow drift down. When I was about ten or so Maggie said she loved the way the snow swirled up off the banks like desert dunes. I sneered at her and said they were Frosty the Snowman farts. She smacked me for ruining her moment of poesy.

I think I'm coming down with something. Bit of pneumonia or bronchitis. I have to put more effort into breathing.

Randal helped me out of the tub the other day. I kept struggling. Every time I reached for the bar and tried to balance myself on the edge of the tub my arm shook and I fell back down, splashing water everywhere. Finally called for the boy. Thankfully I'd left the bathroom door unlocked. He didn't question anything. Helped me right out. Took my arm around his neck and boosted me into my chair, which was draped with towels. Then he stood by and waited to see if I needed anything else. Wanted to hug him. Patted him on the thigh instead. Told him Thanks.

Maggie and I seem to have settled into a lull of strained civility. She goes about her business, I go about mine. It seems to work.

The radio's always playing here, and because it's on a shelf in the kitchen I can't reach the goddamn thing to switch it off. Just yesterday, the CBC was on and there was a discussion about euthanasia and assisted suicide for persons with severe disabilities. They asked people to call in to ask questions and give their opinions. I asked Randal to bring me the phone—Maggie was still at work—and, with some concentration, I dialled the number. I explained who I was and why I was calling and the operator put me through. Ready, Dr. Ripley? she said. Yep, I said. Three, two, one, you're on. Hello there, said the host, who's with us right now? My name is Dr. Dexter Ripley, I said. Hello, Dr. Ripley. Do you have something to add to our conversation? Yes, I

do. I'm a professor of English at the University of Saskatchewan, and my specialty is disability in British literature. One of the things I study is the use of language where disability is concerned, how it's constantly associated with negativity and stigma and worn-out stereotypes. I see, Dr. Ripley, and how does this affect how we think about assisted suicide for the severely disabled? It perpetuates the notion that all people living with disabilities are useless. It allows for the circulation of language and mindsets that are restrictive for persons with disabilities. If we think that people with severe disabilities should be killed, then does that concept not extend to other disabilities simply by relation? These assisted suicides, because they're so widely publicized, they create associations in our minds, and from those associations we create judgements. I see, and what do we need to do to free ourselves from those associations? We create new approaches to language. We use different terms for disability. What sort of terms? Terms that exclude the negative dis in front of ability. I see, thank you for your input, Dr. Ripley. We can also make jokes. Jokes? If persons with disabilities make jokes that use that negative language, eventually that negative language gets twisted so that it no longer has any effect, and persons with disabilities become empowered because they have emancipated themselves from language, they have determined how they will be addressed. Hmm, we seem to be heading in an interesting direction, so we'll give you a bit more time, Dr. Ripley. What sort of jokes are you talking about? Can you give us an example? Are you sure? Yes, go ahead. I looked at Randal. His eyes glittered. His lips parted with anticipation. I grinned and straightened in my chair and switched the phone from one ear to the other. Well, I said, if you'd like a fairly strong example, here's one for you. What did the quadriplegic deaf kid get for Christmas? The host was silent. I raised my eyebrows at Randal. Cancer, I said. The host's voice stumbled. Can we please move to— The line was cancelled. Let's move on to our next caller, the host said on the radio. Who've we got on the line? I held the

phone away from my face. Randal hunched forward, leaning into his laughter. His voice caught and skidded and he lost his breath and he laughed even harder. I laughed along with him. Then I said, Randal? He wiped his eyes and looked at me. Yeah? he said, still laughing. You know why I make those jokes, right? Yeah. I just heard you. Okay, so you know I'm not an asshole, right? He laughed again. No, uncle. I know. You're just doing some good in your own way.

My bedroom door has a lock. But the funny thing is I seldom if ever lock it.

I Do Not Think the Mermaids Will Sing to Me— December 11, 2009

Pneumonia's licked. Or whatever it was that stunted my breathing. It left almost as soon as it came. Nice to know my immune system's still working.

Sat in the bath earlier this afternoon. Forced myself to do it. I smelled like Byron's syphilis. I took my time folding myself into the tub. I inevitably spilled water, but not too much. I sank into the water. I'd locked the door. I needed the privacy for once.

It had snowed the previous night and I felt the cold hulking around me, circling me through the walls and the ceiling. The steam rising from the water dizzied me. I let my head fall back under the water. I closed my eyes, then opened them to the distant wavering ceiling. I let a few bubbles escape my mouth. My limbs, now relaxed, hovered. The privacy thrilled me. Made me ache. I let a few more bubbles out and thought, This is my depth. This is as far as I can go—to the bottom of this bathtub, in this bathroom, in seven inches of water.

I came up for air and went back under. The heat gently gripped my head and face. I had only one tremor and knocked my elbow on the edge of the tub. I stayed until the water went cool. Then I clambered out of the tub and dried myself off.

THE WINTER OF MY DISCONTENT—DECEMBER 17, 2009

Tremors have become aggravating, even exhausting lately. Have been sleeping late. Sucking back vitamin C and ginseng to fight a head cold.

Submitted my final marks today. Out of sixty students, five of them received an A. Didn't fail anybody, though. Didn't want any inquiries or complaints.

Felt a discomforting finality when I submitted my marks. I don't know when I'm going to teach again. As I clicked on the SEND button and sent the marks to McTavish it felt possible that I might not teach again. I'll still work, writing articles and performing administrative work for my various committees. But teaching's the main work. I enjoy the stimulation, the trust my students place in my knowledge and experience. Teaching's empowering for me. Articles and committees give a derivative, vague sense of authority. Teaching's much more direct.

GHOSTS OF CHRISTMASES PAST—DECEMBER 23, 2009

Thinking of Dad. I often do during the winter. It just happens. Winter forces us all inside.

Dad and I look very much alike. Same cheekbones. A cinched pouch of a mouth. Eyes as dark as empty beer steins.

His generosity really came through at Christmas. Because the farm ran on a shoestring budget he and Mom were frugal with their money. Our farm didn't generate much; Dad's main job was selling farming equipment, but he didn't want to let go of his vision of a pastoral existence, so we kept a few cows and a horse or two. Anyways, Christmastime was always rich. Maggie and I always got what we asked for, even if we'd been particularly cruel to one another. On Christmas morning the tree lights would already be plugged in, flooding the living room with a dense dazzle of green, yellow, blue, and red. The bottom of the tree would be more crowded than an ancient spruce bangled with tree huggers. Dad would sit on the couch, cradling a hot cup of coffee, fully dressed and shaven. He'd insist that Maggie and I open our gifts first. He'd watch with the quiet pleasure of a man who'd soundly provided for his family, and I made sure to express joy with each gift, for my joy was his, too.

I think about who might've killed him. Sometimes I wonder if that's the source of my anger. Then I think it can't be that simple. I do feel emptiness at times, but it fluctuates, and I've been angry since I was a young boy.

Maggie has pictures of Mom and Dad on the wall in the living room. One of them, a family portrait, was taken when I was about five or six. Maggie and Mom are half-smiling, like they always do for photographs. My expression is hesitant, like I don't know how to react to having my picture taken. Dad's expression's always puzzled me. His hand is loosely draped over my shoulder. His eyes seem anxious. As if he has something to do and he just wants the picture over with.

When I look at the picture one of the theories about Dad's original disappearance—the one involving him leaving us for an unknown woman—somehow seems credible. In that pose, with that expression, he looks like that sort of man. Then of course the fact of his death wedges in and cancels all that.

I don't know if I'm at peace with his death.

But then I'm at peace with very little in this world.

GOD REST THIS WEARY GENTLEMAN, WHOM EVERYTHING DISMAYS—DECEMBER 25, 2009

I spent last night nagging Maggie about her gift-wrapping and antici-pating Randal's reaction to the gifts I bought him. I was excited, but I did my best to hide it. In the process I forgot to take my pain meds. Woke up feeling woozy. Feeling like my spine was trying to dislodge my ribcage. My arches clenched. When I moved I remembered an adver-tisement on TV from a decade or so ago. The catchline—I forget the product—was big big big BIG! sung to the tune of Beethoven's Fifth. When I woke up, my first thought was, big big big PAIN! I coiled up and called for Maggie. She brought me my meds and a glass of juice. Sat with me as I ingested them. You okay? she said, sitting on the edge of my bed and adjusting her blue pyjamas. Give me some time, I said, closing my eyes. Randal's awake now too, she said, but do you want me to let you sleep? No, just give me ten minutes. Okay. I opened my eyes. Gazed at the ceiling. Groaned at the pain in my back. I adjusted my position. It did no good. You're really in a lot of pain, aren't you? I nod-ded without looking at her. I manage it, I said. I didn't know, she said. Well, I knew, but I didn't know it was this bad. I forgot my meds. It's not like this all the time. A tremor whipped through me, accompanied by a lurch in my head, as though my brain was being squeezed through a cold metal cylinder. The telltale sign of withdrawal. I looked at Maggie. Her face was plain, pallid in the greyish-blue morning light. I studied her face for a moment, and it wasn't until later today, when we were in the living room unwrapping presents, that I realized that the reason she gives me so much guilt and nagging is because it's the only way she can show she cares. Our ability to express affection has been so stunted that we rely on subtler methods like guilt and callous jokes. The usual system of hugs and encouraging words simply doesn't work. Maybe that's why we're so affectionate toward Randal. It's a way to compensate.

I spoiled the boy. I gave him a voucher for a trip to Europe. Any

truly intelligent person goes to Europe at least once, I said. He was sitting on the floor by the tree, dressed in sweatpants and a t-shirt with the old Batman symbol on it. When he opened the voucher he laughed and bounced to his feet and ran over and hugged me. I reciprocated, patting his back. Maggie took a picture. Randal stared at the voucher, bouncing on the balls of his feet, saying he couldn't believe it. When can I go? he said. You can go whenever you want, I said. Just tell me when you wanna go and I'll work out the details for you. Where do I go first? Wherever you want. He laughed again. Could you come with me? I looked at Maggie. I don't know, I said. We'll have to see. Europe's streets can be pretty hazardous for a cripple. Oh Dexter, Maggie said. She stooped over and took an envelope from under the tree and handed it to me. From both of us, she said. Oh yeah, Randal said, grinning. I curved my thumb under the flap and tore open the envelope. Pulled out a card. A snowman on the front. Opened the card. Found a slip of paper. A gift certificate for two months' worth of massage therapy. On the facing side of the card, Maggie had written For Dexter, Beloved brother and uncle. Take this gift and take care of yourself. Love, Maggie and Randal. Thank you, I said. I hugged Randal and nodded again at Maggie, who smiled.

We had dinner at two-thirty. Ham and potatoes. Pumpkin pie that Maggie had forgotten in the freezer in October. Enough chocolate to give Willy Wonka cavities. Maggie let me have a glass of rum with Pepsi. I came back to my room feeling loose and glorious. Like I could stretch my arms around the entire world and embrace it close.

This tidbit much later at night:

Even though I've written several articles about *A Christmas Carol*, in which I've identified Tiny Tim as a flat, vacant character used only to stir up sympathy, every time I watch a film version, I cry at Tim's death. This year I managed to avoid watching it. And now I feel as though I've missed out.

Should Auld Acquaintance Be Forgot?—January 1, 2010

Spent last night here with Maggie. She'd been invited to a party but she chose to stay with me. Didn't want me to be alone, she said. I'd protested. Go, for chrissakes, I said. Go and get the frickin starch out of your system. Get pissed. Get laid. She shook her head. I'm not gonna burn your house down, I said. I can take care of myself. She said no, so we ended up sitting in the living room, impatiently watching the countdown to midnight. About ten minutes before the minute and hour hands aligned, she asked me, as she does every year, if I had any New Year's resolutions. I sipped my rum and Pepsi, which was insultingly sweet. I don't feel any obligation to change, I said. I have no resolutions. Nothing? Nothing you'd like to change, or do, or do better? I knew she was fishing. She was waiting for me to say I want to get proper treatment or I want to repair our relationship or I will start treating her better. I looked at the TV and took another drink. I wanna get back to teaching, I said. Okay. And I wanna teach Randal a few things, and see him come back from Europe. Okay. Maggie waited. Drank her vodka and Sprite. Then she said, I want to try and get on good terms with you. I nodded, and held up my glass. You could add some more rum to my drink, to start with. I'm serious, she said. I want you to feel like you can trust me, and vice versa. Is that unreasonable? Bring me some more rum and we'll find out. How much have you had? Just this little glass. I can hardly taste it. She looked at me and got up off the couch and took my glass and went into the kitchen. This'll be the last one. It's not good for you, with your meds. You know how many times I've mixed alcohol with pain meds? I don't wanna know. It's only dangerous if you overdose. On the meds or the alcohol? Both. I'm only adding a bit more, and a bit more Pepsi. That's all. No! That's all, Dexter. She came back into the living room. My glass was much taller. I smelled it. The rum was

147

only slightly stronger. I slumped in my chair. That resolution of yours must be ironclad, I said. I'm not stupid, she said. How can you trust me, or how can I trust you if you won't do what I ask? I'm not here to do what you ask. I'm your sister, not your servant. Beh. I took a drink. A tiny spark of rum blushed from the crackling sweetness. You should try to find a man, I said. Do you a bit of good. I don't really want a relationship, she said. Why not? They're not good for me. After I divorced Thad [Randal's father], I decided that was enough, at least for a while. Well, then just date. Work the circuit. I'm not that kind of person. Well, what kind of person are you? She looked at her drink. For a minute we didn't speak. Just watched the crowd on the television. You're in your fifties, for god's sakes, I said. That doesn't mean anything, she said. What does it take for you to get life right? I'm working on it. You shouldn't be working on it. You should be settled. When you were a teenager, you seemed settled. You were a bitch, but you were sure of yourself. I was angry then. Why were you angry? Lots of reasons. Like what? Was it because of me? Not you, or just you. What else? She looked at her drink. Took a hard gulp. You remember—no, you wouldn't remember. Remember what? I said. What I'm about to tell you, Dexter, must be kept between us. I nodded. Actually, never mind. What is it? I'm not sure I want to tell you. Why not? Maggie watched the television. I scoffed. Fine, then, but you just started talking about trust. Maggie kept watching the television. Then she put down her drink. Did you know that I had an abortion when I was seventeen? I frowned. She nodded. Mom thought I was going to Saskatoon for a school trip, but really I was going to the clinic. I was two months along. Really? I'm not kidding. Why didn't you tell anybody? Mom would've helped. She wouldn't have judged or anything. I just wanted it over. I didn't want to deal with the questions and the backlash. I was relieved when it was over, but it... Maggie bit her lip. Who was it? What, the father? Yeah. Fred Rutgers. I chortled. Laughed. Hunched over with laughter. Maggie stared at me. That's

fabulous, I said. I'm guessing Randal doesn't know about this. No, he doesn't. If I'd done Fred Butgers, I wouldn't tell anyone either. I don't want you to tell him, Maggie said. Did Fred make that stupid beeping noise like he always made in the hallways? Shut up. It was an innocent mistake. Nobody screws Fred Butgers and calls it an innocent mistake. Look, that's not the point. The point is, I don't want you to tell Randal. I don't think it'll affect him much. He's mature for his age. I'll tell him when he's older, but right now I don't want him to get the wrong idea. Wrong idea? I don't want him to think I don't value him. Jesus christ, Maggie. I've kept a lot from him, she said. It was hard when he was living with his dad. For a while I felt independent, but I also felt alone. And whenever I saw him on a weekend or whenever it was, I just poured everything onto him. I'd just bitch and bitch about work, about home, about Thad, about you. It was very wrong and unreasonable of me to do that to him, so I decided to stay quiet. You can change that, I said. The countdown began on the TV. We watched a bloated porch light descend into a glowing rack of lights flashing 2010. I raised my glass. May auld acquaintance be forgot and never brought to mind, I said. Maggie's face blanked. She sat deep. Drank. The clock above the TV read eleven-fifty-eight.

MOLOTOV COCKTAILS EXPLODE HOTTER IN THE BRAIN— JANUARY 3, 2010

Got an email today from a colleague in the States. Said my diatribe in Scotland had spread around the disability circuit. Asked me if I wanted to publish a formal paper to concretize the debate. I said I'd be delighted. He warned me that I might face even more hostility than I did in Glasgow. Told him that I'd moved and that I was on sabbatical and that nobody would find me.

He also took issue with a few of my ideas. He wrote that many writers would refute my idea that a disabled body purifies the mind and the consciousness. Because the senses provide us with information, which feeds our minds, a disabled body's senses are flawed; therefore the mind is flawed. Beh, I replied. I elaborated that such language was the problem; that the debate needs to focus as much on the language as on the ideas themselves; that these so-called flaws are actually benefits because they allow for a different vision of the world, and thus a different kind of mind, a mind equally as valuable. In the face of Western assimilation, which is prevalent in Canada even though we may not admit it, disability is a crucial reminder of difference and diversity. In a culture governed by extraordinary impatience (the distant incestuous cousin of intolerance), we prefer people to be the same.

I've been trying to come up with a new term for disability, and the urgency to find one ratchets up each day. Everything moves slower in academia. A paper accepted for publication today won't see the light of day until eighteen months from now. And even then, only six or seven graduate students will read it. Only the best (i.e., most accessible) ideas squeak into everyday life…and usually without anyone knowing who came up with them in the first place. The best you can hope for is a little shift in people's thinking. Revolutions don't begin on paper. They begin with voices. And my voice wanes by the day.

Been tired the last few days. My legs feel depleted from non-use. A strange sensation because I never really think about my legs. Doesn't seem necessary in a motorized wheelchair.

What Happens to a Dream Deferred—January 11, 2010

Came back today after a stay in the hospital. Still heavy with meds and the prospect of readjustment. Bumped my chair into the hallway wall. Gonna take a minute here. Let things clear up.

Three or four days after my last entry I was in the bathroom boosting myself out of my chair and onto the toilet. It was taking some time. Because I'm in a motorized chair now I use my arms less and less, weakening them further. I pushed myself up using the silver bar and got mostly out of the chair, but I faltered. My elbow bent. I let go and fell sideways and smashed my head into the edge of the bathtub. Wasn't completely knocked out. Just knocked into simplicity. I stared at the floor like it was the most interesting thing in the world to me. I thought to myself that the corner where the bathtub meets the wall needs to be cleaned out. I fell into a mesmerizing stillness. No pain. Just a soft emptiness. Maggie found me and scrambled. Called the ambulance. I mumbled to her. Moved my head. My forehead flared with pain. My first thought was Maggie had taken the branding iron and seared the cow with wings into my skin. I groaned. Felt dizzy. Bitch, I said to the linoleum. I laughed. Asked Maggie to get me a drink. She came into the bathroom. Oh Dexter, she said. Your head. I rolled over a little and touched my forehead. It'd swollen to a hard lump. It appears I'm growing horns, I said, chortling. Ambulance is on the way, she said. What for? I feel more glorious than I have in years. It was true. My tremors seemed to have calmed. My back didn't bother me. Even my arches had cooled. I worked to sit up straight. Maggie helped me. Wow, I said. I am totally in the juice. Not even Vicodin can do this. Look at me, Maggie said. Can you see straight? God! I said. You should really wax your eyebrows. She frowned. Just stay still, she said. You might have a concussion. Ah, I said. I've always wanted to ride in an ambulance. You think they'll play Twisted Sister as they drive?

Ambulance arrived within minutes. A paramedic shined a light

in my eyes (a rudeness for which I swatted at his arm) and checked my vitals and asked me a few questions, to which I gave some wise answers. Then I was put on a stretcher and wheeled out, during which I cautioned them to watch for the narrow walls, and we were away. The ambulance, all steel and drawers and tubes, rattled like a toolbox. I thought one of the defibrillators would fall on my head. By the time we got to the hospital I was completely caustic. The pain in my head had ballooned to a swift raking pulse, allowing the pains in my feet and back to reassert themselves. My body was a furnace, and my mouth was the vent. I shut my eyes against the hospital's whiteness. Why're the walls so white? I said as I was wheeled down the corridor. I clamped my eyes. Eck! Goddammit! They assault my eyes even when they're closed! Why can't you paint the walls green? And get some orange lights in here! Juice! Sugar! I need sugar! I gripped my temples. Hold on, Mr. Ripley. It's Doctor Ripley! Doctor! Get it right or I'll shit on your glasses! One of the nurses chuckled. Shut up! I said. I clapped my hands over my ears to stifle the infuriating squeaking of the gurney's wheels.

The swelling on my forehead had hardened into a sort of callus, so it had to be opened and drained. After a two-hour wait I was checked for concussion symptoms. Though I was still angry, in retrospect the exam was hilarious. Primary symptoms of a concussion include difficulty balancing, altered motor coordination, incoherent or slurring speech, irritability, and difficulty reasoning. I just tilt my head back and laugh at this exam now. Wishing I'd just relaxed and enjoyed the whole damn thing.

Because of my medical history (meaning my Charcot-Marie-Tooth disease), the doctors decided to keep me in the hospital. I was put in a room with a young boy and an older man. I questioned everything the nurses did. Why are you adjusting that? What kind of medicine is that? What do the doctors say? May I see my chart? Although I was still lightheaded, I still possessed my faculties, and I

didn't want them to use my concussion as an excuse to correct my body. I'd already been questioned by two doctors that day regarding my faltering arm strength. I told them it was an accident and that my arm strength is sufficient.

At night, listening to the young boy draw breaths through his ragged throat (he'd had his tonsils removed), I was reminded of the Residence. Even though the hospital was considerably drier in tone and cuisine, it gave off a similar taste. And I saw that I miss the Residence terribly. I thought of Jeeves and Esmeralda and Dante and Gertrude and Stefan. Across the room the boy woke up and started crying and hit the button to call the nurse. I swallowed against crying.

I had an MRI the next day. Because of my disease, the doctors were unable to correctly see whether I had a concussion. They put me on a white plastic tongue and slid me into the machine's circular mouth. I couldn't help feeling like an hors d'oeuvre. When it was turned on it made a noise like a robot choking. I tried to remain as still as I could. My tremors and the hilarity of their request—Please try to stay still, Dr. Ripley—made it difficult.

Two doctors spoke to me about my head injury and my disease. Said they'd looked over my medical history and were concerned at the frequent refusals for treatment. I said I had a good reason to refuse the surgeries and the therapies. They asked me the reason. I told them. Their expressions softened. They were confused. They asked about my current living situation, my occupation, my lifestyle. I told them. They asked if I'd been mentally evaluated. I asked why. They said that my multiple refusals for treatment formed a strange, even alarming pattern. I told them I wasn't deranged. They wanted to refer me to a mental health practitioner who would evaluate me and determine the soundness of my mind. I laughed and told them no. I'm here because of a concussion, I said. Other than that, I have a perfectly working mind and I'm not letting you pick and prod. I wiped my mouth before any drool could escape. They said they'd speak with my GP and get her opinion.

I told them they'd hear the same thing from her.

I spent that night in the hospital, too. As a precaution, I was told. Maggie brought me some food. I asked her not to talk to the doctors. She asked why. I said to trust me.

The boy was gone but the older man was still there. He lay there quietly. I didn't see his face. He was turned away from me. White beard. Cobbled skin. Might've been Aboriginal.

Had a mantis dream that night. A full-on, raging, Mantiszilla dream. I leapt and hissed, spat and stomped. Saskatoon was my playground. A broad and elaborate sandcastle just waiting to be kicked apart. I mashed tall men into the concrete. I tore up the Bessborough Hotel. Threw a Lays potato-chip truck at the Royal University Hospital. Tipped over four cows at the same time. People clapped and jumped and hollered for me. And as I gleefully spurred through my destructive tirade, I felt a roaring sense of gratitude. I drew a clicking, elative breath. My hard green chest creaked as it swelled. I giggled. I laughed. Out of pure euphoria I clipped off the head of a bodybuilder. Knocked down the Kinesiology building on campus pillar by pillar, corner by corner. Jumped a hundred feet in the air and slammed down on top of the magnificent wreckage. Toward the end I stretched my body and my claws up to the sky and let out a supplicating roar.

Diagnosed the next day with a mild, Grade 1 concussion. Given the name and number of a mental health specialist with the hospital. Maggie and Randal, who'd been with his dad the last few days, came and got me. Left in one of the hospital's wheelchairs, as mine was still at Maggie's. Maggie asked if I was going to call the specialist. I said I couldn't. She asked why. I said, Because I threw his number away.

Days like this remind me of the difference between mind and body. With each passing day, that difference becomes more pronounced and more crucial. I become clearer in my mind, and in my clarity I become more alone.

A TEACHER'S WORK IS NEVER DONE—JANUARY 18, 2010

Brief entry today. Tremors are bad. Difficult to even type. Actually it's not really tremors. It's just weakness. Holding my hands up to the keyboard. Keeping them focused. Thank god for the autocorrect function.

It's three weeks into the new semester and I'm going through a sort of withdrawal from teaching. I've been through withdrawal before—with meds and, at one point, alcohol—but I was able to function then, more or less, working my way around the dizziness and the lack. Now, my entire rhythm is off. Tried to get started on that article concerning the language of disability and I couldn't do it. I felt stifled. Immobile. Without momentum.

Since I can't teach university—I'd even be glad to teach that goddamn Canadian literature course—I've taken to tutoring Randal. Much of what we discuss involves issues stemming from his classes: writing mechanics, the various periods of English literary history, the differences between symbols, similes, and metaphors, and so on. But occasionally we talk about bigger ideas. I've introduced him to nihilism, existentialism, absurdism, empirical thought, Marxism, and Cartesian duality, among others. He listens seriously. He asks questions. Even though he's only sixteen, I get the sense that he'll find some use for these ideas in the future. It makes me happy, for I'm making the most of our time. We're becoming much closer. He asks me questions about my experiences in university and being a professor. Sometimes he asks me about his mother. He worries about her. Though he doesn't always appreciate her dotage, he realizes, on one level or another, that she's insecure, and he asks me how she got that way and did anything happen to her when she was young. I've already told him quite a bit. Maggie's told him very little, it seems. There are some things that I won't tell him, though, not so much to protect

Maggie as to protect myself. Despite Maggie's rigidity, I'm beginning to settle in here, and I don't want to be kicked out. I believe she would do it if I told Randal something I'm not supposed to tell him. For I see, in fleeting samples, in the way her brows deepen in the kitchen light or in how she may put her glass down on the table harder than she intended, that she's retained that vicious edge she had when we were younger. Although I do act caustically around her, I admit that in those rare moments I'm afraid of her. I can't defend myself.

A DAY WITHOUT LEARNING IS PENANCE ENOUGH— JANUARY 22, 2010

Randal's been suspended from school again. He told my quadriplegic deaf joke to another student, and a teacher heard it and hauled him to the vice-principal's office. Because of his prior history with the Gandhi-Manson joke, he got a one-day vacation.

Naturally, Maggie blames me. It's not my fault the boy doesn't have proper judgement, I said. Don't try to turn this onto me, Maggie said. If you hadn't told him those idiotic jokes in the first place... How was I supposed to know he'd use them to impress his friends? He's a teenager, Dexter. What do you think teenagers do with jokes like that? I thought he had better judgement. I'm sorry, I guess I was wrong. Maggie sighed. We were in the kitchen. She stood by the table, her hands planted on the back of a chair. He's going to be graduating in two years, she said, and a suspension won't look good on his school record. Give the kid some slack, I said. He's gonna be fine. You're not his parent, Dexter. I never said I was. But I live here. He might look at me as a parental figure. Then you need to act like it. No more of these stupid shenanigans. I scoffed. Did it occur to you, I said, that if the boy's looking to me for parental influence, that might say something about the job you've done? Maggie straightened. You're a dick, she said. I'm incredibly stressed at work and with you and now Randal. I don't need anything else. I chuckled. You get yourself so worked up about him, but he's more mature than most eighteen-year-olds. I know, I've taught eighteen-year-olds. He's still sixteen, Maggie said, and that's the bottom line. I sighed. Wiped my mouth. My voice felt tired. Maggie waited a moment, then sat down at the table. Look, she said, I'm glad you two are getting closer, and I'm glad he has a sort of semi-father figure in his life who seems to care about him. But I don't want him getting in trouble. He's a smart kid, I said. Smart kids can still get into trouble, Maggie said. Look at you. I guffawed, a twanging

bray. Randal could be somebody great, I said. A folk hero, a leader. He has that heft to him. It's rare, it's beautiful. Maggie hunched forward. Propped her head on her hands. Beneath her cropped red hair, I saw a pimple on her scalp. It'd been popped. I went back to my room.

A Tale Told by a Doctor, Full of Sound and Fury—
January 27, 2010

Maggie took me to the clinic yesterday. Said she was getting concerned with my condition. I told her that my doctor knew perfectly well what I was going through. She took me in anyway. Said it would give her some peace of mind. In my opinion, I think she was just pissed that I drooled onto her carpet.

As I put on my coat, I knew the excursion would be useless. A general practitioner unfamiliar with my history wouldn't know what to say. A neurologist or a musculoskeletal specialist would be needed, but I'd already seen them when I was diagnosed. I was degenerating right on course. Maggie insisted, though. Just for a check-up, then, she said. It can't hurt. I sighed and finished dressing for the cold, thinking that if she heard my words from the doctor's lips, she'd lay off.

Getting around is now a slightly different operation. I transfer from my motorized wheelchair to my regular one because we can't fold up the motorized one and put it in Maggie's car. Maggie then rolls me outside—plickety-plickety-plickety—and helps me into the car. She tucks my wheelchair in the trunk and gets in with me and off we go.

When we got to the clinic, she wheeled me over to Registration. The receptionist was a young chunky woman with solid shoulders and dense clumps of dark arm hair. As she moved her hands above her keyboard I was reminded of a black and white insect movie from the 1950s, wherein giant ants attacked a city. One of the shots in which a hairy ant leg gently sliced through the air and lowered to the ground sparked an uncanny comparison.

Maggie gave the receptionist my health card and tried to speak for me. I didn't let her. I humped forward, my elbows clattering on the table. Despite my detailed oratory of my medical history and reason

for visiting, the receptionist kept looking at Maggie for confirmation. We soon finished registering, and as Maggie led me away I said over my shoulder, You know, Charles Darwin thought that overly hairy women suggested a missing link in human evolution. Maggie pinched my shoulder. I chuckled and wiped my chin.

It's true the muscles around my mouth are weakening, along with my arms and shoulders. My feet feel as though they've crystallized, arrived at their final form. But if there's any group of muscles in my body that gets regular exercise, it's the ones controlling my mouth, so I'm not worrying too much about that right now.

I told all this to the doctor, a man about my age. He listened intently and said precisely what I told Maggie, that any real information could only be generated through a specialist. I smiled at Maggie and told the doctor I wasn't interested. He asked why. I told him why. He smiled a little. I frowned. Reminds me of a patient I had last year, he said. What kind of patient? Maggie said. A cancer patient. She told me she used to be a fraidy cat. Her words. She said something very similar to what you're telling me now, that she thought her cancer toughened her up. I've lived so far, she said, and I'm gonna keep on living. She declined chemo and radiation treatments. I told her she'd regret it. She said she wouldn't. Three months later she ended up in the hospital with severe pain in her chest and her head. Vicodin didn't work. Morphine didn't work. They ended up having to put her in a drug-induced coma, from which she didn't wake. The doctor leaned back against the sink, around which bottles of tongue depressors and cotton balls stood. I studied him. He had a disquieting air of self-satisfaction. Do you think that'll happen to Dexter? Maggie said. I sighed. Charcot-Marie-Tooth's obviously a different condition, the doctor said. I'm simply telling a story. A story with a moral, I said. He shrugged by lifting his folder up from his lap. He seemed remarkably docile, even bored. Nobody likes stories with morals. I know. I study stories for a living. Okay, he said. He sat on his stool, fully relaxed,

crossing one brown shoe over the other. I studied him. He had an expression like a pothead's, like he could watch the Four Horsemen gallop past and then casually bet on who would finish ahead of the pack. Is there a problem? I said. Nope, he said, smiling. I grimaced, then asked Maggie to take me home.

I festered on the drive back, rankled by the doctor's apathy. I'd wanted him to be shocked by my choice and he wasn't. The dick.

Maggie's planning to book me into massage therapy. I'll let her do it. Gratefully.

DEATH SAVES A MAN; THE IDEA OF DEATH DESTROYS HIM— FEBRUARY 1, 2010

Today, Maggie brought home an obituary clipped from the newspaper. Said she'd seen the person in the Residence. When I saw Esmeralda's picture I took the clipping and read the obituary. The picture was obviously from her younger years. Even with the heavy grey newsprint I could tell her hair was bright red. I stared at her teeth. White as Moby Dick's belly. As I stared they seemed to brighten and blossom up from the newsprint. I could tell she flossed, something which, given her declining appearance while at the Residence, she obviously gave up when she moved in.

She died of complications arising from her A.L.S. I felt proud of her for that. She let her disease take its course. She didn't try to clip things off early—or if she did, it didn't work. The obit said her dad and brother were with her. At least she had her family there. Dying in front of strangers is a horrifying idea. I sometimes had that thought in the Residence, like when Old Scratch kicked off, and when I did it upset me.

A clenching ache. Clamped my lips between my teeth. Why does love seem possible for me only in retrospect?

All Noble Things Are Touched with Melancholy— February 4, 2010

McTavish sent me an email telling me who's teaching my classes this term: a sessional lecturer who hasn't even completed his PhD. I cringed. My carefully designed syllabi, plotting delicate but sure inroads leading to the full realization of my chosen texts, are in the hands of a mere apprentice. The world bubbles with little injustices.

Spent the last few days bored. Still can't work up the motivation to do that article. Earlier today I watched a documentary, one of those brown, dry shows they play at midday because they're saving the juicy stuff for the evening. I sat and watched as the camera lazily panned across a village belonging to a South American tribe: thatched huts, earthen floors, that sort of thing. Even the insects seemed aimless. Then the camera framed a small man wearing a red and yellow headdress. He spoke, his mouth moving elliptically against the translator's fluid English. He had around his neck what the translator called his talisman, which he never took off and which he and he alone regarded as a sacred object. His tribe at times teased him for his monomania but ultimately they trusted him because of his vision.

I thought to myself, It's just a frickin claw. I turned off the TV and took out my dog-eared copy of *Moby-Dick*, a book I'd been meaning to finish for a while. If nothing else, the sabbatical frees up time for me to catch up on my reading.

I tend to think in images. If an image bothers me long enough, it becomes something more, a symbol or a metaphor. When I finished the novel—I'd only three chapters to go—two images budged up against each other: Ahab balancing precariously on his peg leg, his little whaling boat tipping and rocking, his harpoon held high above the surging white whale; and the tribal shaman gently shifting his talisman between his fingers. After a while Ahab and the shaman began to splice together so that the shaman held the harpoon and Ahab,

still on the whaling boat, bobbed, the talisman clicking as it loosened and tightened around his neck. Sacred objects, I thought. Objects of their personal mania, sacred to them only. I sat there for a moment. Looked down at my arched feet. My wheelchair. When an idea arises it arises hot. Steam through pumice. To me, my wheelchair is such an object. It is a throne, a talisman that represents what I believe to be the sacredness of disability. But like Ahab's harpoon and the shaman's claw, that sacredness might be unearned, or simply esoteric. That's the danger of monomania. It's too singular to be believed.

My disability doesn't feel like just a disability, though. It feels like more than that. Something I'm continuously trying to define. My chair is my *Pequod*, which I pilot toward either blazing fulfillment or flat tragedy. I don't know if I'll be able to drive a harpoon into the heart of disability and create a new ceremony out of its scattered blood. I'm discouraged right now, so it appears difficult, if not impossible.

THOU SHALT HAVE CRAMPS, SIDE-STITCHES THAT SHALL PEN THY BREATH UP—FEBRUARY 8, 2010

Pneumonia. Coughing and general pain. Pain flaking from the lungs and dusting down into the little crevices of my body. Coughing which forces my diaphragm to heave, sparking pain in the spine. When I cough I hear in my spine a metallic crumple. To breathe is to hoist myself up and let myself down as gently as my tremors will allow.

I've found myself assuming the role of Randal's third parent. Randal came home from school yesterday looking discouraged. I was sitting in the living room reading; he dropped his bag by the door and sat on the couch. I closed my book and asked him what was wrong. Kept my distance; didn't want him catching my illness. You remember that joke I told? he said. This guy at school, he came up to me and started swearing at me. Was like, you don't have any fuckin right to say something like that, you don't know what you're talking about, you can't do that, and yeah yeah yeah. Randal shook his head. He cornered, kind of cornered me by my locker. He plays for the football team. He told me his sister was deaf. I told him I was sorry and that I didn't mean it like that, and he just told me not to do it again. Randal looked at me. I thought he was gonna hit me, he said. Everybody was walking past us and none of them said anything and when they looked at me it looked like they wanted him to hit me. Randal hunched, folding his arms. I didn't want to hurt anyone, he said. I know, I said, coughing. Randal exhaled. Bit his lip. I don't like the people my age, he said. They're just...I don't know, they don't know enough about things. They're teenagers, I said. No, it's more than that, he said. It's like they don't care to know how things really work. Nobody understood my Gandhi-Manson joke. Nobody got it. Only the teachers did. I chuckled. I talk with my teachers during lunch hour, he said. My friends, they're just kind of there. Like, they're nice and everything but they don't really do much for me. You're mature

for your age, and that can either get you ahead or it can get you in trouble. I know. I don't want to get in trouble, I wanna help people. I know. I wiped my mouth. If it were up to me I'd make you my personal secretary, but now's not the time to do it. You need to finish high school, finish your education. I'm sick of high school. It's nothing but *Twilight* and soap operas. I chuckled. I felt the same way when I was sixteen. But I had bigger goals. I wanted to go to university. I wanted to discuss big ideas. And the only way I could do that was by finishing high school. Gahhhd. Randal sat back. Glanced out the window. What's your goal? What do you want from your life? Randal thought for a moment. To be important, he said. To give something new to the world. To be like you. I smiled. Coughed. Looked at myself. My chair. My feet. Are you sure? I'm not exactly the Dalai Lama. He chuckled. You're living your ideas. That's the best way. Don't tell your mom that. Why not? She doesn't see me as the best role model. Randal scoffed. At least you have things you wanna do. You have goals and ideas. Mom doesn't have a clue.

Started coughing and couldn't stop. Came back to my room. Randal followed. Told him to stay away so I wouldn't get him sick. With a short struggle I got into bed. Drank cold tea with a straw. Slept in lapses.

Awoke in the evening to hear Randal's and Maggie's voices in the living room. Randal telling her that Uncle Dexter told him about how she mistreated him when they were young. That he didn't want any more tension in the house. That he hated her insecurity and he loved Uncle Dexter's direction and steadiness. That he had no respect for her. A few minutes later a door slammed. Then someone knocked on my door. Dexter. I groaned. Maggie opened the door; regrettably, I hadn't locked it. She turned on the light. I winced. Did you hear all that? she said. All what? She sighed. You heard it, didn't you? I squinted. What, your son's lack of respect for you, or his unbridled admiration for me? Okay. She stepped forward. Hold on. I

know you're gonna blame me, but I didn't put those words in his mouth. He did talk to me, I'll grant you, but I didn't say anything like that to him. Maggie stood in the middle of my room, the air thickened by my coughs and scraping breaths. Where did he get the idea that I'm withholding things from him? I shook my head. Coughed a few times. When I could gather a full breath, I said, In the interest of preserving and healing my lungs, I'm exercising my right to remain silent. Did you tell him about the abortion? No. Are you sure? No. You're not sure? Sure. Maggie huffed. I chuckled and festered for a moment and then sat up quickly. For god's sakes, Maggie, just go get your son and tell him everything. All right? Tell him your entire life story. Don't look at me like I'm to blame. You're the one to blame for all the secrecy, you're the one to blame for all your problems. You you you. Maggie's hands quivered. Her eyes gritted. Stop looking at me like that. Abortions happen every day. He probably knows a few classmates who've had them. You don't understand, she said. It was a very painful thing for me and I don't want him to get the wrong idea. The wrong idea about what? About whether or not I cherish him. He knows that, Maggie. Besides, it happened over thirty years ago, almost forty years ago now. You might not've noticed this, but Randal's a very understanding young man. You're being much too sensitive. Maggie waffled. Looked at the wall. Neither of us said anything for a moment. I hacked and dredged up mucous. At once Maggie turned and left the room and closed the door. I spat into the garbage can near my bed. As my mouth is weak, instead of a lofty projectile, all I could manage was a heavy drip.

Nothing Like the Sun—February 11, 2010

Must've lost ten pounds since I got pneumonia. Have hardly left my room. Maggie and I aren't speaking again. We say nothing when she brings me food and water. I am a pet, or a plant. When she leaves the room I speak to the door: Petty hag, dried-up Sycorax. I've exposed yet another one of her inadequacies. Spite lingers in the air like rotten incense.

Beset not just with tremors but also general weakness. Difficult to get into my chair. My wasted muscles have been thinned even further by illness. My biceps like toothpaste tubes that've been squeezed empty. My shoulders knobby as cobblestone.

Email from McTavish. The sessional lecturer is apparently doing well with my classes. The students are enjoying the texts. McTavish undoubtedly sent the note out of guilt. I deleted it.

Randal comes to see me for a few minutes each day. No more than that. Don't want him getting sick. Earlier today he asked if I wanted to hear a joke. I said no. Felt too tired to laugh. Realized it's been a while since I've had a good laugh. Such a strong sadness welled up and left me steeped in loneliness.

He asked me if I could help him with his essay on Shakespeare's sonnet "My mistress' eyes are nothing like the sun." Told him maybe, if I improve. He said it's due in a week. Told him not to get his hopes up.

After he left I became alarmed. What if I don't improve? I'd heard numerous stories about people with conditions like mine contacting a common illness and then passing away. I was jarred. I'm not ready. There's still work to be done. I'm not finished yet.

Bukowski Probably Liked Hospital Gowns— February 16, 2010

Just got home from the hospital. Spent four days there. My pneumonia wasn't going away. Breathing was like sucking air from nails and bolts. Lungs and airway felt rusted. My coughing wouldn't stop. Maggie was concerned and took me in. I was hesitant. Didn't want doctors prodding me again. My coughing decided for me.

Shared a room with a six-year-old boy with devil's grip. The paediatric ward was full. Was strapped to an oxygen tank. As soon as the nurse put the mask over my mouth and nose I shook my head and thought, Old Scratch, you leathery bastard. Felt like some strange justice had just been accomplished. For me it was an embarrassment, an outrage. Wondered if Dante's kicked off yet. Wondered if Jeeves is getting bored. Was suddenly disappointed that neither Gertrude nor Stefan has tried to contact me.

The boy had a fever and severe chest pain. He lay on his side most of the time. He's from Cudworth. His mother came every day, a thin woman who somehow managed to look round. She said hi to me, asked me how I was doing. I'd tilt my hand in reply. Then she'd attend to her son. A quiet boy. Dark blue eyes. He looks suspicious even though he doesn't mean to. When he speaks he speaks quickly, gathering his breath and then letting it all out. Like he feels he doesn't have enough time to get out what he wants to say. His mother often told him to slow down because she couldn't understand him. Said that he was mumbling. I studied them. He studied me. When his mother was out of the room he spoke to me in a slower voice. Asked me what was wrong with me. Asked me if I was dying. I shook my head. How old are you? he said, hugging his flank and speaking through his teeth. Forty-seven. My aunt was forty when she died. Okay.

I often fiddled with the tube leading up to the needle that fed medicine into my hand. A bag of transparent fluid hung above my

bed. Made me think of catheters and colostomy bags. I groaned. Fuck you, Old Scratch, I thought. May the fires of hell tickle your ripe old ass.

My last night in the hospital, the boy's mother read to him from a book of fairy tales she'd plucked from the paediatric ward's bookshelf. I followed along. From where I lay, I saw it was an older hardcover volume; the mother held the book so that it faced me. The illustrations were dazzling, even haunting in their clarity, placed on glossy pages in between the crisp leaves holding the text. The wolf in *Little Red Riding Hood* had an enormous head with grizzled, matted fur; I could almost smell its wet-dog musk. Red Riding Hood was drawn in mid-cower, in the act of turning away from the wolf, her face arrestingly sly yet vulnerable.

The mother read an unusual version of *Three Billy Goats Gruff*. The goats, as the story usually goes, convinced the troll to let them pass on the bridge by each saying that his older brother was bigger and beefier. The difference was the troll himself. Rather than the usual ugly little son of a bitch, the troll had a pronounced limp with sharp knobby limbs. The illustration was a full-page portrait of the troll leering in the middle of the bridge, heavily favouring his right leg and pointing a bumpy yellow finger at a goat, whose nose and face poked out of the corner of the page. The illustration was so detailed that I imagined the troll sucking on his lips and spitting as he spoke, his words spurting out from between his few, clumsily distributed teeth.

When the mother finished reading the story, the boy looked over at me. He'd seen my foul rag-and-bone body whenever I went to the washroom. I widened my eyes and took off my mask and smiled at him. I am absolutely a troll, I said, but don't worry, I don't eat goats. They taste too furry. The mother chuckled, and the boy smiled a little, but with his suspicious eyes I couldn't tell if he was comforted or uneasy.

Came home just an hour ago. The boy was still there when I left.

I'm better now. Definitely tired of hospitals. Breathing more or less regularly, though my lungs still feel partially deflated. Arms a bit

stronger. Wrists aching now, though. Haven't written like this for a while. Then again, there wasn't much to report until now. What am I to do about that?

The Vitruvian Man Is the Spokes of a Giant Wheel— February 22, 2010

Got an email from a publicity assistant at Freaky Productions, the movie studio that made *My Left Foot Job*. They want me to watch a few more of their movies and talk about how they represent persons with disabilities in a positive manner. Apparently the studio's come under fire for making a film featuring people with mental disabilities, including Down syndrome. The title of one of the films is *Going Down on Her*. Another is *One Flew over the Cuckoo's Breast*. I've been loosely following the story in the news. Not sure how I feel about it. They say they got the actors' consent beforehand, but some non-profit group is saying that these actors didn't understand what they were being asked when they signed the contracts. That's not the issue for me, though, or at least it's not the primary issue. The primary issue is whether or not the films are sexy. Cerebral palsy is one thing; Down syndrome is another. A disability can sometimes be like a dress. Some people wear them very well, so well that they make them appealing, even enticing. Disability as Prada. If you wear something confidently enough, everyone will want it. Others wear their disabilities like they're pants made of staples and toad flesh. People with mental disabilities often don't know how to wear them, and as a result, they always look uncomfortable. Their brains have been clothed in the wrong bodies. This is one kink in my philosophy: how to apply it to people with mental impairments. How can you use your disability to become stronger and smarter when your mind is unreliable? If you embrace a mental disability, you could hurt yourself and hurt others. That's not what my philosophy is about. But then, if I encourage the correction and rehabilitation of such people, how do I avoid looking like a hypocrite?

In any case, I agreed to watch the films. I don't know if they'll be sexy, but at least this time I have a door that can be locked.

Over the last few years, I've developed a habit of leaving things as they are, even if they can be fixed. With the TV remote, I'm more likely to mash the buttons down or nose the *Pequod* forward and put the remote closer to the TV rather than simply put in new batteries. I used to think I was patient, but I was actually just ignorant. I think this habit's come because of my disability. I think of myself as something that doesn't need fixing, so I apply that notion to everything else—which is wrong. Obviously other things need fixing. Maggie, for instance. She hovers around me even more than she used to. Not just out of suspicion about my influence on Randal, but out of concern for my health. I'm over my pneumonia, but the illness weakened me. I can get out of bed and onto the toilet, but not much else. I bathe every second or third day. Randal helps me in and out of the tub. I asked him if it feels weird or uncomfortable. He shook his head. I told him he's a good man.

It's hard to look at Maggie now. Her eyes look bleached. They linger rather than just stare; the animation's been scraped away from them. Her mouth clenches. Her lips fold between her teeth. I don't know if she's tired or anxious. She has to go to Toronto in a few days for a work conference. She's been looking for a caregiver to take care of me while she's gone but she hasn't found one. I told her not to worry too much about it; Randal and I can survive on our own. Randal told her the same thing. I can help him, Mom, he said. He's not that heavy. I chuckled. Yes, I said, raising and flexing my arm, I'm on Weight Watchers for Cripples. Randal laughed. Maggie sighed heavily. She doesn't like that it's two against one. She said she'd think about it, meaning she'll eventually agree because there's no other option.

She's taking me to massage therapy again tomorrow. There are two masseuses who work with me. Both female. Both fat. Both possess blacksmith's hands that knead and pound my flattened muscles even flatter. I often jar when they work on my back, my arms and legs snapping upwards like a skateboard broken in two. I am a one-

hundred-and-forty-pound cripple completely at the mercy of a pair of two-hundred-and-twenty-pound behemoths with hands like giant potato mashers. Yet, at the end of each session, I emerge feeling like my body's been rinsed with whiskey and Listerine, my muscles humming and tingling, my joints yawning open.

I don't think of the therapy as treatment. It's more of a pleasant excursion. Each session's an hour-long vacation. The masseuses never ask questions. They just do their job, running their heavy hands over the mass of knots that is my body. Despite Maggie's purpose in giving me the therapy—to encourage me to think more positively about my body—I thank her for it. If nothing else, it's something for me to look forward to.

I Felt a New Orleans Funeral, in My Brain— February 24, 2010

I watched the Freaky Productions videos last night (door closed) and found them a bit confusing. Certain bits were sexy; the cast for *Going Down on Her* was composed chiefly of Special Olympians who, with the help of makeup and lighting, managed to look decent. However, at times the actors seemed confused. I wonder if they'd seen a porno before, or if they knew what was expected of them. In one scene, the male obviously comes early, as evidenced by his heightened voice, pinched eyes, and increasingly frantic movements, but just before he reaches orgasm they cut to a different angle of him with a lower voice and slower thrusts. On the whole, it was unclear whether it was exploitive or empowering. In the other film, *One Flew over the Cuckoo's Breast*, one good-looking woman who appears normal is cornered by a male attendant. The attendant says, I need to give you an injection, and whips off his pants. At the sight of his penis the woman starts going batty, slobbering over him, shouting both insults and praise at him as they screw all over a padded room. It was sexy, but it also felt like a parody of mental illness. I don't know what condition the woman had, if any, and I don't know how anybody could take it seriously. I sent the company an email saying I couldn't do a write-up in support of their endeavours. My thoughts on the films are too ambiguous.

There's a hierarchy within the disability spectrum. Bodily impairments are ranked higher than mental, based not only on the person's ability to live with that impairment, but also on the average person's ability to understand and process the impairment. When your disability is visible or physical, it generates sympathy and/or empathy, and so produces understanding. A physical impairment is also much more predictable; a mental illness is more abstract and unstable. We can offer analogies and diagrams, but they only go so far. Humans

are primarily a physical species, and the way we interpret and comprehend ourselves attests to that idea.

I've heard that a quarter of the Canadian population has some
form of mental illness. That number's apparently risen over the past
few decades. I understand that it's the result of deeper and more developed studies, but I also think it's the result of general human weakness. Because of the availability of these labels, we seek a quick diagnosis and then treatment, usually drugs or therapy or a combination
of both, rather than summon the strength to deal with it ourselves.
People say, Oh, they can't deal with it themselves because they're not
stable enough or they're not strong enough or they don't have the
resources. They're right. They don't have the strength. Not anymore.
We're analyzing ourselves into mush. In the case of mental illness, we
should've left that science behind in the fifties, when we were moody
instead of bipolar. So much needs to be left alone. My backbone may
be twisted, but at least I have one.

Ding Dong, the Witch is Gone—February 25, 2010

Maggie left for TO this morning. Just enjoying the enhanced quiet. Enhanced because I know it won't be interrupted.

Got an email from my colleague in the States asking about the paper on jokes and language. Told him I'm still working on it. I've made a few notes here and there but without a single unifying concept—a new name for disability—it's useless.

Maybe I should take my own advice. Leave it alone. What would it do? What would it solve? Who would read it? There are so many doctrines out there that trying to choose wears us out. Maybe we should withhold our ideas and aim for simplicity.

I know I sound discouraged. I know I've worked for years on these ideas and that they're valuable to me. But I'm stumped: Stifled. Paralyzed. My *Pequod*'s grounded. I don't know how to raise its sails again.

Also, in a small but infuriating way, Maggie's admonitions have burrowed into me. I constantly fight against her notion that I'm punishing myself by resisting a full course of treatment. And the idler I am, the more time I spend dwelling, and the more correct Maggie becomes.

OLD NO. 7 BRAND—FEBRUARY 27, 2010

I've never wanted to get drunk more than right now. I spent the entire day searching the house for a bottle of wine or a fifth of vodka. I opened the pantry and tossed boxes of Ritz crackers and chicken noodle soup all over the kitchen, and found nothing. I tried to get into Maggie's room, but it was locked. I crawled down the stairs to the basement and found nothing but empties. When I crawled back upstairs (a task that took me twenty goddamn minutes) I went online to find a liquor store that delivered, and by the time I found one Randal had come home from school. You okay, Uncle Dexter? Yes. Why're you sweaty? You look upset. Just doing my exercises. Are you gonna have a bath? 'Cause I need to shower. You go ahead and shower, then. I'll be in my room.

I am desperately dry. I want to be cradled within Jack Daniel's welcoming balm. The walls around me crinkle, like the tongue of a man long dead of dehydration. It makes me miss the period following my diagnosis, in which I was severely depressed, but also free to indulge. One weekend, I bought four bottles of Old No. 7 and lined them up on my kitchen counter and drank them in succession. In the middle of the second bottle, I sat on my living room floor, my right foot cradled in my lap. I'd visited the specialist a few days before and he'd described to me the symptoms of Charcot-Marie-Tooth disease, so I was extremely self-conscious about my body; the smallest itch or sore demanded my attention. I watched my foot for a long time, expecting it to bend before my eyes. When I took a drink I didn't move my eyes away. Eventually I started to cry, and I grabbed my foot and tried bending it with both hands. Then I stood up and whipped it into the hardwood floor. I drove my toes down; two of them crumpled. I hollered and stomped. I took a long drink and hit myself on the head with the bottle. In a delirious way, I wanted to assert myself: if my disease was going to disable me, I would disable myself first. In

retrospect, it seems grossly proud, something Oedipus would've done as a teenager.

The worst part of that period was how I treated Maggie and Randal. I hardly acknowledged them. Maggie knew I was drinking and so tended to avoid me; we only saw each other once every few months. She'd call ahead to make sure I was sober, or at least civil, then I'd drive to her house. Thad, a grocery-store manager with a horrible moustache, would hold her hand as much as possible. Maggie would offer him small smiles. Randal at that time was five or six. He drank big glasses of red juice and ran all over the yard; in my state I couldn't believe he didn't get dizzy. I still have the two or three pictures of Randal and me from that time, and I can't remember them being taken. The ground of that occasion, holding me up and fixing me in time and space, drains away from beneath me.

And now here we are, all under the same roof. We're definitely closer now, and I owe some of that to my disability, for it's streamlined my life. But the pathway here was circuitous, ploughed by bitterness and circumstance rather than love and affection. I don't know if it was worth it, because I don't know if it'll last, and I don't know if I've changed enough.

A New Ceremony—March 1, 2010

I have it, goddamn it! The answer! Dexterity. Dexterity is the word.

Working on that article now. Riding the momentum of eu-fuck-ing-reka.

This much later in the day. The momentum's subsided. I wrote seven pages today, the most I've written in months. Here's how it came about: I got an email this morning from a disability organization, which I serve as a board member. They sent out a newsletter and my name appeared at the top of the page on the masthead; even though I don't edit newsletters, they put my name on the top to establish credibility. My name was directly above the word disability, and I found myself saying, Dexter, dextrous Dexter, with his lovely disability. There was a pause. I stared at the screen. Then there was a loud click. As though the mechanics in my brain had been scraping and groping for months before finally locking into place with the relief of steam and sweet alignment. I shouted. I began the article that instant.

The basic idea: I don't have a disability. I have Dexterity. In addition to replacing the term "disability," the word also underscores the strength and judgement developed as a result of acquiring a disability. I've also capitalized it to give it the legitimacy of a doctrine.

I haven't eaten yet today. When Maggie tried to interrupt with a plate of food I told her, Woman, bugger off! I'm on the roll of my life and I sure as hell am not stopping for the sake of pork and rice. She left in a huff. I'm light. I'm nimble. My thoughts swish through the air, seeking new depths, curling under doors and kicking up dust. Christ was not so buoyant when he discovered he could walk on water. The geeks shall inherit the earth. The geeks shall inherit the earth.

Much Madness Is Divinest Sense—March 13, 2010

Still working on the article. Up to fifteen pages now. Working slower. My arms feel weaker and my breathing feels stunted. Not pneumonia again. This feels harder. Like my lungs are callusing over.

It's not so much an article as it is a hymn or a gospel. A strange thing's happened as I've been working on it: my conscience, that hissing spitting invertebrate, has blushed blackly into being, resting before me on the computer screen. It's also here, in this journal, ripe with a lifetime of anger. But then what positive changes arise without anger?

A BIG SISTER IS THE APPENDIX IN THE BROKEN FAMILY'S ANATOMY—MARCH 15, 2010

Continuing work on the article. Things have slowed as I check sources and rework a few ideas.

Maggie and I had a spat today. I've sequestered myself in my room as I work on the article, so as a result I haven't been eating much. She came in with a plate of pasta and put it on my desk. Are you going to eat? she said. In a bit, I said. Dexter, look at your eyes, look at your hands, you can hardly type. Thank god for the delete button or I'd look pretty stupid. Dexter, take a break, okay? I don't want to. Maggie stared at me for a moment and then took the grips on my chair and pulled me away from the desk. Hey! She stood between me and the computer. You're not working any more until you eat. You're not gonna starve writing a silly article. Silly! I pointed at the computer, through her abdomen. This is my life's work. Years of thinking and revising boiled down to this one crystal. And how can you continue working if you don't keep up your strength? My momentum keeps up my strength. Now let me get back to work. Not until you eat that plate right there. I nudged my chair forward and bumped her knees. I'm not moving, she said. I pulled my chair back and rolled forward again. She lifted herself onto my desk; her feet came up to my chest and she held me at bay. I kept nudging the chair forward and the desk shook and the plate of pasta tipped off the desk and onto the floor. Goddammit, Dexter. Get off my desk. I'm losing momentum. Maggie rubbed her eyes. Maggie, will you move, please? Maggie bent down to pick up the plate, and then stood up. I'm not picking that up, she said. You can pick it up. She left my room. I started to work again. She came back and put a roll of paper towel and a bottle of carpet cleaner in the corner.

Most of the noodles and sauce remain on the floor. I eventually tried to clean it, but it was impossible. I can't lean down far enough

to pick all of it up; my back plays heavy metal when I stoop that far. I could only grab thick hunks and I couldn't scrub the carpet.

I hope she cleans it up soon, because if I have to go to the washroom or into the kitchen to make myself something to eat, my wheels will roll over it and drag red sauce into the hallway.

Watering a Poison Tree—March 18, 2010

Had a mantis dream two nights ago. I was the giant I wanted to be. I brought my heavy arms down upon a group of clapping school-children. I leapt from one side of the city to the other and kicked apart Credit Union Centre and demolished a hospital, an elementary school, and a row of $900,000 houses. But then I saw Maggie standing in the middle of the road. This was on Spadina Crescent, by the river downtown. Everyone else around her was clapping but she wasn't clapping. She kept her arms sternly at her sides. It reminded me of when she was young. I roared and hissed at her. Her mouth opened and closed. She didn't say anything but the quickness with which her mouth moved suggested she wasn't happy. It was as though her mouth was on fast-forward; it would've been funny if her expression wasn't so aggravating. I reared up and giggled. I brought my two arms together; they clacked dryly, and I swung my entire body down onto her. I came back up and she was still there, untouched. I swiped at her. She withstood the blow and didn't move. I lowered my claw and nudged her. She was as immovable as a possessed protester. I shoved her and kicked her but even with my immense strength I couldn't dislodge her. I collapsed onto my belly and cried at her. Then the dream ended. When I got out of bed and rolled down the hall— the sauce and noodles were still there—Maggie and Randal were eating breakfast at the kitchen table. Randal straightened. You need help with anything? he said. I looked at Maggie. The discomfort from the dream lingered with me and balled up along with the petulance of the past few days. She didn't respect my work. When she'd come into my room with the pasta, she'd never asked if I was hungry. She'd simply imposed. If there's one thing that bothers me more than anything else, it's when other people think they know what's best for me. As I sat before her, I felt outraged; I saw her as a hindrance, an obstacle. I needed to assert myself. Maggie stared at me. I looked at Randal. Did

she tell you about what happened when she was seventeen? Maggie's face darkened. Dexter. I waved her off. If anyone was going to break the tension, it was me. She had an abortion, I said. Now, it's not a reflection on you or anything. She was a teenager. It was just a one-time mistake. Your mother loves you. She just needs to learn to let some things go. Randal looked at Maggie. Maggie's eyes crackled. Is that true, Mom? Maggie looked at him. She breathed. Wiped her eyes. I waited. That…that was not for you to tell. You understand, though, right? I said to Randal. It was a long time ago. She was nearly your age. Dexter! Maggie shook the table, spilling her coffee. Mom, it's okay. Why did you do that? Maggie said. Mom. Randal stood up and went to her and put his arms around her. It's okay, he said. It's all right. It's not a big deal. Maggie said something unintelligible and then hugged him. I got a juice box from the fridge and wheeled back to my room. Maggie called to me; I ignored her. A few minutes later she came in to tell me that I'm unbelievable and that she'd talk to me when she got home from work.

As soon as she got home she came into my room and locked the door. She stood there for a minute looking at the floor, and then she pushed me away from my computer and punched me. Her fist glanced off my temple. Christ! I said. She stared at me for a moment. Her arms shook. She punched me again, under the eye. Maggie! She began beating me. In a minute Randal pounded on the door. Maggie worked with the efficiency of a yakuza enforcer. She punched me and pulled me out of my chair and booted me in the stomach. I squawked. I feebly tried to hit her back. Tremors sputtered down my arms; my hands were jarred spiders. She began crying, then took my journal and emptied the computer-printed pages out of it and dropped it on me. I rolled onto my back and held my face. She wiped her eyes and said, All right, and unlocked the door. Randal dashed in and, when he saw me, swore at Maggie. He ran after her. I heard him shout, Why'd you do that! Maggie's voice wavered and spiked as she tried to get him

to calm down. I lay slumped and awkward on the floor. Wiped blood from my mouth. A tremor made me nudge my nose. Terrific pain all over. I lay there listening to them scrap.

Randal came back and helped me into my chair and cleaned up my things. He put my journal back in order. Said he was thinking about going back to his dad's house but he didn't want to leave me. I told him he was a good kid. I asked him if he had a problem with me telling him about Maggie. He said no. I don't see what the big deal is, he said. I chuckled. My thoughts exactly, I said. I don't know why she doesn't trust me, he said. She treats me like I'm fucking seven. I hear you, I said, lifting my bloody hand. Randal took me into the bathroom and helped me clean up. Maggie had left the house.

I'm still sore. Wondering if one of my ribs is broken. Broken rib plus scoliosis equals splintering pain. Breathing is even harder now. Hardly slept last night.

Maggie came into my room this morning before she left for work. I don't know what to say to you. I've run out. You could say you're sorry for beating the hell out of me. I'm not sorry, though. Oh. Maggie shrugged. Are you kicking me out? I said. I'm not sure. I'm still debating on whether or not that's too cruel, and if Randal will be so angry that he'll go back to his dad's. Last night I had a fantasy of putting you in the car and dropping you off on a street corner downtown, without your wheelchair. Let the streets have him, I thought. You wouldn't do that to me, I said. I came this close, she said. You'd feel too guilty. I could charge you with assault. You wouldn't do that. Why not? You're too proud, too afraid of appearing weak. You wouldn't allow yourself to condescend to being questioned in court. Interesting theory, I said. It's not a theory when it's correct, as you once said to me, Dexter. Well, if that's the case, you won't kick me out. Not for your sake, Maggie said, but for Randal's. Well, I said, when his mother lays a ferocious beating on her crippled brother,

sympathy tends to swing toward the brother. Maggie smiled a little. You're an exploitive asshole, she said. Then she walked out. I locked the door and called her a cunt.

THERE'S A CERTAIN SLANT OF LIGHT THAT OPPRESSES— MARCH 23, 2010

As I found out when I had pneumonia, people with certain conditions aren't as able to heal. I remain bruised. One of my eyes is a royal purple. My arms and sides hurt the most; they absorbed Maggie's kicks. Randal asked me if I'm going to charge Maggie with assault; said he'd help me. The idea's tempting, but Randal can't drive and so can't do the shopping. On a purely practical basis, it's a bad idea. It'd bring the household to a halt.

The air in the house is stilted. I drag it through my teeth. Still working on that article. I do a little bit at a time. Soreness prevents me from going further. My rib feels better, so it isn't broken. My arms are still badly bruised. Every little flex or tweak brings pain. I type as carefully as possible so I don't have to delete and start again.

A Cripple's Venom—March 29, 2010

Email from McTavish. My classes went well. He and the sessional lecturer planned the final exams without my input. Nothing about me teaching next year, either. Sent him a response saying I'm coming back next year and that I want to see the exams before they're delivered. I want to teach a course in disability literature in September. He hasn't replied.

Maggie walks around the house with the posture of an aged and discarded mistress, a dispossessed character straight out of a Faulkner novel. The inside of her mind must look like the house of a long-time hoarder, everything greasy and cluttered. Hard to separate the garbage from the valuables. Everything dulled by association.

Now she and Randal seldom talk to each other. The walls of the house feel blasted and fragile, on the verge of a cave-in. Like when Maggie and I were living together after Mom died. When I lie in bed at night I stare up at the stucco. The shadows prance and play tricks on me.

Work on the article's slowed. I have twenty-two pages. I hit a bit of a snag. I don't know whether to discuss my own disability or keep my analysis purely literary. I'm discussing the metaphorical and symbolic values that've been assigned to disability over the last few centuries. These values—poverty, immorality, weakness, obsolescence, deviance—must be undermined with Dexterity, which attempts to institute stronger values of judgement, intelligence, and uniqueness. But there are no literary examples I can use to demonstrate my idea. Tiny Tim, Quasimodo, Lear, Ahab, Richard III, Oedipus…I need examples that carry weight. Contemporary literature has some Dextrous characters, but they're not as firmly rooted into the Western consciousness. I could use the blind prophet Tiresias, but the meaning of his blindness is complicated by Oedipus's self-imposed blindness. I don't know if putting my own story amongst these others will hinder my argument. I'm also not entirely sure that my story will fully support my philosophy.

As Though of Hemlock I Had Drunk—April 6, 2010

Sick. Sick all over. Each crevice ripe and sweating with flu and depression. The ceiling pushes my breath back at me. My spine creaks. I can never get comfortable. Slightly better sitting than lying down. I'm constantly moving. Even though I shouldn't be. I vomit into a bucket beside the bed. Randal takes it out. He wears yellow dishwashing gloves and holds his breath. I sweat and drink water and pop. Can't even keep my pain meds down. I punch things. Maggie doesn't come in.

Got an email from a colleague in California. Wants me to speak at a conference in July. Committed to it instantly. Something to shoot for. Back to bed.

This later on. Randal just gave me my laptop, along with some meds. I'm writing in bed. I had a frightening dream. I was in my normal body, the body of ten years ago. It was so unfamiliar to me. I studied myself for a moment. Flexed my hands. Looked at my feet. Stretched my back. I jumped up and down. I was worried. Like my normal body was an omen. I was standing in this unknown yard and Maggie showed up. I stared at her. She was trespassing. Bilious outrage. I yelled at her. Slapped her. Punched her. She didn't flinch. I poked her in the eye. Didn't matter. The ground was the colour of sick. Matted brown ribbons curled through the air. They caressed me and then seized me, wrapping around my arms and legs, locking me in place. I was strung out, as on a rack. Maggie came up to me. I spat in her face. She got to her knees and lifted my shirt. I shouted at her. She began gnawing at my stomach, her teeth digging. She made juicy sounds. My flesh was soft, like peat. It didn't hurt. Only tickled. I sobbed.

ANGER'S MY MEAT; I SUP UPON MYSELF AND SO SHALL FILL WITH FEEDING—APRIL 9, 2010

Woke up with gritted teeth. Blue anger on my lips. My limbs charged. A desire to blow the door off my room. I'd had enough of Maggie's apathy, her stiffness. Being ignored makes me feel like less of a human being. I boosted myself into my chair without wobbling. Jerked open my door. Went into the kitchen and saw Maggie. She sat at the table, holding her coffee. Her eyes slanted, cupped by a porcelain shine. All right, I said. I steered the *Pequod* so I was almost touching her knees. I'm tired of this crap. Do you want me to move out? Maggie studied me. Do you wanna fight? I said. Just roll around the kitchen floor here and get it all out? I waited. Maggie! She stirred. Talk to me! She fiddled with her coffee then pushed it away. I don't know what to do, Dexter, she said. I've spent the last few weeks trying to think of something. She shook her head. I'm stumped. I don't know what to do with you. Do you want me to leave? I said. Well, if you left I'm pretty sure you'd have no quality of life. That's not an answer. I want you to go, but you can't. So am I staying? Will I remain your tenant? Yes. Will you continue to resent me? Yes. I waited. So we'll just endure each other? That's a good way of putting it. I sighed. Are you going to apologize for beating me? Are you going to apologize for telling Randal about my abortion? I stared at the wall. Maggie watched me. She said, Does it bother you that neither of us can apologize, just for the sake of apologizing? It bothers me. Do apologies mean anything anymore, I asked. Between you and me, that is. They mean something to me, she said. They don't mean anything to you? Depends on how much damage is done. Hm. She pushed her faint red bangs off her forehead. And the damage I've done is beyond repair? I don't know. Let me ask you something, Dexter. How can someone as intelligent as you be so unaware of other people's feelings? I'm not unaware. Yes, you are. Not of your feelings. I just don't like you, Maggie. Why

not? I've never respected you, not as a person or as a sister. Her brows pinched. You're a depressed, desperate woman. You're much too sensitive and insecure, and frankly, I think that you're weak and ridiculous. Maggie studied me for a moment, and then stood up and swatted me hard on the ear. Jesus! I said. I could report you for abuse. That's no excuse, Dexter. Your philosophy or cult or whatever it is that you follow doesn't protect you when you mistreat other people. I held my stinging ear. It's not a cult, you dumb cow. Another swat on the temple. I hissed and slapped the table. What will Randal say about this? He'll understand. He's on my side, I said. Wait until he sees who you really are, she said. I grunted. If you hit me you're breaking the law, I said. It's perfectly legal to discipline a child this way when all other methods fail. I reached out to hit her, and missed. I slapped a chair instead. Don't you dare call me a child, I said. You're a child, Dexter. That's all you are. You're an angry, lonely, insecure little boy. I leaned forward to try and hit her again; Maggie stood and backed away toward the kitchen sink. Stop running, I said. You're not making this fair. She smiled. You think this is fair? You're a cunt. You're a pathetic fuck. I'm not a child. You're worse than a child. I picked up a spoon and threw it at her. It hit her on the breast. Maggie dodged around my chair and switched it off. Hey! She turned me around and started pushing me down the hallway. I tried to swing my arms backward but they were too stiff. My elbows and hands whacked against the walls. Maggie! She shoved me into my room. You sit in here and think things over. She then closed the door. I could report you, Maggie! I could report you for abuse! Goddammit! Turn my chair back on! Maggie! My cheeks heaved with heat. My lower lip quivered. I drooled freely into my lap. I slapped the arms of my chair. I punched the wall and broke open a knuckle. I bucked and growled and screamed.

After a few minutes I glanced out the window. All I could see was the browning wall of the house next door. I sighed, and began to imagine leaving the house and becoming a street person, cupping my

twitching palms for money. I imagined gathering all the other street people into a corner of the alley and instructing them on the basics of the English language and teaching them how to read using old newspapers and discarded McDonald's wrappers. I shook the thought away when a more realistic image arose: sitting on the sidewalk with my back against a brick wall, my arms and legs limply splayed, my dried face blushing with mosquitoes. I'd try to trip people in an effort to be noticed, but it would seldom work. They'd easily skip over me. Combined with Maggie's resolve, the image incited a tumble in my gut, and I became frightened.

The Still-Small Voice Pronounces Trippingly on the Tongue—April 12, 2010

Have locked myself in my room for the last while and, consequently, finished a draft of the article. Twenty-nine pages. Not quite satisfied with it, though. Feel it's missing something—a jolt. A sustained charge of passion that glorifies a philosophy and gives it momentum. The academy's notorious for resisting passion. Inside the ivory tower churns a rusty iron heart. This is why I love disability studies: passion and logic can intermingle without penalty. I want my ideas to make a dent in the world: a crater, crooked and lovely and big enough to hold everyone.

A rickety peace has settled over the house. Whenever I leave the room I expect a sudden sound to pop out of the walls and surprise me. Randal and Maggie speak in restrained voices. Randal sometimes comes into my room. He talks about school and his friends, nothing else.

Because I've sequestered myself, I've had to keep busy, so the other day I dug through a box of items left over from the Residence. Among single socks that lacked partners and DVDs I stole from the Residence living room, I found the digital picture frame. I slipped out of my chair, hitting my ass on my footrests, and crawled to a wall socket and plugged it in. There were only the three pictures of Randal and me. As the pictures faded into one another I found their rhythm disjointed and the pictures themselves displeasing. I unplugged the frame and sat with my back against the wall. My spine did not comfortably align. My body arched forward.

A Jack in the Box Is a Crippled Son of a Bitch—
April 16, 2010

Called a cab today. It took me to the university and I went to the room where my students were writing their final exam. They'd just begun. When I entered all of them stared at me like I had the wrong room. I rolled to the front with overweening confidence. The instructor, a puny twig of a man who looked like he'd just come out of hibernation, blinked at me and asked me who I was. The little weevil. I designed this class, I said, and I'm insulted that you wrote the final exam without asking my opinion. The man stammered. Glanced at the students, who were no longer interested in writing. I know these texts better than you know your own pecker, I said. A few students exhaled. You've no right to take over my class without talking to me. He stammered again. Looked at the exam sheet he was holding. Blake told me it was fine, he said. Blake was McTavish's first name. I don't care. You need to show respect. And now, I'm going to invigilate this exam. You can leave. Give that to me. I reached for the exam sheet he held. He was so shaken he automatically handed it to me. Thank you. Now you can leave. He looked at the students again. They now studied him as though he were a thief. I smiled a little. I'm supposed to be here, he said. I'll make sure they don't cheat, I said. This is my class, though. No, it's mine. He bit his lip. But it was given to me. I arched my eyebrows and nodded toward the door. I wiped my mouth just before the drool could drop. Get out of my classroom, I said. His hands stuttered. He waffled for a moment, glancing at the students, desperate for support. Finding none, he went and got his things and walked out. The students looked at me, concerned. I piloted the *Pequod* front and centre. My name is Professor Dexter Ripley, I said. I was the original teacher for this course, but due to unforeseen circumstances, I was removed from teaching. I will invigilate the exam today. If anyone has any questions, you can come

up and ask me, but be discreet about it, as your fellow students are writing. Now, you may return to your exams. I started moving toward the desk at the front. The students glanced at each other. I turned my head. Get to work! They stirred and hunkered down and resumed. I looked over the questions on the exam sheet, then put it down and watched them. Many of them looked up from their work. I watched the door, waiting for the instructor to bring someone from security. After the first hour I chuckled and checked my watch and wrote the time on the chalkboard in jittery digits. The instructor came back in at one point. Get out! I said. You're interrupting! He left immediately. After that, the time passed without incident. When the students finished I collected the exams and when everyone was out of the room I read them. I frowned and bit my lip. Their perspectives of the texts were vague at best and irrelevant at worst. None of the essays was whole. I felt gratified. I put the exams in the folder on the table and steered my chair out of the room and down the hall to the elevators. The instructor would mark them; the essays were the product of his teaching, not mine. I got up to the English floor. The secretary saw me and stood up. What happened to you, Dexter? she said, pointing to my chair. You look…shakier. I shrugged. I went from the basic model to fully loaded. I patted my chair and gave her the exams. You look thinner, she said, and you got rid of those damn baseball cards. I coughed and wiped my mouth. She chuckled a little and looked over the exams. You all right? I didn't know you were gonna be supervising an exam today. Well, we cripples are full of surprises. Is Blake here? No, he's not. I groaned. Where is he? I don't know, out and about. If you see him tell him to email me and that I'm coming back next year come hell or high water. Why can't you tell him? 'Cause he won't listen to me. Tell him I'll gather students up and teach them on the goddamn lawn if I have to. She nodded. People have been asking about you, she said. I frowned. Shook my head. Turned my chair around. Just tell Blake what I said.

If my colleagues in the department were truly curious about me, they'd contact me. And even then I'd probably ignore them. Maybe they know that.

I'm taking Maggie and Randal out for dinner tonight. Maggie'll be included only because she'll be driving. We'll go to a hole in the wall—a cavernous restaurant, dimly lit. Maybe Amarello's downtown. For once I need to diminish myself.

THE STRAINING MAN PERCHED ON A CIRCLE PREPARES TO ABANDON ALL SYSTEMS; THE STRAINING MAN PERCHED ON TWO CIRCLES PROPOSES AN ENTIRELY NEW SYSTEM— APRIL 21, 2010

Finished reading Cohen's *Beautiful Losers* today. Hence my heading. It's a gleefully rutty mess, a guttural love song of human error, not so much a Canadian novel as a European novel, so it's forgivable to quote it.

Randal's made a new friend at school, Vivian. Red hair. Tattoo of a butterfly skeleton on her wrist. Shoulders as broad as football uprights. She'd heard his (my) joke and, although she's in a wheelchair, she found it funny. Said it was her kind of humour. When she was here visiting I told her about my work and how I hope it'll help and she emailed me this morning and asked me to come to a meeting for her wheelchair group in two days. I replied that I'll be there. Within ten minutes she replied back saying they're excited to have me. It's mostly teenagers and young adults, with a few real adults. The age group, Vivian said, is fourteen to fifty-two, with most of the group leaning toward the younger end of the scale.

Disability, like war or abuse, blurs the lines of age like rouge and Botox never can. The distortion is internal and results in either a buoyant sense of discovery, because just about every experience is new and thrilling, or an iron depression, because nothing interests you. Sometimes both occur, amounting to a crippling bipolarity, a tragic hesitancy. Over time you withdraw from life because you simply can't make up your mind on how to feel. Your disability is no longer the issue then. It's how you think.

Vivian asked me to read from my article. I'm hesitant. (I realize the irony here. Shut up.) I just don't know if it's ready. I've read it over and over looking for a place, a crook in the elbow of my prose, to inject a heroin shot, something that'll turn my ideas into a drug, because

that's the only way they'll work. That's the only way they'll spread, is if they become a fix. I don't want a Manson family of cripples (though having several female sex slaves is enormously appealing). I want my ideas to work. I want them to flood some previously untouched rind in people's brains with a charged, awakening crackle, as though they've been slammed with gospel. I want canes and crutches to be raised like M16s. I want wheelchair users to roll like tanks into crowded rooms. I want tongues as loose and jittery as mine to hop around the earth like fish suddenly turned amphibious, hollering instead of gasping, chanting instead of croaking. I want the growls and grunts and yips and huffs and shouts and warbles of all my floppy-mouthed comrades to be taken as calls to arms, as wondrous philosophy, as the voices of our times. I want disability, Dexterity, to be known as the ideal condition of the twenty-first century. Here's hoping that I've enough breath in me to infuse my work with the full vivacity of a cavalry bugler.

FOR THINE IS THE KINGDOM, AND THE POWER, AND THE GLORY—APRIL 22, 2010

Took a taxi to the meeting, which took place in a building downtown. Randal came with me. The building was a plain white one-storey office. We entered via a long wooden ramp; splinters prickled up in certain spots. Over the windows hung thick, drawn curtains done in a multicolour pattern that somehow amounted to a vomit-like wash. *The Flu* by Jackson Pollock. It was sunny. I could smell the river. I nudged my joystick forward little by little.

The building had the air of an abandoned elementary school. The hallway smelled like old pipes. Randal and I went forward toward the sound of voices at the end of the corridor. I thought about my article tucked into my bag, which hung off the back of my chair. I expected a small gathering of five to seven people sitting in a circle. Cripples Anonymous. When I entered the room I saw close to forty people, all in wheelchairs or on crutches, talking animatedly. Maggie's word, cult, scratched at the back of my head. The curtains were open so the room was naturally lit. I looked at Randal. He smiled at me and waved at Vivian, who came over and welcomed us. As word got around that I had entered the room people quieted down and began to arrange themselves into rows. There were no desks and only one table off to the side, which held a coffee maker, styrofoam cups, and a box of doughnuts. Randal opened my backpack and gave me my papers and Vivian instructed me to go to the front. You want water? she said. She brought me a cup of water. You want me to introduce you? I nodded. I looked around again. So this is my Sermon on the Mount, I thought. These are my first disciples. Vivian waited for everyone to get comfortable and then introduced me. When she finished nobody clapped. There was a tension of expectation. I swallowed. A strange sensation hulked in me. I felt like I was at the university about to lecture on Dickens and Eliot, but the atmosphere was looser, much

more personal and permissible. I didn't have to react against anything here. My usual classroom tricks of barking instructions and handing out nicknames weren't needed. A velvety swoon in my head, like a glass of Jack had just settled in me. I grinned. I spread my wavering arms and began talking.

I opened with a joke: why did the cripple cross the road? Because he saw a Do Not Walk light. They stirred. A few of them chuckled uneasily. A glorious start. For an hour I talked to them about my condition, about language, hatred, anger, and liberation. I told a few more jokes and asked why nobody (except Randal and Vivian) laughed. I ended with Dexterity. I realize it's a bit egotistical to name the idea after myself, I said, my underarms and back and forehead awash with sweat, but that's how it came about. What we have here is essentially a New Testament that allows us to see our conditions the same way a black man sees his skin, or a Christian sees his religion, as a break- through to selfhood.

When I finished, a dense silence followed. No applause. People nodded solemnly and excitedly. I saw that a few were still sceptical. I was surprised they had stayed throughout the entire lecture. A few members came up to me and shook my hand and thanked me for coming. One young man with glasses and hair clumsily dyed blonde told me he'd never thought of his disability that way before, that he'd just lived his life in whatever way he thought was best. He didn't know there were ideas like mine. He sometimes thought of the group as an enclosure rather than an open and welcoming society. I coughed and thanked him and hoped my ideas worked for him. Vivian then came up and gave me a hug and thanked me for coming. That was wonderful, she said. I was actually crying for a minute there, your ideas are so good. I chuckled and said, Are you sure it wasn't the jokes that got you going? She laughed and looked up at Randal, who grinned at me.

When Randal and I went down the hall and out of the building and down the ramp to the waiting taxi, I exhaled, the sigh of a

spent priest. I held my papers in my hand. I'd hardly looked at them throughout the entire lecture. I came home and began rewriting certain paragraphs, infusing them with the energy I'd felt in front of the group. I deleted two pages' worth of material and added two.

It's evening now. I find it strange that my hands and arms convulse even when I'm so tired. Where does my disease get the energy?

Get Me a File, Young Pip—April 27, 2010

All of the other professors have turned in their plans for next year's courses. McTavish emailed me and said he hasn't decided whether I can come back next year. He also said he'd heard all about my exam stunt and that it's not doing me any favours. I told him that if he doesn't let me come back I'll drag him and the department before a human rights tribunal. It's one thing to put me on administrative leave based on my behaviour; it's another to keep me away because of my condition.

Rereading the article now. My colleague from the States is begging for it after I told him I'm nearly done. More than any other piece I've written, this article will cement my reputation as a pioneer in disability studies. My colleagues will no doubt attack me for my arrogance and lack of critical engagement, but there is no critical theory in disability studies that supports what I have to say, and to borrow from other theoretical systems—colonial thought, sociology, Michel fucking Foucault—would undermine the purity of Dexterity. So screw my colleagues.

I don't know if anything's changed between Maggie and me. The hot air's cleared away; we no longer see each other through an angry simmer. We continue to tolerate one another. Sit civilly at the dinner table. Make small conversation. Help Randal with his homework. If anything has changed, it's that we're more aware of each other, of our limits, where we stand. Maybe that's enough.

Randal wants to go to Europe in July. He badly wants me to go with him. I told him I'd think about it. I have a conference in California to attend in the middle of the month.

My breathing's becoming more stunted. My lungs clack and crinkle. My airway whirrs. My voice, already hampered by my slackening mouth, is an old toad's. The lecture last week sapped me. I preserve my breath for the evening, when Maggie and Randal are home. An

easy-enough task. I do nothing during the day. I talk to no one except myself.

I'm not worried about teaching in the future. Teaching will give me the energy to sustain my voice. It'll be something to look forward to.

Just in case though, I might look into treatment. Just for my lungs. Nothing else.

This late at night, around 1 am:

Just finished masturbating. Watched one of the Freaky videos. Kept replaying this one part from *One Flew over the Cuckoo's Breast* when the female mental patient shoves the male attendant against the wall of the padded room and locks him into her. Her need got me going. Her vulnerability. For some reason, vulnerability arouses me enormously.

But there was something else. As I squeezed myself, with my tremors again adding surprise to the proceedings, I felt myself slow down. My semen lurched out rather than shot, delaying my orgasm. It refused to meet the urgency of the moment. As though my body's entire rhythm has slowed to conform to my condition. I wiped myself off and stopped the video and stared at the blank screen. I thought I controlled that part—not the progress of the condition, but my body's rhythm. I thought I had more control over how urgently I move and react. I don't want to have just one speed. I want many. I want my body to conform to my emotions and thoughts instead of the other way around.

THE READINESS IS ALL—MAY 1, 2010

Submitted the article this morning. Now awaiting editorial comments. Ordinarily such comments might take six months to a year, but my colleague wants to publish it soon, so it'll probably be a few weeks to a month.

Booked the trip for Randal and me, despite Maggie's hesitancy. I'm skipping the conference in California. We leave on July 2 and will spend a month in Europe. Randal won't stop talking about it. Where are the best places? What are the things to see? Do they speak good English there? I warned him we'd have to go slow and steady. He understood. It's a relief. The last time I went to Europe—I was thirty-four or so, still able-bodied—I did a brief whirlwind tour, hitting France, Austria, and Italy in two weeks. This time I can linger and appreciate everything.

Maggie suggested I get an oxygen tank. Yeah, that'll look fabulous on the plane, I said, a convulsing, nervous-looking man who speaks indecipherably and carries a tank that looks like a small missile. She brought one home yesterday and put it beside my bed, leaving it to me to use it. I've resisted so far. I see Old Scratch in the tank's rough glint.

Randal and Vivian are dating now. Thank god the boy came to his senses. Apparently some of Vivian's friends don't like that she's dating him. They and a few others are still miffed about the joke he made. But she's a good girl. Solid and smart. If nothing else she'll help clear Randal's reputation.

TRAVEL NARROWS THE MIND—MAY 4, 2010

No updates on the professing front. McTavish and the faculty committee will soon have a coup on their hands if they don't reinstate me. I've come up with my syllabi and everything. And with my renewed lungs I should be in decent shape to teach.

Since my body can't recover, I'll turn it into a philosophical instrument: a sharpened Vitruvian man, a curved compass needle, my limbs splayed all over the dial. Behind every successful idea, from Apple to Christianity, stands an enormous personality. So I must be larger than life, a giant, a horrible, glorious mantis too big and too pervasive to trap behind glass. I want to open different spaces in people. Spaces that hiss and drip and echo. Spaces crisp with the taste of resurrection and renewal.

Started using the oxygen tank yesterday. I don't use it every minute; just once in a while, whenever I really need a deep breath. The first time the intake was so heady it made me dizzy, and I started laughing. Then I saw myself in a glass picture frame in the living room. I looked like I was inhaling laughing gas, so I laughed harder. Then I started running out of breath and needed the mask again. When I put it up to my face I thought about Old Scratch and held the mask up to the ceiling and choked out Cheers, you ripe old bastard! and just kept laughing. I couldn't stop for five minutes. I was in pain when I finished. The pain forced me to stop. My sides hardened. I swear my spine bent another inch or so. I will die laughing. I'm almost sure of it.

Earlier today, at breakfast, Randal asked me how people with disabilities are seen in Europe. I told him it depends on where you are. France's attitude is fairly progressive, thanks to Monsieur Vanier and the L'Arche program. Germany's guilt over its eugenics past has ensured that its disability programs are much gentler. Italy, however, has been slow to embrace disability. Its narrow streets and its over-

whelming Roman Catholic base have prevented much progression beyond sympathy and charity. When I visited Rome in my thirties and walked from the Vatican to the Colosseum, along the sidewalk there was a line of cripples that extended for four or five blocks: women whose club feet looked like medieval maces, men with no arms, young mothers holding crippled, pathetic children in their laps, men with blank faces holding signs written in stilted English. BLIND PLEASE HELP MONEY. NO HEARING. FAMILY AT HOME. Just outside the Colosseum I was accosted by a woman in a black robe. She limped over and leaned her shoulder into me and held out her palm and begged me for money. I waved my hands and said No change, no change. The shrewd wench pointed at my money pouch around my neck, where a few coins bulged through the cotton material. She pointed to the coins and then glanced up at the sky and held open her arms. Her voice had a scratching urgency. She spoke a mixture of Italian and Latin and kept repeating the word Christe. Christe Christe Christe! I tried to move away. She put her hand on my chest. I told her, in clumsy Italian, to go away. I attempted to step past her. She blocked my path and grabbed for my money pouch. I slapped her hand away and skipped down the sidewalk. Arridiverci! I said. She shouted at me, shaking her fist and pointing to her leg and to the sky. When I came home a week or so later and saw a man begging in downtown Saskatoon, I said to him, Put some effort into it. The beggars in Europe work for their money.

Randal stirred two spoonfuls of sugar into his coffee. I drank from my oxygen tank. Are they still like that now? he said. I don't know, I said. Europeans are usually very open about the body. Much more so than Canadians. I saw a man in Rome pull down his pants in the middle of a busy sidewalk and take a dump right where he stood. Nobody said anything. Nobody seemed to think much of it. But when it comes to disability, especially in places like Italy, the attitudes appear to change. Is it religion that makes it like that? Randal

said. That has something to do with it. Europeans are often traditionalists when it comes to religion. But also some of these places, like in Eastern Europe, they're still recovering from war and economic ruin, so they don't have time to change their attitudes. It's not a priority. Thinking progressively about minorities is a luxury of a stable and economically sound nation. Some nations simply can't afford to think like we do, so nations like ours have to do it for them. Randal frowned and sipped his coffee. Well, he said, but don't those poor nations have more people with disabilities? They often do. I know it seems backward, that the nations with more disabilities should be the ones to do something about it, but it doesn't work that way. Africa, Eastern Europe, the Middle East...disability is not at the top of their lists. In a capitalist society like ours, progressive thinking costs money, and disability and physics and Alzheimer's research and all these things that change our thinking about the world are, basically, the high-end merchandise in the department store of thought. Right now, you and I shop for Apple computers and Armani clothes and BMW vehicles. They're shopping at Value Village. Randal smiled a little. You understand? I said. Yeah, I get it, he said. It's just shitty, though. Yes, it is. Is there anything you can do? Could you give your ideas to people over there? I don't know, I said. My kind of thinking is much further ahead than theirs. They don't have the basic foundation yet. We'll see in two months if anything's changed.

I kept him too long. He was late for school. He said it was worth it, though. I smiled and wished him a good day. Despite his parents' inconsistency, the boy has a strong sense of family. I envy him that. It gives him solidity, a rod in his backbone. My own spine bears the testimony of my distorted familial relationships. It's something from which I can't draw strength. So I have to draw from other sources.

If Only You Could Breathe What I Breathe—
May 8, 2010

This song was on the radio earlier. It's called "Breathe" by a band called Moist. A band of premature ejaculators. Or whining tearjerkers. Who knows with today's musicians? Song's half-decent, though. The chorus flits around my head.

I'm getting hooked on oxygen. It's become a luxury. A cripple's cognac. Maybe because I've been deprived of luxuries for so long, I'll take whatever indulgences I can get.

Maggie and I had a discussion today. Randal was out with Vivian and Maggie and I were in the living room. I was reading Steinbeck's *East of Eden.* Maggie had a copy on her shelf but nobody had read it yet. Its spine was still smooth. I took it off the shelf and opened it and pushed back the cover so the spine made a pleasing crackle. I was just beginning the second chapter when Maggie said, Dexter. I looked up. She was reading the newspaper. She folded it up and put it on the couch beside her. Are you sure you should be going to Europe? I sighed. I knew you were gonna say something. Well? I wouldn't book the trip if I wasn't able to go. Are you going to be able to keep up with Randal? Will you have the energy to go to museums and restaurants every day? That's a lot for an able-bodied person to take. But for someone in a wheelchair, in your condition... I scoffed. People go to Europe when they're practically on their deathbeds, I said. Maggie scowled. This trip isn't for you, is it? No, it's not for me. I admit my health isn't the best. I admit that I'm chugging air like it's Budweiser. I took a swig from the mask. This trip is for Randal. It's kind of a traditional thing. When they finished school, young Englishmen used to take trips on the continent and walk through Europe. It was part of their education. I don't doubt that it's good for Randal to go to Europe, Maggie said. I just want to make sure that you know what you're doing and that you'll be able to make it through. I won't

be there to help. Why do you think I'm going? I said. Maggie tapped her fingers on her leg. I'm giving Randal an international phone card, so he can call me from wherever if he needs to. Are you mad that you're not coming? I said. Maggie's mouth pouched at the corner. Yes. I wish I could come with you, but I have to work and I can't afford it. I studied her for a moment. She wore a green University of Saskatchewan t-shirt; I've seen scarecrows wear their clothes more comfortably. Do you get any joy out of life? I said. Any happiness? Her face slackened. Randal makes me happy. Okay, but you're obligated to say that, because you're his parent. Don't you have any pure happiness? Some little thing in your life that has absolutely no attachment to your family and friends and buoys you every time? I swallowed more air. Does your work lift you up? Your hobbies? Do you even have any hobbies? I've lived here, what, five or six months, and I haven't seen you do anything other than read the paper or watch TV. I used to draw when I was in university. I didn't know that. Charcoal and pencil, sometimes pen and ink. I've tried getting back into it a couple times, but it never worked out. I'd get frustrated, because I didn't know what to draw. I'd lift up a pencil or a pen, but I wouldn't know where to start on the page. There's a box in the basement with some of my old drawings. Bring them up here, I said. You want to see them? Yes, I'm curious. Maggie stood up from the couch and walked out of the living room and into the kitchen and through the door leading downstairs. A minute later she brought up a large box and put it on the coffee table. These are all from college? I said. Most of them, she said. I reached into the box and pulled out of a sheaf of drawings. The topmost was a drawing of a Rottweiler. Thick shoulders. Thick legs. Head shaped like a brawler's knuckles. Its front left paw was lifted and its head was turned to the right; its expression was serious. The pencil rubbings made it seem like it was in mid-stride. This was before or after Mom died? I said. Before. I nodded and sifted through a few more. A fence post with a bent nail sticking out. A clothesline

bent into a wide U because of the wind, the clothes themselves flapping and indiscernible. I flipped through until I came to a portrait of a beetle. I lifted it up and put down the other drawings. Its broad shell and pinched face filled the foreground. The shell shone greyly. In the background, indicated by just a few lines and a telephone pole, lay the prairie, flat and indistinct. By contrast, the beetle was richly detailed. Even though it was done in pencil, the shell was textured with a wide round contour and neatly spaced pocks. The legs were as subtly menacing as splinters and looked as though they would click if it walked on the floor. The cocked angle of its face and the tight glint in its eyes suggested that it was curious, even contemplative. One of its front legs was lifted as though making a point. I studied it, trying to keep my arms as still as possible. Maggie watched me. I want this, I said. Okay. I want to put it in my room. Go ahead. I put the picture on a different table so it wouldn't get mixed in with the others. I went through more pictures but none of them interested me. When we were done Maggie closed the box and I picked up the beetle portrait. When did you do this? I said. A few weeks after Mom died, I think, she said. I'd like to get a frame for this. Okay. I miss drawing. Yeah, some of these are pretty good. Thank you. Maggie smiled a little and took the box back downstairs. I remained in the living room, tilting the beetle portrait so that the light fell on it differently and studying the glint in its pinched eyes.

A Noiseless Impatient Mantis—May 13, 2010

My mouth is all liquid warble. My lips and tongue shapeless gobs from a lava lamp. My voice a useless gargle. I feel like a Muppet. I am a visitor from the planet Cripple. Larga-blarga-flicker-bonk.

Actually, it's not that bad. Randal and Maggie and Vivian can understand me fine. It's just that on certain days it feels like my mouth is imploding. Like my vocal cords are being down-tuned to a severe twang. The extra oxygen doesn't really help. If anything it makes my voice's gracelessness more apparent. My voice lacks the pleasing rake of yesteryear. There's always an undercurrent of fluid. My words surf out.

I've kept all this from McTavish. He said I can come back in September so long as I'm healthy. But there'll be no more shenanigans, he wrote. If I hear that one more student has been mistreated or harassed or insulted, I will raise the motion for your dismissal. I sneered when I read that. Two years ago I wrote a letter of recommendation for a grant application that eventually won the department enough money to hire two research assistants and plan a yearly conference. McTavish told me then that it was my letter that earned the grant. He knows just as well as I do that while students are an important part of the department's reputation, research is even more important. If he fires me, a large chunk of money—along with a considerable amount of credibility—will be gone.

I submitted plans for my usual British literature courses and for a course on disability in literature, the first class of its kind to appear at the University of Saskatchewan. I will shock the farm children, all of whom were raised to kill weak calves and shoot lame horses. They are wheat. I will grind them into bread.

ADAM POTTLE

THE PEACOCK—MAY 16, 2010

Arms hurting. Feet, too. Just this little bit today.

Yesterday Maggie spoke about the time she, Randal, and I went to the Forestry Farm across town. Randal had been seven or eight; at the time my disease was gaining momentum, but I could still walk. It was the middle of July. I don't function well in the heat, and my perpetually hungover state made me parched and miserable. We walked all the way around the zoo. The grizzly bears and lions hardly moved. Maggie and Randal fed the geese and the deer. One of the bald eagles bent over and spurted white shit in our direction. Randal and Maggie laughed; I wiped the sweat from my forehead and adjusted my sunglasses. That bird's a prick, I said. Maggie shushed me. When we finished our tour we sat down at a picnic table outside the gift shop. Maggie gave me a bottle of water; I drank it quickly. She bought Randal an ice cream sandwich. A handful of chickens pecked at the ground around us, and a peacock presided over the area around a garbage can. When Randal finished his sandwich, Maggie helped him clean his hands and asked me to put his wrapper in the garbage. I took my bottle and the wrapper and walked over to the can where the peacock was. Its S-shaped neck seemed to be made of an extremely flexible material. It bobbed its head as though it had a song in its head. When it saw me, its neck straightened. It fluttered its feathers at me. I threw the bottle and wrapper into the trash; the bottle banged against the side of the can. The peacock made a sound halfway between a baby's cry and a dog's bark. It sprang at me, flapping its wings. I backed away. It cried out again and started chasing me. I dodged it and ran. Pain hollered up through my feet; they were already stiff from walking and, at that time, my arches had begun to heighten. I shouted at the peacock. Many people laughed at me. My feet screeched, and I hissed and slowed to a trot, trying to balance on the outsides of my feet where it didn't hurt as much. The peacock's

long neck snapped out and it pecked at the back of my leg. I jumped and ran further. It turned around and ambled back to the garbage can. I looked back. Like everyone else, Maggie and Randal were hunched over with laughter. I swallowed and stared blackly at Maggie. That night I bought another bottle of Old No. 7.

When Maggie told the story yesterday, I laughed with her and Randal. Our laughter fluttered loosely through the kitchen. The house slackened around us.

ASSHOLE DOCTORS—MAY 19, 2010

Received a call from a Dr. Johansson at the Royal University Hospital. He wants to meet with me. Says he's interested in discussing how my disease has progressed. Because nobody's ever let it progress in such a way, he wants to study me. You're an unprecedented example, he said. You could really be a lot of help to me and my colleagues. I told him I would meet with him when he pisses milk and shits mangos. I'm not about to indulge in some doctor's eugenics fantasy. Nobody's going to find a cure or a breakthrough through me.

Speaking of doctors, McTavish is officially a cunt. Said I need a doctor's note to return to work. I fired back an email saying he never mentioned it before, that my word was good enough. Apparently university regulations state that a faculty member requires a doctor's note to return to work if he's put on administrative leave for health reasons. But since I never wanted to go on leave in the first place, and since my leave was called a sabbatical, I shouldn't need a note. If McTavish persists, I'll fight him.

The medical establishment ruins everything for the disability movement. If we take a step forward in the cultural sphere through positive representations in film or literature, the medical establishment forces us to take two steps back. Assisted suicide, prosthetics, cures, experimental procedures, physiotherapy, psychotherapy, speech therapy, behavioural therapy, cognitive therapy. We're over-treating ourselves, and the reason we over-treat ourselves is because every condition, every disease, every disability has a label, and if it has a label, it has a treatment. Fifty years ago, someone with a limp was called a gimp and he just dealt with it. Someone with dyslexia was called slow or a wonky speller. Assigning specific, scientific labels to things is fine (I do this for a living) but sometimes labels take the edge away from life. We've over-compartmentalized the world. We've pigeonholed ourselves so our utility is strictly limited. We're no longer

everymen. We no longer have backbones or intuition or empathy. Sometimes we need to deal with things ourselves. We need to know for ourselves rather than having someone or something know for us. Thankfully, I do, and it's allowed me to maintain a semblance of sanity and serenity.

I said this exact same thing to Maggie the other day. She said again she was concerned about my health. I've apparently lost a bit more weight and have been frequently using the oxygen tank. She's had to replace it a few times now. My hair is thinning a bit at the top. Even though I'm forty-seven it's come a bit suddenly. Even my beard feels deflated. Maggie's asked me to eat more. I've obliged. Hard not to. I've been hungry. On days when my mouth is especially weak I look at Randal and cup my chin with my hand and move my jaw up and down, making sloppy chewing noises. A Muppet scarfing chicken and potatoes. We laugh. Maggie smiles, which is heartening to see. Sometimes it feels forced, but at least it's there.

The Sound Must Seem an Echo to the Sense—
June 20, 2010

In the hospital again. Been here for ten days or a few weeks.

Heart attack. Not massive but not mild either. Enough to do damage. I laugh every time I think of it. The whole attack began with a fart. I was sitting in the living room reading, and my back was sore so I was sitting in such a way that the fart was trapped. It rolled and rolled around like a lottery ball waiting to fall. The anticipation built and then it didn't come. I strained and grunted but the bastard still didn't come. Goddammit, I said. My head was hot. I was blushing and sweating. I lifted myself up and strained once more, concentrating all my resources on shoving the fucker out. Next thing I know my chest is heaving and pain is sprinting through my arm. I smell something strange. Something internal. My body buzzes. I hiss. I clench. In the midst of the buzz a little puff, a brief squeak, is released.

The trip to Europe's off. Poor Randal. I apologized to him. He said forget about it. He found me and has to keep from crying when he visits me. When I had enough energy to speak, and when I was somewhat coherent, I told him to take Vivian to Europe. But it wouldn't work. While Randal and Vivian are mature for their age, two teenagers shouldn't wander around Europe by themselves.

Maggie can hardly look at me. She's reserved about talking to me because I don't think she wants to hear my warbles. They discomfort her. The attack's weakened me, which is funny. Kind of like tossing a grenade into a home that's been destroyed by fire. I should be afraid. But I'm at peace. I laugh a lot. I feel like I don't have much to worry about. The pressure's off. I took the prognosis with a nod and asked for more Pepsi.

Best of all, I had a mantis dream a few nights ago. I remember every smidgen. I saw everything through my telescopic eyes. Seaweed in the Atlantic Ocean. Mosques in Afghanistan. Patches of oil on

concrete in California. Skyscrapers in London. And whatever I saw I decimated. I leaped. I screeched. I giggled. I spat. I dared to disturb the universe and people of all races and all religions and all abilities clapped for me, and I revelled in their applause, and I loved them by mashing them into the concrete, by sweeping them like crumbs into the ocean, by roaring and squishing spiritus mundi.

Note to the Reader

There are several scholars whose work in the field of disability studies informs my own. These authors have established common tropes in disability studies that Dexter echoes. Such authors include Rosemarie Garland-Thomson, Lennard J. Davis, Ato Quayson, Katharine Quarmby, Tanya Titchkosky, Tom Shakespeare, Michael Bérubé, Sharon L. Snyder, and David T. Mitchell. I strongly urge people who are interested in the literary and cultural impact of disability to read books by these writers.

Thanks for reading. Hope to meet you again in the future.

—AP

Acknowledgements

Mum, Dad, and Taylor. Support as warm and solid as a brick shit-house in Kitimat.

Tara Chambers. Good friend and fellow literary raconteur.

Kim Aubrey. Thank you for your encouragement and suggestions.

Dennis Bolen. Ab-fab writer and advisor.

Vici Johnstone. Jane-of-all-trades and master of the small press.

Debbie. Earth angel. My love and joy. So much frickin joy.

THE
REGISTRATION
REWRITTEN

T0287598

Millions and millions, with more every day...

Mantis Dreams

Adam Pottle

CAITLIN PRESS

Caitlin Press Inc.
8100 Alderwood Road,
Halfmoon Bay, BC V0N 1Y1
www.caitlin-press.com

Text and cover design by Vici Johnstone.
Printed in Canada

Caitlin Press Inc. acknowledges financial support from the Government of Canada through the Canada Book Fund and the Canada Council for the Arts, and from the Province of British Columbia through the British Columbia Arts Council and the Book Publisher's Tax Credit.

Library and Archives Canada Cataloguing in Publication
Pottle, Adam, author
        Mantis dreams / Adam Pottle.

ISBN 978-1-927575-25-3 (pbk.)

        I. Title.

PS8631.O7746M35 2013   C813'.6   C2013-905061-2

MANTIS DREAMS

Despite the way their relationship started, and the pain Lynell felt from Zach's hands, his death pushes her to the edge of a breakdown. Somehow, in less than two weeks, Zach became her friend and family. She even dreamt of building a life that included him, her husband's best friend and the cousin she never knew she had, but who she quickly grew to love and trust.

But the dream was shot in the chest, and she watched it disappear before her eyes.

Her phone buzzes, and Lynell looks down to read Ramsey's second text.

Of course, you don't have to answer anything you don't want to, and you'll have your lawyer with you. Don't let this freak you out. Nothing has changed since last we talked. We'll get it handled.

She types back a quick *thank you* before setting her phone down. Thanks to Ramsey's work with the Registration committee and an expedited DNA test, her claim as the true heir was legitimized. And with the might of the Registration backing her, Ramsey assured her that neither she nor Daniel would be charged with murder for the death of Eric or Zach.

Despite his reassurances, a constant thrum of anxiety lives in her mind, like an exposed wire waiting to spark. Ramsey is used to people in power always getting what they want, having things go their way. Lynell isn't. Power or not, she can't stop picturing handcuffs around her wrists, and a judge who pronounces her guilty.

When Daniel gives a soft snore, Lynell puts her phone on the chair and crosses the room. She can't help but smile at Daniel's peaceful face. She may have dozens of daunting tasks awaiting her, but at least she won't be facing them alone.

Lynell crawls into the bed next to Daniel, who gives a little huff but turns without opening his eyes to make room for her. "Can't sleep?" he mutters, voice rough and quiet.

Settling into his side, Lynell rests her head under his chin. She doesn't reply, knowing he'll fall back asleep soon. Sure enough, a few seconds pass before his breathing settles back into a slow rhythm. She shuts her eyes and matches her breathing to his, letting the time pass in peace, until the door cracks open and Ramsey sticks his head in. They make eye contact, and he disappears, clearly waiting for her outside. Lynell muffles a groan before climbing out of bed, pulling on a robe, and leaving the room. Wearing a three-piece suit sans tie, Ramsey stands a few feet away, tablet in hand and beard perfectly combed.

"Good morning," he says, with a quick nod.

She eyes the watch on his wrist, noticing it's barely seven. "Are we always going to be awake this early?"

"Yes."

Lynell presses her lips together and exhales through her nose in reluctant acceptance. "What's up?"

"We have some material to go over before the meeting this afternoon."

Lynell runs her fingers through her tangled hair, dread weighing her limbs as she thinks about the thick stack of files she's only halfway through.

The Registration, a system that provides two weeks every quarter during which any citizen with an unused Registration can legally kill one person, is owned by the Elysian heir. It also has a committee board of eight members: four are elected by the American people and four are chosen by the oligarchs. The Registration is a private business, and the committee is the equivalent of a board of directors. But due to its complicated and important nature, the board often acts as a bridge of sorts between the Registration, the citizens, and the oligarchs.

She's met three of the members so far, but the other five remain a mystery. Ramsey scheduled this meeting while she was still in the hospital over the weekend, hooked up to a morphine drip and without any real concept of how much was required of her. After spending two weeks expecting to die any second, thinking about the future—even a few days into the future—had been an exercise in creative fantasies. And appointments were little more than conceptual ideas, not real events she'd have to attend, much less be prepared for.

But now the day is here. In a few hours, she'll be meeting with people who, two weeks ago, were mythical higher beings. These people have been working to keep the most important business in the country running for years, some since before Lynell was born. Now she's supposed to waltz into a room as their new leader? She can't even walk into what used to be her uncle's house—now hers—without having a full-blown panic attack.

"Mrs. Elysian?" Ramsey says, pulling her from her thoughts. Judging by the way he's watching her, Lynell assumes he said something she didn't register.

She blinks, rocking back on her heels. "Sorry, what?"

Ramsey presses his lips together but doesn't comment on her attention lapse. "I think it best that only you and I attend this meeting. We'll introduce Mr. Carter later."

Lynell frowns. "Why do we need to introduce Daniel at all?"

"He's your husband. The committee needs to know and trust him as well."

"Right," Lynell says, even though Ramsey's words are a shock to her system. It won't be difficult for the committee to learn of Daniel's rebel past. They may already know if they've done any sort of research. "Give me thirty minutes and I'll meet you in the office."

"What about breakfast?" Ramsey asks, a slight note of concern in his voice. If it weren't for his vigilant attention to keeping a schedule, Lynell would've missed half her meals this week. "I can have it brought to your room again."

Lynell nods. "Thanks." They've been back in the Elysian mansion for almost three days and each one has been a reminder of the nightmare this building was two weeks ago. Lynell hasn't gone anywhere in the house but her and Daniel's bedroom, and the office Ramsey had the staff set up next door. Nearly every meal is brought to them, and the nurses come to the bedroom to change their bandages and take their vitals.

"I will see you in the office at eight," Ramsey says, excusing himself.

Lynell returns to the bedroom to find Daniel awake. He pushes the blankets back so she can slide in, and he kisses the side of her head.

"Maybe we should go to my place. You might sleep better there," he says.

Lynell shakes her head. "We can't. You heard what Ramsey said. We need to be surrounded by twenty-four-seven security. Plus, I need to be close to the Registration offices."

"Then pick somewhere else for us to go. You're the Elysian heir. Shouldn't you have the option to choose where you live?"

She shrugs. "Maybe long-term. But right now, we don't have the luxury of choosing where we do business when people are threatening to rip said business from my hands."

"This isn't a place to raise a child." Daniel leans forward, his eyes widening slightly with an idea. "We could find a smaller place that has a guest house where the Raines' could stay. Maybe that'll help convince them."

"Daniel . . ." she mutters, too quietly for him to hear.

Though Anna is their biological child, Lynell put her up for adoption after giving birth. But the couple who adopted Anna, the only parents her child has known, are now dead—collateral in the struggle against Eric Elysian—and Anna's adoptive grandparents, the Raines, are fighting for custody. They are probably worried for her safety if Anna comes to live with her birth parents.

Lynell doesn't blame them. If she gains custody, Anna will be in the spotlight—and a possible target for anyone wanting to get to Lynell.

"And when the people get to know you and realize the good you're going to do for this country, they'll love you as much as I do. You'll keep the business, and we'll have Anna."

The corner of her mouth pulls up, but Daniel's comment has the opposite effect than he probably expected. She knows that he believes the single "good" option is to listen to the rebels and end the Registration. But Lynell isn't so sure. Not when she has no idea yet what it would really look like to choose good.

"Thank you, Danny." Lynell presses a kiss to his stubble-lined cheek before climbing off the bed to go take a shower.

By the time she's finished, their breakfast has already been delivered. Lynell eats quickly and heads to the office, which is right next to her bedroom.

In the hallway, she gets a glimpse of the staircase that leads to the first floor. Her heart flutters. Unbidden, a memory of the first time she crossed the threshold engulfs her mind like a choke hold.

She'd been terrified, standing next to her cousin, who was still a stranger at that point. Every man in her radius posed a lethal threat, and the building was so imposing that she felt no more significant than a worm stuck on hot pavement. The dining room on one side of the front door will forever be the place her life changed, when Eric told her she was an Elysian and she had to die. Across from it is the sitting room, which crawls with nightmares that she'd give everything in her newly-stuffed bank account to burn down.

So much blood, screaming, loss, and pain. A shelter for ghosts that will haunt her till the day she dies.

She bites her cheek to rip her mind back to the present, and with a deep breath, she pushes open the office door.

"Mrs. Elysian, perfect," Ramsey says. The office was once a spare bedroom, but he had it transformed so Lynell wouldn't have to use her late uncle's office.

Simply thinking about the room sends a chill down her spine as she recalls the feeling of her knife sinking into Eric's flesh.

Ramsey stands next to the L-shaped desk sitting in front of two large, fixed windows. Lynell crosses the room to slide into the chair, which holds her body like a perfect mold, grabs the edge of the desk and rolls forward, studying the folders and binders Ramsey has already set out for her.

Sitting in one of the black chairs across the expanse of the heavy desk, Ramsey gestures to the stack of files on Lynell's left and asks, "You've already familiarized yourself with the general files, right?"

Lynell nods, though she feels overwhelmed with the information they hold on the most important events and people in American history, from the war that prompted Gideon Elysian to suggest the Registration, to the evolution of the oligarchs, the Registration committee, and the ever-changing groups of rebels. Of course, like every citizen, she knows most of it, and even knows more about the rebels thanks to Daniel. But the Resurrection, the current largest anti-Registration group, is less familiar. And, regardless, in her current position, all this information takes on new significance.

Ramsey smiles and taps the thickest binder directly in front of Lynell. "We'll go through this before the meeting. It explains the Registration's day-to-day operations, the overview of financials, summaries of past committee meetings and any motions that have been passed, possible laws or policies that have been suggested, upcoming policy changes, and more."

Eyes wide, Lynell looks from the binder to Ramsey. "Should we postpone the meeting to Monday, so I have more time to go over all of this?"

Ramsey shakes his head. "The committee needs to get to know you. We'll be vulnerable until all eight members back your position."

"Why do they have to back it?" Lynell asks. "I have the code, and I'm the only Elysian left." She doesn't mention that her daughter technically has Elysian blood, but judging by Ramsey's pressed lips, it's obvious he thought of the child. "The Registration is mine."

"Yes, well, it's best to have people on your side. Royal blood and a throne may give a man the title of king, but it does not make him king. It is the support of his council, people, and army that gives the king his power. If he does not have the money of nobility and loyalty of guards, then he'll easily be overthrown."

Lynell sucks in her bottom lip, biting on the dead skin as she watches Ramsey talk. Her mother used to call her dad a king, and Lynell grew up imagining him ruling a faraway kingdom. Even Eric compared his position to that of a king. She wonders when, if ever, this office chair will begin to feel like a throne.

"So, you're saying that everything I did to survive was pointless?" She struggles to keep the anger out of her voice, but the lift of Ramsey's eyebrow suggests she fails.

"Not at all. It's much easier for a king to gain the loy—"

"Ramsey," Lynell interrupts, holding her hand up to stop him. "Please drop the king metaphor and speak plainly."

He nods, unperturbed, and continues. "Having the name and blood of an Elysian is essential to gaining the committee's loyalty. You gain all of this as the surviving Elysian heir." Once again, he gestures at the binders in front of him and then around the room, as if to encompass the house and everything and everyone inside. "You inherit money, information, fame, and the loyalty of those who will always follow an Elysian, no matter what. All of this being yours by law is what made you a threat to Mr. Elysian. However, if you don't make an effort with the committee, you'll lose their support, and their support is vital. They are your connection to the oligarchs. They have tremendous sway and influence over the entire country. Who you are has given you this power. What you do is how you'll keep it."

"Right." Lynell nods. "If the committee disapproves of me and actively works against my claim, I lose it all."

"Precisely."

"What about my people? The guards and informants and employees?"

"Most are loyal to you by default. But it would be in your best interest to get to know them and gain their trust as well." Ramsey leans forward and taps a binder at her far right. "This has a list of all positions within the company and their roles, salaries, importance, and how long each employee has been in that position or with the company. I suggest you wait to get to that one until you have the committee and oligarchs on your side, and have had time to go over any important upcoming dates and meetings. Those few dozen people are much more powerful than the thousands of employees on your payroll."

"Got it," Lynell says. She vaguely remembers discussing basic positions in the company and telling Ramsey to make executive decisions for her until she was out of the hospital, but the details of the conversation escape her.

She presses her hands on either side of the main binder. "Where do I start?"

"First, you need to firmly decide who your Chief Operating Officer will be, as they'll go with you to the meeting and help guide you through everything."

Lynell frowns. She'd been thinking of Ramsey as her right hand, but that can hardly be his official title. Pieces of that far away conversation in the hospital room return, and she thinks she remembers promoting Ramsey to . . . something. "Didn't I make you the COO already?"

Ramsey doesn't smile, but Lynell imagines him grinning with fondness. One day, she'll earn that fond grin from him. "You technically promoted me to the position of 'figuring everything the fuck out and keeping my family safe.' I was one of the five Head Regulators, but since that conversation, I've been working as your Chief Security Officer. The last one died when Zach—" He stops short, but Lynell feels the rest of his sentence deeper than if he had said it.

"So, who's my COO?"

"You don't have one yet. I've been handling most of those responsibilities, with assistance from others."

"Who was Eric's COO?"

"Robert Harmon, but he's been wanting to retire for years," Ramsey says. "During the . . . unconventional transfer of ownership from Mr. Elysian to you, Harmon took the opportunity to step down. I've included Mr. Elysian's list of Harmon's possible successors. There's also a list of people qualified to be your CSO, if you'd like me to return to my position of Head Regulator."

Lynell is shaking her head before Ramsey finishes speaking. There are few people she trusts, and Ramsey is one of them. She's not about to lose him to some stranger her uncle deemed worthy of the position. "Actually, I'd like for you to officially take the position of COO."

Ramsey manages not to smirk, but she can still see a flicker of pride in his eyes. "Of course," he says. "And as for your CSO?"

Lynell groans. "There are options here?" she asks, holding up the folder he'd slid across the desk.

Ramsey nods. She picks at the edge of the folder, thinking. Next to Ramsey, there's one other Regulator and employee that she sees herself genuinely trusting, and he's currently acting as her main bodyguard.

"What about Hayes Booth?" she asks.

"Perhaps," Ramsey says. "He's a bit young, but with the proper training, he could do well."

She wants to hire Hayes right then, but her personal feelings aren't enough for such an important role. So, she taps the folder and says, "I'll look through it later, but I want Hayes added to the candidates. Until we can focus on the appointment or start Hayes's training, let the other four Head Regulators deal with it. As long as you don't actively distrust any of them."

"Yes, ma'am," Ramsey says, which feels weird. Lynell is two decades younger than him, not a 'ma'am.' "Now that that's settled, let's begin."

He launches into explanation after explanation while they flip through the binders. Lynell follows as well as she can, highlighting certain sections and sticking tabs at the top of pages. The overwhelming responsibility of her new position seems to flow over her in waves each time she reads something new.

Worse, every other page has her thoughts wandering off to other concerns not at all connected to the Registration.

She reads about Warner Golden, a seventy-three-year-old committee member, and his daughter, whom no one has seen or heard from in years, and this makes her think about the many dangers to Anna. She reads about Michaels Sutton, the only oligarch amongst the seven men who also actively dislikes the Registration, and wonders if she'll have the courage to speak against a system most of the country seems to love.

After a mind-numbing hour, Lynell finishes with one thick file and opens the one on today's meeting and the objectives. As she does, she somehow feels that this is where she was meant to be, right here, tackling this behemoth one bite at a time, but worries she'll drown in responsibilities. This complex world is something she's never imagined to be hers. The magnitude of responsibility, knowing the balance of lives that are in her hands, is an adrenaline kick the equivalent of fifteen espressos on an empty stomach.

She rubs her eyes and props her elbows on the desk, about to read something called "Three-Part-Policy," when she wrinkles her nose at a rich, powdery, bitter smell. She looks up from the file to ask if Ramsey also notices, but her words are drowned in the shriek that fills the entire house. The noise hits beyond her eardrums down to her bones, vibrating an almost painful rhythm. She barely has time to register the alarm before an all-consuming blast makes the vibration in her bones feel gentle.

The world shudders and breaks around her, launching her from the chair. Agony bursts across her arm, forcing her onto her back, blinking up at the ceiling. A sharp ringing replaces all other sounds. Dust and smoke clog her lungs, her eyes stinging from particles filling the tear ducts. Black spiderwebs stretch across her vision.

Slowly, her brain catches up with the last few seconds. She smelt smoke. Heard a fire alarm.

Then there was the boom so loud that only one thing could be responsible.

A bomb.

CHAPTER 2

"Miss Sawyer! I drew you on my letter!" Amara shouts, waving a piece of pink construction paper above her head. She's pushed herself to the front of a crowd of children and is hanging off the counter separating the kids' room from the hallway.

"Did you?" Sawyer D'Angelo smiles and stops in front of the counter. She sets down her coffee cup, reaches out for the paper, and studies the scraggly words that Amara likely copied from the board on the other side of the room. A colorful image depicts Sawyer with purple hair rather than her natural blonde and four fingers. A speech bubble above Sawyer's head reads *"We will resorect!"*

"This is beautiful," Sawyer exclaims, glancing around to see the children all writing letters to the oligarchs, Registration committee, lawyers, representatives, and priests, urging them to join the fight against the Registration. She remembers leading a similar exercise a few years ago. She'd encouraged the kids to personalize the letters by adding stories illustrating how the Registration hurt their families, and how the Resurrection helped.

Since its formation four years ago, the Resurrection has grown into the largest rebel group in the country. Every day, Sawyer is in awe of how far they've come, unable to believe anything she started could be this success-ful. They still have much to do, but she feels pride watching these kids, Res-urrection members' children happily spending their days doing their part in making this country a better place.

"I'm going to make another one with Miss Ellery on it," Amara says.

Grief flares in Sawyer's chest at the mention of her late wife. Ellery has been gone for six years, but her legacy persists. The fact that she was well-known before she died, and that her death was a hate crime, adds to her allure. Keeping Ellery's memory alive is good for the Resurrection. After all, her death is the reason Sawyer started this group.

Before waiting for a response, Amara turns around and runs back to the center of the room where she drops onto a stool next to Gael, a sev-en-year-old boy whose grandparents moved to Dallas to hopefully earn enough money to help their daughter pay for him to have a Registration when he was born. Unfortunately, many Latino families and other mi-norities can't afford Registrations, because few banks offer loans to lower-income families.

Gael's parents joined the Resurrection when he was four, after his baby sister died from complications during childbirth. His parents knew the baby had a low chance of survival, but they didn't have a Registration to end the pregnancy. Maybe if the baby survived, they never would've joined the re-bellion. But she didn't, and the loss turned them against the Registration. Many members have similar heartbreaking stories.

Sawyer heads down the hallway, past several offices. The landlord of the building, a Resurrection supporter, began renting to them at a huge dis-count a month ago, and the extra space will do wonders for their cause, al-lowing people to work in one place and drop off their kids at the daycare be-fore heading to work. She's not blind to the fact that several recruits joined the rebellion for the resources more than the cause. The Resurrection of-fers occasional childcare, educational materials, free meals for people who show up to volunteer or attend a protest, and access to medical care from rebels who are also doctors, nurses, and vets. Very few people will sacrifice time, effort, materials, and money for a rebellion without some incentive or promise of success. Sawyer unlocks her office and pushes the door open, then stops dead, dropping her bag and forgetting everything else as she stares at the mess in her office.

Flower petals scatter the floor, a few dozen black and white photos mixed in. Setting her coffee on the table by the door, she leans down and picks up the closest photo, studying the image closely. The picture shows her unlocking her home front door, hair falling out of a bun and wearing a black workout top revealing several of her tattoos.

Sawyer gasps, and the photo drifts slowly back to the floor. Each one is of Sawyer, taken in the last few days without her knowledge. She struggles to steady her breathing as she takes in the far wall. The giant window overlooking the courtyard has been completely covered by photos, obscuring the outside world. The room feels like a coffin rather than an office.

Her saliva is acid in her throat as she swallows hard and steps closer to the wall of photos. These images all show gruesomely completed Registrations—bodies without a recognizable face after being blown apart by a shotgun, bloodied scalp tissue, gray matter, and brain covering the surroundings. A child lying in her princess bed, purple markings around her neck where someone clearly held her down and choked her. People lying in their own blood with multiple stab wounds littering their chests. Broken corpses with limbs twisted at odd angles after having been pushed off high buildings or bridges. Women hanging from chains, their naked bodies beaten and broken. People reduced to a pulp after being run over by trains or cars or buses.

With each new image, Sawyer's lungs seem to stop taking in air. Blood, bone, bruises, and suffering surround her, a thousand taunting voices of the dead displayed like sadistic art.

Art meant for her.

Several pictures have been tampered with. About a third of the heads are covered by cutouts of her own. Sawyer's face stares back at her, atop the bodies of the Registration's most tortured victims.

In the center of the pictures are two printed news stories. The first is an article about Lynell Elysian, the second is the report of Ellery's death six years ago. *When weeds thrive,* is written in red ink over the first article, and over Ellery's face on the second article it says, *flowers die.*

When weeds thrive, flowers die.

This is the third time Sawyer has gotten this message, and it's clear every time she reads it. As Lynell, the weed, thrives, Sawyer, the flower, will die. Someone seems to believe that Lynell's power will cause Sawyer's death.

Without thinking, she reaches out and touches Ellery's image. Moist ink meets her skin, and she yanks her hand back as if stung.

Whoever did this was here not long ago. In Sawyer's office. They might still be in the building.

How did they get in? How did they have a key to her office? Did no one see them?

The room feels warm, and her back sweats as she takes a deep breath and steps away from the bloody collage of death, her heart thundering against her sternum. She stumbles and catches herself on the edge of her desk as black fills her vision. Her head feels light and dizzy, like she's been lost in a free fall for hours and no longer remembers how to stand on her own feet. Rocks fill her throat, making every breath difficult and painful.

Somehow, she manages to turn away from the wall, but that puts the center of the office on display again. Only now does she notice the type of flower petals painting her floor.

Peonies.

Ellery's favorite.

Sawyer starts to fall. She grabs the edge of her desk and lowers herself to the ground, back pressed against the cold, sturdy metal. Gasping for air, she covers her mouth and blinks several times, trying to free her eyes from burning-hot tears.

CHAPTER 3

Hands grasp her shoulders, and Lynell is lifted into the air until her feet flatten against the floor. Ramsey's scarred face blocks her view. His lips are moving but her ears haven't yet recovered from the blast. Still, she gets the gist of what he's saying.

Run.

She nods and forces her feet to follow him from the room. The smoke curling in the air is darkening, and she coughs, sharp pain piercing the space between her ribs.

They reach the steps leading downstairs when her hearing returns. The alarm is still blaring, joined now by screams. Fire crackles somewhere nearby, and there are distant sounds of crashing, like a wardrobe hitting the floor. Dozens of people exit rooms, fill hallways, and run for the exits. One of those fleeing is Hayes Booth, and Lynell thinks, *If he dies, I'll have to pick a stranger to be my Chief Security Officer.*

Hayes runs up to Lynell's side and yells something to Ramsey she can't hear. She remembers being stuck in the basement of this very house, learning that Hayes hated Eric and his job and growing confident that he would help her escape.

Hayes grabs her uninjured arm, and his touch shocks her into the present. Saliva fills her mouth as she runs down the steps, looks to her left, and gasps at the sight of half the house destroyed, rooms crumbled into rubble. Bright yellow and orange flickering flames climb up the walls like fingers of chaos, intent on consuming everything in their path. Heat slams across her skin as if she walked directly through the fire, while the pleasant smell of a campfire mixes with the acrid stench of melting plastic, with a hint of alcohol or gas.

"Hurry," Hayes says, tugging on her hand. She freezes, jerking away from him, confusion and fear twisting his face. "Lynell?"

Eyes widening, she shakes her head, mutters, "Daniel," and turns to sprint back up the stairs to her bedroom, where she bursts through the door.

Empty.

"Daniel!" she screams, stepping into the room and frantically search-ing every corner. She runs toward the bathroom, but, halfway there, the world rumbles and something crashes, knocking her off balance again. She falls, this time managing to twist and land on her good arm. The impact still sends a shockwave of pain through her body, and the breath evaporates from her lungs.

"We have to go!" Someone grabs her. "The house is going to collapse."

She fights the hold and stands on her own, stumbling into the bath-room. "I need to find Danny, please!"

"He's probably outside already!"

But what if he isn't?

"Lynell!" Two people are grabbing her, yanking her from the room.

She's about to start thrashing when Ramsey says, "I'll find him. You go outside." His words are so urgent and honest that she stops, shakes hair from her face, and turns to him. His eyes are wide, pupils blown so large they nearly overtake the brown irises. "Go."

Lynell stops fighting and follows Hayes's gentle tug to continue down the stairs. Another crash shakes the house, followed by several shattering windows. Shards fly free, raining down on them alongside ash. Lynell lifts her right arm to shield her face, expecting to feel several cuts, but Hayes has completely covered her, bearing the rain of glass.

"Hayes—"

"Hurry!" he interrupts, nodding toward the front door. She might have argued and searched other rooms had she not seen a figure through a blown-out window.

Daniel.

He's outside, on the driveway in front of the porch. Three men are struggling to keep him outside, one pushing at his chest and two holding his arms as he screams and fights against them.

Lynell doesn't wait for Hayes. She jumps past the last two steps and sprints for the opened front door, coughing through the acrid smoke and hot ash. She doesn't slow down until she's outside.

"Lynell!" he screams, the agony in his voice stronger than the pain in her body. When he sees her, his face goes slack and his lips part. His next word is quiet, but she doesn't have to hear him to know what he says. "Lyn . . ."

His pause in struggling makes the guards loosen their hold. He takes advantage of the moment, pulls free, and sprints to meet her halfway. He lifts her, and she wraps her legs around his waist, holding onto him like he's a life vest that'll keep her from drowning.

Her injured arm is pressed between them, sending through her fresh, nauseating waves of pain. Then Daniel groans with his own pain, and Lynell unhooks her legs so he can set her down. Red blooms from his shoulder, staining the shirt where he was shot not too long ago.

The effort of running and holding her must have reopened the stitches. She reaches up, touching the tip of her fingers to the wet section of his shirt.

"Danny, your—"

He shakes his head, cutting her off. "It's okay. Ambulances are on their way. They'll fix both of us."

She realizes then that the wounds on her left hand are bleeding, too. When he rubs his thumb along her forehead, she feels something warm trail behind his touch. He shows her the blood on his hand and the sight somehow gives her brain permission to feel the ache in her head from the cut along her hairline. She must have hit her head when she fell off the office chair, during the initial blast.

"What happened?" Lynell asks.

He shrugs. "I'm sure we'll find out."

As if in response, another crash comes from the building behind them. Lynell spins around, remembering Ramsey is still inside and looking for Daniel, who is already safe from the fire. Her pulse accelerates as her gaze traces the burning house, and she realizes that Hayes hasn't followed her outside either.

He's gone back in to get Ramsey, she's sure of it. If either man dies, it'll be her fault.

A fresh balloon of black smoke fills the air as another corner of the house collapses, and Lynell gasps with the sound. When the smoke splits, two men emerge, coughing and covered in ash and soot. Relief outshines the pain for a precious moment at the sight of Ramsey and Hayes, both safe. They run down the steps, ordering Daniel and Lynell to follow, putting more space between them and the fire.

The first fire truck arrives as the rest of the house collapses.

"There are nine injured and one casualty, a young intern who was gathering information from Mr. Elysian's old study where the bomb went off."

Half of Lynell's brain clings hard to Ramsey's words. The other half can't think past her confusion and pain. It can't get past the primal need to find who is responsible and force them to face justice.

Lynell is sitting up in a hospital bed, Daniel perched on the edge and Ramsey standing in front of them as he relays the information he gathered. Despite being the last person out of the house, Ramsey appears less affected than most. He's still wearing a suit, though one pant leg was cut off so a medic could wrap a small burn on his shin, and his long hair and beard are dark gray from ash, making him appear a decade older than he is. Lynell and Daniel, on the other hand, look exactly like she imagines people who escaped a house fire to look.

Daniel is shirtless, his exposed skin smeared with ash. There's a bandage over the reopened gunshot wound on his shoulder and a butterfly bandage over a cut on his cheek. Lynell's own shirt is cut open on one side so the EMT could tend to her arm and hand.

Several moist towelettes are wrapped around a burn on her other hand, and the cut along her hairline was doctored and secured with a Band-Aid. Both have IVs secured to their arms, pouring fluids and pain meds into their dehydrated bodies. Her tongue and throat are still coated with ash, and every time she tries to swallow the foul taste, a fresh round of coughs wrack her body, despite having worn an oxygen mask for fifteen minutes before they reached the hospital.

Her eyes aren't burning anymore, but an occasional ringing joins the cacophony in her ears as she recalls the thunderous bomb and all that followed. Sirens, shouting first responders, crackling flames competing with shattering glass, and the crashing spray of pressured water pummeling the house.

Now, in a private corner of the emergency room, Lynell listens to nurses walking about, machines beeping, people groaning, and a drunk man shouting obscenities. The hospital's bleached smell gives her vivid déjà vu. A week ago, they were in this hospital, having survived the two-week Registration period. They'd narrowly escaped Eric's house then, too.

"Do we have any idea who did it?" Lynell asks.

Ramsey shakes his head. "The bomb was set off in Mr. Elysian's old office. It's still being examined, but it appears to be a crude homemade bomb meant to destroy the immediate area and spread a fire to the rest of the building. The physical files were destroyed, but we have everything backed up. An accelerant was used, so even if the bomb hadn't gone off, the entire house would've gone up in flames." He gestures to Lynell. "We can assume the bomber hoped you'd be inside when that happened."

The hospital door pushes open and Hayes walks through.

He inhaled quite a bit of smoke and has a large burn on his shoulder but is otherwise okay. Not long after they got to the hospital, he left to take a call.

"What was that about?" Lynell asks.

"We got a call from Ms. Sawyer D'Angelo. She said it was urgent that she speak to you."

Lynell recognizes Hayes's 'business voice,' which is lower and slower than his normal tone. She prefers the latter because the former rarely conveys good news.

"Never heard of her," Lynell says. She looks at Ramsey, whose face has fallen into an angry frown. Then she turns to Daniel, who's wearing a similar expression, though tinged with cautious shock. "You know her?"

Daniel instantly drops his eyes. Before he can respond, Ramsey answers, "She's the leader of the Resurrection."

"What does she want with me?" Lynell asks. Though Ramsey wears a neutral expression, he's clearly not happy with a rebel trying to contact her. After all, as the Elysian heir, they're her main enemies.

Hayes's Adam's apple bobs when he swallows. "She claims someone is trying to kill her and only you can help."

"Absolutely not," Ramsey says before Lynell can open her mouth. "You aren't meeting with Sawyer D'Angelo. Especially not now. Someone just bombed your house. We've already had to postpone the committee meeting because of this."

Lynell bristles. "I think someone's life being in danger is more important than a stupid meeting."

"Your life is in danger," he quips.

"We don't know that the bomb was an attempt to kill me."

"D'Angelo is the leader of the rebels, Mrs. Elysian," Ramsey says. If he wasn't so professional, Lynell might think he's grasping at straws, searching for something to convince her this is a bad idea. "Her death would benefit you."

She glares at the man, heat rising to her cheeks from a strong desire to rebuke him.

"Murder is never a good thing, Mr. Davenport." Ramsey flinches at her use of his surname. "I'm not going to ignore someone who asks for help. What good is power if it can't help those in need?"

"Mrs. Ely—Lynell," Hayes corrects. Lynell grins. Unlike Ramsey, who refuses to call her anything except 'Mrs. Elysian,' Hayes has finally learned to call her Lynell. "We can't ignore the significance that she called two hours after your house was bombed. This woman has made bringing down your family and business her entire life. Perhaps you should send one of us in your stead first, to make sure it's not a trap."

Ramsey nods curtly in agreement. "I wouldn't advise running into a meeting with a known enemy without proper preparation."

"I think they're right, babe," Daniel adds. "I care about her cause, and I understand that you want to help her, but you come first."

"What exactly did she say?" Lynell asks.

"It was a short conversation. All she said was that she's received several death threats that have all mentioned you, and she wouldn't take them seriously if she didn't have reason to believe there was a legitimate danger."

"So, she's not threatening me?"

Hayes shrugs. "It didn't sound like it. She sounded genuinely afraid. But then again, she's a sworn enemy of the Registration, and if she wants to lead you into a trap, she likely wouldn't threaten you outright."

Lynell notices Ramsey's pinched face, but she turns to Daniel and asks, "What do you know about her? Is she trustworthy?"

"I've never met her personally, just know her by reputation, which is good. There's a reason so many rebels joined the Resurrection even after the war ended so badly for us. The Resurrection is the first successful attempt at merging different rebels and their resources into one group that actually stands a chance against the government. She didn't form the group to throw tantrums or plan violent riots without a plausible alternative to the Registration."

"Bombing the Elysian house sounds like a tantrum to me," Ramsey says.

"You think that was the Resurrection? And then she calls me right after the bombing, knowing we'd be on high alert?" Lynell scratches her eyebrow, an ache spreading through her head. "Sounds far-fetched."

"Has news of the bombing already spread?" Daniel asks.

Hayes nods.

"Well, then isn't it possible that D'Angelo heard about the bomb and thinks it's connected to the threats she's received," Lynell says. "Maybe she's trying to *help* me."

Ramsey crosses his arms. "Your theory is that the leader of the largest rebellion heard someone bombed your house and decided to meet you, even though she'd surely be a suspect? What for? To keep you safe?" Lynell shrugs, and Ramsey shakes his head. "The rebels don't care about your safety. The bomb could've killed you. They probably hoped destroying your house and the important documents or money you kept inside would be a win for their cause. And if you get injured or killed in the process, all the better for them."

"Why are you so positive that this was the Resurrection?" Lynell does not want to argue with Ramsey's theory but hopes to expand on his reasoning. It'd be easier to simply trust Ramsey, yet it's too big of an accusation to make without more information or evidence.

"None of the other rebels are organized enough for something like this," Ramsey says.

"How would they know where to set off the bomb?" Lynell asks.

Hayes frowns. "What do you mean?"

"Ramsey said it started in Eric's room," Lynell explains. "If they were after me, then starting it where I'd be sleeping would pretty much ensure I'd die. If they were after Registration files, Eric's office would be the place to start. Either way, they'd have to know where the room is and how to get there without being detected. Otherwise, they could've planted the bomb anywhere. Or even thrown a Molotov cocktail through the windows. That'd be much easier. Safer, too."

"You have a point," Ramsey says. "Mr. Elysian's room isn't easy to stumble across if you don't know where you're going."

"But wouldn't they have seen that Lynell wasn't in there?" Daniel asks.

"Maybe they didn't have time to go searching for her," Hayes suggests. "They'd already risked a lot by entering the building."

The group is quiet for a moment as they consider the obvious. If whoever set the fire started it in Eric's room purposely, they had prior knowledge of the home's layout.

"The rebels must have an informant," Ramsey deduces.

"Maybe it wasn't the rebels," Daniel argues. Lynell looks at him, noticing a war raging behind his eyes. He probably still has a deep-rooted loyalty to any rebel group after fighting on their side all those years ago. Now, as Lynell's husband, he's forced to be an enemy of the rebels in every sense of the word.

"It was the rebels," Ramsey says, a note of finality in his words. "This has the Resurrection written all over it."

"Then why is D'Angelo calling right after?" Daniel asks, bringing the conversation full circle.

The three men talk through the possible motives of the bomber for what feels like an hour while Lynell thinks that whoever planted the bomb most likely has a vendetta against her. She can't fully blame them. She's not merely benefiting from the very organization that has claimed the lives of millions, she's also keeping it running.

"Whoever it was, it's clear you're not safe, Mrs. Elysian," Ramsey says, cutting both Hayes and Daniel off. "We can have a safe house ready within hours for you to stay while we find the bomber."

"A safe house?" Lynell repeats. "You want me to go into hiding?"

Ramsey nods. "The bomber could try again."

"Absolutely not. I'm not going to spend my life in fear. I just spent two weeks running and hiding."

"That was different," Ramsey says.

"It feels pretty damn similar to me."

"You weren't the last Elysian then!" Ramsey presses his lips together and pulls a deep breath through his nose. "It's more important than ever to keep you safe. And you won't be hiding in abandoned houses. We have access to the best safe houses in the country. It won't take long to find the culprit."

Lynell shakes her head. "It's not happening, Ramsey. I can't disappear. What about the committee meeting?" As much as she'd like to, she can't avoid the meeting forever.

"The meeting will be surrounded with security. We'll take you to the safe house after."

"What about Anna?"

"You can't do anything about that yet," Ramsey says.

"No judge is going to grant custody to someone in hiding."

It's unlikely a judge will grant custody to someone in this kind of danger, either. Maybe if Daniel wasn't with her, he could take Anna. Lynell had listed him as Anna's father in the healing aftermath of giving birth. He's her legal father who never abandoned her and isn't in danger. Logically, she should suggest Daniel leave her and fight for custody of his daughter. But she'd spent two years separated from him, and she's too selfish to lose him again.

"Custody cases take months. We'll have you safely back at home long before then," Ramsey says.

"Would I even be safe in hiding? If one of our people is working for the Resurrection, they'll know about the safe houses."

"It's unlikely. Knowledge of these houses and their security measures is controlled. Only a handful of people will know where you are."

Hayes looks between the two of them, his face unreadable, and a flash of suspicion blinds Lynell for a moment.

How well does she know these two men? Is she wrong to trust them? Either one of them could be behind this. Maybe they helped her survive Eric because they knew she'd be easier to control or take down, after Eric was gone.

"I'm not hiding," Lynell says adamantly, hoping her tone conveys strength. "Feel free to do what you need to find the bomber and secure a new house, but nothing else is changing. I'll meet with the committee today and continue with work as planned. Daniel and I will fight for custody of Anna."

Ramsey clearly wants to argue, but he says, "Understood. I'll have a new place prepared by the time we're out of the meeting. I'll leave extra security here with Mr. Carter, and he can head to the house as soon as it's ready."

"Okay," Lynell says.

"However, I insist that you refrain from calling Ms. D'Angelo. It's a risk we can't afford to take," Ramsey says.

Her jaw flexes as she bites down a retort. "Fine. I won't call her or meet her."

Ramsey holds her eyes for several moments as both silently try to read the other's mind, then he finally nods and leaves, the door closing behind him like a vacuum sucking both air and tension from the room.

"It's only going to take a few hours to get an entire house ready with furniture and security and everything?" Daniel asks.

"Yes," Hayes says.

Lynell laughs at Daniel's disbelief, feeling pockets of frustration dissipate within her. He moves closer to her so she can lean against him, sliding his hand into her hair, his fingers scratching her scalp. She'd purr at the sensation if she could.

CHAPTER 4

His eyebrows are singed and he can still feel the heat of the flames racing closer. If he'd waited a moment longer, the fire would've burned him, too. Or the bomb would've blown him apart like it did the girl he'd locked in the office. Her death was regrettable. He takes no pleasure in ending an innocent life, but she'd seen him carry in the bomb and accelerant, so he didn't have a choice. No witnesses, after all. He must keep the bigger picture in mind, the reason for all of this. And that reason is big enough to sacrifice a few nameless people who were in the wrong place at the wrong time. He stayed long enough to see the flames crawl closer to the bomb he placed in the center of the room. It was designed to go off once it reached a certain temperature, which gave him time to set the fire and get out before the explosion.

Afterwards, he lingered until the bitch's rebel husband ran out of the house, a wild look of shock and fear on his face as he looked around for his precious wife.

TJ liked it.

It's not that he relishes pain or violence or even death. It's that they're ruining everything. The girl parading around as an Elysian and her bleeding heart of a husband. They're going to fuck it all up. Both deserve to feel this pain. They need to know what it feels like to lose everything. To fear for your people because someone else has decided to take over.

He smiles at the memory, cold water running over his hands, then pushes the faucet back, cutting off the flow, and grabs a paper towel. Once free of the bathroom, he turns on the TV and flips to the news channel, catching the end of the anchor's sentence.

"... not released suspect names, but speculation of rebel involvement is rampant. It is unclear if Mrs. Elysian herself was one of the injured, but our sources say she was at the mansion at the time of the explosion."

TJ turns the volume down. Whether the Elysian bitch was inside or not means nothing to him. She won't last much longer anyway. She's not prepared for the pressure of leading the Registration. Whether legitimate or not, she's damned herself by claiming the Elysian name.

Lynell will destroy herself.

And he'll be right there to watch it happen.

CHAPTER 5

A handful of times, Daniel has felt the overwhelming fear that somehow dulls and sharpens every sense all at once.

He'd expected to feel it during the rebellion, but it wasn't until he was
twenty-one that he was fully consumed with fear. He'd moved to Dallas to
help his sister care for their mother, who'd been diagnosed with cancer.
Daniel was at the pharmacy picking up medicine when his phone rang. He
knew before answering what his sister was going to say.

Mom was dead.

The second time he felt that fear was when he walked into the apartment he shared with Lynell and saw her packed suitcase. Again, he knew
what was going to happen before it did. Lynell's own fear was controlling
her. She was going to leave and use her Registration to end her pregnancy.

The third time was when Zach admitted he was Registering Lynell.
That fear was with him throughout the fourteen-day Registration period,
until Lynell survived Eric's attempts to kill her.

Now, the fear is crawling toward him for the fourth time.

Lyn leaves the hospital, surrounded by security, to meet with some
of the most powerful people in the country. She's going to sit in the room

where decisions are made that Daniel spent years of his life fighting against. Then she's going to come back and tell Daniel that she wants to meet with Sawyer D'Angelo.

She said she wouldn't, but Daniel knows Lyn better than she thinks. He saw the lie in the minuscule twitch at the corner of her right eye. He noticed the determination to do what she thinks is right in the flex of her jaw as she bit down on her back teeth. He felt it in the air the moment she made a decision she knew others would hate.

All Daniel can hope for is that she'll tell him her plans. Because no matter the fear that nearly erases every other thought in Daniel's mind, he'll support her. He'd rather live in that ocean of terror by Lynell's side than pretend he's not drowning while abandoned on the shore.

"Good afternoon, Mr. Carter," a nurse says before taking his vitals. While she works, Daniel's mind wanders.

He thought he was an adult when he joined the rebellion, but he had no idea what was coming. He didn't know how complicated, painful, and beautiful the world could be.

His own father moved to England rather than stay in a country with something as barbaric as the Registration. His mother, the gentlest person he knew, told him every day that God's love was bigger than any man-made law. She didn't believe in the Registration, but she bought one for her children anyway, because it mattered more that they had everything they *might* need to be happy than forcing them to share her beliefs.

"No one can be forced into goodness. Saints are made in the fight against temptation, not in the absence of it," she used to say.

Daniel grew up wanting to be as good of a person as his mother, so he swore never to use his Registration. He joined the rebellion because he wanted to help bring about a better world, one his mom could be proud of.

Then he met Lyn. He fell in love with her tenacity, strength, and the vulnerability that she hated but allowed him to see anyway because she loved him, even if she waited so long to admit it. The first time he ever considered using his Registration was when she told him about Alan, her stepfather. He almost Registered that abusive son-of-a-bitch, but Lynell could tell what he was planning to do—she could always tell—and she made him promise not to.

"I love you too much to let you compromise your morals for me," she'd said.

But now his morals could be his wife's demise. His connection with the rebels could ruin her. The rebels could kill her. Then he wouldn't have morals, only rage.

Lyn won't stop until she's confident she's done everything in her power to do good. And she won't hesitate to run headfirst into a death trap if she believes it'll help people. She might think he's the one ruled by his emotions and desire to help people, but under all her thick, impenetrable armor, Lynell loves more intensely and selflessly than anyone he's ever known. She'll give away her whole self to improve the world even a fraction.

That's why he will do everything in his power to keep her safe while she's at the front lines. If that means revisiting a life he left years ago, so be it.

He doubts any of his old contacts would know about Sawyer D'Angelo's secret plans, and even if they did, he can't count on old friendships to compromise their loyalty to the cause. But all he needs right now is information on who Sawyer D'Angelo is behind the scenes. What she's capable of and how far she'll go to get what she wants.

Because Daniel doesn't intend to suffer through that fear ever again.

CHAPTER 6

T he drive to the committee meeting gives Lynell's anxiety time to grow. She picks at the edge of the Band-Aid on the back of her hand where the IV was and struggles to listen to Ramsey preparing her. He reminds her of committee members' names, possible topics that'll come up, and what *not* to say.

"We're here," he says, splintering any thoughts that formed in Lynell's mind.

They're in a parking garage, so all she sees is other cars and a sign directing drivers to go right to exit and straight to park. Daniel used to tease her for not knowing the difference between a Ferrari and Lamborghini, but even she can tell that these cars are expensive—Elysian expensive. Oligarch expensive.

"The oligarchs won't be here, right?" Lynell asks.

"Not today. But they've been requesting a meeting. Mr. Macgill and Mr. Underwood are especially eager to meet you," Ramsey answers. "Remember, no mention of—"

"D'Angelo or the rebels reaching out, yeah, I know," Lynell mutters.

Ramsey nods and walks right next to her as they pass through a heavy metal door a guard opens for them. They enter a bare stairwell with cream walls and climb three flights before walking through another door into a wide hallway with a glass wall on one side. Lynell looks through the glass and sees a conference room, complete with two televisions hanging from opposite walls, windows peering down at the city, and a large oval table. Half the chairs surrounding the table are filled by men and women wearing expensive suits and dresses. Each person is older than Lynell by at least a decade.

A windstorm of nerves blows through her stomach.

"You can do this," Ramsey whispers. He opens the glass door and heads through first, nodding for her to follow.

Six sets of eyes fall on them. Lynell's brain tells her to smile, but her lips don't obey.

"Thank you for agreeing to meet later than planned," Ramsey says, walking to the head of the table.

Remembering his lessons, Lynell scrambles to follow them. She's supposed to sit at the head to symbolize her position. The committee members technically work for the shareholders of the Registration, not for Lynell, but she's the only one in the room who inherited her position. She was born into this role, and her movements should reflect that. Plus, the Elysian family started the company and still holds the largest share. *She* holds the largest share.

"Yes, thank you," Lynell says, relieved to hear her voice is steady. She slides into her seat in what she hopes is a graceful manner, and Ramsey sits on her left. Two guards position themselves at the door, their backs to the conference room.

The woman closest to Lynell smiles. Even sitting, Lynell can tell that the woman is small, probably shorter than five foot three. Her hair and skin are almost the exact same tawny color, and her flawless face makes her look younger than thirty, although Lynell knows that the youngest committee member is thirty-six.

"Of course," the woman says. "It's quite clear we have a lot to cover." Her accent becomes more noticeable the longer she speaks, and Lynell realizes this must be Tamara Nelson, the only committee member who wasn't born in the country. Her family moved here when she was seventeen, though Ramsey said no one knows why. Foreigners don't often move to this country, because citizenship means they're eligible to be Registered but they'll never have a Registration themselves.

"Yes, we were presently discussing that," says the older woman seated next to Tamara. Her gray hair is styled into a stacked bob with several thick layers. Her face has that slightly waxy look caused by skin that should be wrinkled but has been smoothed and stretched back by talented plastic surgeons. She glares at Lynell with eyes heavily lined with black kohl, and her synthetically plumped lips are pressed together in clear disapproval.

Robin Jacobs. The oligarchs chose her over thirty years ago, and she's been on the committee longer than any other member. Ramsey explained she, alone, ever managed to control Eric. Lynell makes a mental note to do all she can to get on the woman's good side.

"Apparently, our new Elysian is not only a murder suspect, but has enemies willing to blow up her ancestor's home and make her a murder victim." Robin glares at Lynell, who wonders if the woman even has a good side to be on.

"Mrs. Elysian had nothing to do with her uncle or cousin's death," Ramsey says. "And we have our best people looking for the party responsible for the bombing. At this stage we do not know for sure that Mrs. Elysian was the target."

Robin snorts. "That doesn't change the fact that, in her first week, Mrs. Elysian has been suspected of killing other Elysians so she could assume power, and has been connected to the rebellion, even being called the rebels' savior. If it was an assassination attempt, at least it would make the latter accusation less likely."

Lynell has no idea who called her 'the rebels' savior,' but she knows better than to ask, which would show her ignorance. She can tell that Ramsey wants to say something but bites his tongue when Junior Booker chimes in from the other end of the table.

"Robin, it really isn't productive to begin this conversation when we're missing half of our party." Lynell recognizes his wiry beard and rectangle glasses currently perched on the edge of his thin nose. Booker visited Lynell in the hospital, although he didn't stay long. He also didn't wear the brown cowboy hat now sitting prominently on his head.

"We'll be waiting forever for Izzy," Tamara says, tapping a perfectly manicured purple nail on the table. Lynell can't remember reading about an Izzy, and she doesn't have time to puzzle out who Tamara is referring to before a woman with curly, platinum-blonde hair speaks.

"Tamara, darling, must you push every button available to you?"

Tamara gives a wicked grin, and Lynell instantly likes her. "What's the fun of a button you can't push?"

"We're here to do our job, not socialize," Robin says, repositioning slightly so she's an inch further from Tamara. The two women seem to exist on opposite ends of a spectrum, which must make decision-making nearly impossible.

While the idle discussion continues, Lynell takes the opportunity to look around the table. The blonde woman to Junior's right is Verity McGowan, a woman whose natural skin sporting a scattering of dark age spots makes her appear older than Robin, although her file says she's seventy and Robin is in her eighties. Verity's thin lips shine from a glossy balm, and layers of deep wrinkles cradle her eyes.

On Junior's left is Finnegan Reese, the youngest man on the board. His suit is perfectly tailored to his shockingly fit body, and chest hair peeks through the top of the shirt where the first two buttons are undone. With an impeccably trimmed beard and gelled-back hair, the man radiates confidence.

The conference room door opens and two men walk through, one leaning heavily on a cane and the other with a gut dipping over his belt.

"Apologies," the older man says. He has a thick, rolling, southern accent that instantly puts Lynell at ease. Warner Golden was the first committee member she met, and his calming, grandfatherly disposition made her think life as the new Elysian wouldn't be so bad. Now that she's met more board members, she's not as optimistic. "I hope y'all haven't been waiting long."

Robin huffs as Lynell says, "No, of course not. I'm glad you made it, Mr. Golden."

The man raises one overgrown eyebrow. "Haven't I told ya to call me Warner, young lady?"

Before she can reply, the large man who walked in with Warner drops into his seat with a loud grunt. "Can we skip the small talk? I have another engagement after this."

Robin bristles, and Warner tsks as if reprimanding a child. "We all have busy schedules, Mr. Holmes."

"Yeah, Izzy," Tamara says, and Lynell realizes it's a nickname. By his tensed shoulders and deep frown, Izrael Holmes doesn't seem to appreciate being called 'Izzy.' "None of us came here to diddle spiders."

"For God's sake, Tamara. Speak English," Robin says.

Tamara frowns. "Oh, was I speaking French again? My bad."

Lynell chuckles. All seven committee members turn their attention to her, expressions varying from anger to annoyance to amusement. "I don't think the spiders would appreciate being diddled, anyway," she says, heat climbing up her neck.

Ramsey tenses and everyone else at the table looks unimpressed, save for Tamara and Warner. The older man winks at Lynell, and Tamara grins so wide that her eyes nearly disappear.

"Finally, we have someone with a sense of humor," Tamara says. "I like you, Carter."

The blush moves from Lynell's neck to her cheeks. She briefly wonders if she should analyze Tamara's choice to call her 'Carter' rather than 'Elysian.' It could be a subtle act of insolence by refusing to recognize Lynell's claim to the Elysian name. On the other hand, several stories on her have reported her preference for the name 'Lynell Carter,' so maybe Tamara is being respectful.

Before anyone else can speak, a gorgeous woman in a pressed dark blue dress enters. She has slick, black hair and thin, dark eyes. Her perfect posture and gentle smile make her appear more sophisticated than everyone else. Tilly Nguyen lowers herself into the chair between Tamara and Lynell.

"It's lovely to see you again, Lynell," Tilly says, giving a small nod in acknowledgment.

"You as well," Lynell says. Tilly didn't speak much when she visited, for which Lynell was grateful at the time, but she did explain that her grandparents immigrated here before Gideon began the Registration. Like Tamara, Tilly's focus on the committee is foreign relations and immigrant rights to Registrations.

"Now that we're all here, shall we begin?" Izrael says, clearly impatient.

"Yes, let's," Robin says.

Ramsey nudges Lynell's foot with his. Anxiety seems to suck all gravity from the room, but she shoves the discomfort down and lifts her chin. "I know we have several items on today's agenda, but I think you'll agree with me when I say the most pressing matter is the recent bombing, likely resulting from the mixed responses to my claim to the Registration. We need to discover who is responsible."

"That's obvious, innit?" Junior says, his country accent so prominent that Lynell wonders if he's purposefully emphasizing it. "It's the rebels trying to get rid of the last Elysian."

No one mentions Anna, although they all know about her. Perhaps the fact that she's a child keeps her from being viewed as a possible Registration owner, if Lynell were to die.

"It might not be a rebel," Lynell says, her voice calmer than she expected it to be. "Plenty of people have reasons to want me gone. People who think someone else would be a better fit for my position."

Several people bristle at her words, and Junior responds, "I think I speak for all of us when I say we don't appreciate the accusation that we'd be disloyal to the Elysian family line."

"You don't speak for all of us, Junior," Warner says. The low timber of his voice hasn't changed, but somehow he sounds more intimidating than before. "I didn't feel personally accused by a general statement about a plausible motivation. Perhaps you should examine why you, however, took Mrs. Carter's words personally when there was no indication to do so."

Junior's face grows red and Tamara laughs.

Hoping to avoid an unproductive argument, Lynell says, "I didn't mean to insinuate that any of you were involved. However, I think it's safe to assume there may be people who wish to take advantage of the upheaval. Anyone wanting my position would recognize now as the best opportunity, as I'm the only Elysian truly standing in the way."

"Why go through the effort of bombing your home when all they'd have to do is wait for you to fail?" Robin asks.

Her words are like a pressure against an existing bruise, but there's too much truth to them for Lynell to be insulted. Ramsey warned her about this. The committee is unlikely to have faith in her abilities, and even the members who like Lynell recognize the dangers of having her take Eric's spot after publicly murdering him.

Ramsey, however, doesn't have that problem.

"Mrs. Jacobs, that is quite enough. Mrs. Elysian is the Elysian heir, whether you like it or not. Must I remind you that it was her grandfather who created the Registration?"

Annoyance sparks in Robin's eyes, and she straightens to look down at Ramsey before replying in a contemptuous voice, "My father died in that abhorrent war, and my brother would've been next if it wasn't for Gideon. I don't need a reminder for events that I lived through." Her attention swings from Ramsey to Lynell and her voice settles back into its normal haughty decibel. "I've been on this committee far longer than you've been alive, child. Forgive me if I question your ability to handle the responsibilities that come with this position."

"Robin has a point," Izrael says. "With all due respect to Mrs. Carter, she's not even old enough to be a committee member."

"Neither was Zach," Lynell says, her throat tightening around each word to give them a clip of annoyance. "Yet, if he'd survived and had taken his father's place, I doubt you would've complained."

"Zachary was preparing for the position his entire life," Verity says. "He knew what to expect. You, on the other hand, have blindly accepted a life you cannot imagine. It's you I think about when I express my doubts."

"I appreciate it, Ms. McGowan, but my failure is not a given," Lynell says. Her previous fear vanishes and her gaze pierces Verity as she speaks. "My grandfather wanted the Registration protected by his family exclusively. Must I remind you that I have more of a claim to this position than Eric ever did, given he was illegitimate." She pauses, glancing around the room to catch any reactions to the news. Unfortunately, either the committee knew of Eric's illegitimacy, or they have fantastic poker faces, because no one betrays surprise. "I might not have grown up being groomed for the position, but I'm the only person who knows the code that can control or destroy the Registration. You probably don't need an explanation about the significance of said code, but let me refresh your memories." She leans slightly back and scans each person. "It doesn't matter who likes me or who doesn't. It doesn't matter how young I am or how much training I lack. It doesn't even matter that I'm married to a man who was once a rebel." Ramsey tenses at the last sentence, but Lynell ignores him. "I'm the legitimate Elysian heir, and I have the key to accessing the very core of the Registration. With my key, whether you accept my rightful claim or not, I can manipulate the Registration whenever I want, however I want." Lynell's upper lip nearly trembles with a confusing mix of anger and excitement.

Not a single committee member manages to keep their reactions private. They frown and bristle and glance at their colleagues with a glimmer of fear in their eyes. Their responses feed Lynell's growing confidence.

"It's in your best interest to support me, rather than make this time more tempting to the rebels. Hate me all you want, but be smart enough to realize the only logical action is to help clear my name, get the public on my side, and find the bomber."

Junior cocks an eyebrow. "You're threatening to end the Registration if anyone contests your claim?"

"I'm simply reminding you of the facts."

"That seems like a pretty big motivation for someone to want you gone," Tamara says. Coming from someone else, it might have sounded like a veiled threat. But Tamara presents it like an observation of a possible problem.

Lynell shrugs. "I'm getting used to people wanting me dead. But it might be prudent for anyone thinking of killing me to consider any contingencies I might have. My dad left the code for me to find. I'd have to be pretty dumb not to follow his example."

Robin scowls, synthetic skin tightening along her forehead. "Gideon's grandchild would want to protect the Registration at all costs, not use it as a bargaining chip."

"Gideon's son used the code as a reason to kidnap, torture, and attempt to kill me," Lynell rebuts smoothly. "Am I not protecting my grandfather's legacy by keeping it out of the hands of someone like Eric?"

"How do you expect to protect the Registration from inside a prison cell?" Finnegan says.

"Finnegan, she won't be arrested," Warner says.

"Thank you for bringing us back to the problem at hand," Lynell says. "The murder investigations."

It takes a few more minutes of discussion before Ramsey manages to run through everything they know about Eric and Zach's cases. When he's finished, a few committee members suggest avenues to clear Lynell's name and generate positive publicity for the Registration. Lynell knows these people are some of the most powerful in the country, but she hasn't realized how far their combined influences reach. It seems endless, the list of possible helpful contacts they have amongst them: people in law enforcement, large corporations, major religious organizations, news stations, and more.

Ramsey has been trying to convince Lynell not to worry about being implicated in the murders. Even as people shared pictures of her with devil horns digitally drawn on her head, he promised it wouldn't last. This was but a public relations issue, he claimed. Rumors didn't last and she shouldn't worry about any genuine danger with the law.

But she's never believed him. Not until this moment as she listens to the boundless influence in the room like a front seat to the show *Rich People are Held to Different Standards and the Law Doesn't Apply to Them.*

Then Lynell realizes that *she* is one of those rich people. She's free of the limitations that bind everyday men and women. The restrictions that most people are born and die with, the rules that are so second nature that they become invisible, and the restraints of being a vulnerable person bound by laws no longer affect her.

With that type of security, maybe Ramsey is right. She shouldn't worry about the investigations. Lynell isn't sure why there are still any whispers about her possible guilt in these murders, unless not all the committee members *want* her name cleared.

Nearly two hours of pointless, circular conversation follows. Lynell's back aches, and she'd give anything for a Valium and silence. The brief feeling of invulnerability dissipates when she remembers the other dangers. The law might not be a threat, but that doesn't mean she's safe. She could be hurt. Her family could be targeted. Her reputation could be ruined.

There's a short pause in conversation, and Lynell takes advantage. "Okay," she says, "that's enough for today. We can pick this up next time. I expect you will all be doing what you can to ensure the police move their investigations away from me. Junior, a news station's editor owes you a favor, right? Call it in and have the station announce that I've been cleared and the investigations are moving forward without me as a person of interest or suspect. We could use some good press."

The older man pushes up his glasses with a frown. Maybe they didn't expect her to give orders, but she'd bet the last twenty-four years of her life that Eric gladly gave orders when he sat in this chair. And those orders were likely followed more often than not, and without question.

"I'm not sure—" Junior starts.

"If I look bad, we all look bad," Lynell interrupts. "I'm not going anywhere, so it's time we get on the offensive rather than playing catch up."

"And if the police don't clear you?" Junior asks.

Lynell raises her eyebrows at the man before scanning the rest of the room. "Why wouldn't they?" A few members look like they want to reply, so Lynell adds, "May I remind you I have several souvenirs from my time with Eric?" She points to the three finger splints on her left hand and several bandages. "Yet, I only ever saw good things about the man in every news outlet that wasn't rebel-owned. The murder investigations need to disappear, and my portrayal in the media needs to be much more positive. So, make it happen before the damage is irreversible and the entire Registration goes up in flames."

Lynell pushes away from the table and stands, making several eyes widen and a few people glance at their neighbors. "We'll schedule another meeting after the investigations move on and the media's opinion shifts in our favor. Then we'll discuss every other item on the shockingly long agenda." She smiles and almost feels as if the last three weeks hadn't happened and she's back at her normal job, where she got through each day with a fake smile.

She's about to make her exit when Finnegan leans on his forearms and says, "You don't want to discuss the policy change we're scheduled to announce next Friday?"

Lynell almost decides to ignore him, but confusion and curiosity get the better of her. She can't remember if Ramsey mentioned anything about a policy change. Then again, their morning meeting was interrupted. She looks at Ramsey, who has followed her lead and is also standing, preparing to leave. He doesn't meet her eyes, making him appear guilty.

"Policy change?" Lynell forms the words as a question and slowly drags the heat of her gaze back to the committee. Finnegan is smirking, clearly entertained by Lynell's ignorance. Tamara is wearing an uncharacteristic look of indifference, and Warner looks concerned. The rest appear equally shocked and frustrated that Lynell doesn't know about the policy change.

"The one we voted on at the beginning of the year," Izrael says, as if expecting her to slap her forehead and say 'oh, duh, of course, *that* policy change.' "It'll raise the price of the Registration and give every adult the option to purchase one, whether or not they already have one."

Lynell blinks. The insect-swarm sensation returns with a vengeance, this time in her mind. She can't get a single thought through.

Her confusion must be obvious, because Robin says, "You didn't read the outline for the new policy?"

The instinct to lie flares strongly, but Lynell bites down on her pride. "I didn't have time to go through the entire agenda before my house was bombed." She returns to her chair and takes a deep breath. "Would someone care to explain?"

Thankfully, it's Warner who says, "Eric brought the change to the table again last year, and after some discussion and reworking, it was voted through in January." Lynell notices the use of 'again,' meaning this probably isn't the first time Eric tried to raise the price. From the way Warner tells the story, he was against it but was outvoted. "This is the first of three policy changes. This one will raise the price of every Registration from fifteen thousand to thirty thousand and raise the interest to 2.25% a month or 20% annually."

Lynell barely manages to keep her jaw from dropping. A few years ago, the price rose from ten to fifteen thousand and people complained. How are they going to react to the cost doubling? How many families will be unable to afford it now?

How many more Elizabeths will be forced to stay with Alans because their parents couldn't buy them a Registration?

"In addition, any legal adult citizen will have the option to purchase one Registration for seventy-five thousand dollars, no payment plan available. That way, if your parents couldn't or refused to buy you one at birth, you can do so yourself."

"For seventy-five thousand dollars?" Lynell says, unable to keep the disbelief from her voice. "Upfront? Half the country can't afford that."

Finnegan scoffs. "Maybe it'll incentivize them to work harder."

Lynell's teeth grind together. From the corner of her eye, she sees Ramsey return to his seat.

Ignoring Finnegan, she focuses her attention on Warner. "Any adult can buy one? Even if they already have one?"

Warner nods. "To ensure we aren't accused of discrimination."

"Yeah, because raising the price to be too expensive for half the country isn't discriminatory at all," Lynell says, lips itching to raise into a sneer.

"We take the Registration seriously," Izrael says. "It's essentially how much life is worth, and we think the price should better reflect that."

"Some families can't even afford for their kids to go to decent schools," Lynell says, barely managing to keep her voice level. "Now you're basically asking them to choose between an education and the right to a Registration."

"In that case, they have to decide which is more valuable," Izrael says.

"Anyone can still buy one for their children—lifetime payment plans are available," Tilly says, as if trying to suffocate a flame before it can burst into a fully-fledged fire.

"And the activation clause?" Lynell asks. "Is that changing?"

Most people try hard to pay for their kid's Registration in full, or to pay it off as quickly as possible. But if they have to use a payment plan, the Registration in question is inactive until it's paid off. If a child's parent dies before they've finished paying off the child's Registration, then the child's new guardian or the child themself receives the obligation of either taking responsibility for the debt or to abandon the payments and, consequently, the Registration itself.

"No," Tilly says. "It won't change. It'll simply reflect the new interest."

Lynell is about to mention the higher interest rate when Tamara speaks. "Now, any adult citizen can buy one. Including *new* citizens."

Immigrants. Tamara herself will finally have a Registration. That was probably her main reason for being on the committee at all. To be an advocate for people like her.

Well, people like her with seventy-five thousand dollars lying around.

"You said this is one of three changes," Lynell says. She wants to keep fighting, but she needs the entire map before she can blindly start running into a dangerous forest.

Warner nods. "The next will be a year from now, creating the opportunity to purchase Registration immunities."

Lynell blinks.

"For an upfront payment of ten million, you can add yourself or a loved one to an immunity list, making it illegal for that person to be Registered."

Anyone with enough money can be untouchable.

Like the Elysians.

That kind of power turned Eric into a monster. What will it do to the entire country?

"The last will be five years from now, raising the price once again. This time to fifty thousand per Registration, for both infants and adults, and fifteen million for immunities," Verity says. "The delay is in place to allow people to adjust."

"Five years to adjust from paying fifteen thousand to fifty?" Lynell says. "How does that make sense? The rebels already use the price to prove corruption. You're handing them bombs that they'll be happy to throw right back into your homes."

"We can handle a few rebel tantrums," Robin says, waving her hand in the air.

"Really? Because their last tantrum almost ended you." When no one replies, Lynell says, "How is this legal? Don't the oligarchs have to pass a law to—"

"Nope," Finnegan interrupts. "The existing laws allow for Registrations and immunities, thanks to your family." He winks and Lynell's stomach churns. "With some clever wording, this policy change is simple. For future plans, though, the oligarchs will need to be included."

Lynell suspects from his level tone that he's not worried about influencing the oligarchs.

"I have a feeling they'll be more than willing to cooperate," Izrael says, a cocky note to his voice.

The oligarchs' cooperation wouldn't be surprising. After all, they make money off the Registration. It gives them power. Maybe they knew about Eric's plan for this policy change. Hell, it might have been their idea.

"What future plans?" Lynell asks.

"Your uncle had many intriguing ideas for this business and country," Tamara says. Lynell can't tell if *intriguing* is a bad thing or a good thing in Tamara's opinion.

"You can't tell me that you all are okay with this? These changes will make the divide between those with Registrations and those without grow dramatically. And with immunities? You might as well label half the country disposable and the top five percent invincible."

Warner winces. Several others have the decency to look upset by her words. But Finnegan smiles and says, "What's wrong with that?"

Lynell gapes at him. "Where do I start?"

"Perhaps this can wait for another day," Ramsey says, physically leaning forward as if to push himself back into the conversation.

One look at her most trusted advisor and it dawns on her: he knew about this and didn't tell her.

Even if he was planning to until the explosion got in the way, he still waited until right before the meeting.

"Not if this is happening in a week," Lynell says.

"There's not much you can do about it now," Izrael says.

Lynell feels her face burn with anger.

Then Warner clears his throat. "Actually, there is. These policies were voted through by a committee that no longer exists. It's in the bylaws that pre-activated changes can be re-voted if any member of the committee leaves or is replaced."

Gratefulness for the old man replaces Lynell's anger.

"No board member has changed," Izrael all but growls.

"Warner, we already voted, let it be," Finnegan says.

Warner looks at Lynell, and she doesn't have to read his mind to know what he's trying to say.

"Perhaps not, but the owner has changed," she says. "And the owner is to act as a tiebreaker for any votes." *That,* at least, was included in the materials Ramsey made her read. "Meaning, I am, technically, a member with the right to vote."

"It passed five to three," Izrael says, outraged.

"Then, you shouldn't worry about a revote," Lynell says. Somehow, his anger helps her regain confidence. "If it passes again without a tie, nothing will change."

"And if it ties?" Izrael asks.

Lynell shrugs. "Then my vote will matter, won't it?" A quick glance around the table tells Lynell she's won this battle. They'll have to vote again.

"When will the revote be?" Tamara asks.

Lynell knows that the bylaws state seven days must pass—at least—between extending an issue to be voted on and the actual voting. This is meant to allow time for board members to make their cases to one another. To convince, bribe, or extort. Whatever they need to do to ensure the votes swing in their direction.

Which means Lynell has until next Thursday to convince at least one person at this table that giving people like them more power is a bad thing.

"Next Friday?" Warner suggests.

Predictably, he's instantly shot down. "Seven days is seven p.m. on Thursday," Izrael says.

"We all have commitments outside of this committee," Verity says. "I, for one, would prefer to wait until the following morning."

"There's a meeting already scheduled for Friday morning in preparation for the convention," Warner states. "That seems a convenient time for a revote."

Lynell's memories of the annual conventions are foggy. It's held in a different city each year, and the Registration head and an oligarch always make a speech to announce changes, whether legal or business. They also highlight a notable speaker, but it's always been so exclusive that no more than a handful of people personally attended. The rest of the country, including Lynell, watched live. The conventions were never particularly interesting, but they were important if you wanted to stay up to date with news, laws, and the Registration.

This year is going to be different, Ramsey told her. The event is already scheduled for next Friday here in Dallas, but he plans to use it to officially announce Lynell as the owner of the Registration and generate a ton of good press for her and the company.

"It should be Thursday," Tamara says. "If we vote Friday and it doesn't pass, we won't have much time to update the convention plans."

"The convention plans have already changed quite a bit, haven't they?" Izrael asks, giving Lynell a distasteful look.

The argument continues, which is apparently normal behavior when trying to set meeting times, because Tilly spends the entire time leaning back in her chair, watching the exchange with a slightly bored expression.

Robin also refuses to speak for several minutes. When she gently sets her hand on the tabletop, the entire table falls silent almost instantly. "If an extra twelve hours will change the vote, then perhaps this policy shouldn't be passed. We will vote at exactly 7 a.m. on Friday before preparations for the convention. It's natural to vote the same day. You all know the rules. If you're late or absent, you forfeit your vote. If, once again, the policy passes, everything will continue as planned and we will make the announcement later that day. I also support Mrs. Carter being officially sworn in during the convention. Let's be sure any other . . ." She side-eyes Lynell, synthetic lip twitching as if she wants to sneer, ". . . problems are taken care of before then. We need to present a strong and united front. The whole country will be watching."

Lynell doesn't particularly like the woman, but in that moment, Robin Jacobs becomes her hero. Robin stops talking and no one argues. They agree and begin packing up, as if Robin's decision was the implicit dismissal from the meeting. Both Izrael and Tilly are already gone before

Lynell manages to stand. Her brain is still struggling to catch up with everything that just happened.

One week until nearly half the country becomes nothing more than prey to the richest, most powerful members of society.

She has to stop it.

CHAPTER 7

Time, experience, and plenty of therapy have taught Sawyer how to see through her own emotional sandstorms. In her teens and twenties, her feelings were always bigger than they should've been. She wasn't anxious or scared, she was terrified. She wasn't frustrated or angry, she was enraged. And she wasn't sad, she was devastated. The slightest wind-stirring could become a storm.

But she learned. Not to ignore her emotions or feel guilty for them, but to control them. To live with more organized feelings. The sandstorms became fewer, and when she found herself lost in one, she didn't feel as blind.

Today, though, it takes all her energy to not lie down and let herself be buried. For several hours, her life is endless images of death as she cleans her office. The door remains locked so no one can interrupt her work, and she ignores the occasional knock, though the sound always makes her jump. She's on the edge of a deadly abyss, and each sound her phone makes is a hand reaching out to either push her off or to pull her to safety, she can't be sure. Is the stalker calling her or Lynell Carter? Does it make a difference?

Sitting on the freshly vacuumed floor, Sawyer separates the stalker images of herself from the rest and flips through them with increasingly numb fingertips. In most pictures, she's in public where anyone could see her. But a few are much more intimate, and it's those that feel most like a threat.

One is dark, taken at morning twilight, Ellery's favorite time of day, in a cemetery. Sawyer is lying on the dewy grass next to a tomb, and though it's not clear in the image, she can practically see Ellery's epitaph carved in the stone. Whoever took the photo had to be following her practically twenty-four seven to take that picture. Very few people know about Sawyer's weekly morning twilight visits to Ellery's grave. Only her father, her older brother, Ellery's sister, and Harlow Graham.

Another photo is of her cuddling with her cat, Guinness, in her recliner at home. The picture looks like it was taken from inside her home. From the angle, though, Sawyer knows it could've been shot from the corner of the window over her kitchen sink. Meaning the stalker had to sneak into her backyard and stand on the air conditioning unit to get the specific vantage point.

However, the most disturbing image isn't a stalker photo at all. It's of Sawyer in a kayak on Lake Tahoe, laughing. A candid moment eight years ago captured by Ellery on their anniversary trip. The picture once sat on Ellery's desk, framed. But for the last six years, it's been buried in a box of Ellery's things stored in Sawyer's closet. She tries remembering who packed that specific box, but those weeks after Ellery's death are a blur. Everyone in her family, Ellery's family, and several close friends were in and out of her home, helping her with the dozens of painful tasks that plague the newly widowed.

With a sharp exhale, Sawyer stands and stores the photo in a locked desk drawer, then carries the last trash bag outside to the dumpster. She forgot about promising to meet Harlow at her house until her friend texts to say she's on her way. In record time, Sawyer grabs her things, locks up, and speeds home, beating Harlow by mere minutes.

"Are you okay?" Harlow asks when Sawyer opens the door.

Sawyer grins. "I'll be fine." She's known the other woman for ten months, but in that time they've become like family. Maybe because they've both experienced heartbreaking loss or because they both feel separate from their family or because they both hate the Registration. Whatever the reason, Harlow is the older sister Sawyer never had, which feels almost too ironic to be true.

If someone told Sawyer a year ago that in a few short months her best friend would be Zachary Elysian's mother, she would think they had fallen through a pit to Wonderland.

"Want to share?" Harlow asks, kicking off her old sneakers.

Sawyer shakes her head. "I want to finish this speech."

"Alright," Harlow says. She never pushes for information or expects to be entrusted with Sawyer's problems. Sawyer sometimes thinks that Harlow's over two decades of living in hiding has conditioned her to see secrets as water and currency, both needed for survival and to be shared only for something in return.

Sawyer spreads out the printed pages of Ellery's old speech on the dining room table, passes a pencil to Harlow, and scoots her chair in closer to lean over the papers. They start editing without preamble, updating the words Ellery wrote over six years ago to make them applicable for the present day.

"Maybe you should change this line," Harlow says, tapping the tip of her pencil against the paragraph. "Instead of 'His power thrives on our weakness,' you could say something like 'Even in death, he holds our weakness over our heads, passing all power to the next Elysian?' That'd point to his family retaining their control through passing power from generation to generation."

Sawyer leans back in the chair, thinking. Harlow straddles the space between the Registration and the rebellion more than anyone Sawyer knows. Despite sharing very little about her life before returning to Dallas, Sawyer knows the basics. She was surrounded by the Registration's power throughout her childhood, her father having served on the committee for decades. What complicates matters is that Harlow briefly dated Eric Elysian, an affair that produced her son, Zachary. She could've stayed and benefited from her family's power, but fear of Eric eliminating her for knowing he was illegitimate drove her away, and she had to watch her son grow up on a screen.

Harlow said she returned for Zachary—undercover, to help the Resurrection stop the Registration so he could be free. In short, she came back, risking her life to be a rebel, to reunite with her son and save him from his father. When, almost two weeks ago, she learned that her son was dead—murdered—and Lynell Carter the head of the Registration in his place, her conviction strengthened.

Unfortunately, Harlow's bitterness and anger mixed with that motivation now needs a new target, which Sawyer fears will become Lynell Carter.

"We should be careful not to villainize Carter. Until she gives us a reason other than her heritage to see her as the enemy, I don't want to paint her as such."

Harlow's perfect poker face doesn't provide a reaction. "I understand as well as any that no one has control over their family. But they do have control over their actions."

From the statement, Sawyer wonders if Harlow blames Carter for Zachary's death. She wants to ask, but they haven't discussed Zachary, and Sawyer won't be the one to bring him up.

"If we tell Carter she's our enemy, then she will be," Sawyer counters. "Better she think of us as a friend, no matter how we see her."

Harlow doesn't reply, and the two continue their work on the speech. Sawyer glances at the woman, taking in her familiar appearance. She's beautiful, but years of stress and grief have taken its toll. Her blonde hair is turning light gray. Deep wrinkles line the space between her eyebrows, webbing out from her eyes.

Sawyer is thirty-five, over a decade younger than Harlow, but she, too, has seemingly permanent bags under her eyes that disappear primarily under the influence of concealer. The last six years have left massage-defying knots along her shoulders and back. Even the color of her auburn hair has been fading, as if her body can't be bothered to produce enough melanin.

"Did you meet with Henry today?" Sawyer asks, referring to a member of the Resurrection's board of directors. Though she alone started the group four years ago, it quickly grew as more recruits joined, bringing more money and possibilities. To handle the growing demands, Sawyer formed the board of directors three years ago.

Harlow nods. "He's confident in the information he's gathered so far but, of course, he wants more."

"Has he asked you to reach out to your dad again?"

"Every day." Harlow sighs. "He wants as much knowledge about Friday's convention as possible to avoid surprises. He said Carter's involvement is changing things. Already, dozens of vendors have been invited to set up booths."

"I'm not surprised."

"Also, Ramsey Davenport is increasing the convention's security." Harlow pauses, turning a slightly worried gaze on Sawyer. "Maybe we should postpone. You can give the speech whenever."

"What?" Sawyer frowns in shock. Harlow is cautious by nature, but she's enthusiastically supported this plan since its inception. "You know we can't do that."

"We could use the inevitable fallout from the convention to our advantage."

Sawyer leans forward.

The Resurrection has been preparing to hijack the convention's live feed for months. She's been pouring over Ellery's speech, trying to make it perfect for next Friday.

If everything goes well, the entire country will turn on their TV to watch the convention and instead see Sawyer.

"Where is this coming from?" she asks.

Harlow shrugs. "It'll be dangerous."

"Everything we do is dangerous, Harlow."

"Not like next Friday will be. Especially to you. We can't guarantee your safety."

The conviction in Harlow's voice grazes the warning bells in Sawyer's mind. But before they start ringing, she remembers how much her friend has lost. Of course she's scared for Sawyer. She doesn't want to lose anyone else. Sawyer understands. She sympathizes. But then her eyes slide along the speech and land at the top of the first page. Those six words are etched in her memory.

'Be a Peony by Ellery Klein.' The last thing her wife wrote. The speech she didn't live to deliver. The world deserves to hear Ellery's beautiful words. Sawyer will make sure of that. She *has* to.

"Safety is never guaranteed. That doesn't mean we spend our life hiding." She doesn't mean the words as an insult, but Harlow still flinches. Before Sawyer can apologize, Harlow responds.

"You're right. Then let's make this the best damn speech in history."

An hour after Harlow leaves, Sawyer receives a call from Henry. She told him to look into the bomb at the Elysian mansion this morning, and has since been waiting for an update.

"'Sup, Boss?" he greets in his typical jovial tone.

"What did you learn?" she asks, because giving Henry any time for distraction makes it much more difficult to force him to the point.

"I received a tip from one of our lower-level informants in the Elysian security team. He said all the employees are being questioned after the bombing, and by the questions he was asked, he thinks they suspect a traitor working with the bomber. The speculation among the employees suggests that the traitor is someone close to Carter."

"But not one of ours, right?" Sawyer asks. Over the years, they've managed to get a few Resurrection members onto the Elysian payroll and convince a couple others to be informants, but none of them are in positions of power. Eric Elysian was paranoid and meticulously careful about who he let into his home and trusted circle.

"Not directly, I don't think."

"What does that mean, Henry?" No one connected to the Resurrection should've been involved in the bombing.

"Well, we also intercepted a somewhat problematic message. We haven't figured out the intended recipient, but it was sent by someone who had to have been in the same building as Carter during the committee meeting earlier today. It reads 'Stay close to the peony for surveillance while the weapon focuses on the weed.'"

Heat drains from Sawyer's limbs before she fully understands the message. She's quiet as she attempts to interpret the words, but Henry doesn't let the silence linger long.

"We need to learn more, but it seems as if the Registration traitor gave orders to watch you while they're focusing on Carter."

"So, Carter isn't the only one being betrayed," Sawyer says.

Henry seems unwilling to instantly respond. She hears rhythmic clacking in the absence of speaking from his cane hitting the floor while he walks. When he speaks, it's in a somber tone she's never heard from him. "No, she isn't. We think whoever is behind the bombing is working with someone close to you."

Without much else to share, Henry ends the call a few minutes later. Sawyer stands in the middle of her living room, mind numb and unable to fully process the information. Anxiety fills her like a thousand tiny feet crawling along her veins. She senses a storm of emotions brewing and, without thinking, she does what she always did as a kid when trying to survive the onslaught of overwhelming feelings.

She runs to her dad.

She doesn't want to cry about her call with Henry or share her fears about the threatening notes. She just wants to be with him.

She spends the half hour drive doing the breathing exercises her therapist taught her. By the time she arrives at the small two-bedroom house at the edge of the metroplex, she feels more stable. She lets herself in with her key and passes through the quiet house to the sunroom bursting with color from varying flowers. Lincoln is exactly where she expected: in his chair, a pipe in one hand and a bucket filled to the brim with walnut shells at his feet. His old pug, Eisenhower, jumps up at her arrival and rushes over for attention.

"Dad," Sawyer says, patting the dog's head as it snorts.

"Hey, baby," Lincoln D'Angelo says, raising his pipe in greeting.

Sawyer takes a seat in the chair next to him and picks up the abandoned nutcracker.

Eisenhower paws at her leg, but gives up fairly quickly and drops to his stomach with a huff. Sawyer places a walnut in the cracker's jaw and squeezes until the satisfying snap sounds. Prying the pieces of shell off, she asks, "Have you heard from Uncle Paul today?"

Her great-uncle has been incrementally losing his memories to dementia, and his independence soon followed. He never had children of his own, but Lincoln has plenty of money to hire a private nurse, so Paul hasn't had to move into a home yet.

"I visited on Monday, and he asked me how I was," he says, extinguishing the remaining tobacco in his pipe.

"That's a good sign, right?"

Lincoln scoffs. "Well, he thought I was Jude and wanted to know how my infant son, Lincoln, was doing."

"Ah," Sawyer says, dropping another de-shelled walnut into the bucket.

"He thought he was still married to Paige, too," Lincoln says. "He talked about how they were going to start trying to get pregnant again for a good ten minutes."

Sawyer pauses in her nut cracking. "What?"

Lincoln shrugs. "He seemed confident that it was going to work 'this time.'" He makes air quotes with his fingers.

"But . . . Grandpa always said that Paige left Paul because he didn't want kids," Sawyer says.

"He must've lied, because the way Paul was talking, it was like the thought of having a child erased all of his pain." Lincoln scratches his chin and makes a gesture as if to wave away a fly. "Honestly, you wouldn't believe the things he's told me since believing I'm my father."

Sawyer digs out another walnut and watches her dad closely. "Family secrets?" She and her siblings used to joke about the closet of skeletons her family hid. After Grandpa Jude died, her older brother, Fox, wanted to hire a private investigator to dig up some of those skeletons, but Sawyer has no idea if he ever did.

"A few," Lincoln says. "He asked if I—Jude, I mean—was still planning on going behind Gideon's back."

Sawyer meets her dad's hazel eyes, the single physical characteristic they share. In every other aspect, Sawyer favors her aunt Sally. "Wasn't it the other way around?"

Lincoln shrugs. "That's what Dad always said. That after fighting by Gideon's side and vouching for him with the other senators, Gideon lied through his teeth and claimed the Registration was all his idea. Classic partner betrayal." Her dad says it all with little emotion. Any time Gideon Elysian is mentioned, Grandpa Jude told the same story about Gideon ruining his life by cutting him out of the Registration. He also claimed his wife left him for Gideon, but Sawyer thinks she left because no one wants to hang around someone who won't let go of the past.

"Who's to say if any of it is true. Paul's losing it," Lincoln says. "You can't take anything he says seriously."

A sour taste fills Sawyer's mouth. She's always been closer to Paul than anyone else in the family. He was estranged for several years, so she didn't meet him until after her grandfather's death. Paul showed up at the funeral, and Sawyer recognized him from family photos. She'd wanted to march up to him and ask all the questions Jude and her dad never answered but was too scared. Shockingly, it was Lincoln who invited Paul to the post-funeral barbecue.

It didn't take long for Sawyer to learn the main reason for his estrangement was his rebel involvement. She'd give anything to talk to him about next Friday's convention. But her dad is right. Paul is in no condition for those conversations. So she settles for her father, who might disagree with her political opinions but wouldn't let it interfere with their relationship.

"Dad, I have a question."

Her father smiles, wrinkles curling around his eyes. "Shoot."

"If you were fighting for something you believe in and someone threatened you to stop, would you stop or keep going?"

"Who's threatening you?" he asks, voice dropping in anger.

"Dad."

"Honey, I'm never going to tell you to do something that would put you in danger. What you do," he pauses, clearly struggling with his child being one of the most well-known rebels in the country, "is dangerous enough. I've wanted you to step back for years. Look what happened to Ellery."

"But shouldn't I stand up for what I believe in?"

"You have stood up. You've been standing up. You're allowed to sit."

She knew he'd respond like this. Maybe that's why she asked him. The rebellious lurch in her gut, telling her not to bend to threats when thousands suffer every day, is exactly what she needs. Her father telling her to put herself and her comfort first makes her want to become an even bigger target. Maybe then the hunters will aim for her, rather than the innocents falling from their bullets.

Sawyer firmly believes that, when someone dies, pieces of them live on in those they loved. Their sense of humor goes to a best friend. Their love of writing letters goes to a sibling. Their taste in music goes to a child. Sawyer got Ellery's stubborn desire to fight injustice against all opposition. Ellery was never more intent on fighting than when someone told her to drop her fists.

"You used to tell us being disliked was a sign we were doing something right."

Lincoln digs his fingers into his eyes, groaning. "Your memory can be quite inconvenient, you know? Like your mother."

Sawyer smirks. "Sorry," she says, though they both know she's not.

"Being disliked isn't the same thing as being threatened. Honey, none of this is worth your life."

"How much is my life worth then, Dad?"

He frowns, probably sensing a trap but unsure how to avoid it. Predictably, his paternal love beats his internal political chess player. "Your life is priceless, honey. It's worth everything."

Trapped.

"According to the system *you* support, my life is worth exactly fifteen-thousand dollars, like every other American citizen. The Registration puts price tags on human life. Isn't that worth fighting against?"

She watches her dad struggle with the desire to argue. But in the end, he shakes his head. "I don't want to have this conversation, Sawyer. I merely want you to be safe."

"I know, Dad." Love for her father replaces her anger. She drops the uncracked walnuts back into the bucket and stands. "Why don't you show me what's going on with your computer?"

Clearly grateful for the subject change, Lincoln pushes himself up, groaning with the effort. "Damn thing won't save any of my documents."

She listens to him complain, knowing the fix will be simple. Instead of annoyance, she finds herself soaking in every second with him, wondering if this'll be the last time she hears him complain about something he doesn't understand. Wondering if those threats are real and someone is planning to kill her before she can give Ellery's speech on Friday.

If the target on her back is as big as she thinks, then she'll be gone in eight days. She'll never see her dad again.

Or anyone else.

Except for Ellery.

CHAPTER 8

"**I**t was in the binder, the policy," Ramsey says, once they're back in the SUV. "I didn't intentionally keep it from you."

Lynell studies him. Stray wiry strands stick out of his beard. From this angle, she can see the valley caused by the scar piercing his beard and ending at his chin. The effect makes him appear altogether like a menacing assassin and a lovable lumberjack.

She's always found that, when someone offers a defense before the accusation can be made, it's because guilt prompted them to.

"Yet, you deemed each committee member's family tree as more important and demanding of a spot at the beginning of the binder. Don't you think learning about an imminent policy change would've been a better use of my time than reading about Finnegan Reese's brother's habit of jumping in and out of rehab?"

Ramsey's face remains emotionless. "I didn't count on being disrupted by a bomb."

"We only lost a few hours. Even without the disruption, I wouldn't have had time to learn anything but the existence of the policy. I'd have barely been more prepared than I was."

"This meeting was your chance to make an impression on the committee, an introduction of sorts. I prioritized your knowledge of the committee because I thought that would be the best way to carve your place among them."

"If Finnegan hadn't brought it up, then we wouldn't have this chance to reconsider it."

She's not trying to sound accusatory, but there's an edge in her voice, nonetheless.

"I—" He pauses, and the way he swallows is so unlike him that Lynell softens. "I didn't know a revote was an option."

It's the first time Ramsey has sounded truly ashamed and embarrassed. "I'm sorry," he adds. "It wasn't an intentional omission."

Lynell chews on the inside of her cheek, watching him with a frown. The apology feels tangible between them, but her anger isn't that easily subdued.

"I can't look like I have no idea what's going on. You're the one who said I need them on my side. I need their respect, or they'll always see a spoiled little girl who scarcely graduated high school, married a rebel, and was handed a position she didn't earn because the family she didn't know were all murdered."

"You're on your way to getting their respect," Ramsey says. "You did well in there." Pride travels from his eyes to his voice, and Lynell tries not to sit up straighter at his praise.

They don't talk for the rest of the drive to the new house. She pulls out her phone, prepared to look up past policy changes and voting history of the committee members.

Instead, she types in Sawyer D'Angelo's name, curious about the rebel leader now that the immediate threats of the bomb and meeting are in the rear-view mirror.

She clicks the first link, which is a news article that was published two days ago.

ANTI-REGISTRATION REBELS CONDONE
ELYSIAN MURDER

Outspoken Anti-Registration Activist, Sawyer D'Angelo, Calls Lynell Carter "The Rebels' Savior" and Says the Deaths of Eric and Zachary Elysian are "A Huge Win for the Cause."

A popular live podcast, *The People's Regulators*, was recorded near the Elysian property on Sunday afternoon, which included a short interview with Anti-Registration activist and leader of the Resurrection, a large rebel organization, Sawyer D'Angelo. The Resurrection leader gained notoriety after her heartbreaking song "You Promised" went viral four years ago. The song, which includes an excerpt from a speech given by Eric Elysian, memorializes D'Angelo's late wife, a transgender activist who was Registered as a hate crime by local religious zealots. D'Angelo now speaks boldly against the Registration and calls for justice for all who have lost their lives to the Registration. On Sunday's podcast, D'Angelo admits that the rebel groups have experienced a win that could "change the course of history."

"Eric Elysian was a heartless snake who turned a deaf ear to the cries of the American people," D'Angelo says on *The People's Regulators*. "Whether she pulled the trigger or not, Lynell Carter has freed the country of a tyrant."

When Marjorie Dunn, *The People's Regulators'* co-host, explained her worry of simply trading one Elysian for another, D'Angelo defends Carter, who has also been referred to as "Mize," saying that no one can choose their family.

She ends the interview by imploring the protestors outside of Carter's home to stand down. "Right now, Lynell Carter is the rebels' savior," D'Angelo said. "But if we're not careful, we may turn her into our greatest enemy."

Despite not being halfway through the article, she stops reading and types "Sawyer D'Angelo wife" into the search bar and picks at a growing hangnail on her thumb while waiting for the search results to load. When they do, she scrolls through them, icy sympathy filling her chest. Ellery Klein, D'Angelo's wife, was one of twelve LGBTQ activists who were Registered and killed six years ago by a group of "Sin-Fighting Warriors" who claimed they were doing the Lord's work. Because the killings were legal, none of the men faced legal consequences. However, four of the "Sin-Fighting Warriors" were Registered and killed by grieving family members, but the man who Registered Ellery Klein, Thomas Johnson, is still free and travels to churches across the country, encouraging others to follow his lead.

Lynell feels sick. She can't imagine what Sawyer D'Angelo must have gone through. And she can't blame her for fighting the Registration.

But what about the four family members who were able to get justice on their own through the Registration? D'Angelo could have done the same, and Ellery's killer could be dead right now, if D'Angelo had an unused Registration. The "Sin-Fighting Warriors" used the Registration to back up their twisted views the same way they use religion to validate those views.

The Registration isn't supposed to be a weapon in the hands of evil. It's supposed to be a tool in the hands of good. She deletes the tab and notices a recent article about the bomb. Knowing it's probably a mistake, she clicks the article. It's short and straightforward, giving the facts without speculation. The comments below, however, are bursting with theories and opinions.

Is anyone really in doubt that the rebels bombed the Elysian house? I mean, duh.

Why would Sawyer D'Angelo publicly defend Lynell Elysian only to bomb her house? Someone else is probably trying to pit them against each other.

L Elysian shouldn't have inherited the Registration. She's basically a high school dropout with no education, a nobody until she killed her family. She should be in prison, not a mansion.

This is a classic case of pitting women in power against each other. When Lynell Elysian replaced her uncle, she became an immediate threat to the men in America. There are now women controlling two of the largest organizations in the country, and that's a nightmare for misogynists and anyone who benefits from a divided country.

what a surprise this is sexism too! women will do anything for attention

It's more than possible when studying history and the politics of other countries to see evidence of individual parties hijacking their local government in order to control the society from behind the scenes. For example, there are several case studies of what's called a "shadow state" or "shadow government" made up of unelected people wielding nearly all the power without the knowledge of the public at large, in places such as Uganda, Brazil, and yes, here in the US.

lol ok conspiracy nut. how were the alien probes?

Lynell drops her phone and closes her eyes, pulling long breaths through her nose. It's always a mistake to read the comment section. She can't identify the emotions building from the comments, but they feel suspiciously like fear. They don't know who planted the bomb or if it was meant to kill her.

It could've been one of the committee chairs or oligarchs, unwilling to let an untrained girl who is hardly an Elysian take over. If that's the case, then she might as well dig her grave now. She barely managed to survive Eric. Now, enemies as bad as, or even worse than him could be hungry for her blood.

The SUV pulls to a stop in front of a house at the end of a cul-de-sac. It's Tudor Style and about a third of the size of Eric's house, probably four-thousand square feet, with a black wood accent trim. The shrubbery and garden are pruned to perfection, and the lawn is deep green. Lynell waits for one of the guards to open her door before she climbs out and walks up the sidewalk, Ramsey following close behind. The front door is open, and the moment Lynell steps inside, she loves the house.

There are no ghosts haunting her in the hallways, no dungeons where prisoners are kept and tortured. She walks past the staircase and formal dining room to the right of the entryway, into a large open space complete with a fully stocked kitchen, open space living room, small dining nook, and a clear sliding door that leads to the back patio. At her entrance, the door at the back of the house opens and Daniel steps through, smiling.

"Nice, isn't it?" he says. "There are three more bedrooms and bathrooms, a family room, and an office upstairs."

"Damn," Lynell says, turning slowly to take in the space. The house probably costs more than she could afford if she'd saved a lifetime for it. Now, in a blink, it's hers. No month-long wait before closing or hefty bank loan needed.

"Mrs.—Lynell." Hayes walks toward her from the staircase, so clean that he might never have been in a fire. "I hope your meeting went well." It's clearly a rhetorical sentence, because he launches into an explanation of the house before Lynell has time to reply.

Despite hoping to keep the location a secret, he and Ramsey agreed on stationing six guards at the house day and night. The group will work in shifts, one at each entrance, one circling the property, one inside the house, and two sleeping in the spare bedrooms. While he speaks, Lynell returns to her fleeting idea of promoting Hayes to CSO. He's young but a hard worker, and with Ramsey teaching him, she's confident he'd do well.

She'll deal with her staffing problems later, she decides. After thanking Ramsey and Hayes, Lynell excuses herself, requests to have dinner sent to them, and pulls Daniel to their bedroom. She jumps onto the Texas

King-sized bed, her muscles relaxing. Daniel climbs on next to her, and she feels his blue eyes staring at her profile.

"How are you feeling?" she asks, voice barely above a whisper.

"Fine."

She reaches up and pinches the collar of his shirt, carefully pulling it back to see the bandage over the re-stitched wound. "Does it hurt?"

Daniel shrugs before reaching up and grabbing her hand. He pulls it to his mouth and presses a kiss to her palm. "I'll live. Plus, the pain meds will help," he says with a smirk.

Studying her husband closely, Lynell almost considers not telling him about the vote next Friday, or her plans for contacting D'Angelo. But she promised she'd never lie to him again, and she knows from experience that having him by her side makes the impossible feel achievable.

She takes a deep breath that turns into a sigh. "I need to tell you something."

His wild eyebrows pull together in worry, but he stays silent while she talks. His reaction to the policy change is predictable and not much different than her own. By the time he finishes ranting about the injustice and horror of such a change, he's paced the large bedroom dozens of times.

"You have to stop it," he says.

Lynell nods, now sitting at the head of the bed. "I'm going to try."

"You have to," he repeats. "Use the code if necessary."

She looks down, noticing that she's somehow picked at several hang-nails on her right hand, despite her left being useless.

Eric had her Registered, kidnapped, and tortured for the code that could practically give the holder unlimited control to the Registration. Anyone using it could edit the lists, give people more Registrations for free or take people off the list. They could even shut down the Registration all together.

Lynell didn't know she had it until a few weeks ago. Her father had secretly given it to her through a letter, and though she deciphered it, she hasn't done anything with the code yet. Zach warned her that using it could make the Registration's system vulnerable to hackers and might throw the country into a chaos so devastating there'd be mass fatalities.

"I still need to see if I can verify what I think it is," Lynell says, "and learn how to safely use it."

"How are you going to do that?" Daniel asks.

"I need to talk to an expert in the field."

"But you can't give the code to anyone. Or tell them it exists and you have it. We don't want another Eric situation."

She tucks her hand under her leg and nods. "I know. But when I was going through the different departments in the Registration, I noticed the head of the IT security and IT management and administration departments were both hired by my dad before he died. Owen and Summer Meadows, siblings. They were both included in Ramsey's list of employees in management positions that he thinks we can trust. At least, those who weren't overly loyal to Eric."

"That's a good sign," Daniel says. "But I'm still not sure consulting anyone else is smart."

"Danny, I need help. We're out of our depth here. What if I try using the code, then screw up and accidentally open the Registration for anyone to go in and steal lists or edit them for their advantage?"

"Then you end it," he says, like it's the most obvious course of action. He seems to have forgotten that she never hated the Registration like him. She didn't consider the possibility of it ending until a few weeks ago. "Lynell, you're the only person who can end it. And now's the perfect time. The rebels are stronger than ever, and the oligarchs and committee are vulnerable."

She's surprised it's taken them this long to have this conversation. She's been expecting Daniel to tell her to end the Registration since Eric's death was validated, making her the Elysian heir. She's suffered through sleepless nights, wondering how she'll reply when he inevitably asks her to end the Registration.

But he hasn't said anything. He hasn't even asked her what, exactly, the code is.

"You heard what Zach said," Lynell says. "Using it could be disastrous. That's something we'd have to plan for."

"If you wait, what's to keep the committee from passing something worse next? Or the oligarchs from changing the laws?" The policy seems to have erased any hesitancy to talk about this. She hasn't seen that fire in his eyes in years. He steps closer to the bed and his voice is softer when he says, "Baby, I know you want to do what's right. I trust that you will. But I'm worried you don't have as much time to do so as we thought."

"If I use the code without a plan, then it'll start another civil war," she says. The last *real* civil war the country had, not including the attempted resurgences like the one Daniel fought in seven years ago, nearly destroyed them. The only thing that stopped the fighting was the creation of the Registration. "What if the result is worse than what we have now? And what about the good things the Registration gives us? Without it, women will have no control over their own bodies. They'll never be able to end an unwanted or dangerous pregnancy." She averts her eyes from Daniel's face when she says this, the feeling of shame still sharp in her chest. "And people who are terminally ill or in constant pain will be forced to endure it. Criminals will get to go free. And—"

"New laws can be added to address all of those things," Daniel interrupts.

"There *were* laws, remember? But no one could agree on what they should be, and our country was caught up in a civil war for years. All I'd accomplish by ending the Registration is returning us to that misery. I'm not saying I don't want to end it, just that I need to think it through first. Make sure we have a plan and alternate solutions."

As Daniel's jaw tenses, he runs his fingers through his thick curls. "I know," he admits, though frustration makes the words sound like a growl. "You're right, I know you can't end it without making us even more vulnerable."

Silence settles, and before she can speak, someone knocks at their bedroom door. Lynell jumps at the sound and Daniel answers, letting Alex, a young female guard with pitch-black hair and three nose rings, step inside, pushing a little cart filled with two covered plates and cups into the room.

"Thanks, Alex," Lynell says before the young guard leaves.

Their bedroom has a couch and coffee table at one end. Daniel pushes the cart over, helping Lynell move the food and drinks to the low table. She uncovers the plates to show two bowls of chili, bread, and a side of green beans. Her mouth instantly fills with saliva at the smell. In silence, she starts on the green beans and is halfway through before Daniel speaks.

"If you're going to ask those IT siblings, the Meadows, then you should have Ramsey or Hayes run a background check first."

"Good idea," Lynell says. "But even if I do talk to them, I'm not going to outright tell them a code exists or what it is. I need some guidance. Someone to explain how the database works."

"It would be helpful if one of us was an expert technician or programmer."

"I think the real skills we need are those of a hacker."

Their conversation lulls as they focus on their meal. Lynell's bowl of chili is still a third full when she leans back on the couch, hunger satisfied.

"We need allies," she says.

"Yeah." Daniel nods, still leaning over the table while he finishes off his chili. When his bowl is empty, he reaches over and grabs Lynell's. The action is so second-nature for him that a smile tugs at Lynell's lips.

She shakes her head, forcing her thoughts back to the matter at hand. "I'm going to meet with D'Angelo."

Daniel drops his spoon and sighs. "I figured. Is there any point in trying to change your mind?"

"You're the one who wants me to end the Registration, Danny. We need someone like Sawyer on our side to make that work. And you said she has a good reputation."

"I don't care what reputation or intentions she may have. She's a rebel, Lyn. As much as I agree with their cause, my loyalty is to you. She'll see you as nothing but the enemy."

"You fought with the rebels, but you don't trust them?"

"This isn't the same rebel group, and you're an *Elysian*, Lyn. I'd be an idiot to trust them not to make snap judgments about you."

"Okay, but *she* reached out to *me*. There must be a reason for that."

"Maybe the reason is to lure you into a trap."

Lynell knows that's possible, but her instinct disagrees. Still, it'd be stupid to ignore logic in favor of a gut feeling.

"I guess my big strong husband should come with me for protection."

He rolls his eyes. Then, without warning, he leans forward, forcing her to fall back on the couch. He cages her in with his arms, hovering above her as his eyes travel along her face like he's been on a journey for several years and finally reached the destination. When his gaze drops to her lips, Lynell's breath nearly stops in her lungs.

"You are terrifying," Daniel says.

Lynell blinks, her brain sluggish. "What?"

"You're one of the smartest, bravest, kindest, and strongest people I know. You could easily rule this world. Now you have the power and money to do so. Anyone should be afraid of you."

"Are you afraid of me?"

"Of course I am," Daniel says. "You're my biggest fear, Lynell Carter, because you have my heart. You are the one person in the world who could destroy me completely."

"I would never do that," she says, even as memories of having done so plague her every day.

"Then you can never die on me." Emotion thickens his voice. She knows his pleas are fueled by the fear of what could happen when they meet with Sawyer D'Angelo.

"I won't if you won't," she whispers. "Because you're my biggest fear too."

CHAPTER 9

After Mrs. Elysian disappears with her husband, Ramsey delegates evening jobs, then shuts himself in the upstairs office of the new house to read through reports and return to the bombing investigation.

He works through the night, taking occasional breaks to warm his muscles, keep his mind sharp and his vision from blurring. He's aware of time only because the open window faces east, so the sunrise brightens the office.

Someone knocks as he marks a bombing suspect as cleared.

"Come in!" he shouts.

The door opens and Hayes Booth steps into the office, holding two cups of coffee. "Good morning, Mr. Davenport," he says, setting one cup on the desk.

Ramsey doesn't acknowledge the gesture, choosing instead to focus on the kid in front of him. He's taller than Ramsey, but the eagerness to prove himself subtracts from a possible imposing manner. He wouldn't be Ramsey's first choice, as Mrs. Elysian's primary bodyguard or CSO, but she'll choose him. For reasons Ramsey can't understand, Booth has bonded with Mrs. Elysian.

She trusts him.

Ramsey doesn't yet. He also doesn't rely on trust or instinct. He already privately assigned two men to investigate Booth. If they provide similar reports, Ramsey will be confident in the results. If there is outlying information, however, then he'll need to look closer, and he steels himself for the possibility that Booth may need to be eliminated.

"What updates do you have for me?" Ramsey asks.

"Nothing about the bombing, but the team is still investigating. They should be sending you their morning reports. Also, I called Daphne Bloom to handle the custody situation, but I couldn't get ahold of the other lawyers you mentioned."

"Why not?"

"I called, but their assistants said they were bus—"

"No," Ramsey interrupts. "People aren't busy when we need them. You work for *the* Elysian. Unless speaking to an oligarch, always demand immediate attention."

With wide eyes, Booth nods and shifts his weight between his feet.

"Confidence, Booth. Don't wait for respect. Assume you already have it, because you should."

"Yes, sir."

"Call Willhite back later," Ramsey says. "She'll be Mrs. Elysian's head lawyer for the criminal charges. Knowing her, she might already have them dropped." He stands and walks around the desk. Booth adjusts his stance as Ramsey moves so he's always fully facing him. "Have Mr. Elysian's *Midnight Files* been salvaged from the old house yet?"

"I—"

Detecting the uncertainty in Booth's voice, Ramsey lifts a hand, interrupting what would undoubtedly be an insufficient answer. "There are no digital copies of those files. The safe Mr. Elysian stored them in is the best available. It survived the bomb, and we need the files."

"I'll get them myself, sir."

"You'll get the safe. I'll have it opened to retrieve the files," Ramsey corrects. He's never read the *Midnight Files*, but he knows what they are.

As one of five Head Regulators, Ramsey was privy to information most weren't. Including several orders given to Mr. Elysian's private Researchers. They were the best in their field at gathering knowledge that shouldn't exist. Their most valuable discoveries went into Mr. Elysian's infamous *Midnight Files* and were locked away until needed.

Ramsey doesn't need to know the specific content to know those files are worth more than a hundred Researchers. The time when such delicate information will make or break a leader isn't far away.

"Yes, sir," Booth says.

"The team assigned to guarding the child?" Ramsey asks.

"They sent a report fifteen minutes ago. All is quiet. Anna is safe."

Ramsey nods. "And D'Angelo?"

"No further communication since the initial call. I have two people looking into her and the alleged threats."

"Make that five people. Mrs. Elysian doesn't need any distractions." Ramsey likes Mrs. Elysian, much more than he expected to after hating her uncle for so long. But she's young and, despite the horrors she's experienced, still harbors a youthful idealism. Ramsey fears she'll ignore logic in favor of satisfying a need to protect by attempting an alliance with the rebel leader.

"Yes, sir."

"I'm relying on you to handle all of this while I focus on the bomber," Ramsey says. "Don't disappoint me."

Booth juts his chin out and nods, his hands locked behind his back. "Of course, sir."

Ramsey dismisses the boy, kicks the office door shut, and lets out a breath. His shoulders fall and his posture relaxes, allowing aches from the bombing to return. Digging his fingers into a tight knot on his upper trap, he rolls his head to one side, stretching his neck. Nearly fifteen straight hours of work and he has about the same amount of information as yesterday.

He stares at the bomb diagram again. He's looked at it so many times since receiving it yesterday that he has it memorized. It's a brilliant design. No mere rebel could've built this bomb alone. It's much too sophisticated.

The memory surfaces again, like it's compensating for years of neglect.

They were lying on an old couch, she on top and him still dragging fingers along her soft skin. He'd been lost in her. Everything about her swallowed him whole, the way nothing else ever did. He would've given anything to never leave that apartment, to explore her body and mind like it was his life's purpose.

Despite their similar pasts, their present only had space for occasional meetings. They tended to dedicate the rare moments to nothing but each other. But the Elysians, the Registration, the rebels, all of it inevitably intruded on their peace. They both hated Eric Elysian but couldn't extend the hatred to the Registration itself. It was one of the reasons he felt free with her.

"Do you ever want to leave?" she had asked, breaking the silence.

"I can't leave," he'd answered. Which was true. They both needed him there, working on Eric Elysian's security team.

"Do you ever think the rebels have the right idea?" His hand stilled against the base of her back at the question. She had never supported the rebels before. *"Not all of them. Just . . . they're doing something, you know? They're fighting. Choosing a side."*

"I have a side,." Ramsey replied. *"Yours."*

She lifted her head to look down at him. *"But we're not even together. Not really."*

Ramsey didn't say anything. She was right, and the fact was too painful to face.

"If Eric was gone . . ."

"Don't," Ramsey said. He might not have liked Mr. Elysian, but the man was his boss. Ramsey's job was to protect him.

"Remember your last visit?" she asked.

He nodded.

"Well, I've been thinking about it, and . . ."

Then she climbed off him and came back with the paper. She had taken their idle musings of a possible bomb and turned it into a real design.

"You wouldn't even be there when it went off," she said. She was smarter than people gave her credit for.

"It's too unpredictable," Ramsey said, after they imagined the possibilities of one well-placed bomb.

It *was* too unpredictable. The design was good, but neither of them were experienced bomb makers. Anyway, they weren't actually going to do anything so drastic. It was nothing more than talk. A way to let out their frustrations.

They saw each other once more before she disappeared. Ramsey hasn't seen or spoken to the woman he loved in five years. He thinks he knows why, but he never found out for certain. And he hasn't thought about their bomb since then.

Until yesterday. The bomb that destroyed Mr. Elysian's mansion was better made than their old design.

Then again, Ramsey is smarter, too. He's learned a lot in those years.

He's also lost a lot. He's not the same loyal, hopeful man he used to be.

He's a liar. A traitor. A murderer.

And before the day is over, he will find and present to Mrs. Elysian a viable suspect for the bombing.

CHAPTER 10

E ven as the Elysian heir, contacting the committee members is akin to receiving quick and productive assistance from an insurance agent. Both situations fill Lynell with frustration till her bones feel like they could pop at any second.

The first one to answer is Warner Golden, her favorite amongst the committee, and he volunteers his advice and knowledge without prompting.

"In addition to myself, Junior Booker and Robin Jacobs voted against the policy change last time," Warner says.

The call is on speaker, so Lynell has both hands free to take notes. She's sitting cross-legged on her desk, having long ago kicked off her shoes and unpinned her hair.

"You need one more to vote no, then you can cast the tiebreaker vote, but I would suggest at least two more in case someone surprises you and changes their vote."

"Are you hinting plans to back out on me, Mr. Golden?" Lynell asks in a lilting, joking tone.

"Do you have such little faith in me, Mrs. Carter?"

She laughs. "How confident are you that Junior and Robin will vote no again?" She's specifically thinking about Robin, who doesn't seem like the open-minded type.

"If I still gambled, I'd bet my committee seat on them both. Junior might not seem it, but he truly cares about the people. *All of them.*"

Lynell notes the stressor in the last three words and leans down to write *cares about all ppl-meaning?* next to Junior's name on her notes.

"You won't find anyone more loyal to the traditional ways than Robin," Warner continues. "She's voted against every possible change since I joined the committee over thirty years ago. My suggestion would be to focus on the remaining women. Verity McGowan was the least certain of her vote last time. Tilly Nguyen votes solely on logic, so if you have a strong argument, you might have a chance convincing her. Tamara Nelson will empathize with your position as a woman and as the youngest person at the table."

Lynell transcribes his words, though she doubts her chances with Tilly and Tamara. Both have strong reasons to support anything that helps immigrants.

"Thank you, Warner," she says. "This is really helpful."

"Of course, darling. Any time." He's quiet for a moment and Lynell is about to check if the call was dropped when he says, "How well did you know Zachary?"

Lynell drops her pen and straightens her spine. The question is so unexpected that she has to turn it over in her mind a few times before answering. "Well, I didn't meet him until a couple of weeks ago, when he Registered me." She hops off the desk and walks to the bookshelves built into the far wall. "It took a few days before I learned who he really was, then it wasn't until he risked his life to save Daniel and me that I started trusting him." Images of Zach standing between her and several armed men flitted across her vision.

"So, you liked him?"

Zach Registered her, kidnapped her, and tortured her. But he also saved her. More importantly, he saved Daniel and Anna. And he was her cousin.

"Yes, I liked him," she answers with full conviction. "He was a good man." Then, yearning to ease the ache of the abused part of her heart that longs for a family, she asks, "Did you know him well?"

Warner takes a shaky breath. His voice is more delicate now than when they were discussing business. "No, but we met several times. He grew more callous over the years. I worried he was becoming more like his father."

Lynell never saw Eric's cruelty or desperation for control in Zach, even in the beginning. She couldn't rationalize why Zach thoughtlessly obeyed until he explained that Eric had threatened his mother's life.

"Did you ever meet his mom?" she asks. Zach said he hadn't known his mom until five years ago, but Warner joined the committee years before Zach was born.

Warner's breath catches and his voice is thick and quiet when he says, "Not well." Then, before she can reply, he adds, "I should be going. Good luck with your meetings."

Lynell is left confused when the call abruptly ends. She stares at the phone, unreleased pressure behind her eyes and nose causing emotional vertigo.

To steady herself and set aside the odd conversation for now, she opens the committee members' binders to hunt for any helpful information before attempting to contact them again. She dives in, reading until her eyes strain. It takes four hours, but she manages to make two appointments for the following day, one with Tamara Nelson and one with Verity McGowan. She's scanning immigration laws when someone knocks on the office door.

"Come in," she calls, setting her highlighter down and looking up, catching the time on the clock as Ramsey walks in. *Seven p.m.? When did it get so late?*

"I see you managed to secure two meetings tomorrow, well done." Her eyebrows pull together, and he adds, "I have access to your calendar."

"Oh," she says. Now that her focus is broken, she feels the exhaustion settle over her like a weighted blanket. "Right."

"I can assist in preparations, if you'd like," he offers.

"Maybe in the morning. Any news? On the bomber or anything else?"

Ramsey's years of perfecting his professional attitude makes it nearly impossible to tell what he's thinking. Still, Lynell senses a moment's hesitation before he answers, "I've narrowed down the suspect list to these people." He passes her a piece of paper that has fourteen names, each with the suspect's age, vocation, and connection to Lynell. "Please let me know if any of these stand out to you, and I'll look into them more carefully."

"The bomber wasn't caught on camera?"

"Not his face. But we have an approximate height and weight, which all these men fit."

"What is it?" Lynell's eyes move from the paper to Ramsey's face.

"About five feet, nine inches and a hundred and fifty to a hundred and seventy-five pounds. His clothing made the weight difficult to determine."

She scans Ramsey's body and thinks back to his file. She read it while still in the hospital, but the memory is crisp. "That would be about your size, wouldn't it?"

"Yes, ma'am."

When he doesn't say anything else, she presses her lips together and nods. "Do we know anything else about him?"

"He's Caucasian. Street cameras gave us a potential car, but we traced it back to an eighty-year-old woman who reported it stolen six days ago. The cops put a BOLO out. No news on possible DNA results yet, but I'll let you know when there is. I'm sure we'll find the responsible party soon."

"I'm sure you will. Anything else?"

"I've confirmed that you will be officially announced as CEO next Friday during the convention. Both your father and Eric had rather large parties to mark their succession as the Elysian heir, so this convention will be a perfect event to do so. The planners are adjusting accordingly; increasing the guest list and media presence, inviting vendors to open the event, ensuring the entire affair will be live streamed for the rest of the country, and more."

"Do we have to—"

"Yes," Ramsey interrupts. "It's a notable moment in our country's history and vital that your incumbency begins with sufficient significance and credibility. Traditions such as these give countries confidence in their leaders."

She huffs but acquiesces. "Fine. What else?"

Ramsey runs through a list of reports, most of them unremarkable, before excusing himself. Lynell mulls over what she's learned while rubbing her eyes, letting her mind sift through the details. After a few minutes, her stomach urges a gear shift, and she leaves the office to hunt down Daniel for a late dinner.

She doesn't get much sleep that night and finally gives up, pulls on a pair of sweats, and quietly returns upstairs to her office. After settling into her chair and switching on a lamp in lieu of the overhead light, she studies the names on Ramsey's list and draws stars next to the ones she recognizes. She can't, however, think of a personal reason any of them would have to target her.

She sighs and sets the list aside, then dives into the stack of files waiting for her to play catch-up on years of the Registration run by her uncle. Daniel finds her several hours later, a steaming cup of coffee at her elbow while she pores over minutes from past committee meetings.

"Don't worry. If anyone can convince these people, it's you," he says, pressing a kiss to her lips. "I'm seeing an old friend of mine today. Maybe he can help."

"An old friend?"

Daniel nods. "Grant Woods. We fought together."

"He's a rebel?"

His eyes crinkle with a smile. "Don't worry, Lyn. I'll take a guard and won't meet with any other rebels without you. I'll be safe."

"If someone sees you . . ." She hates that she and Daniel have to live their life conscious of the public eye now. But if she's going to make the system work for her, then she has to play by its rules. Meaning Daniel does too. At least, in public.

"We won't be seen, promise. Besides, it's not like Grant is a famous rebel."

She wishes Daniel could stay secure and safe in their house all day, but he's her partner, and they need to work together for this life to work.

Before he leaves, Lynell stands to give him a proper kiss, each promising they'll be safe, and it takes several deep breaths after he leaves before she's ready to return to her mountain of work.

Running on coffee and last night's meal, Lynell skips breakfast, hurrying to the first meeting of the day, with Verity. And though the other woman listens to Lynell's pitch, she doesn't make any promises or seem overtly inclined to change her vote. Without time to fully dissect the conversation or drum up a detailed argument beyond simply feeling out the stern woman, Lynell heads to Tamara's office.

In the car, she sits in the back seat, silently rehearsing her pitch while one guard drives her from place to place like a chauffeur and another sits in the front, acting as her bodyguard.

Unpredictable as always, a memory surfaces, lurching Lynell to the back seat of a different car, this one holding Zach, too. She didn't know him yet, but got her first glimpse of his true nature in his visible fear that seemed to heighten the closer they got to his house.

"*Who are you?*" she'd asked.

He laughed and replied, "*The question is, who are* you?"

Over three weeks later, and she still doesn't have an answer to that question.

She pushes her cousin from her mind, and twenty minutes later, they're parking outside a gothic-style commercial building with the name "NELSON & COLLINS" on the front. Tamara purchased one of the largest publishing houses in the country a few years ago, changed the name, and moved the headquarters from New York to Dallas after accepting a chair on the Registration committee. All independent publishing houses, media conglomerates, and production companies are owned by a committee member or oligarch, whether directly or indirectly through parent companies. With religious organizations and news stations still active, the country has the illusion of free speech, but the eight committee members, seven oligarchs, and Registration owner have their hands in all the companies that might produce anti-Registration and anti-oligarch materials.

Which is why Lynell doesn't understand why there's so much negative news about her—between the sixteen of them, they should be able to control it.

Like Lynell alluded to in yesterday's committee meeting, among the sixteen of them, there shouldn't be so much negative news coverage on Lynell. Not if the committee and oligarchs didn't want such material published.

Lynell can't help but marvel at the building's architecture and interior on her way to Tamara's office. The company's success breathes through the bustling atmosphere while employees rush about the open floor plan, even on a Saturday. Covers of the publisher's bestsellers are blown up to fill the walls top to bottom, thousands of books are strategically placed on shelves and desks, and the space is naturally lit by tall domed windows. She feels a strong yearning to curl up with a good book and dive into a world that doesn't involve boardrooms, the Registration, or bombs. But she tamps it down and focuses on the task at hand.

Tamara meets Lynell at the door with a bright, purple-painted smile. "Carter, welcome to paradise."

"Thank you," Lynell says, following Tamara into her office and telling the guard to wait outside. The driver stayed in the car, probably to keep an eye on the building's perimeters.

"Would you like a cuppa?"

"That would be lovely. Black with cream if you have it."

"Of course." She orders their drinks as a young intern closes the door on his way out, giving the two women complete privacy.

"So, I assume this visit isn't about a book you'd like published?" Tamara asks. Her Australian twang makes everything she says captivating, helping to settle any nerves lingering in Lynell's empty stomach.

"I wish," Lynell mutters. "I've been reading books from this publisher my whole life."

"I did get a good one, didn't I?"

They dribble away with small talk, until the intern returns with their tea. Once they're alone again, Lynell seizes the moment to launch into her pitch, but she's hardly a few sentences in before Tamara interrupts.

"You get why I'm supporting this policy, right?"

"Of course," Lynell says, stirring a wooden stick around her tea. "But what if you can get what you want without this specific policy passing?"

"This is the first policy that gives immigrants a chance of having a Registration," Tamara says. "I'm a committee chair and have never had a Registration."

"But it doesn't have to be the last." Lynell is immensely grateful for the large oak desk between them hiding her bouncing leg. "Only adult immigrants with plenty of money to spare will benefit from this policy. We can do better. Rather than the rich gaining more power over life and death, let's give everyone the opportunity. Anyone who never had a Registration, whether because they're immigrants or because their parents couldn't or refused to buy them one, can purchase their own at any time—for the same cost."

"Tried it, failed," Tamara says.

Lynell remembers that policy, but it was before Tamara's time. "Three chairs have changed since then. It's a new committee," she says.

"Not really," Tamara answers. "Even the new members make decisions primarily based on monetary value. A policy like the one you suggested would discourage parents from buying a Registration for their children. They'd think 'Well, they can buy their own later in life.' Soon, it wouldn't be as standard to have and use a Registration. People wouldn't buy until they needed one, meaning they may never buy one at all. Fewer people would have and use Registrations. The company would make less money. Citizens would start questioning the success of such a system. Rebels would have time to corrupt minds and sway opinions before someone spends their own money on a less acceptable right of control. When people don't grow up with something from childhood, they're less likely to accept it as adults."

Lynell allows herself a moment to process Tamara's words before pushing the disappointment back. "Okay, so we pass a policy that any immigrants can buy their own when they become a citizen."

"I suggested that already." Seeing Lynell's frown, Tamara adds, "Off the record. I wanted to test the waters for hungry sharks before going swimming. It was instantly obvious the others would shut down any policy that would invite immigration without producing enough money in return."

"But this policy wouldn't invite immigration?"

"Not at the price point. The immigrants that the oligarchs want to keep out of the country won't be able to afford it."

The meeting continues with Lynell making suggestions that Tamara consistently refutes. Her untouched tea is cold by the time Tamara announces she has an appointment and stands, gesturing for the door.

"Listen, I like you, Carter," Tamara says, her hand on the doorknob. "I admire your passion. But you're fighting against rivers that have been flowing for longer than you've been alive. Be mindful of the rapids. I don't want to see ya' drown."

"Right." Her fondness of Tamara isn't enough to quell the desire to punch the next person who tells her she's too young and naive to be the Elysian heir. "I like you, too, but don't forget that I own these rivers, and I have no intention of letting half the country drown."

She leaves then, stealing the last words for a second of satisfaction, which fully evaporates by the time she's back in the car. In its place is the anxiety from that morning, now doubled in intensity. The ride seems to pass quickly, Lynell lost in thought, fighting a tickling dread that she won't win this fight. She needs allies, and she needs votes.

THE REGISTRATION REWRITTEN

She's not comfortable taking the risk of the code yet, given Zach warned her how lethally dangerous it could be. The code is her last resort. Regardless of Daniel's advocacy for using it, she simply can't.

Not yet. Not at this stage, without enough information on how it even works.

Seeing Ramsey waiting as she steps inside the house reminds her that there are several other problems, with their own swarms of anxiety, that she has to deal with.

"What is it?" she asks, draping her silk cardigan over the couch.

"I found him."

She kicks off her shoes. "Who?"

"The bomber," Ramsey explains. "I know who he is."

"Wait, really?" Her full attention snaps to him. "Who is it?"

"Thomas Johnson."

The name sounds familiar, but Lynell can't place it. It's the type of familiarity that leaves a coldness at the base of her stomach rather than a warmth through her limbs. "Was he on the list?" she asks.

Ramsey shakes his head. "He doesn't have a history of hatred toward you, your family, or the Registration. He's a local religious fanatic. You might recognize him as the man who Registered Ellery Klein six years ago."

The memory surfaces at the same moment Ramsey speaks, and the coldness turns to nausea in Lynell's gut. "The Sin-Fighting Warriors."

Ramsey nods.

"Why would he bomb Eric's house?"

"I'm still working on that. Our best men are looking for him, but he seems to have gone underground. I doubt he'll try anything else now that we know who he is."

Ramsey runs through his process of finding Johnson and their next steps, but Lynell only half listens. She knows the information is meant to put her at ease.

Knowing the enemy's identity is better than trying to protect against a ghost, after all.

But Lynell's thoughts are consumed with the fact that Thomas Johnson killed Ellery Klein, Sawyer D'Angelo's wife. The man who targeted Lynell is probably the sole person D'Angelo hates more than anyone with a Registration, including Lynell herself.

D'Angelo and Lynell now have a common enemy. Meeting with her is now pretty much a necessity.

CHAPTER 11

O ut of habit, Daniel shoves the front door shut with his shoulder, which sparks fresh pain from the gunshot wound. "Fuck me," he mutters, inhaling sharply.

"Are you okay, Mr. Carter?"

Daniel looks up at Hayes Booth standing by the car, a Maserati, by the looks.

"I thought one of the others was coming with me," Daniel says.

"Lynell requested that I take you."

Daniel rolls his eyes. Of course, in the forty minutes since he saw Lyn, she replaced a nameless guard with one she trusts. "I'll drive," Daniel says, holding out his hand. He's never been a fan of the passenger's seat.

Hayes tosses him the keys, and the two climb in, Daniel pushing the seat back to adjust for his height.

They're both silent during the drive, and as he's parking, Daniel says, "You can stay in the car."

"Lynell said I should come with you."

"Fine, but you're not coming into the apartment."

"I should check it first for—"

"Look, I appreciate your obedience to my wife, but Grant is a friend, and I'll be fine. I don't want him to know I come with a bodyguard now, so, please, just . . . stay out of sight."

Hayes reluctantly agrees and falls several feet behind Daniel. It's a small complex, built several decades ago and refurbished to look nicer without actually *being* nicer. Grant's apartment is behind the pitiful excuse for a dog park, on the third floor, which Daniel assumes he got to appease his worry-prone mother.

With Hayes several doors down, Daniel knocks using their old pattern, waits five seconds, and does it again.

"Jesus, dude!" comes a shout from the other side of the door. "Patience!"

Daniel knocks again, solely to annoy his friend.

The door swings inward before the pattern is finished, leaving Daniel's fist hovering in the air.

"You're early," Grant says.

"You look like shit," Daniel replies. Grant is wearing torn jeans and a stained tank top, and his once-thick mane of copper-tinged blonde hair is a short, shaggy mess.

"Not all of us came into a billion dollars recently," he grumbles. Then he smiles wide and Daniel follows suit, pulling Grant into a hug.

"Now, let's get in there. I have some questions."

"Didn't anyone tell you faster isn't always better?"

"No one ever had to." Daniel winks. "Besides, I'm on a deadline."

"Oooh, big important guy with the fancy wife has deadlines now," Grant teases, dropping onto the center of what looks like a new couch.

Daniel takes in the space and is slightly surprised to see nearly all new furniture. Six years ago, everything was secondhand. "Why haven't you moved?"

"I did, briefly. Then I came back," Grant answers.

If Daniel had been lying about the deadline, he might've asked for the obvious story behind Grant's answer. But he hadn't, and he has a wife and child to protect, so he asks, "How secure are you in the Resurrection?"

"I mean, I've been with them since it was formed. I'm not on the board of directors or anything, but they know they can trust me."

"Even Sawyer D'Angelo?" Daniel asks, sitting in the chair opposite Grant.

"Dan, what's going on? We haven't spoken in years, and you suddenly call and ask to meet, and now you're poking for information on my boss?"

"Not poking. Asking questions."

Grant crosses his arms, displaying a new tattoo on his tricep. "Ms. D'Angelo is protective of her privacy and careful about who she confides in."

Daniel's not surprised. He saw plenty of Ellery Klein back in the day, but Sawyer avoided the spotlight until she started the Resurrection.

"Speaking of, do you know what the Resurrection is up to? Have you . . . heard anything about Lynell?"

"Dan, you're asking a dedicated rebel to give the husband of the Elysian heir information on the Resurrection's plans? Really? I thought you were smarter than that."

"She's my wife, Grant."

"She's Eric Elysian's niece. Don't think I forgot who you used to be. You hated Eric Elysian more than anything."

"She didn't know he was her uncle until two weeks ago," says Daniel. "She's innocent in all of this." The low-burn heat in his gut hints that he might not believe his own words, but Daniel extinguishes it. Lynell might not be innocent, yet she isn't responsible for what her family has done to this country. "Look, I'm not asking you to betray the Resurrection. I just want to protect my wife. And to possibly help D'Angelo."

"Help her? What do you mean? What's going on?"

Daniel rubs his forehead and manages to hold in a groan. Scraping through his mind, he finally says, "I'm trying to find a way to get Lynell out of the position she's in. She's not an Elysian. Biologically, sure. But that's not *who* she is. Neither one of us will ever be safe or happy if she's forced to become a true Elysian."

Grant is quiet for too long. Daniel is about to start panicking when Grant finally says, "Fine. I don't have a lot of information for you, but my ex might. Drea's on the Resurrection board of directors."

"Drea Chapman? You dated her?"

Grant laughs. "Don't act so surprised. Your boy has game."

Daniel smiles and lets out a heavy breath, his chest relaxing. "If you had game, would she have broken up with you?"

Grant gives a mock gasp of offense. "What makes you assume *she* broke up with *me*?"

Dropping the smile and raising an eyebrow, Daniel gives Grant an unamused glare.

"Okay, yeah. She broke up with me. But it ended on good terms. She wants kids, and I . . ."

The calm atmosphere between them shatters. Daniel leans forward and squeezes Grant's knee once. "I'm sorry, man."

"Yeah."

Grant once had a wife and a son. But some psychopath Registered his son and kidnapped him. Took the kid straight out of school. They found the body two weeks later, a few hours shy of the end of the Registration period. It was clear that the last two weeks of the boy's life had been hell on earth. But because he'd been Registered, the man who killed him could only be charged with rape, not murder or kidnapping or anything else that he deserved to go to jail for. Worse still, there wasn't enough evidence to convict the guy.

The next quarter, Grant's wife Registered and killed the man who tortured and murdered their son. Then she killed herself.

Grant decided never to have another child. The experience broke him.

"Anyway," Grant says, a thickness hinting to unshed tears in the word. He clears his throat as if to break up the emotion. "Drea and I are still friends. I'll see if there's anything she can tell me, but no promises. The Resurrection is a lot more organized than we were back in the day. The board doesn't share secrets or plans willy-nilly with any rebel that comes asking."

"Anything could help." Then, before he forgets or decides it's a bad idea to ask, Daniel adds, "Have there been any threats to the Resurrection recently? Or specifically to D'Angelo?"

"We're chronically threatened. You should know that, living in the lion's den."

Daniel's toes press hard against the ground, relieving some vexation. "Someone aside from the typical Registration loyalists. Like, a new person hanging around or anyone trying to take her place?"

The tip of Grant's tongue peaks between his teeth as he thinks, a habit Daniel recognizes from when he met him nine years ago. "How new? We've had an upswing of recruits in the last six months, and a new board member recently joined." A short pause, then his eyes lift and he adds, "I heard my guys discussing Bruce Macgill, the oligarch? Apparently, he's been going to church, one primarily for anti-Registration folks, including Ms. D'Angelo's great-uncle. Macgill was asking about Ms. D'Angelo and her family. Nothing overtly weird, just how they all are. If he wasn't a selfish, rich, Registration-supporting oligarch asshole, I'd think he's being nice."

"But he is a selfish, rich, Registration-supporting oligarch asshole," Daniel says.

"Exactly. So his niceness is probably ill-intentioned. But he hasn't done anything to suggest he hates Ms. D'Angelo or the Resurrection more than anyone who profits off the Registration would."

Daniel nods. "Okay. Thanks, man."

"No problem. Let me know if I can do anything else."

"Thank you."

Likely hearing the disconnect in Daniel's voice, Grant says, "I'm serious. I miss you, Dan. A bunch of us do. If you ever want to relive your rebel days, we'd be happy to welcome you into the Resurrection. Even if you are married to an Elysian."

Daniel smiles slightly. "Sure. Thanks again."

He leaves, any warm nostalgia lost in the intense heat of his love for Lynell.

Once home, Daniel calls Fenn Vaughn, Anna's social worker, and their family lawyer to prepare for a possible custody battle. He wants to reach out to Catherine, Zoe's younger sister, since Anna is staying with her until custody is decided, but everyone advised him against it. All he can do is try to prepare for the custody battle, which he does for several hours before taking a break to go on a bike ride. He's pleased—but not surprised—that his personal bike was brought here from his old apartment.

He rides until the sun begins setting, then heads back. Still in tight running shorts, with sweat soaking his thick waves of dark hair, Daniel heads inside. His cleats clack on the wooden floor all the way to the bedroom, where Lynell is pacing back and forth, a fingernail between her teeth and hair bun falling apart.

Daniel steps in front of her and curls his hands around her chin and the back of her neck. "Lyn, baby. Breathe."

But she's not hyperventilating, and her pupils aren't blown. She doesn't seem lost in a panic attack. He drops his hands and steps back to give her space.

This is one of the most difficult things about being Lynell's husband, but it's also one of his favorites. A husband unwilling to learn the intricacies and various supportive needs of his partner isn't a man, he's a leech.

Lyn isn't a simple video game where learning the correct sequence guarantees a win every time. No, she is a myriad of activities. Her trauma and anxiety are a tight dance between two partners. She needs him close, his skin against hers and his movements gently leading her. It's a chess match, her devious and reckless curiosity that likes to jump before looking over the edge to see what would happen. He reacts to her plays while looking several steps forward, because someone needs to be there with anti-itch cream or a bungee cord. Her simple childlike joy is a paint by numbers canvas, where the directions are there but neither she nor Daniel have any plans of following them. Art, after all, is in the eye of the beholder.

This element is mostly in her head. The scheming brilliance that always sees the path to success is a tall cliffside, perfect for rock climbing. Without her other aspects, this could warp her into a more selfish, inconsiderate tyrant than Eric, because she'd have the wisdom, strength, and tenacity to be unstoppable. But she's more than one thing, she isn't alone, and Daniel knows his role here, too.

Step back, watch her climb, and be ready to catch her or pull her back down.

"What happened?" Daniel asks.

"Not much with Tamara or Verity but, Danny, he found him. Ramsey found the bomber." Her smile is so at odds with her words and tone that he wonders if she's already climbed too far.

"Who is it?"

"Thomas Johnson. The Sin-Fighting Warriors. It's him. Or them."

Her energy is difficult to match because he doesn't know its source. She's not happy, but the news still inflates her with eagerness. "Okay . . . Did they catch him?"

Her smile falls. "No, but don't you get it? Johnson killed Ellery Klein out of some perverse justice because he disagreed with her life and values. Name me a more obvious suspect for who could be threatening D'Angelo?"

He realizes it's not joy or eagerness she's feeling. Its justification and motivation. Because they know now that D'Angelo and Lyn can help each other. "You think he's the person also threatening her."

"Don't you?" Lyn asks.

Before he gets the opportunity to answer, someone knocks at the door. They both turn to see Ramsey step through, his jaw tight and his knuckles nearly white from gripping his phone.

Instantly, Daniel's entire body goes into alert, his bones recognizing the danger before his brain can register the events unfolding.

"What happened?" Lyn asks.

Ramsey's expression isn't instantly recognizable, probably because Daniel's never seen the emotion on his face.

Fear.

"It's Anna," Ramsey says.

The shrill roar of a hurricane's center fills Daniel's ears. He's enveloped in a cold darkness, like he fell into his own shadow.

"She's gone."

CHAPTER 12

T error replaces the air in Lynell's lungs. Her heart thuds so hard that she feels the pulse in her fingertips.

"All the guards on duty are being questioned. There are signs of a struggle but no blood. No one died as far as we can tell. They took Catherine, too, which is a good sign," Ramsey says, referring to Zoe Raines's younger sister and Anna's adoptive aunt. "They'll want someone to take care of Anna. Like how Eric took Zoe and Anna."

His words unearth the buried image in Lynell's mind. Eric aiming a gun at Zoe, pulling the trigger. Anna sitting next to Zoe's corpse, crying.

"Maybe you'd like to see how it feels to have a child taken from this world in front of your face."

She can't breathe. Her lungs bow under the weight of horror. The words impale her eardrums and chain her to the spot, unable to think clearly or feel anything but molten dread.

"I pulled everyone who is not assigned to your protection," Ramsey gestures to Lynell and Daniel, "to help find Anna."

"Fuck my protection," Danny says. "Put those guys on this too. Put everyone on it. *Find* my daughter!"

"That could be playing into their hands," Ramsey says.

"I don't give a shit!" Daniel yells.

"You don't care if they go after your wife next?" Ramsey's voice is maddeningly calm. It's like he thrives when everyone around him is panicking. "They likely want your protection lessened so they can go after Mrs. Elysian next."

Daniel seethes but doesn't respond. Lynell can practically feel the radiant heat of his anger and fear.

"They won't hurt Anna."

"How the fuck do you know?" Daniel demands.

Dimly, Lynell thinks this is the most she's heard him cuss in such a short time. Even on the day she left him and he thought she was going to end the pregnancy, he hadn't cussed once. He didn't need to. His words were still effective. *"If you leave, leave. Stay gone. Don't come back,"* he'd said.

"Because she won't be useful to them dead," Ramsey says.

"Useful?" Daniel repeats. "She's our daughter, not a fucking tool!"

"The moment she's no longer valuable, they'll get rid of her. You don't want that."

"Who are *they*? Who took her?"

"I don't know, but—"

"Then find out!" Daniel interrupts.

"I will, sir," Ramsey says, his own volume not wavering. "I promise, this is our top priority."

"How did they even take her in the first place? I thought you had her protected!" Daniel's voice rises in volume with each word. Lynell flinches away from him, a decades-old survival instinct triggering her desire to run. To hide. Her stepfather's verbal and physical abuse has done that to her.

The tears she's denying are drops of burning rain and any second she's going to combust. She has an emotional fever and, out of self-preservation, her body lowers its internal temperature until ice walls form in her chest.

"She was. They got past security somehow and the guard inside had been drugged. They're all being questioned extensively."

"When did this happen? How long has she been gone?"

"The last check-in was at six this afternoon when the guards changed shifts, so it must've been sometime after that."

"That was over three fucking hours ago!" Daniel shouts.

"I know, sir. But the man stationed in the house only checks in every three hours. When the team didn't hear from him, they searched the house and found him passed out. They reported it immediately. We're working as fast as we can."

"Where is Thomas Johnson in all of this?" Daniel's volume falls, but the demanding, ferocious, distressed tone remains.

"We're looking for him."

"You mean you don't know where he is? Do you know anything?"

"I know this is scary, but I promise—"

"Your promises mean shit!" Daniel interrupts. "You were supposed to protect Lynell and she almost died in the explosion. You were supposed to protect Anna and she was kidnapped. You were supposed to find Johnson and he's still out there, free to kill again!"

"I know, I'm sorry."

"Fuck your apologies! If my daughter is hurt, I swear on the bones of everyone ever Registered, I will kill you, Ramsey Davenport."

The voice sounds nothing like Daniel. Lynell has never heard it before. This man isn't her husband—he's a survivor born from the misery of war and fury of a father's worst nightmare.

"I understand. But I'll need your help. You need to calm down."

"Calm down?" Daniel's body jerks like he's going to attack Ramsey, and Lynell reaches out and folds her fingers over his wrist. Her consciousness returns to the present moment, like a helical spring meeting in a tight spiral.

"He's right, Danny." He looks toward her, but she has the impression he's not seeing her. He's seeing nothing but his own bright fear. "We're no help if we break down." She keeps her hand on Daniel and turns her attention to Ramsey. "What can we do?"

Ramsey's chin dips in an imitation of a nod. "You need to continue as if nothing is wrong. A public reaction will only force them to escalate their plans."

"Continue as if nothing is wrong?" Daniel says. "Shouldn't we send out an Amber Alert or make a public plea for her return?"

Ramsey shakes his head. "This isn't a typical kidnapping. We've searched the area around the house and sent teams to search any place connected to Catherine and Anna, such as family and friends' homes, questioning everyone who knows them. We're watching Catherine's bank accounts for suspicious activity and surveilling all suspects, especially major rebels."

"What about Registration people?" Lynell asks. Whatever flimsy ice surrounds her emotions now shudders against the pressure of her fear. She can't afford for the ice to break, though, not with her daughter's life on the line.

"Who do you mean?"

"Employees who hate me, committee members who distrust me, the oligarchs, even," Lynell says. "Let's be real, everyone is a suspect. I'm not the country's favorite person right now."

"Everyone on payroll will be questioned, but we have to be careful not to alienate those in power," Ramsey says.

"I don't care about that now. Turn me into the greenest, most tentacled alien out there and check the committee and oligarchs." An internal tremor sends a crack spiderwebbing across the icy walls.

"Yes, ma'am. But I strongly suggest that you don't show outward suspicion to anyone. Pretend like you know nothing until the kidnappers reach out."

"What makes you think they ever will?" Lynell asks.

"What other reason would they have for taking Anna? You're the most powerful person in the country right now, and your daughter is the perfect bargaining chip. Your enemies will think that whoever has Anna controls you. I urge you not to let that be the case."

"She's our daughter," Daniel says. "We'd do anything for her."

Ramsey's lips straighten into a grim line. "I'm afraid they're counting on that. Mrs. Elysian, the best thing you can do for Anna right now is nothing. Keep doing your job. Focus on the vote and convention on Friday. Leave the rescuing up to me."

"How am I supposed to read memos and have meetings like nothing is wrong, knowing my child's life is in danger?" Lynell asks. The heat surging through her veins reaches her eyes. But she can't cry. If she starts, she's not confident she'll ever have the strength to stop.

"By remembering that the best people are working to save her, and she needs you to make the world safe for her return."

If Ramsey could say anything to convince her, it was that. Remembering the policy change and the destruction it would cause recenters her. If this law goes through on Friday and the convention goes smoothly, then Anna would be saved only to live in a world that treats human life as little more than a paycheck. Right now, the Registration is a gift largely used with good intentions. But this vote will turn it into a tool for destructively selfish intent.

Sure, as the Elysian heir, Anna is safer than the average child. It'll be illegal to Register her. But what kind of lesson will that teach her? Lynell can't let Anna see her mother as a complicit cog in a murder machine, all for the sake of control.

Nevertheless, agreeing to Ramsey's plan cuts off a layer of Lynell's self-respect. She's lived a life of abuse, pain, loss, fear, guilt, and torture, but this is the hardest thing she's ever had to do.

She nods. "Okay."

The look Daniel gives her pierces her heart. "You're kidding?"

Her throat burns but her eyes stay miraculously dry. "Just because I have to play a game of normalcy, doesn't mean you have to, Danny."

The moment he understands is clear in the raising of his brows and parting of his lips.

"I might be restrained by the rules, but you're not. There are no laws, morals, or expectations that apply to you saving our daughter."

He seems to struggle momentarily with the implications of that—of possibly sacrificing his ethics to find Anna—before he nods.

Lynell imagines a future where her kind-hearted, blameless husband learns there is nothing more noble than sacrificing your own soul for the life of someone you love. She'll let that happen if it comes to it. But she hopes it won't. If she can save both Daniel's soul and Anna's life, she will.

She will become the villain, to let her husband remain the hero he was born to be.

CHAPTER **13**

"**Y**ou're welcome to join the interrogations, but let me ask the questions," Ramsey says, from the closet doorway where he followed Carter. Mrs. Elysian has locked herself in the office upstairs to work, but her husband is a wild card who could ruin everything.

He watches Carter pull a small box from behind his shoe rack. For a moment, Ramsey is confused. Then he realizes it's a small safe gun case that Carter must have hidden there as soon as they moved into the house.

"I'm not asking you to do nothing, just not to do anything drastic," Ramsey says.

"Why?" Carter asks without turning around.

"Because I'm trained for this, you're not. I have this under control."

"You're not her father. I am."

The gun case now open, Carter pulls out two weapons and several rounds of ammunition. Ramsey has to bite his tongue to keep from calling the man a reckless idiot. He clearly thinks that his short time fighting in that pathetic rebel army, eight years ago, makes him qualified to take on these kidnappers.

But he has no idea.

"Which means I think logically and am not guided by blind emotion," Ramsey says. "You getting arrested or killed won't help anything."

"I won't be killed, and I'm sure you have the resources to get me out of jail if it comes to that. Laws don't apply to the rich, do they?"

"That's not the point, Mr. Carter. Image matters now." Ramsey is amazed with his own ability to keep the irritation from his voice.

"Yeah, I know," Carter mutters, checking the gun barrels.

"What do you expect to find that my best men haven't in the last twelve hours?" He knows that neither Carter nor Mrs. Elysian slept last night. They most likely spent the time restless and panicked, coming up with some inane plan to save Anna on their own. They're used to facing crises alone, and that type of solitary attitude doesn't change overnight.

Carter finishes loading the guns before he answers. "I know how to keep a low profile," he says, standing and tucking away the guns. "Don't worry about me. Do your job and find my daughter before I have to do something drastic."

Ramsey steps to the side, allowing Carter to walk past him to the bedroom. He's tying the laces of his shoes when Ramsey asks, "What are you planning to do?"

"Protect my family," Carter says, then storms from the room, down the hall, and out the front door.

Ramsey shakes his head and opens his phone, calling Jeremy. The guard was probably the closest to Zachary, and his loyalty switched with ease from him to Mrs. Elysian.

"Yes, sir?" Jeremy answers.

"I need you to follow Daniel Carter from a distance. Keep an eye on him at all times, but don't let him see you unless he's about to do something stupid or dangerous."

"Where is he now?"

"Probably going to do something stupid or dangerous," he says. "He took the Rover. Air tag number eleven." All the Elysian vehicles are tagged with trackers, so Jeremy should have a live map of Carter's location.

"Got it. I'll keep you updated."

Ramsey hangs up and puts the husband from his mind so he can focus on the daughter. He needs to find her soon so Mrs. Elysian can focus on the convention. What was supposed to be a two-hour event with a thousand guests, one speech, and the policy change announcement has officially turned into a full day event with thirty thousand guests, vendors, keynote speakers, a dinner, and the official announcements of the policy change and Mrs. Elysian's succession as Registration heir.

The country's best event planners are working overtime to get everything ready before Friday, but Ramsey has personally taken control over increasing the convention's security. He wants the best at every entrance, trailing Mrs. Elysian, and keeping out threats like the rebels.

Unfortunately, he can't fully dedicate himself to the convention until Anna is saved. The fact that his men have yet to find Anna or Thomas Johnson is outrageous. Eric Elysian would've already killed someone as an example of his displeasure for the lack of results. His niece is a completely different person, though, and wouldn't appreciate such measures.

She probably wouldn't like blackmail or threats, either, but the moment Anna is back, she won't care what Ramsey did to make it happen. And she doesn't know about the *Midnight Files* locked away in Eric's industrial-grade safe currently sitting in Ramsey's garage.

Ramsey leaves through the back door and takes his personal motorcycle, which isn't tagged, to the crumbling ruins that used to be Eric's home. He leaves his bike between a thicket of trees deep in the backyard and lifts his hood before walking to the trapdoor a few feet away.

For someone who spent several days locked in Eric's dungeons, it's shocking to Ramsey that Mrs. Elysian hasn't considered that that part of the house may have survived the bomb. It was, after all, underground, built of sturdy concrete, and several times reinforced. Large portions of it aren't even directly under the house, such as the tunnels Ramsey climbs into now.

He turns on his flashlight and walks the path he memorized years ago. Eric often assigned him to the dungeons, both before and after his promotion to Head Regulator. The cells were typically for Eric's enemies, or people he said, 'needed motivation to do the right thing.'

One of Mrs. Elysian's first orders after she woke up from surgery, nearly two weeks ago, was to let anyone in the dungeons free. Ramsey obeyed. Of course, he obeyed. But it seemed a shame to waste all that space.

Now, every cell is occupied not with Eric's enemies but his supporters. Regulators, Researchers, and employees who tried quitting after Eric's death. Not everyone who abandoned their post—Ramsey understands their desire to be free of the Elysian name—only those who were so loyal to Eric that they refused to work for his killer, even if she is his niece.

Mrs. Elysian disagreed with Ramsey and Booth's idea to imprison Eric's supporters, but she was high from the medication and not thinking clearly. She didn't realize how dangerous letting them go would be.

He stops in front of a Regulator standing at the entrance to the dungeons. "Any developments?"

"Prisoner three hasn't eaten his last five meals," Kenneth says.

Ramsey assigns three at a time to the dungeons, one he trusts and two who might need a reminder about what happens to disloyal employees. Kenneth is the former.

"Sick or defiant?"

"Defiant, I think," Kenneth says.

Ramsey considers the problem. He's not a murderer, but he's also not going to force his enemy not to starve himself.

"Continue giving him meals. It's his prerogative whether he eats or not. If you begin to suspect there's a problem outside of insolence, call me and we'll arrange medical attention."

Kenneth nods. "Yes, sir."

"Keep me updated," Ramsey says. "Now, I have some business to discuss with prisoner seven." He opens the door and steps into the dungeons. He ignores the scattered yells, insults, and threats as he walks through the halls. They're thinning out, more prisoners losing hope with each passing day.

He stops in front of the cell where Mrs. Elysian was kept, chained naked to a bed, enduring torture.

"Morning, Reggie," he says, looking through the bars on the door.

Sitting curled in the corner of the room, Reggie doesn't look the least bit intimidating anymore. Nose crinkling at the smell of shit and piss, Ramsey thinks it might be time to have someone come clean out the buckets.

Reggie looks up at Ramsey's voice. His eyes are red, and he sneers. "What the fuck do you want?" He used to rage, slam his fists against the door, and swear vengeance. But he's breaking.

"Turns out, you might actually be of some use to me," Ramsey says.

"Fuck off."

"I need every one of Eric's passwords, and I know you know them." The safe is password protected and Ramsey already tried every password he's familiar with, plus the passwords two other Head Regulators and the Head Researcher knew. None of them worked.

This prisoner is his last chance before trying brute force. Reggie wasn't a Regulator or Researcher, but he was one of Eric's most trusted employees. He was the best at torturing information out of people. He might be crazy with bloodlust, but Ramsey can't think of anyone else Eric would've trusted with such important information.

"Suck my dick."

Ramsey sighs and shakes his head. "You know what comes next, Reggie. You've been through this dozens of times." The difference is Reggie is now the victim, not the torturer.

Ramsey grabs the small cage hanging on the hook next to the cell door and holds it up for Reggie to see. For the first time, Reggie truly reacts. He gasps and sits up, pupils blown.

"Did you miss your old friend?" Ramsey asks, looking in disgust at the squeaking rat in the cage. It's even more malnourished than it was when Reggie kept it as a pet. "Because Arnold missed you."

CHAPTER 14

T J once believed death was a last resort, something drastic that needed careful handling. He might hate someone and believe they were irredeemable, but God was infinitely bigger, and could turn any life around.

He'd been an ignorant coward. Thankfully, he met the Elders, and they helped open his eyes to the truth: God chose TJ. If believers are God's hands and feet, then they must be willing to act in His stead. TJ has to be willing and able to carry out justice through death. If violence and death wasn't sometimes necessary for God's plans, then why would he have given us the Registration? That's a logic TJ can work with.

The first step was joining the Sin-Fighting Warriors and proving their loyalty by Registering those false prophets intent on leading the country to evil. Then, the real work began.

TJ is honored to be a part of such an important change in this country. Every life he takes brings the whole country closer to the promised paradise the Elders are envisioning.

That's what he's thinking about, while drawing the knife along the man's throat. The hot blood, spurting free and sliding over his hand, is a physical reminder of the good he's doing.

He drops the man, now gurgling and choking on his own blood.

"Should've chosen the right side," TJ says, looking down at what is now a corpse. Moments like this test TJ's faith, because this man didn't have to die. If he'd never sold himself to the Elysians, then he never would've been watching this house and wouldn't have died when he discovered TJ.

Squatting, he wipes the knife on the guard's shirt and watches the flow of blood slow now that the heart isn't beating. He sighs, reminds himself of the Elders' promises, and stands to properly clean his knife and hands. Then he calls Elder Finnegan Reese.

"What is it?" Reese asks when the call connects.

"One of their Regulators found me."

The Elder groans.

"I'm sorry," TJ says, though it wasn't his fault.

"How did he find you?"

"He was monitoring Sawyer D'Angelo's home and saw me arrive. I've already dispatched him."

"Why were you at the rebel's house?" Reese asks.

"I was going to leave another message, per Elder—"

"Stop! No names on an open line," Reese interrupts. Then, in a mutter to himself, "Fuck, won't he just give it a rest?" He sighs. "Alright, I'll talk to him, but for now, get rid of the body so no one finds it."

"Yes, sir."

"We'll need to move the child."

TJ knows Elder Reese is thinking out loud, but asks, "Why? No one saw me drop them off yesterday."

"What do you think Carter's team is going to think, when the guard assigned to the rebel goes missing? They'll assume they were killed for seeing something they shouldn't. Then they'll focus their search on anywhere and anyone remotely connected to the rebels."

TJ frowns. "But, the child isn't with the rebels."

"Use your head!" Reese says. Even from a distance, his disappointment and frustration make TJ flinch. "Who technically owns the house?"

And TJ understands. The house is listed under a rebel's name. If Elysian's people decide to search every property connected to a prominent rebel, then they'll eventually find Catherine and Anna.

"Would you like me to go collect them?"

Reese shakes his head. "No, I'll handle that. I need you to make the ransom demand."

"Now?" TJ asks. The Elders had told him not to give the ransom until Monday afternoon, after the Elysian bitch had plenty of time to become desperate. Also, the Eldress was going to take advantage of that desperation to fully befriend Lynell, something she's uniquely qualified to do as the only female Elder.

"Yes, now!" Reese shouts. "It'll throw them off the rebel trail."

Of course, TJ thinks. He's always considered himself a smart man, but the Elders' wisdom keeps him humble. "Yes, sir."

"Make it fast, then lie low before they can trace the call," Reese says.

TJ knows what to do. He's gone over the plan dozens of times: Kidnap Anna and Catherine without being seen or killing anyone. Drop them off at the secure lake house where the Eldress was waiting. Set believable false trails for Davenport. Wait forty-eight hours, then use the encrypted phone to deliver the ransom. Destroy the phone and return to the lake house to help guard the child.

The D'Angelo detour screwed everything up. The fucking guard whose blood is now dripping off the back porch onto the grass below ruined the plan. Anger fills TJ, dulling any lingering pre-Elder inhibitions that'd make the imperative next steps difficult.

"Yes, sir," TJ says, before hanging up the phone. Then he retrieves a tarp from his truck, wraps up the body, and stuffs it in the back seat. He scrubs Sawyer D'Angelo's back porch until there's no hint of blood and departs without leaving any notes, peonies, or photos. There's no time for such theatrics.

He has a body to cut apart, and a ransom demand to make.

CHAPTER 15

There's more blood than Sawyer expected. The majority puddles in and around the toilet, painting white porcelain light red. But the walls of the stall have clouded streaks, and fat drops trail along the light blue ceramic tile floor toward the counter. Despite a constant flow of water from the tap, pinkish blood residue still surrounds the sink.

In the horrific bathroom scene, Sawyer's focus is glued to the spot a few inches to the right of the sink. Amongst the surrounding blood, spanning no more than seven inches, is a clearly defined handprint.

Her stomach lurches with the need to vomit.

Blood has never bothered her, but she's also never seen quite this much in one place up close. Only in photos and videos.

All breath leaves her body at the horror of whatever injury could cause so much blood loss. If she's not careful, a desert storm of fear and grief will ravage her mind.

". . . four students that are absent," Phoebe says, having finished a sentence that Sawyer didn't realize she'd started.

Sawyer blinks and manages to rip her gaze away from the countertop, so she can look at the school's principal. "What?"

Phoebe frowns, causing the ever-present wrinkles in her forehead to deepen further. "We don't know which girl did this," she repeats. "We're offering individual counseling, but we can't enforce it without parental approval. And law enforcement could run this for DNA, but unless the girl is in the system or has a close relative in the system, it's unlikely they'll find a match."

"I hope they don't," Sawyer says. "This girl needs support and medical attention, not criminal investigation."

The uniformed officer standing with his back to the door looks at her with vivid disagreement in his eyes. Thankfully, he doesn't respond.

"I don't know why she thought this was her only option," Phoebe says, her voice thick with unshed tears. The woman is several decades older than Sawyer, and her age shows in wiry gray hair and a slight tremor in her hands. She's been claiming she'll retire soon for the last four years, but Phoebe will likely die before relinquishing her office to a new principal. "We could have helped her."

"She was probably scared," Sawyer says, trying not to envision what must have been going through the poor girl's mind while she was in that bathroom stall, hurting herself in such a horrific way.

Phoebe shakes her head, causing loose skin under her chin to swing back and forth. "Why would she be scared?" Then, with a degree of pride, she adds, "We don't kick girls out for getting pregnant, and we work with several organizations that help girls in trouble."

Sawyer presses her lips together, thinking that, whether the boarding school would expel her or not, a pregnant teenage girl is unlikely to ask for help from an administrator of an all-female Catholic school. Especially if she wanted to end the pregnancy. Any organization Phoebe would direct the girl to would suggest adoption, not help her find a safe way to abort the fetus.

"A few more photos and we'll be good," Sawyer says, struggling with every second to keep from puking.

Lawrence, the Resurrection's media expert, nods once and angles his camera toward the handprint on the countertop. The cops have already taken dozens of photos of the crime scene, but they won't share with the Res-urrection. Showing people the devastation caused by the country's legal sys-tem is one of the best ways to sway others to their cause. They don't typically manage photos of anything other than publicly completed Registrations, but it's important to show that the Registration causes pain and death outside of the legal murders. Like forcing teenage girls, that don't have the privilege of a Registration, to take drastic measures to end an unwanted pregnancy.

"That's enough," the uniform says, holding his hand out to stop Law-rence from taking more photos. "You've had your five minutes."

Sawyer doesn't protest as they're led from the bathroom. Getting even five minutes was more than they could've hoped for. The only reason they knew about the back-alley abortion was because Phoebe called Sawyer right after hanging up with the police. If it weren't for her, this story would have been taken by some pro-Registration media company. Now, they have full control over how to present it to the public.

Sawyer's stomach spins at the thought. This is the part she hates most about her job. Using someone else's suffering to make a point. Unfortunate-ly, tragedies turn into opportunities when you're fighting a war.

And that's what they're doing. Fighting a war.

"Thank you for calling me, Phoebe," Sawyer says as the bathroom door slowly shuts behind them.

"Of course. I didn't want someone using this as some sort of justifica-tion for the Registration." The disgust in Phoebe's words is almost tangible.

"They probably still will," Sawyer says, already envisioning the head-lines. They'll say that this is what happens when people don't have a Regis-tration to use. It'll be assumed that the girl is a part of some devout religious family that refuses to purchase Registrations for their children because it happened at a Catholic boarding school. They'll use this as a perfect exam-ple of what the Registration was created to help avoid.

Sawyer doesn't like to admit it, but she understands that justification. She also knows there are ways to avoid these situations that aren't the Reg-istration.

And she knows anyone can use this to convince people their side is right, and the other is to blame.

"I know," Phoebe says. "But at least this way, we'll be first."

Sawyer nods, hearing Ellery's voice in her head stressing the importance of controlling the narrative. *"It's all about perception,"* Ellery would have said. *"A compelling story will always go further than a boring truth."*

"This is going to terrify the students," Phoebe says, leading the way down the hall. As judgmental as the older woman can be, no one cares more about these students than Phoebe. She shakes her head again, and Sawyer has a mental image of a turkey puffing up its feathers, wattle swinging under its beak. "They already deal with more travesty than any child should have to."

Keeping her strides short so she can walk by the principal's side, Sawyer nods and gives wordless hums or grunts in response as Phoebe continues about everyone who has died so far that year, whether they were Registered or not.

By the time they reach the offices on the first floor, Sawyer is exhausted from listening to Phoebe talk. She knows that the principal's husband wears hearing aids and suddenly wonders if he ever turns them off to keep from hearing her talk anymore.

The idea nearly makes her laugh.

"Well," Sawyer says when Phoebe stops talking to take a breath. "I need to get going, but please let me know if you learn anything else."

"Yes, of course I will. Hey, I was thinking that it might help the students to hear from someone outside the school. An expert."

Brows furrowing, Sawyer asks, "An expert in what?"

"You know," Phoebe gestures forward, as if to encapsulate the entire school. "All of this."

"You mean an expert in living in a world with the Registration?" Sawyer asks. "I don't think such a person exists."

"They need to hear from someone outside of the staff that they have options other than hurting themselves or accepting the system."

"Oh." Sawyer lifts her chin in acknowledgement. "You want someone to come give the students a 'The Registration is evil and you should join the Resurrection' speech?"

"I wouldn't dream of telling children to join a dangerous rebellion. But it couldn't hurt to remind them there is a better, safer way to deal with things."

"I'll see what I can do," Sawyer says.

"Thank you."

Sawyer has to lean down to give Phoebe a hug before turning to leave. The moment she's free of the school, her gut roils and she barely reaches a trashcan before vomit pushes up her throat. She heaves until there's nothing left in her stomach. Abs sore and forehead sweating, Sawyer wipes her mouth with the back of her hand and heads to her car. She fishes a water bottle from the back seat and swishes and spits several times until her mouth feels clean enough to drink.

Once home, she wastes no time getting into the shower. Scalding water hitting her back, she realizes she hasn't felt clean in years. She doesn't think she'll ever feel clean again.

CHAPTER **16**

○——————————————————————○

DANIEL

Sunday Late Morning

Daniel calls and messages everyone he can think of, but gets nowhere. He even considers Alan had something to do with Anna's disappearance, but Lynell's abusive stepfather is currently in jail in Mississippi, having gone on a bender after Daniel and Lynell gave him a car in exchange for using his house as shelter when running from Eric a few weeks ago.

Since apparently Thomas Johnson is a ghost, Daniel decides to track down the other Sin-Fighting Warriors.

Of the seven who weren't Registered, five live in other states and couldn't have taken Anna, and one swore his innocence. Daniel believes him, mostly because he seems to have turned over a new leaf after joining a more accepting church three years ago.

He's since spent much of his time volunteering at a center for homeless LGBT youth.

The last lives two hours away, and Daniel is about to drive there when Lynell calls.

"Hey," he answers.

"You're alone?" she asks.

"Of course."

THE REGISTRATION REWRITTEN

"Perfect. Ramsey messaged Alex, the younger female guard with the nose rings."

"I know the one," Daniel says. The woman in question is usually stationed at the front of the house in the mornings, but she wasn't there this morning. "Isn't she questioning the employees who left after Eric died?" Last night, Ramsey gave them a report on his plans for finding Anna, including other guards' orders.

"That's what the report says," Lyn says. "But he gave her a new assignment this morning. She's now in charge of the rebels. His exact message is, 'Annemarie is taking over. I need you on the Resurrection. Use the directors' individual weak points and make them talk.'"

"The board of directors, I'm assuming," Daniel says.

"Yes. Sawyer D'Angelo, Chuck and Kerry Wright, Henry Doyle, and Drea Chapman."

Drea. Grant.

"What are their weak points?" Daniel asks, dread slithering between his ribs like a snake.

"I'm not sure. The rebel files don't mention weak points, but I imagine it's anything that could be used to manipulate them. Like children or secrets."

"Ramsey is ordering Alex to threaten children to get answers?"

"We did say to do whatever it takes."

"Not threaten children."

"Danny, they have our child," Lyn says.

"I know," he says, careful not to snap at her. He's been unable to think of anything but what Anna must be going through. He doesn't need a reminder from his wife.

His impatience must be obvious, though, because Lynell says, "I'm sorry. I'll try to figure out Ramsey's plan, but I finally got a meeting with Tilly Nguyen in an hour, so I can't miss that. Maybe see if you can contact one of the Resurrection directors. Don't tell them what Alex might be doing, but if you can get information before her, then she won't have to do it."

"Yeah, okay." Daniel doesn't believe the rebels had anything to do with the abduction, but he's not taking any chances. Everyone, regardless of their political beliefs or personal relationship with Daniel or Lynell, is a suspect. "I'll call you later."

"I love you."

"I love you too." He hangs up and changes directions, heading to Grant's apartment instead.

He's positive that if Drea Chapman's weak point is a person, then it'll be Grant.

Daniel hasn't yet decided whether he's planning to warn Grant or exploit that weak point when his phone rings again.

"Got something already?" he asks.

The silence before Lyn's answer makes the snake of dread crawl faster in his chest, leaving trails of frozen slime in its wake.

"The kidnapper called."

Daniel slams on his brakes and veers to the shoulder of the road, ignoring the honking.

"They asked for a ransom," she continues.

"How much?" Daniel asks. "We'll pay it. Of course, we'll pay it."

"It's not money, Danny. They're demanding that I let the policy change pass—or we'll never see Anna again."

CHAPTER 17

T ires screech outside. Lynell jumps from the couch and rips open the front door just in time to let Daniel step through, his arms going around her. Lynell lets out a pained, involuntary squeak from the tightness of his hug.

"Sorry," he says.

"It's fine." Lynell links their fingers together and pulls him back to the living room, where Ramsey and Hayes have turned into their command center. Fenn Vaughn, Anna's social worker, should arrive soon to join the group.

"Mr. Carter, good," Ramsey says. "We were going over the situation."

"Which is?" Daniel asks. His hold on Lynell's hand is so tight that she can feel her bones press together, but she doesn't care. The sensation is keeping her grounded.

"Mrs. Elysian received a call about half an hour ago from an unknown number," Ramsey says. "The voice was disguised, but I have someone working on cleaning it for a possible identification. Here it is." He leans down and presses a button on one of the laptops covering the coffee table.

Lynell has heard the message so many times she has it memorized.

"Your daughter is alive and will be returned after the policy change is announced during Friday's convention. Should the policy not pass, you'll never see her alive again. Every rescue attempt will result in the loss of one of her senses, starting with her vision. Do nothing and she will remain unharmed. This will be my last communication."

The recording ends, but the words continue in Lynell's mind. They swirl around her brain like flies circling a corpse.

"How do we know he's telling the truth that she's okay?" Daniel asks.

A sudden knock on the door prevents anyone from answering him. Hayes goes to the door, holding a gun in one hand. He checks the peephole first, then opens the door.

Lynell expects the social worker to be an overworked woman chasing retirement and hiding behind thick librarian glasses. Instead, a stunning woman, looking no older than thirty, walks inside. With her heels, Fenn is about two inches taller than Lynell. Stylish gold glasses frame striking light blue eyes, made more mesmerizing by a brown birthmark against the left iris. She has a blonde pixie cut that somehow complements her round face and a hoop in the center of her nose. She's wearing a matching gray blazer and pencil skirt set with a pink undershirt faded from too many washings, like she has to stretch the lifespan of her clothing as long as possible. Lynell can relate. Until recently, she wore clothes past their time to save money.

"Thank you," she says to Hayes. Her rough voice, the main reason Lynell expected an older woman, likely comes from a smoking habit. Fenn carries the odor of cigarettes that Lynell knows far too well from living with Alan.

"Ms. Vaughn?" Daniel says in confusion.

"Mr. and Mrs. Carter," Fenn says. "I regret that we're meeting this way. But I thought you needed to see this email I received." She holds out her phone and Daniel takes it, a strangled cry ripping from his chest. The sound is like a metal strap tightening around Lynell's chest.

She knows what to expect from Fenn's earlier call, but that does nothing to prepare her.

There's no subject line or text in the email, only one photo. It's Catherine Imes, sitting with her back against a black wall, Anna in her lap and a tablet in her hand. On the tablet's screen is an article posted that morning announcing that Lynell's official succession will take place at the convention.

"There's your proof that she's alive," Ramsey says, unnecessarily.

Daniel, still staring at the phone with tears streaming down his face, drops to the couch.

"What do we do?" Lynell asks the room at large, not expecting an answer.

"Nothing," Ramsey says.

Daniel's head snaps up to stare at Ramsey. "Just give them what they want? A country at the mercy of a few power-hungry people who aren't afraid of killing children?"

"Yes," Lynell says. Daniel's eyes, now filled with shock and incredulity, swivel from Ramsey to her. "She's safe right now, Danny. If we impulsively act, they'll hurt her."

"But the poli—"

"Isn't until Friday," Lynell interrupts.

"The kidnappers made a mistake with this message," Ramsey says.

The confusion lingers heavy in Daniel's eyes. "What mistake?"

Lynell answers for Ramsey, a taste of hope on the back of her tongue. "They gave us time."

CHAPTER 18

While Ramsey and the others discuss the ransom and possible plans of action, Lynell takes Daniel to the second-floor office, where they won't be overheard. She locks the door and turns on some music to mask their voices.

"You know what else the kidnapper told us with that message?" she asks.

"That he's a psychopath?" Daniel mutters.

Lynell rubs her hand down his arm, gripping his wrist. "That they're not rebels." She sees the moment it clicks in Daniel, as the clouds of confusion pass from his eyes.

"They're committee members."

"Or oligarchs or both," Lynell says. "Thomas Johnson is probably working with them."

"You want to meet D'Angelo."

"Yes, but I don't think we should tell her about Anna."

"Why?"

"The kidnappers might not be rebels, but we shouldn't take any chances. The less people who know about Anna, the better, don't you think? We don't want them feeling threatened. Also, I doubt it'd be good if they found out we met with the leader of the Resurrection."

"Good point," Daniel says.

Lynell smiles. He reaches out, tugs her closer, and tips her chin up. "I love you."

She stands on her toes to capture his lips in a kiss, pressing her palm to his chest to feel the moment his racing heart begins to slow.

"Now, we have to call her and convince her to meet us somewhere secret. Shouldn't be hard," she says, sarcastically.

"Actually, I think I have an idea."

They put the call on speakerphone and lean side by side against the desk.

"Hello?"

"Sawyer D'Angelo?" Lynell says.

"Yes?" D'Angelo answers, the word going up at the end like a question.

"It's Lynell Carter. I hope I'm not catching you at a bad time."

"No," the other woman clears her throat. "No, this is a great time. I didn't think I'd ever hear from you."

"Yeah, well," Lynell says, then looks back to Daniel. He silently mouths 'death threats' and sees her attention slide back in place. "My associate told me about the death threats, and I think you're right. I may be able to help."

"Really? What makes you say that?" A door closes on the other end and a slight echo accompanies D'Angelo's voice, suggesting she's in a hallway.

"I'd rather explain in person," Lynell says. "Why did you call me in the first place?"

"It's complicated. But the threats tie us together. Each message was accompanied by news articles about you and the phrase 'When weeds thrive, flowers die.'"

"I'm a weed?" Lynell asks. Daniel's eyebrows raise.

"I can explain further if we meet." Another sound of a door shutting and a whoosh of wind mingles with D'Angelo's voice.

"Meeting probably wouldn't be smart," she says. "Neither one of us can trust the other." She ignores Daniel as he drops his forehead into his hand.

"We wouldn't be very smart if we trusted each other. And you don't strike me as a stupid person."

"Thanks?" Lynell gives Daniel a silent confused look.

"But we could be useful to one another," Sawyer says.

"Meaning?"

"You're a wild card. You could be sympathetic to our cause. Or at least willing to discuss peacefully, unlike your predecessor. If you were gone, there's no guarantee the next leader wouldn't be Eric 2.0. You know what they say, better the devil you know than the devil you don't."

Lynell almost smirks at D'Angelo practically calling her the 'devil.' The boldness of such an offhand statement makes her relax a fraction. "You think manipulating me will be easier."

Daniel looks her way and she simply shrugs. If she was in D'Angelo's position, that would be her thought. Lynell is a twenty-four-year-old girl who has been publicly hurt by the Elysians and was recently thrown into this position. She's pretty much a dream for anyone wanting to manipulate her from behind the curtains.

"Maybe," D'Angelo says. "But I'm not in the business of underestimating people. Especially people who could either be my best friend or my worst enemy."

"Well, we are enemies by trade."

"No, our trades are enemies. You and I are strangers who have been all but forced into roles by family and circumstances outside of our control."

"This is all very dramatic," Lynell says.

Daniel gently shoves her in admonishment. He's probably wishing she'd take the situation more seriously. But she learned long ago that humor is one of the only things that keeps her sane when she's surrounded by misery.

"Our lives are built around the business of life or death—it's dramatic by nature," D'Angelo says.

"So, we agree that we don't trust each other but we should meet anyway?" Lynell says.

"Yes."

"Great. When's good for you?" Lynell asks.

"As soon as possible."

"How about in half an hour?"

"Where?" D'Angelo asks.

"I figured you wouldn't want me to choose, and I sure as hell don't want you to choose," Lynell says. "So, I propose a solution: neither of us pick where we meet."

D'Angelo pauses and says, "I trust your people even less than you."

That's Daniel's cue. He leans closer to the phone and says, "Ms. D'Angelo, this is Daniel Carter, Lynell's husband."

Silence. Followed by a car horn. Then, "I wasn't aware of your presence, Mr. Carter."

"Call me Daniel."

"Daniel, is there anyone else?"

"No. You might not know me, but I fought with the rebels eight years ago."

"I know," D'Angelo says.

"Lynell's new position doesn't change my beliefs," Daniel says. "I knew of you and your wife. We believed in you. So, maybe you can't trust my wife, but I hope you can trust that I support your cause. Yes, I'll always put Lynell's happiness and safety above anything else, but I believe she'd be the happiest and safest in a world without the Registration. I'm her husband, but before that, I was a rebel, and I still have rebel friends. Perhaps I can be the middleman here. I have a secure place where we can meet. That way, neither one of you have the upper hand of choosing the location."

"This will still be a bigger risk for me," D'Angelo says.

"A buddy of mine has been a loyal member of the Resurrection since you began. I went through him to find a meeting place. Does that help?"

"Who is he? Is he also aware of this meeting?"

"No, he's—"

"Do you want to meet or not?" Lynell interrupts, an impatient bite to her voice. Daniel lays a hand on her forearm.

"Very well," D'Angelo says. "Just the two of you, correct?"

"Yes," Daniel says. Lynell pushes off the desk and starts pacing the office, leaving him to finish the call.

"I'll be bringing my bodyguard. For security."

"We understand."

"Download MessengerGuard to send me the address. It'll encrypt our messages. I'll be there soon."

A click signals the end of the call, and Daniel stands, blocking Lynell's path. "Ready to meet your archnemesis?"

"So dramatic," she says with a groan. Daniel chuckles. "Where are we going? Who's this rebel friend of yours?"

"Tell you later. Now, let's go. I'm driving."

CHAPTER 19

S awyer pulls up next to a duplex. Seconds later, a door labeled with a wooden "B" opens to reveal a tall man with dark skin, broad shoulders, and arms covered in intricate tattoos.

"Hey, Malakai," Sawyer says when he's in the car. "Thanks for agreeing to come on such short notice."

Malakai, a man of few words, shrugs. "It's my job."

It's more than that. Malakai Morrison has been her bodyguard since the beginning, and he spends most of his time by her side, practically on call twenty-four seven. Still, she doesn't know much about him beyond the basics. He spent a decade in the Marine Corps, lives alone, and lost his nephew several years ago. The boy used his Registration to kill his mom who was slowly and painfully dying from cancer, but the grief and guilt drove him to drugs, and an OD quickly followed.

As she starts the drive, Sawyer feels an obligation to offer an explanation.

"Someone broke into my office on Thursday and left another threat," she says. He glances at her, revealing nothing in those deep-set eyes. "Carter called me earlier. I need to stop these threats and she—Carter, I mean—said she can help. Maybe that's playing into—"

"I know," Malakai interrupts. "I trust you, Sawyer."

That's it. No further explanations or questions. They don't speak again until Sawyer parks in front of a building two blocks from the main street.

"This isn't what I was expecting," she says. The place looks like it was built by a team that couldn't agree on the design. The front resembles a hotel or hospital with a circular driveway under a brick porte cochere and sliding glass doors. The back is made of metal and would make more sense as a gym or barn. The ceiling is flat over this section and rises to a point at the front.

"A church?" Malakai asks, reading the large sign in the brown lawn that says, "ONE DIVINE ONE COMMUNITY."

"Doesn't look like any church I've ever seen."

She opens the encrypted app and reads Daniel's last message aloud, where he directs them past the front door to a secluded entrance in the back. Malakai leaves to scope it out before Sawyer. While waiting, she studies the building's front and the dozens of signs plastered to the doors: fliers for church services, AA meetings on Tuesdays, morning childcare, ESL classes, and dance classes.

"Clear!" Malakai shouts, and Sawyer follows a stone path to the back, where he's holding open a metal door. Inside is a ramped hallway on one side and a check-in counter on the other. The counter is bare, showing off a laminate top with cracked edges. The floor is gray carpet and the walls are a light blue, like a grade school.

"This way." Malakai tilts his head to the right. They go past the ramp and down another hall that opens into a large room, with several closed doors and a rock-climbing wall lined with cushions. Kids' drawings fill the empty wall.

Straight ahead is a man standing next to an open door, roughly of Malakai's height, hands in the pockets of his washed-out jeans. He's young, probably a decade younger than herself, but his short beard already has a tinge of gray. Or maybe that's due to the building's awful fluorescent lights.

"Ms. D'Angelo?" he asks.

His voice, though not as gruff as Malakai's, has a dark kind of confidence. Sawyer imagines Malakai's voice to be lightning slamming against a cliff face. If so, then this man's voice is the wind stalling over ocean waves right before the storm hits.

"Daniel?" she replies.

He nods and removes his hands from his pockets, extending one in invitation. Sawyer steps forward and accepts the gesture, her hand nearly disappearing in his. He gives her a quick shake, nods to Malakai, and gestures at the open door behind him. "In here."

The room has off-white walls, a whiteboard on wheels, several pamphlets on a table, and a circle of several folding chairs.

Sitting in one of the chairs is Lynell Carter. Sawyer recognizes her from the photos in the articles and posts about her. Unlike in most photos, where her hair is dark brown, Lynell's current style is closer to cabernet with a red hue. Heavy circles hang under her eyes, like plum-colored hammocks. Her lips stretch into an uncertain smile at Sawyer's entrance. Her left hand has several bandages, and three of the fingers are held straight by splints. The bruises and cuts on her face and arms are fading, and soon the trauma she's experienced will be invisible to the rest of the world.

Even without pictures, Sawyer would've known Carter. She carries the knowledge of her identity in the set of her shoulders, and the burden of her position in the exhaustion in her eyes and her stress-cracked lips and inflamed skin. More than that, Lynell exudes a confidence that only comes from experiencing and overcoming the worst life has to offer.

"Ms. D'Angelo?" Lynell says as she gets up.

"Sawyer." Sawyer side-steps an upholstered folding chair and extends her hand.

"Lynell." She shakes hands twice, then let's go to sit down again. Daniel closes the door and crosses the room to sit next to her.

Sawyer picks the chair closest to the door, and she can practically feel Malakai's approval. He doesn't sit, and both Carters give him a questioning look, though neither comment.

"Where are we, if you don't mind me asking?" Sawyer looks around the space and crosses her feet at the ankles.

"A multipurpose building," Daniel says. "Several organizations use it, like a Baptist church, the rec center across town for overflow classes, AA and NA both use it for meetings, and several others."

"Why did you pick here?" Sawyer asks.

"My friend's sister owns it, and he's one of your people, so I thought it'd be a decent compromise."

"The cameras?" Malakai asks, nearly startling Sawyer out of her seat. She strains her neck looking back and sees him staring at a black dome in the corner of the ceiling.

"They're off, but you can ask Grant to see the feed if it makes you feel better. I didn't tell him why I needed the space, so it's up to you whether you trust him or not."

"Grant Woods?" Sawyer asks, her lips pressing together.

He's been a loyal, hardworking member for years, but recently she struggles to see him as anything except Drea's ex. She refuses to share the reason for their breakup, swearing he didn't do anything wrong, but several nights of her sobbing tells a different story.

"Yes," Daniel says.

Sawyer wants to question him further about the man, but Malakai doesn't give her the chance. "Traffic cameras could pick us up, but unless someone is actively looking for us, it would take them a long time to locate us on any of those. No one has one of those chips?" Malakai gestures to his neck where the tracking chips are inserted. They're similar to the chips people put in their pets, but aren't activated unless that person goes missing. They're rare and became legal a decade or so ago, but more and more people are voluntarily getting them in their children in case their kids are kidnapped.

Lynell shakes her head. "Hell no," she says. "My stepdad suggested it once to my mom, and it was one of the rare times she threatened to leave him. She was vehemently against that kind of tracking."

"You know I don't," Sawyer says.

At the same time, Daniel says, "Me either."

"Alright, now that we've established that," Lynell says, reclaiming everyone's attention. Then, to Sawyer, "I saw what you said on that podcast. Thanks for not assuming I'm a monster like Eric."

Sawyer shrugs. "If we were all judged based on our blood connections, then no generational curse would ever be broken."

"I've never thought about it quite like that," Lynell says. "But you're right. Expecting someone to be exactly like their family members doesn't give much incentive to change for the better."

Sawyer imagines several conversational paths could branch off that sentence, but the palpable urgency in the room helps her ignore them and focus. "I received a third threat on Thursday."

She opens the photo app on her phone and pulls up the most recent picture. Leaning across the circle, Sawyer passes the phone to Lynell. "This was how I found my office yesterday." She should have taken more photos, but her priority had been making sure the place got cleaned before anyone else saw it. "I'm no stranger to hatred. Harassment is inevitable when you contradict the default norm to which the public clings."

Unbidden, an image of Ellery fills her mind. No matter the hate thrown her way, Sawyer's wife never sacrificed an inch of her identity or happiness. "But these don't feel like empty threats. Not with that kind of pageantry and violation to my office and home."

Lynell returns the phone to Sawyer. "All three have used this phrase? 'When weeds thrive, flowers die'?"

Sawyer nods. "And they've all had news clippings about you." She opens the small album of photos she'd created earlier and hands the phone back to Lynell. "Scroll right." Silence returns as Lynell scrolls, Daniel peering over her shoulder.

"This is your mailbox?" Lynell asks, turning the phone around.

Sawyer nods. "That was the second threat."

"No address or stamp. They personally dropped it off."

"Exactly," Sawyer says. "I don't share my home address with many people, but clearly, someone has been following me."

"These are all recent?"

Sawyer knows she's referring to the stalker photos. "Within the last week."

"What does 'she is not a peony' mean?" Lynell asks.

"Peonies are flowers," Daniel says.

Lynell rolls her eyes. "Yes, Danny, I know."

"Are these flower petals from peonies?" Daniel asks, looking from the phone up to Sawyer.

Sawyer's back straightens, a bead of sweat dripping down her spine. "Yes."

"What's the significance?"

Sawyer feels Malakai tense behind her, and Daniel frowns in confusion. "It's a reference to Ellery. They were her favorite flowers."

Lynell and Daniel display the mix of emotions everyone feels when they witness or hear about a horrific tragedy—sympathy and sadness for the victims, anger and fear that such a thing can happen in this world, curiosity to learn more, and relief that the tragedy didn't happen to them.

Perhaps her own experience with trauma and grief keeps Lynell from pushing the point any further.

Whatever the reason, Sawyer's grateful when Lynell reads, "'You've dug the grave, but will you be alone in it, or will she join you?'" She looks up from the phone, and, despite the grim conversation, there's a spark of interest in her brown eyes.

"I think you're the 'she,'" Sawyer says.

"I'm positive I'm the 'she,'" Lynell says.

She glances at Daniel, not for confirmation or permission, but, Sawyer thinks, to make sure he's on the same page as her.

Lynell turns back to her and holds her gaze. "We know who bombed my house."

Sawyer uncrosses her legs. That's not what she'd expected. "Who?"

Closing her eyes Lynell takes a heavy breath. She opens them again when Daniel grips her knee, as if it was the switch of courage needed. "Thomas Johnson."

Moisture drains from Sawyer's body, starting at her mouth and spreading to her eyes, brain, chest, and arteries. That name is her own personal Medusa, turning her to stone and damning her to relive the worst time of her life in a bruising loop.

"Sawyer?" Lynell mutters.

Then Malakai leaves his post, something he never does, and sits by her side, folding her hands in his. "He's not here, Sawyer," he whispers.

That's what people don't understand.

Thomas Johnson is *always* here. Just as Ellery is always with her, so is her killer.

"I'm so sorry, but it was him. And that got me thinking; if someone is threatening you in relation to me and someone is bombing my house, then wouldn't the logical conclusion be that it's the same person?"

"Lyn, baby, give her a second."

"Sorry."

Sawyer squeezes her eyes shut, ignoring both Lynell and Daniel. Emotions whip alive in her mind like a sandstorm. Her skin tingles as she breathes rhythmically until the storm is a manageable wind.

"Johnson bombed your house?" she whispers.

"Yes," Lynell says.

Sawyer clears her throat, the picture of Johnson crackling to pieces in her mind's eye.

"Did he leave a message?"

"No."

"It might not be the same person," Sawyer suggests, though the idea is hollow. Coincidences might happen, but not like this. "Johnson had an issue with Ellery, not me. Eric's people have been more of a threat to me and my job in the last six years than him."

"I would've left a hitman in your office, not potpourri," Lynell says.

Malakai tenses and Daniel shakes his head, but Sawyer welcomes the light tone. It helps her relax and think clearly. "I don't think you have anything to do with it. But they're your people."

"Thousands of people work for me," Lynell says. "What do you want me to do? Send out a company-wide email saying, 'Hey, whoever is messing with Sawyer D'Angelo, please stop. It's not nice.'"

Sawyer laughs, though more at Daniel's exasperated look than Lynell's quip.

"Besides, we already know who it is. Whoever left the threats to you mentioned both of us," Lynell says. "He called me a weed, suggested I would be in your grave with you. So, it makes sense that the same man bombed my house, especially when he has a history with your family."

"What does he mean by this deadline? 'Before Friday?'" Daniel asks, pointing at the phone still in Lynell's hand.

"Next Friday," Sawyer says.

"Friday?" Lynell repeats, sharing a significant look with Daniel that's full of meaning Sawyer can't understand. "The convention?"

"Yeah, I guess." She rolls her tongue and meets Lynell's eyes, thinking. Sawyer can't afford to change her plans now, no matter who Lynell Carter turns out to be.

Collateral damage can't be avoided. Not completely.

Suspicion seems painted in Lynell's raised eyebrows and pressed lips, but she lets the comment go. "So, what does he want?"

"I'm not sure," Sawyer lies.

"It can't be to stop the convention," Daniel says.

"We think Johnson is working with someone else who's invested in the convention running smoothly," Lynell says.

"What makes you say that?" Sawyer asks.

The two have another short, silent conversation, solely through their eyes. They probably don't even appreciate how remarkable it is that they can communicate with only a look. Sawyer didn't until she lost the person with whom she could do it.

"My COO, Ramsey Davenport, has information on several people, Johnson included," Lynell says. "He's confident that Johnson isn't working alone, but he doesn't know yet who that might be. Maybe there's something in these threats that can help us figure that out."

Sawyer takes the phone back from Lynell. "If there was, I would've found it already. I've read these dozens of times."

Lynell huffs like a child who got the wrong birthday gift. "There's something here we're missing."

"I agree," Sawyer says.

"We need to find Johnson. He'll have the answers," Lynell says.

"How do you suggest we do that?"

"By working together."

It's what Sawyer wanted, but alarm bells ring in her mind at how easily Lynell has agreed. "Helping me isn't in your best interest. So, why would you do it?"

"Because I understand what it's like to have your life threatened. I understand the need to survive and the monstrous task it is to survive alone." She fidgets in her seat, and Daniel grabs her hand, kissing the knuckles before resting their interlocked fingers in his lap. Her chest rises with a deep breath. "Plus, you're not the only one he threatened. Johnson bombed my house. He put my family in danger."

Sawyer refuses to admit how much she has in common with the Elysian heir, but she will acknowledge her similarities with Lynell Carter, a scared young woman who doesn't want to lose anyone else she loves.

That's someone Sawyer can align with.

"You know what they say about a common enemy. They'll unite even the oldest rivals and make them twice as dangerous."

CHΛPTER **20**

L ynell studies the photos Sawyer sent through the MessengerGuard app while Daniel drives them home. The threats have their own voice that slams against her skull until a headache forms.

You are nothing against a nation sold to a false god. She will see you burned. The very thing you fight will kill you, and we'll watch you rot.

You've dug the grave, but will you lie in it alone or will she join you? Your beloved was silenced by the blade, and she was wrong. She is not a peony. She won't resurrect.

Neither will you. You'll be beneath the flowers before Friday.

And the final line, tying together the first two notes and the vandalized office: *When weeds thrive, flowers die.*

Individual words float off the phone screen, twisting and layering on top of each other in a blurred kaleidoscope. She drops the phone, closes her eyes, and rubs her temple, wishing she could command her brain to work without receiving enough sleep.

Johnson threatened Sawyer, but clearly hates Lynell too. She comes from a family of unkillable weeds that strangle the flowers of the world.

Did Johnson see Eric as a weed or a flower?

Daniel rests his hand on her thigh while he drives. She wonders if he only agreed to help Sawyer because they took Anna. Lynell made her decision days ago, before Anna.

There are countless reasons not to align with the rebel leader, the Resurrection rebellion against the Elysian family legacy only one of them. Sawyer could be lying. The kidnappers could find out. It could ruin Lynell's tentative control over the Registration.

None of those reasons matter. All Lynell could think about during the meeting was Sawyer's desperation and her own desperate need to save Anna.

Then she looked at Daniel, searching for fear or uncertainty in his eyes, anything that signaled he changed his mind. But her husband's bleeding heart was on full display and all she found was the desire to play hero one more time.

It's not clear whether Sawyer is trustworthy yet, but they do know she didn't take Anna. That's enough for now. And Lynell privately thinks this could be her answer to doing good. It could be her compromise between ending the Registration and letting the committee turn it into something worse.

This could absolve her of any remaining guilt.

They turn into the neighborhood of their new house, and Daniel breaks the silence. "They're going to want to know where we've been."

"I know," Lynell says. They left earlier by climbing through the office window, as if they were teenagers sneaking out. From there, it was an easy jump from the roof to the portico to the ground. "Maybe they won't know we left, and we can sneak back in."

But the hope vanishes when Daniel turns the car, and they see the house at the end of the cul-de-sac has two cars parked in front of it and a handful of guards milling around the entryway. Ramsey is pacing in the front yard, a phone pressed to his ear.

He looks up at their arrival, his eyes piercing the windshield and landing firmly on Lynell.

"Fuck," Lynell groans, heat climbing up the back of her neck.

"Remember, you're the boss," Daniel says.

Lynell breathes deeply and climbs out of the car, slightly tilting on her feet from a ripple of dizziness.

Ramsey is of average height, yet he towers over them.

"What did you do?" he demands in lieu of a greeting.

"Nothing," Lynell says, proud at the lack of an apologetic tone.

"We agreed not to act. If the kidnappers—"

"I know," Lynell interrupts. "It had nothing to do with the kidnapping. Don't worry about that." She lifts her chin and walks past Ramsey toward the house.

Ramsey matches her pace. "You can't disappear without telling anyone."

"I'm an adult. I can do what I want."

"No, you can't," Ramsey says. "Not anymore. You're not solely an adult. You're one of the most important and powerful people in the country. Need I remind you that half the population hates you and the other half is waiting for you to fail?"

"Well, that's encouraging." She walks inside but before they can head to the bedroom, Ramsey steps in front of Lynell, forcing her to stop walking and meet his gaze. It takes a beat too long for her eyes to focus on his face.

"You can't make decisions alone. Even decisions about where you go in your free time. You have an entire team of people working for you, dedicated to your safety."

Distrust of that team bubbles in her gut. "Yes, and how successful that team has been so far."

"There's much more at stake than your safety or your family. I can't do my job if you don't talk to me." Ramsey crosses his arms, making the short sleeves of his collared shirt dig into his biceps. "Where did you go?"

She could refuse to tell him, but then he'd get suspicious. She could lie, but no good excuses come to mind. So, she decides on the truth.

Lynell looks around, sees Hayes and another guard within hearing distance, and sidesteps Ramsey. "Come on," she says, striding to the main bedroom.

Daniel shuts the door behind them and frowns at Lynell. It's not a frown of disapproval or sadness but the kind signaling that he is working out a difficult puzzle. Ramsey's frown, however, radiates displeasure.

"We were going to meet with Sawyer D'Angelo."

Daniel freezes. Ramsey rubs a hand down his face and shakes his head.

"You are the Elysian heir," he says. As if Lynell could forget. "With all due respect, you have no idea what that means. You don't know what the job entails. I do. I worked for Mr. Elysian for over two decades. Hundreds of other employees have been working for the Registration longer than you've been alive. If you want to keep your position, gain the respect of the committee, oligarchs, and American people, and save your daughter, then you must heed our advice. Nothing about your life is as simple as it once was."

His words seem to compress Lynell until she feels smaller than a toddler. In her peripheral vision, she sees Daniel fill with anger. Before he can defend her, Lynell swallows to lubricate her dry throat.

"I know life isn't simple. It never was for me. And I know you're more familiar with the logistics of my new position than I am. That doesn't change the fact that I'm your superior and I'm allowed to make decisions that you may disagree with. I couldn't ignore Ms. D'Angelo's request. However," she quickly adds, "when we arrived, I realized you were right."

She knows her story can easily crumble with one look into Daniel's phone location or the GPS history of the car, but she keeps talking anyway, hoping Ramsey won't need to verify.

"I can't trust her and don't want to do anything that could endanger Anna further. So, we didn't go in. We left. And I . . ." she looks down at her feet and lowers her voice to a near whisper. "I don't know what happened, but when I realized Daniel was driving us back here, I freaked. We went to the park where we first met. We didn't get out of the car," she says in a rush, looking back at Ramsey. Her eyes burn and she doesn't let herself think about why the story is affecting her. "No one saw us. We sat there for a while. Then we came back." She doesn't have to fake embarrassment. The emotions are there, even in the lie.

After a beat of silence, Daniel says, "We needed a little time."

That seems to sell the story to Ramsey. "Tell me next time. Please."

Lynell nods. Once alone, Daniel pulls Lynell against his chest. She's not sure how much time passes before he pulls back to kiss her forehead. "You're my favorite person," he says.

She sobs, clinging tighter to him with one arm than she ever has with both.

"It's going to be okay. We'll get her back."

Daniel doesn't usually lie to her, but she's grateful he does now. It's the permission her body needs to drop into a heavy, much needed sleep.

CHAPTER **21**

RAMSEY
Monday Afternoon

Mrs. Elysian lied to him. He tells himself it doesn't mean anything, but the steadiness in her voice and conviction in her eyes as she lied to his face kept him up all night.

Eric was incapable of respecting others enough to be honest with them. He surrounded himself with lies like landmines. Ramsey was tired of watching his steps for fear of detonation. Mrs. Elysian was meant to be different.

She's supposed to respect him. Trust him.

But she lied. The moment Ramsey knew she was gone, he looked up the vehicle's location. He couldn't hack into the building's security, but street cameras showed Sawyer D'Angelo and her bodyguard arriving. That, plus Jeremy's report that Daniel spent time with Grant Woods makes Ramsey more than worried about Mrs. Elysian's association with the rebels. He needs to intervene.

He can't put it off anymore. Especially after his guard went missing while watching D'Angelo's house yesterday. This has to do with the rebels, and they only have four days until the conference. There's no time to delay the inevitable.

So, he makes his excuses and leaves Mrs. Elysian.

His awareness of his own body grows to an uncomfortably sharp level by the time he arrives. She's staying in a townhome in the middle of a dozen identical units. She's always felt safer as another faceless, nameless copy in a sea of unremarkable people. Ramsey rings the doorbell and faces the camera. He keeps one hand in his pocket and pinches the skin of his thigh as hard as possible to help master the nerves.

He knows she sees him because there's a small gasp on the other side of the door.

"Please, let me in," he says.

The wait is excruciating. Then the door opens inward, and Ramsey sees the woman he loves for the first time in five years. His lungs refuse to inflate for a second. Then he sucks in a lungful of air, his eyes traveling every inch of her body.

The years have been brutal, but she's as gorgeous as ever. She's wearing a tank top and loose shorts. Her blonde hair is piled on top of her head, and her green eyes are like peak springtime. Her skin has lost color, the faint freckles along her shoulders now more visible.

"What are you doing here?" Harlow Graham asks.

Ramsey lets out a breath, cursing his mind for being so easily distracted. "We need to talk."

She grips the door handle with white knuckles, looks over Ramsey's shoulder, and backs into her townhome. He doesn't breathe until she nods and steps aside so he can enter.

"When did you get back?" he asks.

"Almost ten months ago."

His eyes slide closed, pain rocking his core.

"I'm sorry I didn't get in touch. I just . . ."

Ramsey turns around. She's not even looking at him. "It's okay," he says. "I get it. You wanted to join the Resurrection." Harlow had more reason to hate Eric Elysian than anyone in the world. She was forced to abandon her child and go into hiding because Eric was going to kill her for knowing he was illegitimate.

"I wanted my son back."

"Zachary, the Elysian heir?" Ramsey doesn't understand. Joining the rebellion would've increased the danger to both her and Zachary.

"He found me, you know," she says.

Ramsey expected as much but never knew for sure.

Harlow walks past Ramsey to the armchair behind him. She's so small that the chair nearly swallows her when she sits. "He followed you the last time you visited. I was scared that if he found me, so could others. So, I moved and never told you because . . ." Her voice breaks with a gasp. Ramsey sits across from her on the edge of the coffee table. "Zachary told me his father was more paranoid every day. It got worse when the Resurrection began. Eric had a Head Regulator killed for no reason other than suspecting the man had rebel friends."

Ramsey remembers that, except Eric told them there was proof the man was a traitor. That was when Ramsey was promoted, taking the dead man's place as Head Regulator.

"I couldn't risk your life by continuing to see you," she says. The tear bubble along her eyelids breaks, dropping wet regret down her cheeks. "And two people visiting would double the chances that I'd be found."

It hurts, but Ramsey doesn't blame her for choosing Zachary over him.

"About a year and a half ago, Zachary stopped coming. I couldn't get in touch with him. I was terrified. I knew he wasn't dead, but that didn't mean he was safe. I searched for a way to free him from Eric's control for months. Nothing worked. The last option was if Eric and the Registration were gone completely."

"So you moved back to join the Resurrection."

"Not simply join, but help run it. I moved back to befriend the leader."

"Sawyer D'Angelo."

Harlow nods and sniffs.

"But not just for the Resurrection, right?"

Her eyes widen a fraction, as if afraid that he'd guess her true plans. Then her shoulders droop. "I believe in the Resurrection. You might think

I'm crazy, but I've gotten to know these people, and I think they have a chance. Their dreams for a world without the Registration make sense. It could be ... better."

"Come on, be honest with me." He doesn't want to argue with her about politics. "What do you want from Lincoln D'Angelo?"

Ramsey has been meticulously going through Eric's *Midnight Files* since Reggie provided the information needed to open the safe, and was surprised to find one on Lincoln D'Angelo. It was thinner than the others but still provided plenty of shocking information on him and his family. One particular thing about his uncle, Paul D'Angelo, has been burning a hole in the back of his mind, growing hotter every hour he doesn't tell Mrs. Elysian.

"I wanted his help stopping Eric." Her eyes fall to the floor, and he knows she's not telling the full truth. Her hands sit in her lap, fingers gripping each other so tight that it must be painful. "But then Eric and Zachary—"

Her words shatter against a fresh sob. Ramsey's heart breaks at the sound. He drops to his knees in front of her, one hand draping over hers and the other behind her head, fingers sliding into her hair. "I'm so sorry," he whispers.

Harlow's cries are so intense that her entire body shakes. She goes limp, and he supports her weight. She falls apart, knowing that Ramsey is happy to keep her together.

"What happened?" she asks between sobs.

He hesitates, lightly scratching her scalp and staring at the blank wall behind her.

"Ramsey, please." She turns her hand over, pressing their palms together, and leans back. The full force of her grief and attention pushes him over the edge so he's in a free fall.

"I don't think ..."

Desperation in every tear, she repeats, "Please!"

Ramsey looks from one eye to the other, forgotten corridors in his heart crumbling under her pain. "It was quick," he says. He wasn't in the room when Zachary died, but he's heard the story directly from Mrs. Elysian. "He was brave until the end. Protecting his family."

"Eric—"

He shakes his head. "No. His cousin, Lynell, and her daughter, Anna. He was protecting them *from* Eric."

Hatred flashes in her eyes. Her nails dig into Ramsey's skin when she squeezes his hand. "And Eric?"

"I killed him," he says. Harlow doesn't need to know more details about either man's death.

Not now, at least.

He slides his hand from the back of her head to her cheek, wiping away the tears. Mustering every ounce of patience, he waits for her cries to subside and her breathing to settle before speaking again.

"What are your plans now? With the rebels and D'Angelo?"

"It doesn't matter," she whispers.

"Yes, it does," he says, hoping she can't hear his eagerness. "Mrs. Elysian—Lynell needs my help. Her family is in danger now." As informative as the *Midnight Files* are, there's not enough in them for Ramsey to find Anna. He could try using what he's learned to blackmail answers out of certain oligarchs or committee members, but it's too dangerous. Using the files is his last resort.

"Tell her to get as far from the Registration and Elysian name as possible," Harlow answers. But he hears more than sadness in her voice. There's anger, too.

"She's the best chance any of us have," Ramsey promises. Then, leaning on the implicit trust he once had for the woman in front of him, he adds, "She's working with Sawyer D'Angelo."

Harlow's head snaps up, her eyes wide. "What?"

"They met secretly last night."

"Why would they work together?"

"Mrs. Elysian is young, but she's lived a harder life than most," Ramsey says. "She sees herself as the villain in the story."

He's not sure Mrs. Elysian realizes it, but it's become obvious to him in the short time he's known her. She was raised by pathetic excuses for humans. Her family tree has poisoned roots that spread their toxins through most branches. Her personal guilt is a cancer on her soul. "But she desperately wants to be the hero," he adds.

"So, she's helping Sawyer to be the hero?"

"Both have been threatened, I think by the same person. Mrs. Elysian probably thinks that too."

"Who would threaten the leaders of the Resurrection and the Registration?"

Ramsey's focus moves an inch above Harlow's eyes. "I don't know yet," he lies. "I thought you might know, being so close to the D'Angelos."

"Only Sawyer. Lincoln takes more work to win over."

Ramsey carefully and slowly grazes his fingertips over Harlow's pulse. "I need your help, Harlow. Zachary loved Lynell. She's your family now too. Help me help her, please. What is D'Angelo planning?"

Her pulse jumps forward as she studies his face, then settles into a normal rhythm. Finally, she nods, and relief settles over Ramsey. He has her again. After five years, Harlow Graham still trusts him, just as he still loves her.

CHAPTER 22

L ynell stands in the still-unfamiliar kitchen, glaring at the wall like it'll suddenly grow a mouth and tell her where the hell the toaster is.

"We've talked about this, baby."

Lynell jumps at the unexpected voice, sending a splash of juice from the glass in her hand to the tile floor.

Daniel chuckles and rips free a paper towel. "Manifestation doesn't work for cooking."

She sets down the glass and accepts the towel, heart still thudding. She wonders when she'll stop flinching at the smallest things. It's like her fight or flight response had been locked into overdrive for nearly a month and can't remember how to return to hibernation.

"I can't find the toaster."

Daniel reaches to the side of the counter, and moments later, a hidden compartment rises at the back of the countertop. It stops just shy of hitting the cupboard above. Three shiny, sleek, black appliances sit inside, one of which is a toaster.

"What is the point of that?"

Daniel shrugs.

"Probably meant to make the kitchen look cleaner. There's another one on the other side with a spice rack." At her confused look, he adds, "Hayes gave me a full tour of the place when you were at the meeting on Thursday. I can show you later."

"Are there more unnecessary hidden compartments?"

"Of course there are. Why would anything be simple?"

She grins, is about to ask where the bread is when someone knocks at the front door. A guard peers through the window beside the entrance, finger pressed to his ear as someone probably relays information into the wireless speaker and microphone each guard wears. Then he opens the door and steps to the side, giving Lynell a perfect view of their uninvited guest as he saunters into their house.

She doesn't recognize the man but feels like she should. He exudes money. From his silky, straight, tailored, navy suit to his shiny watch that probably has a four-syllable name Lynell could never pronounce. He carries himself with the confidence only a life with money can give you. His short hair is gray but thick and styled so that it looks distinguished, not old. His common, unassuming appearance could've made him appear like a forgettable, everyday man, but instead, he looks like the very mold that generic white men strive to emulate.

"Mrs. Elysian, it's a pleasure," he says, stopping a foot in front of her. He doesn't offer his hand or acknowledge Daniel's presence. "I apologize for not introducing myself sooner. As I'm sure you understand, we've all been incredibly busy."

We? Lynell thinks.

The man smiles. His teeth look more like a set than individuals. "My name is Michaels Sutton."

Suddenly, everything about him—and the odd feeling of reverence rushing through Lynell's blood—makes sense.

"You're an oligarch," Daniel says.

Michaels Sutton looks at Daniel for the first time. Lynell can't tell if his eyes are blue or green. "Much to the chagrin of my brothers."

"Brothers?" Lynell asks.

Sutton's gaze returns to her. His eyes don't flick or jump. They glide like a canoe riding a flowing river. "The other oligarchs. Of course, none are my biological brothers, but the term best describes us."

"But they don't like you . . ." Lynell says. Sutton is incredibly unpopular. He took over for his father when he died, and has since been unabashedly vocal against the Registration.

"You've caused quite a stir, Mrs. Elysian. I must be honest—my brothers aren't happy."

"I'm not surprised," Lynell returns, the words coming from somewhere instinctual rather than intellectual.

"Your uncle's untimely passing and your unprecedented claim to power has disrupted their work. My brothers don't appreciate disruptions."

"What are you doing here?" Lynell can practically feel Daniel's release of breath at her abrupt question.

"Well, I'm here because you appear to need my help."

Her mind is struck by the picture of a captive Catherine, holding a terrified Anna. "Why would I need your help?"

"Shall we sit?" Whether speaking or not, Sutton's mouth somehow stays in a permanent amused smile. It makes Lynell feel uncomfortably humbled.

A rebuke is on the tip of her tongue, but Daniel beats her to answering. "Yes, of course. Why don't we go to Lyn's office? Would you like anything to drink? Or eat?"

"I'll be speaking with Mrs. Elysian alone, thank you," Sutton says.

"Daniel can hear whatever I do."

"I prefer this be a private conversation."

Burning annoyance fills Lynell's lungs. "Well, I prefer—"

"It's fine," Daniel interrupts, hand gently grabbing the back of Lynell's neck.

"Daniel . . ."

"Mr. Sutton is here to speak to you, Lyn. Don't worry, I'll be waiting."

His words help douse the fire in her lungs, and she's able to take a clear breath as she nods. "Alright."

She leads Sutton up the stairs to her office. He shuts the door, and Lynell sits behind her desk, desperately needing the table as a barrier.

"Okay, what do you want to help me with and why?"

Sutton takes his time surveying the room, before deigning to face Lynell. Then, with the same leisure he seems to do everything, he says, "Because, you're only helpful to me if you remain in power, of course."

Lynell feels a hint of sincere respect for Sutton. "Everyone wants to use me."

"Of course. Just as you want to use everyone else."

"I don't—"

"Spare me. Do you not befriend specific people or speak to committee members because you need something from them?"

Lynell's back straightens and she tastes resentment like bile on her tongue. "Using someone is different than working with them. I want to help people, to make this world a better and safer place."

"As do I. Neither of us are fans of the Registration. But the nobility of a cause does not erase the selfishness needed to carry it to fruition."

"That's a strikingly negative outlook."

"Negative or not, my point stands. I've spent the entirety of my time in office, hoping to end the very thing that my brothers value above all else. The Registration is everything humans crave—control, influence, peace, and freedom. It's the opportunity to become a god while preserving a delusion of purity and innocence. For my brothers and your committee? The Registration is money and power. That is not an easy thing to take away."

Lynell both agrees and doesn't agree. It's a confusing dichotomy, one she hasn't had sufficient time to explore. Sutton isn't wrong, but it's not the whole truth.

The Registration is more than that. It's the peace felt when someone chooses to die rather than suffer through another day of their terminal illness. It's the freedom retained when a young girl is able to end a pregnancy she never asked for. It's the justice deserved when a victim Registers their lifelong abuser.

She doesn't have nearly enough energy to have that conversation with an oligarch, though. So she says, "We agree there."

"That's why I want you to stay where you are. You taking control of the Registration has been the first real opportunity to end the system. My brothers see that threat too. It's not enough to survive this time, Mrs. Elysian, you must thrive. You must become untouchable. You'll never get anything good done if you're constantly fleeing death."

Do good.

He's right, Lynell knows. And that fact pisses her off.

"So, what do you suggest? What help do I need?"

"First, your relationship with Sawyer D'Angelo."

Lynell carefully doesn't look surprised. "What about it?"

"My brothers have taken note, which is unadvisable. Any relationship, whether friendly or not, with the leader of the rebellion will strip you of credibility."

"How do they even know?"

"Nothing you do is secret."

"How ominous."

"You're the two most watched women in the country. Did you truly think you could meet without notice?" He rests an arm on the desk and rhythmically taps with all five fingers.

"I'm not declaring Sawyer my enemy on principle."

Sutton's constant grin lengthens. "I'd assume not. But perhaps use a different device for your contact with D'Angelo."

Lynell fights a frown.

One message couldn't have done so much harm, so quickly, that an oligarch decided to show up at her house.

"Aside from her rebellion, Sawyer D'Angelo is an unwise acquaintance to keep in your present situation. You must know by now that family relations and history are important."

There again is the feeling that Lynell should know something she doesn't. It's infuriating, but she has jumped into the deep end with both feet, so she has to learn to swim—while avoiding sharks. "What do you mean?"

"Have you not looked into her past or family?" Sutton asks.

"Do you mean her wife? Because she—"

"No, not Ellery Klein. I am, of course, referring to her biological blood relatives. Specifically, her father, grandfather, and great-uncle."

Now feeling slightly panicked, Lynell racks her mind for any hint of who Sawyer's family could be. Had Ramsey told her anything?

Before she can ask, Sutton says, "Her grandfather, Jude D'Angelo, was Gideon Elysian's business partner."

Everything, including her panic, freezes.

"Jude was a senator before the war and became one of the first oligarchs after the war. He was the man to introduce Gideon to my predecessors."

Lynell manages to break through the ice that keeps her frozen. "But her father isn't an oligarch?" It's half a statement and half a question.

Sutton shakes his head. "Jude didn't remain an oligarch long. He had a falling out with Gideon and resigned. Or was forced to resign. Sawyer's father, Lincoln D'Angelo, never had the opportunity to take over. Worse still, Jude's own brother, Paul, supported the rebels."

"Wait . . . really?"

Sutton raises a brow as he fixes his gaze on hers and holds it. "Her family has tainted itself, and they have a history of tainting anyone they work with. It's a wonder Sawyer has gotten as far with the Resurrection as she has."

"Maybe her work has nothing to do with her family."

Sutton's fixed smile turns patronizing, his blue-green eyes filling with the same sympathy that several of the committee members wear when they look at Lynell. "Living vicariously through others is not living at all."

"Please leave one-liners aside and speak to me like a real person," Lynell says. "I get it, don't be friends with Sawyer because our grandfathers had an argument. What else?"

"I'm sorry?"

Lynell leans against the desk so she's closer to the oligarch, whose essence seems to fill her office. "Why else do I need your help?"

"Very well." He finally seems ready to get to the point. "I've always known several of my brothers scheme together behind my back. They manipulated your uncle and I'm sure Registration committee chairs for their means. I've yet to learn their final goal, beyond control, of course."

"Because as oligarchs, you're sadly lacking control," she says.

"Control is a drug like any other. Once you have a taste, you always need more." Sutton sighs, like a deity pestered by human nature. "I will only go so far against my brothers. But I cannot stand by as they resort to . . ." he sneers in distaste, "primitive methods. An assassination is out of the question, as I believe they fear your death will make you a martyr. So, instead, they've taken your daughter in the hopes of forcing you to do what they want."

The sentence is a tether on her heart, yanking her forward. "The oligarchs have Anna? Do you know where she is?"

"Unfortunately, I don't. Whoever took her is incredibly talented at remaining hidden."

"Whoever took her?" She slaps her hand against the desk, standing so forcefully that the chair falls. "You said it was your *brothers!*"

"Yes, I think so, but I'm unsure which ones."

"All of them, probably!" Lynell yells.

"It's unlikely." Sutton's voice remains maddeningly calm. "I trust Oswald fully and can't imagine Austin would put a little girl in danger. He has four daughters himself."

"I don't give a shit how many kids they have. Who has my daughter? Where is Anna?"

"Please sit, Mrs. Elysian."

She sucks in breath. Sutton's composure is a bucket of ice water, shocking her system back into reality, where she knows logic will get her miles further than emotion. Her legs shake as she picks the chair up and sits back down.

"Who do you think has her?" Her teeth grind as she bites out the words.

"I doubt any of them physically have her. She'll be somewhere that can't be traced back to them. But I'm sure whoever she's with is being supported and manipulated by one or more of my brothers."

"Which. Ones?" Lynell asks, teeth practically cracking.

"The only one I know for certain is connected to this whole ordeal is Bruce."

Bruce Macgill, Lynell thinks. He's a legacy oligarch, the third Macgill brother to take over after the first two died untimely deaths. Fear curdles her stomach.

"What am I supposed to do? How can you help me get Anna back?"

"I can help you satisfy my brothers and keep your position."

Swallowing a lump of pride, Lynell asks, "What's your plan?"

"You cannot fight the policy change. It will pass, no matter how convincing your arguments may be. So, accept that. Let my brothers manipulate you. Do what they want, get your daughter back, then become their puppet."

"Why would I do that?"

"Because no one expects much of a puppet but obedience upon pulling their strings. But I will hand you a knife."

CHAPTER 23

S awyer stretches her left leg, relieving the pressure on her back. A constellation of red imprints paint the side of her thigh, where it had been pressed into the carpet for nearly an hour. Her cat purrs from his perch in the corner of the room, where he watches her with half-lidded eyes, probably judging her in his own feline way.

Her bedroom floor is starting to look like the murder board of an obsessed stalker, or a conspiracy theory board. Recent articles about herself and Lynell fill the border, followed by the edited version of Ellery's speech and a digital flier for Friday's conference. In the center of the spiderweb of images and texts is a picture of Thomas Johnson and a typed message she hasn't looked at in five years.

```
Brothers, our words are as empty as the hearts of
those we despise if there are no actions behind
them. We must prove that we are worthy of these
beliefs. That we are worthy to be soldiers in
this never-ending war against the love of sin.
As our founding Elder said, "A man who speaks but
```

does not act is not a man at all, but a declawed
house cat mewling for food he cannot hunt."

Let us emulate his example and make a stand
none can ignore, just as he fought for his beliefs. This once great country, broken as it now
is, has gifted us with a weapon to begin ridding
the world of the infectious disease that too many
have both ignored and accepted. Let us earn the
title of Sin-Fighting Warriors and silence the
opposition's loudest voices. Rise, brothers, and
make our Elders proud!

Her lawyer found the manifesto weeks after Ellery died. Sawyer, fueled by anger, wanted justice outside of the Registration. She didn't have a civil case against Johnson, not for defamation, discrimination, or a misused Registration. But her lawyer said they could try suing someone else, claiming they coerced Johnson into Registering Ellery. If they could prove that Johnson was pressured, forced, or manipulated into Registering Ellery, then they might be able to sue the manipulator. Unfortunately, they never found the 'Elder' referenced. She scans the conspiracy board again. This time, though, her eyes snag on an article about the Resurrection she's read a dozen times.

THE RESURRECTION AVOIDS LEGAL ACTION

The Rebel Group Known as the Resurrection was Nearly Sued for Unlawful Assembly

On Friday last, thirty-one members of the Resurrection were apprehended in Salt Lake City during an anti-Registration protest and threatened with prosecution for unlawful assembly. Sawyer D'Angelo, the rebels' leader and granddaughter of the late Jude D'Angelo, flew to Utah to speak with the district attorney.

Sawyer stops reading, her finger pressed under Jude's name. She hasn't been described as his granddaughter in years, not since she became more well-known than her family's sordid history. At the beginning of her career, she was always named in reference to her grandfather, uncle, or father.

Ellery used to say, *"I never get lost. I just have to start over and pay better attention to the path."*

Deciding to start over, Sawyer stands, grabs her keys and phone, and hurries out to her car, driving to the large home several miles outside of the city limits. An older nurse wearing black horn-rimmed glasses framed in plastic gems answers the door.

"Sawyer, what a pleasant surprise," Melissa Redd greets her.

"Hi, Mrs. Redd," Sawyer says. "Where's Uncle Paul?"

"In his chair."

"Thank you." Sawyer walks to the den at the back of the home. Her uncle is sitting in the recliner where he spends most of his time these days, an IV taped to his hand and a monitor behind the chair. "Hi, Uncle Paul." Sawyer settles at the corner of a couch next to the recliner. Paul blinks, taking several seconds to focus on her.

"Sally, darling," Paul says. His strong voice is at odds with his thinning limbs and broken memory. "What are you doing here?"

Sawyer's smile stems more from sadness than happiness. Paul often confuses her for her Aunt Sally, who she favors more in appearance than her own mother. "I wanted to visit."

"Do the others know you're here?"

"No," Sawyer says. She's learned to allow Paul to lead conversations until she knows what year he thinks it is.

Otherwise, he grows agitated if she says something that opposes his current memories.

"My brother wouldn't appreciate his daughter speaking with the family disappointment," Paul warns.

"I won't tell him," Sawyer assures him. She spends a few minutes following Paul's lead, simply keeping her aging uncle company. Then, after about half an hour, she asks, "I was wondering, what is it that Grand—Father calls cowards?"

"Hmm . . ." Paul hums as he thinks. "You mean men who use words over brute force?"

"Yes."

"I believe the term is 'declawed house cats.' My brother never did appreciate a well-formed argument. He says he respects action, but I think he fears appearing stupid."

Sawyer's body goes cold.

A declawed house cat mewling for food he cannot hunt.

Her grandfather Jude was the founding Elder of the Sin-Fighting Warriors.

She feels herself walking into a blinding desert storm of grief. Paul continues speaking, oblivious to Sawyer's inattention.

Thomas Johnson and those other men were encouraged by her grandfather's words. Jude hated the Elysian family because he believed Gideon betrayed him. He also hated the rebels because he thought they were cowards, afraid of society progressing under the influence of the Registration.

But he died when Johnson was a child. So, how is he still influencing the Sin-Fighting Warriors?

"Paul, what church does Jude go to again?" Sawyer asks, though she's not sure her grandfather ever went to church. No one in their family is particularly religious.

"Oh, he doesn't. He says the weak willed go to church, needing a higher power to tell them what to do."

"What did he do after Gideon betrayed him and took the credit for the Registration?"

Paul frowns. "I'm not sure what you mean, Sally darling."

"I mean, did he leave the oligarchs immediately? Or did he stick around?"

"He left fairly soon, but not quietly. And he wouldn't surrender the influence of knowing such powerful people."

"You mean he kept in contact with the oligarchs? Is he still friends with them? Or anyone on the Registration committee?"

"Well, he was a few years ago. That's one reason we don't speak anymore. I told Jude that if he supports the Registration, he should be the bigger man and step aside. But he refuses to let Gideon win."

"What is he doing? How is he betraying Gideon?" she asks, remembering what Lincoln said on Thursday about Jude going behind Gideon's back.

Paul's attention has broken, though. He stares into the room with no fixed point of focus. Then his eyes fill with tears and his hands start to shake.

"Uncle Paul?" Sawyer stands in alarm. "Are you okay?"

Paul gasps and shakes his head. "No, don't leave me, please. I'm sorry. I'm so sorry."

"What is it?" Sawyer asks. Paul seems to be looking at someone a few feet in front of him. She knows no one is there, but Sawyer looks over her shoulder anyway.

"I ended things with Juniper, I swear."

"Who?"

"It meant nothing. She meant nothing, I promise." In his agitation, Paul starts pulling at the IV chord in his hand.

"It's okay, Uncle Paul," Sawyer says, trying to reach through time and soothe a man living decades ago.

"It was just Juniper. No one else. You're all who matters to me, Paige. Please."

"Who is Juniper?"

"Mr. D'Angelo!" Melissa rushes to Paul's other side.

Sawyer lets go of her uncle and jumps back, giving the nurse space to work. Rattled herself, Sawyer turns and leaves the room, both her heart and mind racing.

The entire drive home, she replays everything Paul said, unable to get two facts out of her mind.

First, her grandfather is the reason she is a widow.

Second, Paul, Sawyer's biggest role model, cheated on his wife with a woman named Juniper.

CHAPTER 24

Without any leads, Lynell and Daniel are practically forced to go along with Sutton's plan of doing nothing and playing the part of puppets on strings. The lack of action fills her with a new type of adrenaline somehow more uncomfortable than the immediate fear of death when she was running from Eric. She walks circles in the living room and kitchen until her bare feet hurt.

"Alright, that's it." Daniel jumps off the counter where he'd been sitting, watching her pace.

Lynell stops walking. "What?"

"We're going to talk to those tech siblings. The Fields."

"The Meadows?"

"Whatever," he says, retrieving a pair of shoes for them both.

"But Sutton—"

"He said not to do anything about Anna or the vote. He didn't say not to do anything at all. You still have a job."

"I'm waiting for Ramsey to get back from his meeting."

"Well, we can still be productive while you wait. You said it yourself—you can't use the code until you know how to use it."

She grins and kisses his cheek before taking the shoes. "You're brilliant."

"I try," he says.

Lynell calls the office in advance and, at first, the receptionist tells her the soonest she can schedule a meeting with both Owen and Summer Meadows is June third. But the Meadows' availability suddenly allowed for a meeting in an hour after the receptionist realized who exactly had called.

Marveling at the power of a name, Lynell asks Hayes to drive them, and he insists on bringing two other guards. As they pull up, her system finally filling with a sensation other than dread, she notes that the office building is more like a tower with thirty-two floors. It's covered in windows that reflect the blinding sun, making Lynell wish she'd put on sunscreen.

With Hayes in front and the two guards following, Lynell and Daniel head inside and take the elevator to the fifteenth floor. They ride up in silence and step out into a lobby brightly lit by sunlight shining through tall windows. Hanging from the ceilings are gardens of vines and moss clinging to long, thin, rectangle metal baskets that look like square bird feeder cages. A wooden bench is built into one wall, and the other has geometric lights embedded in the deeply grained wood. In the middle of the room is a circular desk, inside of which sits a young woman around Lynell's age, a tiny headphone visible in one ear, the other covered by a swoop of pink hair.

"Hello, how may I help you?" she asks. Then her eyes widen and she sits straighter. "Mrs. Elysian. Welcome. Mr. and Ms. Meadows are ready for you in the first room on the left."

Lynell smiles and nods. "Thank you."

The guards, Hayes included, stay stationed in the hallway while Lynell and Daniel enter the office. It isn't as large as Lynell expected. There's a bookshelf on one side, a desk on the other, and a coffee table between two couches in the center, one of which is occupied by two nearly identical people. Both look about fifty, but by their clear skin, vibrant dirty-blonde hair and athletic builds, Lynell guesses they're a decade older and have simply taken good care of themselves.

THE REGISTRATION REWRITTEN

They stand at Lynell and Daniel's entrance. She extends her hand to the woman first then her brother. "Owen and Summer Meadows, I presume?"

"Yes, welcome," Summer says. "We're happy to meet you, Mrs. Elysian. And you too, Mr. Carter."

Daniel returns her smile, shaking their hands next.

"How can we help you?" Summer sits and crosses her legs, showing off the tanned skin of her thigh.

Lynell follows suit, privately hoping she'll age as well as Summer. "I'm meeting everyone who works for me, and I'm starting with the department heads. Tell me how your experience working for the Registration has been. What works, what doesn't. What does a normal day look like for you? How are all the employees in your department? Are there any issues that need addressing? Basically, anything and everything you think I should know."

Owen and Summer share a quick glance, and Lynell gets the feeling they had expected something different. Owen looks at Daniel next, his confusion deepening.

"My husband is my partner, so he joins me when able," Lynell explains.

"Alright, I guess I'll start," Summer says, interlocking her fingers around her knee. She's efficient while she speaks, running through daily operations, how many employees she oversees, and assuring Lynell that everything is working smoothly and they don't have any issues.

Then it's Owen's turn, and he talks slower than his sister but has much less to say, which is unfortunate because the security side of IT is what interests Lynell more than anything else.

"We have several teams dedicated to updating firewall protection, prevention of data manipulation, and unauthorized third parties," Owen says. "The system is already the strongest I've ever seen. I mean, I've worked for the biggest insurance companies, private security agencies, and did some freelance work for intelligence agencies, and I've never seen anything as impenetrable as the inner powerhouse of the Registration data network."

"Inner powerhouse?" Lynell asks.

Owen nods and leans forward, searching the coffee table in front of them. Seeing nothing but magazines and coasters, he stands and heads to the desk where he grabs a pen and paper before returning. "Think about the Registration's entire cyberinfrastructure as several layers—like an onion." He draws a small circle then encloses it in a larger circle. He does this several more times until the biggest circle nearly touches the edge of the paper.

"Each layer includes different aspects of the Registration. Anything from the list of employees to the media department to the actual Registration list—all of it stored in different layers. The outermost circles are for data that either doesn't require additional security, or that we need easy access to. Such as public information on different websites, like the history of the Elysians and the Registration, names of the committee members, and photos from press conferences. The deeper in the layer, the more secure it is. Phone numbers, addresses, and records of past committee meetings."

Owen touches the pen to the center circle and gives Lynell and Daniel a wide smile. His teeth aren't as pristine as his sister's but his face lights up with excitement as he speaks, making up for any imperfections. "The innermost powerhouse of the layers is the database for the Registration itself. The list of every citizen who can be Registered and everyone who owns a Registration. Also, the constantly changing list of who has been Registered and by whom. Typically, any data that has to be updated as often as this list can have limited security. But this one?"

Owen's smile softens and he shakes his head, as if disbelieving what he's about to say. "The security is constantly being updated. The software system is as complex as it can be. I've never seen a database or a system as strong as this."

Lynell hears Zach's voice as if she'd put in headphones and hit play. *"Think of the Registration database as a large house. Every room is locked. It's pretty much impossible to get to that center room."*

This is her opening, she knows. The moment to bring up her real intention for the meeting. She glances at Daniel, who nods once in encouragement.

"What if someone had a master key to that center circle?" she asks. "Something to unlock that specific database."

Owen gives the widest smile yet and looks from Lynell to Summer, whose expression mirrors his.

"I knew it!" he says.

"Yes, you did," Summer says.

"You knew what?" Lynell asks.

Owen returns his attention to her, and Lynell recoils at the intensity of his gaze. "That there was a master key. I've been saying it for years. I even brought up the possibility with Mr. Elysian once, but he seemed certain there wasn't. One of Gideon Elysian's laws that's still active is that we update the defenses every year, but we can only do so with the closest layers to the center. That way, by the time anyone actually managed to penetrate those layers, they'd be updated, and they would have to start all over. But the powerhouse? Even I can't touch that. I tried once to create an SQL injection that would allow me to manipulate the database, but the security system destroyed the code faster than I could blink."

He doesn't seem abashed to admit to his boss, the Elysian Registration heir, that he tried hacking into the system. But perhaps doing so is part of his job. If he can break in, then so could someone else.

Lynell remembers Zach telling her that they changed the 'language' of the coding and the network every year. He'd also said that a handful of people can cross the digital barriers and access the database.

"If the head of security can't touch it, then how does the Registration even continue?" Daniel asks. "You said it yourself: the list is constantly being updated."

"Right, yes," Owen says, nodding quickly. "I, and a few other people, can get close to the center. We have keys, so to speak, to the closest layers. And I have enough information to input data changes that will automatically update the list, but I can't manually get to the list. Basically, when someone Registers another person, that information is passed through several layers and communicated to the center ring in a type of computer language.

Then the list updates itself. Same thing when someone is born, then entered into the system as a possible person to Register and maybe as someone who has a Registration."

"What if the list changes for other reasons?" Lynell asks. "Like when someone dies, or a Registration isn't fully paid off and abandoned, or if someone legally changes their name?"

"Same thing," Owen says. "Our system has a sort of private, direct pathway to governmental civil registry. Say Summer gets tired of having a weird ass name," Summer shoves her brother and rolls her eyes, but Owen continues without interruption, "and she goes to court to change her name to Summer Normal-last-name. That legal name change is processed by the civil registry, then automatically communicated to our system. The computer takes that information, digests it through the layers, and creates an automatic code that slips into the inner powerhouse to update the Registration list. Now, when someone goes to Register Summer, our system and the civil registry know they're talking about Summer Normal-last-name. It's the same process when birth and death certificates are processed."

"What if something goes wrong?" Lynell asks.

Owen shrugs. "Nothing goes wrong. Computer language on its own is perfect. Written code isn't, because it's only as good as the programmer who wrote it, and issues arise that need manual fixing. But what Gideon and his team did with *this* system is groundbreaking and has never been successfully copied. The internal core basically self-repairs if compromised. It was set up well, and no one pokes at the inner ring, so it continues processing information the same way it has since the beginning."

"There's no such thing as perfect in my experience. So, humor me," Lynell insists. "If someone managed to poke the system and disrupt the process, what happens? How do you fix it?"

"You'd need a master key," Owen says, still smiling wide. "Gideon Elysian was a brilliant man. He'd never have locked himself out of his own creation."

He didn't, Lynell thinks. She shifts, crossing her legs at the ankles and leaning forward as if to better look at the drawing of layered circles. Daniel inconspicuously touches her lower back. "But wouldn't it be dangerous to use a master key? If you unlocked it, could you control who could access the list?"

"Theoretically, yes."

"Theoretically?"

Owen picks up the pen, flipping it between his fingers as he thinks. "With the right skills and enough time, you could slowly unlock it, then lock it again behind you. Or, better yet, if you have an interim DoS, a Denial of Service, you could temporarily shut down the network, making the Registration inaccessible while you're using the master key. But it wouldn't work forever, and you'd have to lock everything back up before the DoS fails and the entire system becomes vulnerable.

"Plus, that would screw with any citizen updates in the civil registry that occurs while the DoS is active." He pauses, tapping the pen against his jaw. "Or, I guess you could do something similar with a virus. Like a trojan horse, you insert a code that infects all programs, and while everyone is focused on healing the virus, you're breaking into the center ring. But that's messy and usually used for people hacking into a network, not using a key. It might not work, because anybody watching and waiting for an opening wouldn't care about a virus as long as there's a way into the database." Owen presses the end of the pen between his lips as he looks up at the ceiling.

"So, it wouldn't work?" Lynell asks.

Owen pulls the pen away and shrugs. "Nothing would work completely."

Lynell presses her palm to the side of her head as if to manually force her thoughts to slow down. The more Owen speaks, the less she understands. It's a completely different language than the one she grew up speaking.

"Okay, the DoS. What does that look like?" she asks.

"It depends."

"On?"

"On the system. And the existing codes. I could create a DoS that might work but what you'd really want is a specifically created companion cloaking code, or a CCC, that was designed to work alongside your master key as partners-in-crime. The CCC plays a loop of the network looking normal, like a security camera that screams 'nothing to see here' while you use the key and get inside without anyone noticing."

"And you can't create that cloak—the CCC—now?"

"Like I said, I could, but it wouldn't be perfect. The true partner code would be made at the same time as the key. If Gideon created a master key, he would've destroyed the key mold and any evidence, right? So, the best I could do is create a generic DoS. *But* if you made a CCC with the same key mold, then it would be designed to work."

Lynell nods, absentmindedly pulling on her bottom lip. Her brain seems to vibrate with the information. She squeezes her eyes shut, desperately trying to straighten her thoughts.

A companion code.

Her code, the master key, unlocks the Registration. But like Zach said, it'd unlock it to everyone, and, once opened, she wouldn't be able to control the consequences. Chaos would ensue.

But if there was a companion key? Something to cloak her actions? That would fix everything.

"He's a businessman. He wants to grow his business," Zach had said about his father. Eric desperately wanted the code to use it. Lynell never understood why or how he would do so without destroying the very business he was so in love with.

With a CCC, Eric could manipulate the Registration as he saw fit, without the threat of losing control. Knowing that makes Eric's extreme efforts in retrieving the letter, and the subsequently hidden code, much more understandable.

Is there a CCC out there? If so, did Eric know what it was? Where is it now?

"How would I find this CCC?" Lynell asks.

"So, there is a code? A master key?" Owen asks.

"And you have it," Summer says the statement like a fact, not a question.

Lynell neither confirms nor denies. In her non-answer, and perhaps in her eyes, Owen and Summer see the truth.

"Mrs. Elysian, I'm not sure you realize the power you have," Owen says.

I do, Lynell thinks. Every day, she's becoming more and more aware of the power she inherited the second her knife sunk into her uncle's gut.

But the power is still incomplete. "The companion code. How do I find it?"

"If it's hidden, you'd have to find out where. The most logical place to start would be with whoever hid it. You'd have to find the person who knows the CCC. Only they could tell you what it is."

CHAPTER 25

R amsey lets out an involuntary hiss after shoving his hands under a stream of water. Small jagged pain pulses from the cuts on his knuckles. He bites his bottom lip and breathes through his nose while scrubbing his hands with soap.

He got carried away questioning one of the prisoners in the Elysian dungeon. Compared to Ramsey's knuckles, the man's face fared far worse. His nose will now forever be crooked, and he'll never get those teeth back, but he's alive. It was pointless questioning. Ramsey learned nothing helpful.

It appears none of Eric's most loyal men know anything about Johnson and his bosses.

Back at his house, Ramsey locks himself in his office, punches in the safe's password, and pulls out the stack of *Midnight Files*. He flips through them until landing on Warner Golden's profile. Most of the committee members' files are filled with the typical bullshit: affairs, drugs, mysterious deaths, proof of abuse, bank statements, tax fraud, and more boring blackmail material.

Golden's file is different. Nearly every inch is dedicated to anything that might tell Eric where Harlow was hiding. That's not what Ramsey is interested in, though. He studies its early pages, created several days before Gideon and Eli died. Ramsey doesn't know if that means Gideon started the *Midnight Files* and Eric took them over after killing his brother, or if Eric started collecting information long before he was owner of the Registration. There are four photos of Warner Golden with Paul D'Angelo and one with Lincoln D'Angelo. Most committee chairs avoided the D'Angelos back then, but Golden seemed to have been working with them.

There's also pictures of three bank transfers. One is fifty-thousand dollars from Golden to an unknown account made twenty-eight years ago. The second is fifteen-thousand dollars from an unknown account to Golden's twenty-five years ago. The last is hours after the second, fifteen-thousand dollars from Golden to Elizabeth Crane. Ramsey had wondered how Elizabeth could afford buying Lynell a Registration. Now, he knows. But he still hasn't figured out who sent the money to Golden to send to Elizabeth.

At the bottom of the page, Ramsey writes, *First time Eric thought Eli might have another child.* It's the only thing he learned during the questioning. Eric discovered this wire transfer and became obsessed with finding Elizabeth Crane and her possible child. While interesting, it's not helpful for Mrs. Elysian's current predicament.

Ramsey returns the file, pulling out Macgill's. He practically has these files memorized, but he reads through each of the oligarchs' again, looking for a hint of their plans with Mrs. Elysian. It's not until Sutton's file that he finds something interesting that puts a new light to Harlow's information.

There's the blurry photo of Sutton exiting a building, Ellery Klein slightly visible behind him. Before, Ramsey didn't think much about it. The picture is one of dozens, Sutton with a different activist or rebel in each.

Written after the photos is, *Sutton digging into Elysian and D'Angelo secrets—high surveillance.* Ramsey dismissed the sentence the first time he read it. Sutton hasn't proven a threat to Mrs. Elysian, and she was a child when these photos were taken, unconnected to the Elysian name.

The image is becoming clearer with what Harlow shared: that Sawyer wants to give Ellery's speech, which Harlow believes Sutton might have helped Ellery write. If Sutton had Elysian secrets and helped Ellery write a speech, there's no telling what it might contain.

Ramsey already doubled security for Friday's conference, but perhaps he should add more. One oligarch already derailed plans by taking Anna. He won't let another ruin things further because of his earlier failures in rebellion.

CHAPTER **26**

"You're an Elysian. You're my niece and I care about you."

"All you need to do is share the letter with me, and together we will make this world a better place."

"Be a part of this family."

"I'm offering you a choice."

A repeating playlist of everything her uncle ever said to her plays in Lynell's mind. Eric ended the life she knew, forced her through unimaginable pain, and left her with blood on her hands and an empire of death to rule. All because he wanted the information she had so he could become more powerful.

Now she's in Eric's position. She has the power of the Elysian heir. She owns the Registration. She *is* the Registration.

And there might be information out there she needs for more control and power.

Lynell has a front row seat to history repeating itself.

"It might not exist," Daniel says. They're in the living room, Daniel sitting in an armchair and Lynell lying on her back, stretched out on the couch.

"If it does . . ."

"Lyn, don't let this send you into a spiral. Searching for this might get the attention of the oligarchs and Anna's kidnappers. We can't aggravate them into hurting her."

"Danny, this is what we've been needing to safely use the code and re-write the Registration our way."

Daniel leans forward, kicking Lynell's foot to get her to look at him. "Before you go storming into peoples' offices, let's think this through. What did Zach say about the code?"

"That when Gideon first created it, he split it up into parts and gave those parts to several people," Lynell says. She's gone over every detail of her conversations with Zach about the Registration and the code since leaving the Meadows' office two hours ago. "Maybe this one is the same. Maybe it's in parts. Or, maybe one of the people Gideon gave a part of the master key to used it to create the CCC."

"Exactly. So, let's make a list." Daniel stands and retrieves his journal and a pen, flipping through pages until he finds an empty one. "Who do we know or think had a key?"

"Most of them would be dead."

"But they would have passed it on, right?" Daniel returns. "The way your dad did."

Lynell nods and sits up, cradling her injured fingers close so the splints don't bump against anything. "Robin Jacobs, she's been on the committee the longest. Although her dad died in the war, so maybe not . . ." She closes her eyes and pinches the bridge of her nose as she thinks. "All of the legacy oligarchs," she says, "the ones whose family members knew and worked with Gideon."

"Which ones are legacies?"

"Sutton, Roman Mills, Zane Long, Oswald Vanderberg, and Bruce Macgill."

"Macgill," Daniel repeats. "Didn't Sutton say he was involved with kid-napping Anna?"

Lynell nods, opening her eyes.

Daniel is gripping the pen with a vibrating fist.

"She's going to be okay," she whispers.

Instead of responding, Daniel asks, "Are there committee member legacies?"

"Verity McGowan, Izrael Holmes, and Junior Booker."

He writes down each name as she says them with so much pressure that the pen nearly tears the page. They continue building the list of people who might know of a CCC until Ramsey arrives, holding two bags of takeout food.

"I hope you two like pho," he says.

"Love it," Lynell answers, following Ramsey to help unload the containers. She notices bandages on his knuckles but doesn't ask where they came from. She has the feeling she doesn't need to know. "What's the occasion?"

Ramsey leans against the kitchen island and gives them both a rare, dazzling smile. "I have a lead on Anna."

Lynell drops a packet of chopsticks.

Daniel hurries to the kitchen. "What? How?"

"I met an old contact who has a unique insight into the committee. She's certain that at least two chairs have used blackmail and threats in the past to further their agendas."

"Who?" Daniel asks.

"Which chairs?" Lynell asks.

"Finnegan Reese and Tamara Nelson," Ramsey says.

She's both unsurprised and surprised. Since meeting him, she expects Finnegan knows more than he's letting on. The man is way too charming not to be a devil in disguise. But Tamara? She's perfected the act of innocence.

"My contact received an intercepted message between those two in which they discussed the transportation of the bargaining chip. I'm certain Anna is the bargaining chip."

Daniel grabs the counter with one hand, leaning his weight on the arm. "They're moving her? Why?"

"Probably to keep us from finding her," Lynell answers.

"Which means they're worried we will," Ramsey says. "And moved, past tense. The message was from a few days ago."

Lynell digs her nails into the palms of her hands. "And we didn't know until now? We're running out of time. Fast."

"And we still have no idea where she is," Daniel says.

"Actually, I put one of my best men on Macgill after your conversation with Sutton—don't worry, he wasn't seen. He's a professional," Ramsey adds, seeing Daniel's incredulous look. "Macgill hasn't gone anywhere suspicious, but he did meet with Finnegan Reese yesterday, so I added a tail on him. Earlier today, Reese called an unknown number, and my guy managed to patch into the network to hear the last part of the call."

He sets an old model smartphone on the counter, taps the screen, then clicks a red play button. Lynell immediately recognizes the voice coming from the speaker as Finnegan Reese.

"Your relief will be there in an hour. He just left Golden's. And don't kill the woman. If she tries escaping again, lock her and the kid in the basement. There are enough provisions down there to keep them alive until Friday."

Ramsey stops the recording. Lynell's eyes stay glued to the phone until she hears a choking sound from Daniel. He covers his mouth, his eyes squeezed shut like it'll block out reality.

"Golden," Lynell mutters, turning back to Ramsey. "Not Warner? Can't be him."

He nods. "No, he's not working with Reese."

"But—"

"They're having Warner followed," Ramsey says. "They don't trust him."

"How do you know?" Lynell asks, trying not to wince at the sound of Daniel's broken breathing by her side.

"He's my contact's informant on the committee. He knows he's being followed, which is likely why he hasn't spoken to you directly about any of this. But he has a pre-arranged way to get private messages to my contact."

"You keep saying 'my contact,'" Lynell says. "Who are they?"

Ramsey's satisfied grin falters. "That's not important."

"Yes, it is." She glares at him, the silence stretching uncomfortably. When he doesn't show signs of answering, Lynell says, "You don't keep secrets from me, Ramsey. Not now. Not about this. Who is your informant?"

He feels like a different person as he holds her gaze uncertainly. Finally, his chest falls with a sigh, and he says, "It's Harlow Graham."

Both Lynell and Daniel gasp. She knows the name because she studied the files on the committee members so deeply. "Warner's daughter," she says.

"And Zach's mom," Daniel adds.

Ramsey nods. "She came back to town a few months ago and has been working with the Resurrection."

Lynell reaches out for a stool and sinks onto it. Names bounce against her skull at an agonizing pace. Harlow's name repeats over and over. She doesn't know much about the woman, only that she spent most of her childhood summers with Warner, and that's how she met Eric Elysian. She disappeared not long after giving birth to Zach, and no one knew where she was or even if she was alive.

Until Zach found her five years ago, of course. Lynell remembers Zach telling her about finding his mother, then losing her to Eric's threats all over again. That conversation with her cousin was the first time Lynell truly understood Zach. Even trusted him.

While Lynell muses, Daniel's attention has snapped back to the most pressing matter.

"So, where is Anna?"

"I'm not positive, but I'm working on it. Knowing the house she's at has a basement and is an hour from Golden's narrows the search considerably. I'm looking into any place that might have a connection to Reese, Nelson, or Macgill."

"What if more oligarchs and committee chairs are working with them?" Lynell asks.

"It's likely, but these three we at least know for sure. I'm personally checking any house with suspicious activity. But we know something else from Reese's call. It seems they plan to honor their word to return Anna and Catherine on Friday."

"After the vote passes and the entire country is under their thumb," Lynell mumbles.

"Even the best chess player has to make sacrifices," Ramsey says. He pockets the phone again and finishes unloading the food.

Though the conversation is over, Lynell doesn't feel free from its clutches. Most everything Ramsey told her was good news, or at least helpful news, but it did nothing to make her feel better.

Both Ramsey and Sutton have told her to sacrifice the country for Anna's safety. To play the game and her daughter will be okay. But the other side continues to cheat, and they haven't made a single sacrifice.

Lynell is sick and tired of obeying the rules. She'll never make real change if she plays their game.

She has to invent a new one.

CHAPTER **27**

LYNELL

Tuesday Late Afternoon

L ynell wants to stay home and discuss their plan for finding Anna, but Ramsey reminds her that she has to attend a pre-rehearsal for Friday's convention.

"Pre-rehearsal? Isn't that overkill?" she asks through the cracked bathroom door, pulling on a soft pantsuit while Ramsey waits in the bedroom.

"Not for something as big as this convention," he says. "Do you realize how much work has gone into updating every detail about this event? These things typically take months."

"We could've postponed my succession and let the convention happen as originally planned." She runs a brush through her hair, then pulls open the bathroom door.

Ramsey looks her up and down, nods, and heads for the door, Lynell at his heels. "You would've been okay with the oligarchs and committee members who kidnapped your daughter using this event for their advantage, knowing the whole country will be watching while they announce a lethal policy change?"

She huffs, unable to argue with the logic. She doesn't say anything until they're in the back seat of an SUV. "What should I expect at this rehearsal?"

"It'll be quick. We'll just go over the schedule and your roles."

"Will the oligarchs be there? Or any committee members?"

Ramsey scoffs. "I doubt it. They've been doing this every year for a long time. They don't need to rehearse."

She'd love to argue that she doesn't need to rehearse either, but as soon as they arrive at the massive convention center, it's clear she does. A short man with long red hair meets them at the front doors and introduces himself as Hugh. He guides them inside and spends twenty minutes giving a tour of the building. He has a slight lisp and offers much more information on the building than necessary.

The tour ends in the auditorium where her succession, speech, and the policy change announcement will occur. The space is more populated than the rest of the building. Several security guards and employees involved with the event planning, according to Hugh, roam the space, attending to tasks Lynell can't imagine.

Once backstage, Hugh excuses himself and gives Lynell an awkward half bow. She turns around, scanning the large backstage area. She's studying an impressive collection of screens, cameras, and speakers, when a tall woman with dark skin and thick black curls approaches her.

"Hello, Mrs. Elysian." She holds out a well-manicured hand. "My name is Jessica." She smiles, showing off a gap between her front two teeth and a shiny gem on her lateral incisor.

Lynell accepts the handshake, confusion tugging her eyebrows together.

"Jessica has been running point on convention plans," Ramsey explains. "She's the reason everything was updated so quickly to accommodate your succession."

"Oh. Nice to meet you," Lynell says. "This is all very impressive."

"Thank you, but I can't take all the credit. I have a great team."

"Yeah, I've met part of your team."

"Hugh?" Jessica asks. "He's one of the best. This is the fifth annual convention he's helped plan. Though it's also the biggest, by far." She pauses long enough to take a breath, then says, "Which is why I requested this pre-rehearsal with you. It's important that you're prepared for every step, especially surrounding your succession."

"Right," Lynell says.

"I think we should go through everything once or twice so you're comfortable. It shouldn't take long. Do you have your speech ready?"

"I . . ."

"Yes, we do," Ramsey says, filling in Lynell's pause of uncertainty. She gives him a short look. He sent her important points of the speech on Sunday morning, but she was too preoccupied with Anna to give it any thought, much less write anything.

Jessica nods. "Perfect. I suggest reading through that once, too. Everyone here has signed an NDA, so nothing you say will leave these walls. Are you ready?"

"Uhm, yeah," Lynell says, though she doesn't feel ready.

"Great." Jessica leads her to the greenrooms backstage and opens one of the doors. "So, this will be your dressing room."

They go over where Lynell needs to be and when, how long the oligarchs will talk before she's introduced, how long her speech will be, when to introduce the committee member who will be announcing the policy change, and contingency plans for the most likely problems—like someone being sick or a camera dying in the middle of recording.

Lynell attempts to follow every step, but her mind screams that none of this matters. She should be home with Daniel talking about the CCC and Anna and what they're going to do with Sawyer to try and stop Johnson and the policy change. By the time she's standing in the middle of the stage where the oligarchs will swear her in to the office she already has, her nerves are frayed. Ramsey gives her a page titled 'Succession Speech,' and Lynell's not sure she'll be able to read the whole thing without exploding.

"My grandfather, Gideon Elysian, had dreams of a better future for this country. My father, Eli Elysian, worked hard to help keep these dreams alive and thriving. Serving you through leading the Registration is in my blood.

Family is everything to me. There is nothing more important. But for me, my family doesn't stop with the Elysians, it extends to our legacy, the Registration, and all the good it can do for the people of this country. As the Elysian heir—" Lynell falters, the words suddenly turning to glue in her throat.

She can't do it. She can't stand here and read a speech about how great her family is, knowing full well that her inherited last name drags along death and pain everywhere it goes.

She can't practice saying this bullshit when her *real* family, her husband and daughter and friends, are in danger. They need her. She needs to be with them. Not here practicing a speech she doesn't want to give.

Lynell looks up from the paper crinkling in her tight grip and finds Ramsey a few feet away. One look and he nods, clears his throat, and says, "Alright, I think that's enough for today."

"But, the speech—" Jessica starts.

"She'll practice," Ramsey interrupts, "but it's not here and now. Thank you very much for taking us through the convention schedule." He crosses the stage, plucks the page out of Lynell's hand, and smiles at Jessica. "I'll call you in the morning to go over final details."

"You'll both be here for the formal rehearsal on Thursday, correct?" Jessica asks.

Ramsey nods. "Of course! We wouldn't miss it, but we really must be going. Thank you again, Jessica."

Lynell mumbles a "thank you." Her vision blurs from a strange shaking like the tremors before an earthquake. Her ribcage pushes against her heart and her lungs squeeze out air too fast.

She's panicking.

Why is she panicking?

Several moments later, she realizes that Ramsey has grabbed her arm and is leading her out of the auditorium. She looks over her shoulder to see her guards following in their typical formation. Ramsey holds her upright, keeping her from stumbling. They don't speak until they're back in the car.

"I'm sorry. I don't know what happened," she says.

"I do," Ramsey replies. "You froze."

"I froze."

"Yes, you did. Anyone would."

"I can't freeze. There's too much at stake."

Ramsey sighs. Runs a hand over his beard and says, "You aren't alone anymore, Mrs. Elysian. Everything isn't on you."

That's not what it feels like, Lynell thinks. "But the speech is," she says.

"The speech is still three days away. We have time to change it and practice. First, you need to get some rest."

"I can't sleep while my daughter is out there with some crazy kidnapper."

"Killing yourself won't help her. And I have people looking for her. You can't do anything until we know where she is. When we get home, take the night off with Mr. Carter. Eat. Sleep. Then, tomorrow, we'll get back to work."

"One day, I'm going to get tired of you being right all the time."

Ramsey smiles. Genuinely smiles. Something she's rarely seen before. "One day, you won't need me to be right all the time."

Unsure how to respond, Lynell nods, leans back and rests her head on the top of the seat. Lynell doesn't want to give that speech. She needs to figure out how to keep this convention, and the announcements, from happening as planned.

CHAPTER 28

SAWYER

Wednesday Afternoon

S awyer is useless all day. She zones out during a meeting with the board of directors, and stumbles over her words while practicing the speech for Friday. The event is two days away, and everyone else in the Resurrection has done their part to prepare.

They've dedicated months to planning how to hijack the broadcast so Sawyer's speech would play instead of live feeds of the convention. Every aspect has been tested and is ready to go.

Every aspect but Sawyer. Because she's still mentally stuck in her great-uncle's den.

Driven to near madness, she decides to call her father. But when he answers, she panics and rather than bringing up Paul, she tells Lincoln about what she found in the bathroom at the Catholic boarding school. Guinness jumps in her lap, and she gratefully pets the cat while she practically dumps the story onto her dad's lap through the phone.

"You know, one of my dad's hopes for the Registration was to make that stuff more accessible for women," Lincoln says. "He even thought people should be able to have an extra Registration for pregnancies. That's one of the things your little group talks about, right?"

"It's not a little group, Dad," she mumbles, knowing the contradiction is pointless. The Resurrection could have a billion members, and her father would still call it a 'little group.'

"Well, your grandfather would've agreed with you."

Her hand stills on Guinness's back. The cat mewls, kicking at her arm to get her to continue petting. "Actually, Grandad is sort of why I called."

"Oh?"

"Yeah . . ." Sawyer swallows and licks her lips. "I visited Uncle Paul yesterday. He mentioned Grandad and said he refused to let Gideon win even after he was no longer an oligarch. Do you know what that means? What did he do to try and . . . defeat Gideon?"

Her father's sigh crackles through the phone's speaker. The sound startles Guinness, who jumps off Sawyer's lap and saunters to the windowsill.

"Honey, you shouldn't take anything Paul says too seriously. He's not all there anymore."

"He's not stupid," Sawyer argues. "And he's not making stuff up. He just doesn't realize who he's talking to or what year it is."

"Exactly. He's probably mixing up events from several points in time."

She almost asks about the Sin-Fighting Warriors, but the words are too thick with emotion to pass through her throat. "Okay. But he also mentioned a woman named Juniper. Do you know her?"

Lincoln answers with silence.

"Dad? Can you hear me?"

"Yeah, yes, honey. I'm sorry, I . . ." he clears his throat. "I haven't heard that name in a while. You're sure he said Juniper?"

She sits forward, perched on the edge of the couch. "Yes, I'm sure. I think he had an affair with her."

"Oh, honey. I wish you wouldn't let this stuff bother you."

"This is my family, Dad."

"You do too much. With that dangerous rebel stuff and everything. Why don't you take a break from it all? You could visit your brother in France."

"Don't change the subject," Sawyer says. "Who is Juniper?"

"Like you said, she's a younger woman Paul had an affair with for a short time. It ended after Paige found out."

"How do you know about it?" Sawyer asks.

Lincoln sighs again. "That's enough, Sawyer. Forget about all of this. It doesn't matter. It was over fifty years ago."

"It does matter, Dad! How long was he cheating on Paige? Is that why they got divorced? Did you know Juniper?"

"Let it go, Sawyer." Lincoln's 'dad voice' makes Sawyer snap her mouth shut. She pulls her feet onto the couch, grabbing her knees like she did as a kid when she got in trouble. "I'm sorry, but bringing this all up can't do any good. You don't have to unearth every bad thing in this world. Don't let this become your next obsession like the Resurrection. Let it all go. None of it is good for you. If you keep trying to get justice for everyone else because you can't get it for Ell—" He abruptly stops talking, but not before his words punch Sawyer in the chest. "I'm sorry, honey, I didn't mean that."

"Yeah, I know," Sawyer says, her voice smaller than ever. She presses her forehead to her knees. "It's okay."

"I am sorry. I hate seeing you in pain."

"I know, Dad. It's okay," she repeats. "I need to go, but I love you."

"I love you too."

She ends the call, feeling worse than she had when it started. It's not only what her dad said that bothers her, it's how she reacted. If she would get angry just once like Ellery, then maybe she wouldn't keep walking into situations that suck her into an emotional storm. Even through her biggest act of defiance, the Resurrection, she's always hesitant to do anything too drastic. Friday's conference will be their biggest move yet, and all she's doing is giving a speech her dead wife wrote.

She's in the midst of brooding about her own failures when her phone starts ringing. She picks it up and flips it around, expecting her father's name on the screen. Instead, it's Lynell.

Relieved, Sawyer answers.

They decide to meet at one of her dad's vacant rental properties. Malakai's eyes track Sawyer as she paces the hallway, occasionally flicking to the back door where Lynell and Daniel should enter when they arrive. Sawyer opens the clock on her phone, watching the second hand tick in a circle until someone knocks on the back door.

"Nice house," Lynell says, neck straining to look at the high ceiling. The living room, foyer, kitchen, and dining room are a large, open-concept box. Tall windows fill the walls, but Malakai pulled the blinds shut before Sawyer even stepped foot inside. "It's not yours, is it?"

"Of course not," Sawyer says. "It's a rental, currently without occupants. No cameras." She watches the couple take in the area, Daniel's body nearly as tense as Malakai's. Lynell looks both relaxed and stressed, as if she can separate fear of an immediate threat from anxiety of future dangers.

"You okay?" Lynell asks, dropping onto one of the cream velvet chairs the interior decorator picked out for staging. The entire house is filled with old contemporary-style furniture and decoration. Bold accents, such as the geometric blue rug in the living room, break up the generally monochromatic earth tones. "Have you gotten any more threats since last we talked?"

"No, nothing. He's gone silent."

"Not silent. We have plenty to update you."

Lynell launches into the story, Daniel dropping in a morsel of information every few sentences. At first glance, he carries all the stress for them both, but the longer Lynell speaks, the more Sawyer sees hints of a deep turmoil.

Lynell picks at a scab on her forearm while explaining their recent history with Anna, information that didn't make it to the papers, like Eric threatening her and Zach sacrificing himself to save her. Lynell's foot shakes and a hitch in her breath ends every sentence when she talks about someone kidnapping Anna.

"I'm so sorry." Sawyer personally knows how weak those words are when your world is falling apart around you, but she has nothing else. A weak hand reaching out is better than being completely alone.

"We'll get her back," Lynell says. "But . . . that's one of the reasons I needed to talk to you. The kidnappers gave us a ransom."

Sawyer frowns. She has money, sure, but so does Lynell. "You don't have enough money?"

Lynell shakes her head. She stops scratching the scab and presses her thumb against the bleeding edge. "It's not money. I had my first committee meeting on Thursday. Earlier this year, they voted for a policy change to go into effect next week. I called for a revote on Friday. The last one was three against five, and I was trying to get one member to change their vote so I could break the tie, when Anna was taken. The ransom is to let the policy change happen and they'll give Anna back."

"What is the policy change?" Sawyer asks.

Lynell hesitates. She pops the knuckles on her good hand and looks at a spot above Sawyer's head, while taking several long breaths.

Then she explains.

It's worse than Sawyer had feared. Harlow passed along information she learned from her father, so they knew the committee was planning a change involving the price of the Registration but not much else. This will make the lives of anyone who can't afford or doesn't approve of the Registration virtually worthless. The rich will be able to kill without consequence. More so than they already can.

The silver lining is that Lynell and Daniel seem to hate the policy change as much as Sawyer. The fact that Lynell told Sawyer at all is a near miracle. But if Sawyer had a child and her child was taken, she would also align with anyone to save her kid.

"What can I do?" Sawyer asks.

"I remembered you mentioned Friday last time we met. There's something about the convention you didn't tell us," Lynell says. "We need to know everything before we come up with a plan."

"Right." Sawyer unleashes a shuddering exhale. "The Resurrection has spent the last few years growing and planning. We've never had more money, resources, or recruits. Our sources told us that the Registration committee plans to make changes to the laws, but we had no idea to what extent. Still, we figured it's time to take more direct action. We're hoping to make a statement, a call to action, but we want it to be as impactful as possible. As soon as the date for the annual convention was announced, we started planning a way to use it in our favor. We realized we don't have to be on site to speak or take over, we just have to be able to hack the broadcast."

Lynell's eyes widen a fraction. "How are you going to do that?"

"It's difficult, but we have people smarter than you and me about technology and virtual broadcasts. We needed a handful of our people in the convention to help hack the hardware encoder and streaming network communication to replace their video with ours."

Lynell leans toward Sawyer as she listens, and Daniel occasionally reacts with a sound of understanding, approval, or shock.

They're a good audience, Sawyer thinks. And that's a vital characteristic of a good leader. Ellery used to practice listening because it was one of the only things that didn't come naturally to her.

She wanted to reply, to take action, not sit in silence trying to listen to someone else speak while her mind had already moved way beyond the conversation.

"We were going to do it during the typical speech an oligarch gives every year at these conventions, but we've altered our plans slightly since they announced your succession, which last I heard, will be before any announcements, like the policy change. Is that right?"

"Yes," Lynell confirms. "That's what they told me at a pre-rehearsal yesterday. Also, who does that? Has a pre-rehearsal? Isn't a rehearsal all the pre you need?"

Daniel, who has mostly been silent until that point, grips her knee and whispers, "Lyn."

She looks at him. Her shoulders quiver slightly with a breath.

Sawyer realizes that for every small hint of stress she's caught in Lynell, Daniel has felt a dozen more. He's probably more in tune with her feelings than she is.

Watching them makes the pages in her back pocket seem to heat up. She'd grabbed the printout of the speech at the last second before leaving, some unseen force driving her actions. She's not sure if it was a desire to have Ellery's words close to her, or if something deeper wanted her to be prepared in case she needed to share the speech with Lynell.

Part of her doesn't want to. She isn't ready to share this part of her wife with anyone, much less the Elysian heir. But in less than forty-eight hours, she'll be giving Ellery's words to the entire country, and despite barely knowing the woman, Lynell is already more than just the Elysian heir.

Her hand is moving to pull the speech free before she's made up her mind to do so. "Maybe this will help," she says.

No one hears her because at the same time, the air splits with the sound of Malakai screaming.

"GET DOWN!"

In a blink, Sawyer watches everything around her move without a moment of hesitation. Daniel lunges forward, grabs Lynell, and yanks her to the floor. Malakai, a gun in his hands, is running toward Sawyer, waving at her to drop.

The window closest to them breaks, glass flying through the air and shattering onto the floor. Sawyer's eyes follow the object that broke the window, landing with a sprinkling of glass in the center of the room. A small blinking device.

Bomb.

Then there's an echoing pop and the object goes off. Rather than an explosion that melts the skin from her body, smoke bursts from the device.

Sawyer coughs and finally drops to the floor, unable to see or process everything she's hearing. Someone is shouting. Two people, maybe. There's another shattering of glass, but Sawyer can't understand why. The building is already heavy with smoke.

The storm in her mind has finally freed itself and become real. She's legitimately stuck in a sandstorm, and she'll never be able to see or breathe clearly again.

Her heart speeds up. A nauseating wave of dizziness washes over her.

More glass shattering and shouting, and she realizes it's not smoke bombs being thrown through the windows.

It's bullets. Three of them so far. Or maybe four.

"Sawyer!" This voice breaks through to her consciousness like the others hadn't. Maybe it's because she hadn't expected it. Or maybe it's because the voice is feminine rather than masculine. It's not Malakai shouting orders or Daniel yelling for Lynell.

It's Lynell, her voice filled with fear—fear for Sawyer.

"Lynell, we have to go!"

"Get Sawyer!"

"I got her."

Sawyer hears the words but can't distinguish who says them through the chaos. A large hand grabs her wrist and pulls her up. Sawyer can't make out distinct features, but she knows it's Malakai pulling her toward an exit he likely already had mapped out.

"Go! Hurry!"

They're running, and the smoke is starting to dissipate. Whoever threw the smoke bomb is going to be inside soon. They're going to catch them and kill them. Or worse.

Sawyer speeds up, her brain finally caught up with the events, clicking into the clear urgency to follow Malakai and escape.

But with the clarity comes awareness of the feelings in her body. Sharp stings of cutting pain jump around, as if trying to confuse her about its origin. She's not sure what caused it. Was she shot? Was it the glass?

She sees the exit, a side door through the house's laundry room, and relief starts to emerge amongst the fear and pain.

The relief shatters with the glass behind her, and a woman's scream fills the air.

CHAPTER 29

TJ

Wednesday Evening

T J sets up in a neighboring house that's empty while the residents are out for the evening. The child's bedroom window offers a perfect view into the living room. After kicking aside a few dolls with unnaturally large eyes and cinched waists, he sets up the gun and peers through the scope. Ten minutes pass, and a large Black man fills the windows. He frowns as the man pulls the blinds shut, obscuring his view.

No worries, he can still hear everything said in the living room. He planted a small microphone earlier.

TJ patiently waits, listening to their conversation. Each passing second pulls at his muscles until he feels so taut that a mere breath would snap him into several pieces. The bitch's voice is like boiling water, seeping into the tissue of his brain. His teeth are pressing so hard together it's a shock they don't crack.

Both women in that house are so stupid and delusional.

One is wasting her life fighting against a system that works because she's pissed that it wouldn't let her continue living in sin. And she can't even fight the system well. She's a brainless, boneless, pitiful imitation of stronger people.

The other is arrogant because she accidentally survived the Registration. She thinks she knows what she's doing and can have it all. Power, control, and a family. She doesn't even seem to care that her daughter is in danger.

They're going to ruin everything. Especially Lynell. The girl who can't pick a last name because she has no idea who she is or what she's doing. Lynell Carter is a sinful young woman who loves a man but doesn't know how to be a wife or a mother.

Lynell Mize is a bitter product of a system that lets inferior men do whatever they want. Lynell Elysian? She doesn't really exist. She's an illusion. A *hope*. A rag doll for the country to fight over until it's ripped apart at the seams.

He can't take it anymore. He's heard enough. He'll have plenty of information to take back.

The smoke bomb launcher is already prepared. He lines up the shot, presses the button, and watches as the tiny device propels past two yards and crashes into the window. It bends part of the blinds, giving him a small circle of visibility.

Pressing his eye tight against the gun's scope, he watches smoke fill the room. He can't quite see, but imagines all four have dropped to the floor. He carefully aims at the top corner of the window and shoots. Then he repositions the gun slightly and pulls the trigger again. The blinds covering the window crumble and fall, giving him a much better view into the building. Unfortunately, the smoke still makes it nearly impossible to see anything.

He pulls the trigger without aiming to add to their fear. They're screaming, but nothing that sounds like a scream of being shot.

He pushes his eye into the scope even harder, knowing that a deep red indent will linger around his eye for a while.

The group has started moving for the exit, and the woman is being covered by that brute who follows her everywhere. He shoots the wall above the man's head, causing him to duck.

But the woman is out of view too. Letting out a deep breath, he watches them stand and run for the exit.

One last time, he aims the gun.

He pulls the trigger.

The microphone catches a scream.

He smiles.

CHAPTER 30

Blood oozes between her fingers. She sucks in a sharp breath as another pulse of pain overtakes her. The years have increased her threshold for pain, but she still almost fell unconscious from the burn of a bullet slicing through her skin.

With Daniel's help, she manages to stay upright until they reach the car parked down the street.

She slumps into the seat, and Daniel wraps his fingers around her wrist, pushing her hand against the wound on her left arm. "Press hard," he says. The pressure is a punch to her gut but she obeys, holding the blood inside her body.

Daniel leaves her side and Lynell blinks, her mind struggling to catch up with the last few minutes.

A smoke bomb. Shooting. Running. Pain.

Now she's in the back of a car she doesn't recognize. She takes in her surroundings, finding Sawyer in the adjacent seat.

The woman's skin, which is normally a few shades darker than Lynell's, is now utterly blanched. Their gazes meet, Sawyer's eyes wide, pupils dilated. Her lips are parted, and her stare slides down Lynell's face, landing on her arm. An inch further and it would have hit bone. Instead, it pierced the edge of her bicep.

"Are you okay?" Daniel asks, turning from his spot in the passenger's seat to watch Lynell.

The car is moving but Daniel isn't driving. She frowns, then remembers Malakai, and sure enough, he's behind the wheel, hands gripping it tight as he speeds to safety.

Lynell nods. Nausea roils in her gut, and she shakes her head. "Probably." Her voice is steadier than she expected. "Hurts like hell, but it could be worse."

Daniel smiles wide, showing off white teeth. The gesture is so out of place in their current situation that Lynell feels her lips mimicking his, climbing up in a grin.

"That's my girl," he says. "Badass."

The car hits a bump, and her smile falls into a breathy hiss and groan at the renewed flash of pain.

"Sorry," Malakai says.

"'S fine," Lynell mumbles. Looking back at Sawyer, she almost lets go of her bleeding arm to reach for her.

Sawyer has grown paler in the last few seconds. The haunted look in the woman's eyes is the type you feel in the center of your chest rather than see. For someone whose wife has been killed and who's been running the largest rebellion in the country for the last few years, Sawyer doesn't seem too familiar with life-threatening danger.

Either that, or she's the kind of person who faints from the sight of blood.

"You good?" Lynell asks. When Sawyer doesn't answer, Lynell leans closer, ignoring the pulsating pain in her arm. "Sawyer?"

Sawyer flinches and her eyes re-focus on Lynell. "You're hurt."

"Flesh wound," Lynell says. "What about you? There's blood on the back of your neck."

Sawyer twists, despite not being able to see her own back.

"Glass," Lynell says, squinting to see the small glint of a shard lodged in Sawyer's neck. "Probably from the window breaking."

"We'll need to clean everyone's wounds," Malakai says.

Lynell nods. "At least no one died."

The word 'died' seems to act as a fuse in Sawyer. She gasps. In one breath, she says, "Oh, my god. Someone shot at us. How did they find us? Who was it? What do we do? Malakai—"

"Take a breath," Lynell interrupts. "We can figure this out."

"We need to go to the hospital," Sawyer says, her words still coming in a rush.

Lynell almost laughs. People keep calling her naïve, but Sawyer is showing off her ignorance with every second. "We can't go to the hospital," she says.

"Why not?" Sawyer asks. "We're not criminals. You're not on the run from a Registration."

"Someone shot at us," Lynell says. She must sound annoyed, because Daniel takes over for her.

"The people Johnson is working for have a lot of influence. At least one oligarch and two committee chairs. They'll know if you go to a public hospital or the cops. If they find out you didn't die in there, they're going to come after you."

"Lynell was shot!" Sawyer yells.

"Not the worst thing I've walked away from," Lynell mutters.

"I agree with the Carters," Malakai says. "I have emergency first aid kits. We can handle the wounds ourselves."

Lynell turns to Daniel and asks, "Did you see who it was? The shooter?"

"I saw an outline of a gun and man when I looked through the blinds," Malakai answers. "But then the smoke bomb hit, and I couldn't get a better look."

"I'll bet it was Johnson," Daniel says. "Malakai, where are we going?"

Malakai shrugs. "Away. We need to ditch this car."

"This is my car!" Sawyer says.

"Which means it's easily trackable," Lynell says.

"Lyn's right," Daniel says. "We need a new car."

"We also need to get rid of our phones," Malakai says.

Lynell grumbles. This is a brand-new phone. Ramsey got it for her over the weekend because she had to destroy her last one when running from Zach after he Registered her.

She rolls down the windows but doesn't toss the phone before Daniel says, "Wait, don't."

"I don't like it either, Danny. But Malakai is right. We can't take the batteries out and turning off the phone doesn't stop it from being tracked." As she talks, she grins at Sawyer's shocked expression and Daniel's private smile of amusement. "And you thought my incessant listening to true crime podcasts was pointless."

Daniel chuckles. "I was going to say we should call Ramsey first."

"Oh, right," she says, rolling up the window. Her new resources are like a new sense she's yet to grow used to. Like she's lived her entire life without the ability to hear anything and, now that she can, she forgets to listen. Muscle memory and habit has her plugging her ears rather than letting the sense work for her.

"Ramsey Davenport? Absolutely not," Malakai says.

"He can help," Daniel says.

Malakai continues shaking his head. "He works for the Registration."

"I own the Registration," Lynell says.

"That's different," Sawyer says.

Lynell sighs. "Look, I get the distrust, honestly. I spent a good amount of time unsure about him. But I think we can trust him. He'll have access to the best resources and will get us somewhere safe."

"He worked with Eric until a few weeks ago," Sawyer says.

"He also killed Eric." Lynell shifts, gritting her teeth as she repositions her aching arm. "You trust Harlow Graham, don't you?"

Sawyer's eyes freeze open in shock. She doesn't reply until Malakai drives over a bump, making Lynell grunt. "How do you know about Harlow?"

"Ramsey."

Sawyer seems to feel Lynell's answer like a powerful wind, because she leans back against the window, yelps at the pain, and sits forward again. "How does he know?"

"Apparently, they have some sort of history. He called her his old contact." Lynell briefly explains what Ramsey told them a few hours ago, about Harlow returning to town to join the Resurrection, learning Finnegan Reese and Tamara Nelson are part of the group who kidnapped Anna to get the policy change to pass, the call recording from Reese, and Harlow's father, Warner Golden, being her informant.

The car slows. For a moment, she thinks Malakai is parking, but she looks through the windshield and sees a stop sign. She's disoriented by their unfamiliar surroundings.

"Harlow didn't tell me all of that," Sawyer whispers. The look on her face is recognizable as the same uncertainty Lynell has felt about everyone all week, save for Daniel. "She's never even mentioned Ramsey."

"Informants don't typically display their informant status," Lynell says.

"She's my friend."

Sawyer sounds on the verge of heartbreak, and Lynell quickly adds, "I'm sure she is. Maybe she was planning to tell you but hasn't had the chance. Ramsey didn't say when she got all that information."

She wonders again how Ramsey and Harlow know each other. For all intents and purposes, Harlow went missing twenty-eight years ago. Ramsey was a Registration kid, born into the life because his parents and grandparents worked for the Elysians, but he was still young when Harlow left, barely an adult.

"Ramsey could've been lying to you," Sawyer says. "It all could've been a ruse to regain your trust."

Lynell frowns.

Daniel speaks up then in an authoritative voice that commands attention. "And Harlow could be lying to you. Hell, any of us could've betrayed the others and told Johnson where we were. Nothing is guaranteed, and we have no way of knowing for certain who has our best interest in mind. The only people we can know for certain didn't pull that trigger are those of us in this car. But if Lynell trusts Ramsey, that's good enough for me. We need somewhere safe to go, and he can make that happen better than any of us."

They drive down three blocks in silence before Malakai says, "I don't like it."

"I don't like that my wife is once again bleeding from an attack, but that's the world we live in. So, I'm going to call Ramsey while you switch cars."

"We don't have a choice but to trust each other," Lynell says. "At a certain point, you have to trust the person who might be your enemy to outlive those you know are your enemies."

"The devil you know," Sawyer says.

Lynell nods. She watches Malakai's profile as he struggles with the idea of calling Ramsey. Finally, he says, "I'm watering my neighbor's plants while he's on vacation for the rest of the month. His car is in his garage. We can take it."

"Do you have the keys?" Sawyer asks.

Malakai gives an inaudible response. He'll probably steal the keys from the house. Or hotwire it.

Everyone in agreement, albeit a taut and feeble one, Malakai changes direction for his house, and Daniel dials Ramsey's number. The call connects, and Daniel offers as little information as possible, probably mindful about the chances of being overheard. The other side of the phone call is little more than an indistinct mumbling, but by the mumbling's tone, Lynell guesses Ramsey is just as unhappy about Sawyer and Malakai's presence as they are with accepting his help. Less than two minutes pass, then Daniel ends the call and relays the safe house address to Malakai. Next, he rolls the windows down and tosses his phone. Lynell follows suit, wondering when she'll be able to buy one and have it longer than a week before her life is in danger again.

Once all phones are gone and the windows back up, Lynell leans her head against the back of her seat, breathing through the pain. Scarcely a second later, she hears a seatbelt unclick.

She opens her eyes to see Daniel moving to his knees so he can lean into the back seat.

"What are you doing?" she asks.

"We'll be in the car for a bit," he says. "I need to wrap your arm so you don't lose too much blood."

Lynell abruptly registers how lightheaded she is.

"Turn for me," Daniel says, the words partially muffled by the shirt he's holding between his teeth. Holding the hem in both hands, he pulls back with his head and rips a large strip of fabric off his shirt.

Lynell angles her body, baring her left arm for him. She lets go of the wound and blood promptly starts dripping down her arm, staining the bandages on her hand. She lifts her fingers to keep the splints clean.

"Do you have any water in the car?" Daniel asks Sawyer.

She nods and reaches into the cargo space, pulling out two plastic water bottles. Daniel takes a bottle, uncaps it, and tells Lynell to hold her breath. Then he's pouring the water over her arm, drenching the entry and exit wounds next to each other on the side of her arm. The water falls into her lap and the seat until she's sitting in a puddle. She almost feels bad for making such a mess in Sawyer's car, but the bullet hole in her arm commands too much attention for her to spare any on a vehicle.

"Fuck," Lynell groans, the pain both a surface sting and a deep throbbing.

"It's through and through," Daniel says. "Not that bad. Half an inch to the left and it wouldn't even have grazed you. It didn't hit bone but got the muscle, so that's probably why it hurts so bad." He drops the empty water bottle before wrapping her bicep with the fabric. He ties it so tight that she yelps, a flash of black filling her vision.

"Sorry," he mutters. "It needs to be tight."

"I know," Lynell says, her eyes filling with tears.

"It's not the most sanitary wrap, but it'll do for now." Daniel leans closer and kisses her arm then her mouth. "Badass," he whispers against her lips, so only she can hear it. She smirks and Daniel returns to his seat, re-buckling the seatbelt.

Malakai circles back twice, though any tails they might've had were definitely lost half an hour ago. When he slows down and finally parks, Lynell looks up, squinting at the dashboard clock. She expected it to be past midnight, but the bright numbers read 11:41.

She and Sawyer wait in the car while Daniel and Malakai get out and cross the street to a shabby duplex. Daniel stands with his back to the front door while Malakai bends over it. A second later, the door opens, and Malakai disappears inside, Daniel remaining behind. Lynell watches as he surveys the street until the garage door opens and an old dark blue sedan backs out. Malakai stops the car on the street, and Daniel returns to pull Sawyer's car into the garage.

"Come on," Daniel says, motioning for the women to follow. The car is so old that Lynell is shocked it's still running. Nevertheless, she's careful not to get any blood anywhere when lowering into the seat.

She never thought she'd meet anyone more paranoid than Eric, but she thinks Malakai might win in that category. Daniel directs him, waiting patiently when Malakai purposefully takes wrong turns and drives in the opposite direction for long stretches. The drive would've been long without the detours, but with them, it takes nearly two hours before they're pulling into an old neighborhood close to Denton.

Lynell looks out the window as they drive through a residential area and onto a commercial street of small shops. There's an electric car charging station identical to the others populating the city, a hole-in-the-wall burger joint, a small bookstore, and several more shops that blend together in the night.

He turns down a new street and the businesses disappear in favor of newly built homes. They're so uniform that only the numbers on the mailboxes and varying sizes of crape myrtle trees set them apart from one another. Each house has slanted ceilings, gray vinyl exteriors, a single car garage on the right side, and a window above it that might be an attic.

The garage door of their safe house opens as soon as Malakai turns into the driveway. Ramsey is visible through the windshield, his hand over a square button that he presses again once the car is fully inside the garage. He turns and walks back into the house as the door shudders as it closes behind them. There's no other car in sight, so Lynell has no clue how Ramsey got here, but then she remembers he has a motorcycle, which is easier to hide from view. He probably drove that over, then parked nearby.

Lynell and Daniel walk inside first and Ramsey greets them by demanding, "What on earth happened?"

Lynell shoves past him, briefly glancing around the small house. The living room, dining room, and kitchen are all in one open space to the right of the garage door. Ramsey turns to keep his eyes on her, ignoring anyone else.

She can't muster the energy to feel small or guilty like last time. "Don't worry, we're fine."

"Oh really?" He raises his eyebrows and gestures to the tight bandage on Lynell's arm, where a small circle of red has bled through. It, along with the few cuts they both have from the glass, makes it obvious that *something* happened.

Lynell shrugs. "Flesh wounds. I'm fine."

"You look like you haven't slept in a month."

"I haven't," Lynell says.

She looks over Ramsey's shoulder at Sawyer still at the garage threshold. Meeting her eyes, Lynell dips her chin, signaling that it's safe to come inside. Malakai, of course, walks through first, broad shoulders acting as a barrier between Sawyer and Ramsey.

"Ramsey, I'm sure you know Malakai Mo—" Lynell starts.

"Malakai Morrison and Sawyer D'Angelo," Ramsey interrupts. He's turned to the newcomers, but Lynell can hear the glower on his face.

"Ramsey Davenport," Malakai says.

Lynell rolls her eyes. "Guys, can we not do this?"

"Do what?" Ramsey asks.

She steps forward, gesturing at the foot of space between them. "This 'we're enemies' standoff. Just for five minutes, leave your dominance bullshit at the door."

Everyone looks at her and she stares back, unblinking.

Ramsey is the first to respond. "Yes, of course."

Then, still glaring at the other man, Malakai says, "I'm checking the house. Sawyer?"

"I'm fine," she says. "Lynell will stay with me."

Lynell shrugs and leans against the wall next to Sawyer. Without moving, she sees that the house is sparsely furnished, with a fridge, couch, and four-chair dining room table. Meanwhile, Daniel and Malakai explore the house and Ramsey waits a few feet from Lynell at the head of the kitchen, his eyes following Malakai's every move.

"Do you know anything about Anna?" Lynell asks when Malakai and Daniel head into what's likely a bedroom.

Ramsey answers without tearing his eyes from the bedroom door. "Not much more. I wouldn't worry, though. They won't do anything with her with the vote still on the table."

"But you don't *know* that," Lynell says. Clearly, their meeting with Sawyer wasn't secret. As painful as the gunshot is, what dominates her mind is the fear that Anna will be punished for *her* actions.

His arms fall and his shoulders relax. Detaching his gaze from Malakai's direction, he looks back at Lynell. "No, but I have my suspicions. There's nothing you can do now, though." His eyes drag along her arm and wounds again. "Not in your state. You need medical attention and sleep." Then he walks away to a nearby bathroom and comes out with the largest first aid kit she's ever seen.

An earthquake of pain momentarily blinds her, stealing all coherent thoughts. She manages to find and drop into a chair while Ramsey snaps on a pair of gloves. He starts cleaning small cuts on her face she didn't notice until then. He presses a small bandage over her forehead when Daniel and Malakai return, both satisfied with the house's security. The latter ignores Ramsey and gestures Sawyer over. She flattens her hands on the table, groaning as Malakai inspects the wounds with freshly gloved hands, cutting open her shirt for better access to the shards of glass he has to pick from her skin.

At the same time, Daniel takes over doctoring Lynell's wounds and unties the fabric from her arm. With her other hand, she grips the arm of the chair so tight her knuckles turn white while Daniel cleans the wound. He pours more water over it, this time catching the majority with a rag.

"I don't see any broken bullet pieces. The bleeding has stopped, but the exit wound is a little too big for my liking," Daniel mutters.

Lynell keeps her teeth pressed together, rather than muttering a response that she knows Daniel isn't expecting. He's talking to himself more than to her, likely to keep his mind off the fact that someone, once again, tried to kill his wife.

"I'm going to stitch this up, okay? There's a suture kit here."

Eyes going wide, Lynell whips her head around to stare at her husband. "You're going to sew my arm?"

"I don't have to, but the wound is big enough that I'd feel better if I did," he says.

Sawyer sits in the chair next to Lynell and rests her hand over Lynell's free one. Malakai has finished cleaning her wounds and is now standing with perfect posture, observing the other four, though Lynell bets most of his attention is on Ramsey.

Lynell flips her hand over and Sawyer gives it a squeeze. "Don't break my hand," she says.

Lynell grins. "I'll try not to."

Then, Daniel says, "Alright. It's going to hurt, but I've done this before, Lyn. Trust me."

The fear is like a poisonous fog in her mind, but she trusts Daniel. So, with a determined breath, she nods.

"You're going to want this," Ramsey says, holding out a semi-clean rag. She frowns at him and he explains, "To bite down on."

The fog of fear thickens. Still, she lets go of Sawyer's hand long enough to take the rag and stuff it in her mouth.

Daniel holds the needle against her skin and says, "Ready?"

She shuts her eyes and nods. The pain of the needle sliding in and out of her skin is white hot. She lets out a muffled scream and grasps Sawyer's hand, hard.

"I'm sorry," Daniel says. "Almost done. Just a couple more."

"You're good at this," Ramsey mutters. Lynell's eyes snap open. Ramsey is watching Daniel over his shoulder, visibly impressed with his work.

"Thanks," Daniel says without his attention faltering.

Intense dizziness threatens to knock her unconscious, then she hears a *snip* of scissors and Daniel says, "All done. Just some antibiotic ointment and a bandage."

Lynell lets go of Sawyer's hand and removes the rag from her mouth, noticing for the first time that her cheeks are hot with tears. While Daniel applies ointment to the wound, Lynell attempts to focus on the breath cycling through her nose, into her lungs, back up her pharynx, and out of her mouth, lips curled into a small 'o.'

Only a few breaths pass before he's dressed the wounds with gauze and wrapped a bandage tightly around her arm. He kisses her skin above the bandage before grabbing some painkillers from the first aid kit.

"Got any water?" Daniel asks Ramsey. He nods, goes to the fridge, and comes back with four cold bottles. Daniel hands Lynell and Sawyer several pills each, and they swallow them synchronously.

"Alright, explanation time," Ramsey says.

"Anna—"

Ramsey interrupts Lynell, saying, "I need to know what's going on to make informed decisions regarding your daughter."

She decided in the car to trust Ramsey, for better or worse, so, she explains. When her voice turns hoarse and mind begins to shut off, Daniel takes over the story. Without the effort of talking, she's able to study every tick in Ramsey's face. Yet it tells her nothing beyond the obvious frustration and fear for Lynell's safety.

"No one but the four of you knew you were meeting?" Ramsey asks.

"We didn't tell anyone. Did you?" Lynell asks Sawyer, who shakes her head. Lynell adds, "Either someone heard our call or was following one or both of us."

"It's safe to assume that the shooter was Johnson," Ramsey says. "I'll send Booth to check out the area."

"How do you know where we met?" Sawyer asks.

Ramsey raises his eyebrows and Lynell grins, finding it refreshing that people still exist who don't instinctively know the answers to questions like that. "We had our phones. He can check our locations," Lynell says.

"Should've left them at home," Malakai grumbles.

"Yes, well, you didn't." The tension between Ramsey and Malakai turns the air to sandpaper. "I wouldn't expect any less from a reb—"

"Ramsey," Lynell interrupts, eyeing the way Malakai swells with rage. The man is several inches taller than Ramsey, has more combat experience, and probably wouldn't hesitate to attack anyone and anything that might be a threat to Sawyer. "We're allies now. Act like it."

He's tangibly displeased even as he nods. "Yes, ma'am."

Before the discomfort has an opportunity to fill the room, Sawyer digs her eyes into Ramsey. "You know Harlow."

Not much rattles him, but those three words knock him off balance. He steps back and presses his hand to the wall behind him. "How . . ." he looks to Lynell.

"Had to convince them to trust you," she says with a one-armed shrug.

His eyes close and his next few breaths are wobbly. Her brain wakes in alarm, not prepared for what Ramsey says next.

"We were together for a while."

"Together?" Daniel repeats. "Like . . . *together?*" It's reminiscent of middle school when kids say they 'like *like*' someone.

Ramsey nods.

"She never told me," Sawyer whispers.

"We didn't tell anyone," Ramsey explains.

"Zach . . ." Lynell trails off.

Thankfully, Ramsey doesn't require an ending to the sentence. "He didn't know. No one did." His voice is unrecognizable, tainted with the memory of a lost love.

"Is that why you hated Eric?" Lynell asks. Unprecedented relief that maybe she wasn't the only reason Ramsey killed Eric inflates her lungs.

"Partly," Ramsey answers. He shakes his head and clears his throat, as if to physically rid himself of the conversation. "It doesn't matter. It's all in the past. What matters now is your safety, Mrs. Elysian."

"Ours," Lynell corrects, gesturing to the room at large. "And Anna's."

"Of course." Ramsey rubs the back of his neck under the bun of long hair. The act doesn't suit him.

Desperate for the typically composed Ramsey, Lynell asks, "What's next?"

He gives her a grateful look. "Booth will go to the house where you met. I'll handle your cover for tomorrow because you can't leave this house, especially not for the convention rehearsal. All four of you need to stay here. It's secure enough for now, though we should probably move you somewhere more remote soon."

Lynell shakes her head. "No. We still have the vote and convention on Friday. This doesn't change anything."

"You were shot at. That changes everything."

"*We* were shot at," Lynell says. "There has to be a reason. I need you to figure out what that is so we know for certain they won't take it out on Anna next."

"Lyn and I haven't done anything the kidnappers told us not to do," Daniel insists. "Not really."

Lynell adores her husband's ability to hope for the best in others. Unfortunately, she doesn't have that luxury. "We met with Sawyer. They might have overheard our conversation. I can't imagine they'll be happy about us working with the rebel leader and telling her about the policy."

"I've known the committee chairs longer than any of you. With the vote still happening, they won't jeopardize it by hurting their main leverage source," Ramsey says.

Hearing Anna referred to as a 'leverage source' makes Lynell want to crawl out of her skin, but she knows Ramsey is right.

"As long as you didn't discuss a rescue attempt or concrete plans to ruin the vote, then we have to continue with the assumption that Anna is alive." Ramsey pauses for a breath. "But we also can't expect them to return Anna fully safe and unharmed after the policy change is in effect. Not after this."

"So, what do we do?" Lynell quickly asks, sensing how close Daniel is to the edge.

"I'll do my best and come back tomorrow afternoon to check on you. We're narrowing down the possible houses where Anna is, so if we find that, then we can rescue her before the convention."

"If you attempt to save her and fail, they'll hurt her," Daniel says.

"Ramsey doesn't fail." Lynell says it more to convince herself and hopefully keep Ramsey confident than because she fully believes the sentence. Their other option is to trust Anna's kidnappers to keep their word.

"I won't do anything until I'm confident in the result," Ramsey says. "I need a few more hours, then we'll know enough to make a more informed decision for our next move. For now, you all stay here. There's plenty of food and water. Mr. Morrison, you know what to do."

There's no hint of the earlier scene between the two men as they nod at each other. Ramsey has probably read all about Malakai and therefore knows his ability to keep someone else safe. Political or personal disagreements won't matter as long as the main priority for them both is the safety of Lynell and Sawyer.

"Get some rest tonight. I'll be back tomorrow. I have a key, so don't let anyone in who knocks."

With that, Ramsey leaves, locking the front door behind him.

CHAPTER 31

S he slept deep, like she was drugged, pulled down into darkness. She
wrestled with nightmares that itched at her soul, taunting her with
blades plunging into flesh and Anna crying in the distance, never able to
find her, reach her, hold her.

She wakes with a headache and her eyelids feel hooked to bricks, though
still more refreshed than she's felt in a long time. She quietly slips out, expecting to find solitude in the living room. But Sawyer is sitting at the dining
table, dragging her finger along the rim of a glass. She's wearing nothing but
sweatpants and a crop top sports bra. Most of her exposed skin above her
elbows and on her back is decorated with gorgeous color tattoos. A particularly captivating one depicting the galaxy wraps around Sawyer's side,
extending past her hip and disappearing beneath her waistband. The tattoos
are marred by a dozen small cuts littering her neck, shoulders, arms, and
back, each now cleaned and covered with small Band-Aids.

Sawyer gives no indication of hearing Lynell until she sits across the
table from her. Sawyer lifts her chin enough to meet Lynell's eyes for a beat.

She thinks, *Couldn't sleep?* but doesn't say it out loud because the answer is obvious. An indefinite length of time passes in which the only sounds

are their breathing, and an occasional whistle from between Sawyer's finger and the glass's rim.

"Are you okay?" Lynell eventually asks.

Sawyer's hand pauses. She shrugs. "I don't know what I feel."

"I get that."

"It's just . . . people have hated me for years. Either because of who my family is, my sexuality, my wife, or my work with the rebels. But somehow, during all of that, it was still . . ." She trails off, her eyes finding Lynell's again. She shakes her head. "I don't know."

"It was still worth it," Lynell finishes for her. "You knew why they hated you, and it was worth it."

Sawyer's eyes widen. "Yes, exactly. But this is different."

"Because now the hate has turned into real, life-threatening danger and you don't know why."

"I mean, I get that they hate me for leading the Resurrection, but why now? Is it seriously all about the speech?"

"Speech?" Lynell asks. "Is that your plan for the convention? To give a speech?"

Sawyer grips the base of her glass, staring into the water like it'll tell her how to answer. "Ellery was scheduled to be the keynote speaker for a conference in Orlando six years ago but was killed a week before. She wasn't big on planning, preferred to live impulsively, but she spent months preparing for that conference. Not many people read her speech, or knew what she was going to say. To this day, I don't know how they got ahold of it, but two weeks before she died, a lawyer sent her a cease and desist. Apparently, the speech could've gotten her sued for defamation against the Elysians."

Lynell notices Sawyer's lips twitch and wonders if she's fighting a smile. Whatever thoughts pass through her mind must give her strength, and she lifts her face to Lynell while she continues explaining.

"She'd never focused on the Registration during her activism until then. That would've been the first time she openly spoke against it. Unfortunately, she didn't pick a great time to shift focus. The oligarchs clearly didn't want any more incited rebellions, because they aggressively shut down anything anti-Registration. So, Ellery was only one of hundreds to be threatened with a lawsuit."

"They didn't have a legal leg to stand on," Lynell says. "Unless the speech contained personal claims against a specific individual, then it's not illegal to share your political opinion."

"I think they were hoping to scare her into silence. I still have no idea how the Registration's people got a copy of the speech. I didn't share it with anyone else for years after she died. Not until I decided to . . ." She trails off, allowing time for Lynell to mull Sawyer's words over in her mind.

"You're going to give Ellery's speech, aren't you?"

Sawyer nods.

"So, Ellery is Registered before she can give the speech, and now you're being threatened into not giving it?"

"I guess," Sawyer says.

"What is in that speech that they're so afraid of?" Lynell asks.

"*I would bet anything he secretly hid the code inside the contents of the letter he wrote you all those years ago,*" Eric seems to whisper in her ear.

History repeats itself. That truth lives in every twinge, ache, and memory in Lynell's body. Could it also live in Ellery's speech?

But why would Ellery know the companion cloaking code? And why would she put it in a public speech?

"Maybe you can answer that for me," Sawyer says. She leans forward and pulls several crinkled and dirty pages from her back pocket. The edges are slightly stained with blood, and one page has a tear nearly all the way down the middle. "I don't know why I brought it yesterday. But I did."

Cautiously, Lynell reaches out. When Sawyer doesn't pull the papers away, Lynell takes them and reads the title at the top of the first page, *Be a Peony*, with the subtitle, *Learning resilience in the face of certain death*. She notices several handwritten corrections throughout the typed paragraphs, probably where Sawyer has made updates.

"'Be a Peony,'" Lynell reads. "The note and petals in your office."

"Yeah. Ellery was going to talk about resilience and finding a way to live despite being surrounded by death. About how the Registration causes death and devastation every quarter. Peonies were her favorite because they die every winter and return every spring to bloom again." She pauses and Lynell turns away, pretending not to see the tear that slips from Sawyer's eye. "Johnson must have gotten a copy of the speech somehow. I deleted every file of it from my computers and rarely left this copy lying around."

"Maybe whoever threatened to sue Ellery gave it to him. An oligarch or committee chair. If they're behind all of this now, then maybe they coerced Johnson to Register Ellery."

Sawyer's eyes widen with recognition.

"What is it?" Lynell asks.

"After Ellery died, my lawyer found this sort of manifesto." Sawyer explains the discovery, her conversation with Paul, and the realization that the 'founding Father' was probably her grandfather. Her words sound frayed at the edges, something Lynell intimately understands.

"I guess you can join the Shitty Grandfather Club."

Sawyer grins. "That's not a membership I ever wanted."

"It comes with a healthy dose of trauma and trust issues. Lucky us," Lynell says, finding solace in the humor. She takes a heavy breath. "Look, I don't think it's just Jude. I'm pretty sure Finnegan Reese, Tamara Nelson, and the oligarch Bruce Macgill are involved too."

"Jesus," Sawyer curses. "How many of them are behind this?"

"We should probably assume a lot. I mean, they've threatened and stalked you, bombed my house, kidnapped Anna, and shot at both of us. The policy change is important to them. They can't have me trying to stop it or you interrupting the announcement during tomorrow's convention. They definitely don't want us working together. We're clearly a threat to them."

"Being a threat sounds good in theory, but it sucks in reality," Sawyer says.

Lynell remembers the comments under the article about the bombing a week ago that mentioned shadow governments and women in power being a threat to the patriarchy. Maybe there's more truth in them than she originally thought.

"Let's see what's in this speech that's so dangerous," Lynell says. She lays the papers out and starts reading. A few sentences stand out, independent statements from the surrounding text.

"Every year, winter ravages any flowers that manage to grow. And every year, peonies return, rising from the dead to bloom once more."

"Every quarter, the Registration ravages this country. And every day, we, the outcasts, the rebels, the survivors, rise from violence to bloom once more."

"Our country is ruled by a devil disguising himself as our heavenly ruler. They want us to believe he is pure, but he's not."

"Their lavish homes are stained with our blood. What they call paradise is our purgatory."

"They condemn us to death and call it a kiss."

"Our very lives are paychecks to them, and the longer we accept the Registration, the more compliant we become to our lives being sold like rotten fruit."

"The Elysians spread death like weeds, hoping to choke the life out of those of us who dare to challenge their values."

"Winter will keep coming. Weeds will keep growing. The Elysians will keep throwing death at us. But like peonies, we will not stay defeated. We will come back every year."

And the last sentence, which Lynell silently reads in Sawyer's voice, "Against all odds, we will rise again."

She knows each previous rebel group had their own idea of how the country should run. Some were formed from times before the Registration and simply evolved along with the country. Some fight solely on the basis that certain things should be legal outside of the Registration, like abortion, but don't try to fight the Registration itself. Others want the Registration to end completely, so everything it allows will become illegal, no matter the circumstance.

The group Daniel fought with was one of the biggest. It became possible when all the groups worked together. After their defeat, the groups mostly dispersed, licking their wounds. Many of the rebels stepped away from activism. It wasn't until four years later, two years after Ellery died, when the Resurrection formed, that those lost rebels found somewhere to belong again.

"I've read it over and over trying to see it from their perspective," Sawyer says. "To figure out why they have a problem with this speech specifically . . . it can't just be because of our plans to interrupt the conference. They could reschedule the announcement or something."

Lynell frowns at the words on the page, experiencing intense déjà vu from three weeks ago when she, Zach, and Daniel were trying to figure out the code. "It's obviously anti-Registration and anti-Elysian. But that's not a new thing."

"The funny thing is, the harder they fight to keep this speech buried, the more convinced I am to give it."

Chuckling, Lynell leans back in the chair, ignoring the pinch in her arm. "You sound like me."

"I sound like Ellery," Sawyer says with a smile of equal sadness and fondness. "The easiest way to get her to do something was to tell her not to do it."

"I've never said I'm sorry for your loss," Lynell says. "I can't imagine losing Daniel."

Sawyer's smile loses some of the fondness and she whispers a soft, "Thank you."

"I heard your song. It's beautiful. It was noble of you to invite others into your grief with your music. Grieving is difficult enough when done in the safety of one's own heart. But now I'm learning how much more complicated and difficult it is when the world seems to have an opinion on your loss."

"Yeah, it's . . . odd. To grieve so publicly. I'm sorry for your loss, too. I know they were horrible, but Eric and Zachary were technically your family."

Lynell feels her spine straighten at the mention of those two names. The mix of hatred for Eric, guilt for his death, and crushing sadness over losing Zach makes her lungs feel too heavy for a full breath. When she speaks, the words sound strained: "Thanks. Eric is no loss. He was nothing but awful. But Zach . . . he was one of the bravest people I've ever known. He would have broken his generational curse."

Sawyer's brows lower and her lips thin. Lynell wonders if she and Harlow ever discuss Zach or if it's an unspoken agreement not to. Does Sawyer think Zach is a copy of his father, or does her friendship with Harlow give her a different perspective?

The Zachary Elysian that the public knew was a man who thought he'd find safety and happiness in loyalty to his father, torn between parents, trying to protect his mother while supporting his father and all that entailed. They saw the man who did whatever he was told, the man who supported the Registration. The public Zachary Elysian thrived off the legacy of death his family left him.

They didn't know the Zach that Lynell had begun to meet before he was taken. The man who gladly sacrificed his life for hers, Daniel's, and Anna's. The man who turned his back on his father and all the power, money, and control that came with his last name because he wanted to do what was right, what was good.

Lynell desperately needs the subject to change. "Tell me about Ellery. What was it like being married to her? What brought her joy?"

Sawyer studies Lynell for a moment, who doesn't blink until she passes whatever invisible test Sawyer is grading.

After a long silence, she rolls her lips together and nods, uncertainty dissolving.

"Being married to her was . . . difficult but beautiful. Ellery was stubborn and determined and assertive. People might have hated her if she didn't work her ass off to love them well." She pauses, drops her eyes, and smiles softly. "The first few years of our relationship were hard because Ellery didn't understand my emotions, so she'd dismiss them. We had starkly different upbringings. It would've been easy for her to write me off as a spoiled, entitled girl who chased drama for the attention. But she worked to understand me like no one ever had before."

Lynell listens, knowing each word is a priceless gift. She can't decide if she wants to smile or cry. The love in Sawyer's voice is heartbreaking, but it also gives Lynell hope more than anything else.

That kind of love is not only healing; it's fortifying.

"That's what gave her joy. Understanding things that didn't make any sense to her. And fighting against injustice. And fighting in general." Sawyer laughs, shaking her head at some memory Lynell can't see. "She loved arguing. Nothing gave Ellery joy quite like having a productive, respectful conversation with someone who disagreed with nearly everything she said. That's why she had friends you'd never expect a transgender, lesbian activist to have. A preacher, a member of the NRA, and a traditionalist pro-lifer, to name a few."

Lynell would whistle if she could.

"And good food. Ellery loved good food. She had the most sophisticated palette. It made going out to dinner nearly impossible. She was so picky."

"My mom was like that too," Lynell says. "She'd eat whatever we had, but she used to talk about gourmet meals she'd had as if they were ex-lovers." She wonders, for the first time, if her father had taken Elizabeth to fancy restaurants when they were dating. Eli Elysian would have had plenty of money to treat her to the most expensive meals. Elizabeth never talked about her own family, but Lynell always assumed they were poor and that's why her mother never had a Registration of her own. If that was the case, then it was likely that any gourmet meals she'd had were courtesy of Eli.

Not for the first time, Lynell mourns everything she doesn't know about her family. And not for the first time, she struggles to contain the rage against Eric Elysian for killing her father and sending Elizabeth into hiding to keep Lynell safe from her own family.

But her family is gone now. Dead. She's the only one left.

"Why didn't you Register Johnson? For revenge?" Lynell asks. Sawyer might be a rebel, but her parents weren't. They would have bought her a Registration when she was born.

Sawyer pushes her cuticles back with her thumbnail, thinking about her answer. "I wish every day that Ellery would come home. Or that I could get revenge for her death. But desperation makes you sloppy. Besides, there are other ways to get revenge."

The way she says the last sentence makes Lynell burn with curiosity. She wants to ask, but a voice in her mind—sounding suspiciously like Daniel—says it's not her place. Thinking of Daniel while Sawyer's eyes fill with tears over her dead wife snaps a string in Lynell's heart. She tastes bitter anger and injustice on her tongue. Ice-cold resentment raises goosebumps on her arms and legs.

What is the point of having the power, money, and influence of the Elysian name if she can't do anything about it? What has changed, really, in the last few weeks? She's again hiding in an unfamiliar house, and can't go anywhere because it's not exclusively her life on the line anymore. It's her daughter's, her husband's, and her friend's.

She nearly gasps at the thought that Sawyer is her friend. It feels right, even unsaid in her own mind. She isn't the enemy the world built her up to be.

"I'm so fucking sick of playing defense," Lynell mutters.

"What do you mean?" Sawyer asks.

"Since I was Registered, I've been on the defensive. Every move has been about surviving. As soon as I try to fight back, to play by the laws of the system, they change the game again. I've never had the ability to win or even make a move that's not running away."

"Offense isn't much better. It's just as dangerous."

"But it's *action*. I'm tired of reacting." A certain rage flickers in her. She knows this type of inner fire is dangerous, that it could burn her and the people close to her, not just their enemies. But now she doesn't care. She's felt cold for too long. The heat of the flames is intoxicating.

"Action can start wars, Lynell."

"Wars can be won."

Sawyer shakes her head. "But the only thing war guarantees is death, not good change for a better life. Don't you want that?"

"Death is inevitable. Let's use it to our advantage."

"You're not thinking clearly. You're hurting and angry and sleep deprived."

"Of course I'm angry. We *should* be angry." Lynell is dimly aware that her volume is rising and there are other people in the house trying to sleep, but she doesn't care. All she hears is the roaring fire.

"I know that. I've been angry for six years. I've also been leading a rebellion. I understand the desire to do something no one can ignore. But the last time this country went to war, we came out of it with the Registration holding us by the throat. We have to be careful with every step we take."

"What has being careful done for you, Sawyer? Four years you've led the Resurrection, and the committee is still going to pass this policy tomorrow."

Sawyer leans against the table toward Lynell, her cuts and bruises more visible than ever. "We'll keep fighting."

"We'll never win if we're not willing to fight like them."

"When has stooping to the enemy's level ever worked?"

"This isn't a movie, Sawyer! We're not heroes guaranteed a happy ending."

"Okay, you're right."

Lynell is so surprised to hear Sawyer agree that she doesn't know how to reply.

"We won't win by playing it safe," Sawyer continues. "But we don't have to become *them* either. We can fight our own way. Together."

CHAPTER 32

S omething about Lynell's demeanor or words must've scared Sawyer because, after another few hours of sleep, she begins the day so determined that she's nearly unrecognizable. She makes their breakfast, which consists of instant oatmeal, canned fruit, and old coffee, and reviews security protocols with Malakai.

At some point that week, Daniel studied the convention plans, security, and schedule and relayed the information to Sawyer. They decided to take the Resurrection's plans and expand them. The hijack won't just be digital. With Lynell, Daniel, and Ramsey helping, the rebels can physically take over the convention.

Lynell watches from the couch, air conditioning leaving goose pimples on the back of her neck. She's still hot from the indignant fire, even after attempting to sleep. Her feet are on burning coals, and she wants to run, fight back, call every Registration employee and Resurrection member to action. She wants to find Thomas Johnson, Finnegan Reese, Tamara Nelson, Bruce Macgill, and any other person who thinks they can manipulate their way into total control and put a bullet between their eyes.

She wants a war.

The only reason she doesn't storm recklessly from their safe haven is Daniel and Anna. Her love for her family is the only thing stronger than her desire for bloody revenge.

After a meager lunch, Sawyer joins Lynell on the couch and asks, "Which oligarchs and committee chairs do we know for certain aren't our enemies?"

"Michaels Sutton and Warner Golden," Daniel answers. "Booker and Jacobs voted against the policy change last time, so maybe them too."

"I wish I could call Harlow," Sawyer says. "I have so many questions."

Daniel nods. "Me too. Zach talked so highly of her."

"Was he that different from his father?"

"Yeah, he was. He struggled with it, but Zach's heart was good. You know the nature versus nurture debate? His entire life was basically a personification of that."

"You think nature was stronger?" Sawyer asks.

"I think Zach's nature was fighting hard against his upbringing," Daniel says. "My mom used to say, 'Saints are made in the fight against temptation, not in the absence of it.'"

"Zachary Elysian wasn't a saint," Sawyer says.

"No, he wasn't. No one can be forced into goodness, they have to choose it, and Zach was doing all he could to choose good." Daniel turns to Lynell. "Don't you agree?"

But Lynell isn't listening. Her mind has traveled beyond this conversation to an idea that dims the fire of rage. Lips parting in realization, her pulse quickens, and she's hurtling toward a finish line. She stands, grabs Daniel's hand, and pulls him toward their bedroom.

"Lyn, what are you doing?" he asks.

"Are you okay?" Sawyer asks.

"One minute," Lynell answers. Ignoring their confusion, she drags Daniel to privacy.

Once the door is shut, Daniel asks in a whisper, "What's going on?"

She looks up at him, too stunned by her deduction to smile. "I know who has the companion code."

Daniel's face transforms to mirror the shock on hers. "Who?"

"Lincoln D'Angelo," Lynell whispers.

He backs up, slowly lowering to the bed. His eyes flick back and forward, like he's reading invisible words hanging in the air between them. "How?"

"What Sutton told me. Jude D'Angelo was Gideon's business partner until Gideon cut him out of the Registration. If they were partners, Jude probably knew Gideon's plans, including the plan to create a master key. He had strong reason to create something Gideon would need later, a way to maintain his control even after being betrayed. Jude had motive, means, and opportunity to create a contingency plan, a way for future power or revenge. And if they thought the same way and Gideon left the code for Eli then Jude would have left the CCC for Lincoln."

"Oh, my god," Daniel mutters.

Lynell smiles wide, renewed with pride and purpose at her own discovery. "If Macgill or any of the others knew about the code, then maybe they know of the CCC, too. Sutton said they haven't killed me because they don't want me to be a martyr, but maybe it's because they don't want the code to die with me."

"Torturing you didn't work for Eric, so they're playing the long game," Daniel says, jumping on Lynell's revelation train. "Except the vote threw things off, so they took Anna."

"I won't be surprised if they let Johnson take the blame so they can continue manipulating me. They'll try to get close, to trick me into giving them the code. *Then* it'll be safe to finally kill me."

"That could be true for Sawyer, too. Maybe they think Lincoln passed the CCC to Sawyer already. Which is why they haven't killed her."

"Maybe," Lynell says. "But she has an older brother and . . ." She trails off when a horrible idea occurs to her, stumbling from the magnitude.

"What?" Daniel asks.

"Sawyer thinks the 'founding Elder' mentioned in that manifesto is Jude because he used that 'declawed house cat' term. But kids pick up

their parents' sayings. Saints are made in the fight against temptation."
She watches Daniel, silently pleading for him to tell her she's on the wrong
track. What she's thinking can't be true. It's too abhorrent.

He doesn't.

Their eyes meet, sadness passing between them.

"Didn't the manifesto make it seem like the 'founding Elder' is the
reason the Sin-Fighting Warriors did what they did?" Daniel whispers, his
voice shrinking with sympathy. "The reason Johnson Registered Ellery?"

She nods. "And if he's alive, he's probably working with Macgill and
the others."

"Ordering Johnson to bomb our house, threaten Sawyer, shoot at us,
take Anna . . ."

"If we need one person to blame, I would stake my life on it being the
founding Elder." Lynell turns and sits next to Daniel on the bed, her body
weak with the chance that her hypothesis is correct. "Everything is pointing
to it, Danny. Sutton's information, what Ramsey told us, the manifesto, and
Sawyer's conversation with Paul. The founding Elder behind everything for
the last six years, since Ellery died, is . . ." Her voice fails, leaning against
Daniel's ability to verbalize the terrible truth for her.

"Lincoln D'Angelo."

Lynell nods. Sawyer's father.

CHAPTER **33**

"What was that about?" Malakai asks, staring at the closed bedroom door.

"Probably something about Zachary. They were close to him," Sawyer says. "Are you almost done?"

Malakai nods. He's sitting at the dining room table, reading Sawyer's recent edits to the speech. It's the most she's changed so far, but she doesn't feel the same guilt she did every other time she edited Ellery's words.

For a moment early that morning, Sawyer wasn't watching Lynell lose herself in the need for vengeful justice, she was watching Ellery. Sawyer didn't realize she'd fallen victim to the pitfall of death turning a flawed human into a goddess. Ellery was a wonderful woman in so many ways, but she was weak in others. It took Lynell breaking in front of Sawyer for her to remember that. The look in Lynell's eyes was the same one Ellery had in the days before she died. Sawyer explained away the unease in her gut, telling herself it was righteous anger against injustice, that Ellery's motivations were pure.

She won't make that mistake again. She'll find a middle between Lynell and Ellery's rash, dangerous actions and her own passive inactions. She has to if they're going to find a respite from death and grief. Regrettably, there is only so much she can do, stuck in this house with no way to contact the others.

"Maybe we should leave," she says. "We don't have to obey Ramsey Davenport and we aren't being productive here."

Malakai surprises her by shaking his head. "Keeping you alive is the most productive thing we can do."

"You can't trust Ramsey."

"I don't. But you trust Lynell and Daniel, right?"

"Sure."

"They trust him. This place is secure. We should stay. For now, at least."

She relents. "You're the security expert."

"This is perfect, by the way." He holds up the speech, giving her conversational whiplash. "I see both of you in it now."

Unsure how to respond, she feebly says, "Thank you."

Lynell and Daniel stay locked in their room for so long that Sawyer is on the verge of knocking to check on them when she hears a click coming from the front door.

Malakai jumps to attention, gun in hand, and positions himself between Sawyer and the front door. He raises the gun, pointing it at the door as it swings open, not lowering it until Ramsey becomes visible with his palms already out to show empty hands.

"Ramsey's back," Sawyer calls.

The next second, Daniel and Lynell exit the bedroom, both looking oddly solemn.

"I'm glad to see you're all in one piece," Ramsey greets them.

"What have you learned?" Lynell asks.

"Booth confirmed that Johnson was the shooter yesterday. However, our knowledge of Johnson says that he's an excellent shot. He doesn't often miss, so it's odd that he fired four times yesterday and only grazed you."

"The place was filled with smoke. The blinds were pulled. He couldn't see properly," Daniel says.

"The blinds were shot off. It looks like they'd been mounted inside the window seal, so a talented sniper could shoot the brackets. And he threw the smoke bomb. If he wanted perfect visibility, he wouldn't have done that," Ramsey says. "Plus, he could have used a laser sight for more accuracy. I'm sure his intention wasn't to kill."

"Then what was it?" Daniel asks.

Lynell answers, her attention still on Ramsey. "Probably to scare us or to keep us from working together."

"I'd agree with the former, but if he wanted to do the latter, he wouldn't have given you a common danger. Johnson isn't stupid. He knows that facing death with someone unites you," Ramsey says. "If it were me, I would kill one of you and not the other. Johnson probably wanted to distract you from the main issue."

"Was he following orders or acting independently?" Lynell asks. She glances briefly at Daniel and tugs at a string on her shirt hem.

"No way to know for certain, but I'd assume following orders. Johnson alone has no reason to leave you both alive. I think we'll know if he stops obeying superiors because he'll become much more dangerous."

"More dangerous than bombing our house and shooting at us?" Daniel seethes.

"Yes." Ramsey says everything with a matter-of-fact tone that matches expressionless eyes and thin lips. He reminds Sawyer of Malakai more than Daniel does. They're both trained soldiers who put the job above their feelings.

"What about Anna?" Daniel asks.

"I think I know where she is."

"Really?" Daniel and Lynell say in unison.

Before they can say more, Ramsey adds, "But I won't attempt a rescue until I know more about the security. Booth is keeping an eye on the house now. It doesn't seem overly protected, but my assumption is that they don't want to draw attention to the house. They're probably relying on the location remaining secret."

"If you can save Anna, then maybe Lyn can keep the policy from passing," Daniel suggests.

"I don't think we have enough time, Danny," Lynell says. "Unless we have leverage over a committee member."

"Mrs. Elysian is right."

"Besides, it might not matter if the policy passes," Lynell says.

Sawyer frowns, wondering if she misheard. That statement doesn't fit with Lynell's behavior and comments in their conversation early that morning. Hours ago, she was prepared to throw the country into war to stop the committee and oligarchs. Now she doesn't care if they get what they want like this policy change?

"What do you mean?" Sawyer asks.

Lynell avoids the question and Sawyer's eyes, speaking directly to Ramsey. "Are you willing to help us, even if it means hijacking the convention and my succession?"

Ramsey's eyebrows pull together and the scar across his face creates a severe, unhappy look. Sawyer expects him to disagree. He doesn't.

"Of course. My loyalty is to you and you alone, Mrs. Elysian."

Unlike Sawyer, Lynell doesn't look surprised at his response. "Is it safe for us to leave here?"

Now Ramsey hesitates. He sniffs in disapproval even as he says, "If you're cautious, yes. We can leave. I brought these, but don't turn them on until you have to use them." He pulls four phones from pockets inside his jacket and passes them out. Sawyer accepts hers and studies it, noticing it's a thick older model but still a smartphone without buttons on the front screen.

"Perfect. Because we have work to do if we're going to pull this off."

Sawyer has no idea what caused this shift in Lynell, but she's not going to question it. "What are you thinking?" she asks instead, looking for direction, needing to be in the loop, scratch the itch to do something other than sit and stare at the blank walls.

"I'm thinking you were right. Our best chance is working together. But we need someone else on our team." Lynell pauses, her eyes moving from

Sawyer to Ramsey to Daniel, who gives her a small nod of encouragement. "We need Harlow Graham."

Out of all the options for someone to work with, Harlow is at the top of Sawyer's list, so she's not sure where her unease comes from. Her body senses danger when her mind can't see anything worth worrying about. She shoves the feeling down so she can plan with the others unimpeded by pointless anxiety.

They stay long enough to agree on next steps, and a time to meet later in the evening. Then the five of them leave the safe house, Ramsey driving Lynell and Daniel while Sawyer and Malakai take the car borrowed from his neighbor.

She's silent during the drive, hoping it'll help alleviate the persistent anxiety. Once at her house, Malakai opens the front door, she steps in, her head down as she turns on the phone when someone gasps and throws their arms around her.

"Sawyer, thank god," Harlow says, her shoulders digging into Sawyer's chin. Several long moments of hugging pass before she pulls back, gaze bouncing around Sawyer's face. "You scared us to death."

"Us?" Sawyer repeats. Harlow steps aside to reveal several people in her living room, all of them now looking at her with wide eyes.

Henry Doyle, leaning against his cane, spins from where he was standing next to the couch by Sawyer's thriving Ficus. Lying on her back on the couch is Drea, dark circles cupping her small eyes and Guinness snoozing obliviously on her chest. Her legs lie in the lap of a man Sawyer recognizes as Grant Woods, longtime member of the Resurrection and Drea's ex. Finally, an older man is standing in the corner of the room, his face pale.

"Dad?"

He crosses the room and stops a foot in front of Sawyer to stare at her, as if uncertain whether she's real or a figment of his imagination. Then he envelops her in the tightest hug they've ever shared. Sawyer is momentarily lost in her thoughts and hesitates in returning the hug because she swears in the second before her dad grabbed her, he looked guilty. She could see regret clear as day in his eyes.

But what on earth would he have to feel guilty for?

When he lets go, Henry and Drea are there, waiting for their turn to hug her.

Sawyer looks between their pained expressions. "What's going on?"

"Seriously?" Drea says. "We thought you were dead! Or kidnapped or something."

"Why would you think that?" Sawyer asks.

"First of all, Henry found this on the floor of your office." Drea turns, scoops up something from the coffee table, and hands it to Sawyer. It's one of Johnson's stalker photos. Sawyer must have dropped it when she was cleaning the office. "Then there was this."

Drea grabs the TV remote and presses buttons until an hours-old news report replays on the screen. A reporter with red hair framing her face takes up most of the screen, bright red and blue lights flashing behind her and a text box at the bottom of the screen that reads, *Gunshots heard at house owned by Lincoln D'Angelo.*

"The police refused to comment on whether or not bodies were recovered from the home, but the way they said it made everyone think that you were dead," Drea says. "None of our calls could go through, and Henry couldn't find your location . . ." She trails off, but Sawyer doesn't need any further explanation.

"What else did the news say?" Sawyer asks, thinking about Lynell.

Drea frowns. "What do you mean?"

"Were there any other witnesses? Did they mention anyone else?"

"Who else would they mention, sweetheart?" Lincoln asks.

Sawyer rolls her lips together, unwilling to share her plans with Lynell and Daniel yet. "Never mind."

None of them seem happy with the response, particularly Harlow and Lincoln, but no one argues.

"So, what happened?" Drea asks.

"I received a threat along with the photos." She lifts the picture up to face the room. "And I was worried. So, Malakai and I were looking for possible safe houses in case I needed one. When we were checking out one of Dad's rentals, someone shot at us, but we're fine."

"You don't look okay, sweetheart," Lincoln says, eyeing the cuts along Sawyer's neck and face.

"Glass from the window breaking." Sawyer suddenly feels claustrophobic. "I'm okay but I'm tired. Everything is still on for tomorrow, so I'm going to shower and get some rest before the convention."

They seem to understand, because they all start their goodbyes, expressing their relief that she's okay, telling her to be safe, and agreeing to see her the next day before the convention.

Harlow is the last to give her a hug, and Sawyer whispers in her ear, "I need you to stay." She walks with her father on his way out, then locks the door, closes the blinds, and pours a glass of water.

Finally alone, Sawyer sits Harlow down and tells her the truth.

"Did they . . . mention him?" she asks, her words so quiet that Sawyer almost wonders if she imagined them.

"Lynell said he was the bravest person she knew. And that he would break his generational curse." Sawyer still can't quite believe the love Lynell seemed to have for her cousin, the man who Registered her. How could she have said such kind things about him? Zachary never showed a hint of goodness, or expressed sympathy for the people who lost loved ones to the Registration.

He spoke to crowds on behalf of his father to condemn rebels and spout the same bullshit about how the Registration is good and they all need to fall in line with how the world works. He looked and acted exactly how she expected the son of a tyrant to look and act.

Yet Lynell, Daniel, and Harlow all knew him personally and have a completely different opinion on the man. As little sense as it makes, Sawyer trusts all three of them.

Nothing in the world seems as straightforward as it once did.

The green of Harlow's eyes expands as tears begin to form. "Thank you," she whispers.

"So, are you in?" Sawyer asks. She knows Harlow would help the Resurrection, but she's not sure if Lynell's involvement will change things. "Will you help us?"

Harlow nods. "Of course."

CHAPTER **34**

LYNELL

Thursday Afternoon

Daniel calls Grant minutes after they're back at the house, which has three times the amount of security it did yesterday, and puts the call on speaker so Lynell can listen.

"Learn anything for me?" Daniel asks.

Grant laughs. "You suck at greetings. But yes, I did. I was going to call you soon, actually. You knew that Ms. D'Angelo was in danger, didn't you? She got shot at yesterday."

Daniel turns on his heel, pacing the length of the bedroom while Lynell's eyes follow him. "How do you know about that?"

"Dude, it's all over the news. Where have you been?"

"Oh, right. I try not to watch the news," he says.

"Right." Grant draws out the word. "Well, I was with Drea when someone called her about Ms. D'Angelo missing. Drea didn't want to be alone, so I went with her to Ms. D'Angelo's house. By the way, have you been there? It's kind of small. I expected something more . . . grand, I guess."

"Focus, Grant." Daniel resumes pacing.

"Patience. I was there when Sawyer and Malakai Morrison returned. She was pretty banged up but seemed okay."

"Now do you see why I'm trying to get some answers? Lyn is in constant danger. So is Sawyer, it seems."

"Yeah, I get it. Anyway, Mr. D'Angelo, Sawyer's dad, was there and I overheard him talking to Harlow Graham."

At the mention of Lincoln, Lynell crosses her legs and Daniel's grip on the phone tightens. "What did they say?"

Lynell throws her hands up, mouthing "Act surprised," but Daniel doesn't seem to understand. At the same time, Grant says, "What, no shock that Zachary Elysian's mother was talking to Ms. D'Angelo's father?"

"Grant, I'm shocked," Daniel lies. Lynell falls back on the bed, covering her face with her elbow. "Now, what did they say?"

"Dude, how are you not claustrophobic surrounded by all those secrets?"

"Grant!"

"You used to be fun," Grant grumbles. "Fine. I overheard her talking to Lincoln D'Angelo, and I think you'll find this interesting. Harlow told Lincoln he needs to decide how important family is to him before he does something he can never take back. Lincoln claimed he didn't know what she was talking about, and she was the one who let her father think she was dead for twenty years. I couldn't hear the next bit of their conversation, but I'm pretty sure Harlow plans on using the rebels to get some sort of revenge. Or maybe Lincoln said to use her dad and the committee to get revenge. I only got pieces of their conversation."

Lynell removes her arm from her face, muttering, "Revenge?" under her breath. Who does Harlow want revenge on?

"What the hell . . ." Daniel whispers.

"Yeah, my thoughts exactly. I tried to keep listening, but Drea was waiting for me, and I was supposed to just be pissing. Then Ms. D'Angelo showed up an hour later."

"Was Harlow accusing Lincoln of putting Sawyer in danger?" Daniel asks, his eyes finding Lynell's. She sees her own dread reflecting back.

"Dunno," Grant says. "Maybe? But he seemed pretty fucking relieved when she got home alive."

"Weird."

Every second that passes, Lynell becomes more uncomfortable in her skin, as if simply existing with this information was a virus eating her alive.

"Does Sawyer know that Harlow is using the Resurrection to get revenge?" Daniel asks.

Lynell whispers, "Revenge on who?" Daniel flaps his hand in her direction in a signal for her to be quiet. She responds with an overdramatic pout.

"I don't think so," Grant says.

After a moment of silence, Daniel mutters, seemingly to himself, "What the hell is going on?"

"You tell me," Grant says. "You show up to visit me after years of silence and the next thing I know, everything is upside down."

"You almost sound like you're blaming me." The playful, joking tone in Daniel's voice isn't something Lynell hears often. A corner of her brain worries that meeting her sucked the joy from his life. Then she mentally chides herself for falling into old patterns of insecurity and guilt.

Daniel had already left the rebels when he met Lynell. He still had plenty of friends during their relationship. Everything that has happened in the weeks since they reunited has not been her fault. And, most importantly, Daniel is a grown man who can make his own choices. If he wants to leave her, he can leave her, even if the idea makes Lynell feel like a discarded ice cube melting in the sun.

Lynell abandons the swirling thoughts to find that Daniel has already ended the phone call. The silent moment is electric, forebodingly so.

"We have to tell Sawyer," she says.

Sawyer and Lynell. Two of the biggest powers and threats in the country. Both because of their families. Their grandfathers and fathers.

Does Sawyer have any idea about what kind of man her father is? Will finding out destroy her?

Lynell never really had a father, but if she had and he was using the Sin-Fighting Warriors to gain power over the Registration, despite having put his own daughter into the line of fire . . .

She shakes her head and looks back at Daniel—his oasis blue eyes that she would happily drown in, the dark curls designed for her hands to run through. A dimpled smile so genuine that each time she sees it, Lynell rediscovers joy.

Her chest aches. It can't hold the love she feels for this man. She's not sure any chest would be sturdy enough to contain her deep feelings for him.

"It'll be okay," Daniel says, misinterpreting her expression.

She drops her eyes and rubs her temple. "Should we wait to tell her until after tomorrow?"

"You know we can't do that."

"Tomorrow will be dangerous enough without Sawyer being distracted by all of this."

Daniel leans against the bed, grabbing her leg and distractedly rubbing his thumb against her calf muscle. "But if Lincoln is who we think he is, then we need her *and* Harlow to know. They have a better chance of getting the CCC from him than anyone else."

"I can't believe you're not trying to talk me out of any of this."

He laughs. "I've never been able to talk you out of bad ideas."

"You should work on that," Lynell says, a teasing note in her voice.

He rolls his eyes. "I don't think you can work on the impossible."

She allows herself a moment to stare at the ceiling and brood about what they'll have to do next before sitting up with a huff.

"Alright," she says. "Let's call in the troops. We've got shit to do."

───

Ramsey leaves. He offers excuses without his typical assertiveness, saying he needs to go over the convention's security and begin implementing their plan. He doesn't look at Lynell, who sees truth in the spaces between his words.

He doesn't want to see Harlow.

Especially not with an audience.

In preparation for his absence, he stations extra security detail around the house. Only Hayes stays inside the house once their guests are brought through the garage, unseen by anyone else. Hayes is the first one through. He walks to where Lynell is standing in the hallway between the kitchen and living room and stops at her side, saying nothing about who their guests are.

"You deserve a raise," she quietly tells him. She digs her bare toes into the hardwood floor while Daniel greets them at the door to the garage.

"Hey, welcome," Daniel says. He's mere feet away, but his voice travels through a tunnel to reach her ears. "Harlow, it's so nice to meet you." The tunnel steals the rest of his words, reducing them to a roar.

Lynell's gaze falls on the older woman as she steps inside accompanied by Sawyer and Malakai. She's unfamiliar but recognizable. They are strangers and they have known each other forever. Her eyes are professional thieves, searching for every detail about Harlow, stealing them for her own memory.

Harlow doesn't share many physical aspects with Zach. He had dark hair, busy brows, and a large frame. Harlow, on the other hand, is small, shorter than Lynell and thinner than Sawyer. She has long, naturally blonde hair. Zach might have gotten his mom's nose, but Lynell isn't positive. She's already forgetting the details of her cousin's appearance.

Not his green eyes, though. Harlow's are lighter, more like fresh spring than emerald, but for the most part, looking into Harlow's eyes is like going back in time and staring at her cousin's, wondering if he got them from his mom and being jealous that she shared his father's brown eyes.

Lynell blinks and returns to her body, remembering where she is and what she's supposed to be doing.

She clears her throat and says, "Harlow?"

The older woman nods.

"I'm Lynell."

"I know." Her smile softens the edges of her voice.

"Thank you for coming," Lynell says.

"Thank you for caring," Harlow replies. "So, would you like to share your plan?"

"Yes, I will. But first . . ." Lynell tugs her attention free of Harlow and gives it to Sawyer. It takes every ounce of determination in her bones to say, "Sawyer, we should talk."

CHAPTER 35

Sawyer has a recurring dream where she's late to an important event and she leaves her house without getting dressed. She has to go through the entire event, whether it's a meeting, wedding, party, or protest, completely naked. In the dream, she's half aware of her nakedness. That dream now bleeds into her reality. She feels the same displacement and amnesia, where she's missing something important that's on the edge of consciousness but doesn't know what it is.

Shaky and self-conscious, Sawyer follows Lynell to the back bedroom, the eyes of Daniel, Malakai, and Harlow carving holes into her back. Some intuitive makeup in her DNA knows that what Lynell is going to say will change everything.

Then Lynell explains, and it doesn't just change everything; it shatters everything into a million raindrops, falling from the cloud's embrace into oblivion.

Each word Lynell says sucks peace and security from the room until Sawyer is stranded in the worst sandstorm of her life.

"I'm so sorry," Lynell says.

It can't be true.

"Harlow should be able to help. Maybe she'll know more and can explain."

Sawyer's chest grinds together, shutting off the flow of air from her lungs and heart until she's dizzy from lack of oxygen.

"If Ramsey is right and Johnson had orders not to kill or harm you, then maybe your fath—"

"Stop," Sawyer interrupts. She squeezes her eyes shut and sucks in as much air through her nose that her lungs will hold. For a blink, she can see and think clearly. During that second, one word fills her mind. It's so loud and bright and big that nothing else registers.

Betrayed.

She's never felt this betrayed. Out of all the loss and pain and anger in her life, she had one thing. She had trust. There was a clear line between the good and the bad. Lynell muddled that line for a while, but she eventually found her place firmly on one side and everything made sense again in Sawyer's mind.

Now the line is obliterated. There isn't a trace of it left. Not a piece or shadow or ghost that proves it once existed.

Sawyer blinks away tears made of tiny glass shards. Anger swells, enveloping the betrayal and grief until it's one monster spinning in her chest. The pressure of it pushes more tears to the surface. It tightens her lungs further. She wants to scream as loud as she can, if only for a modicum of relief. Sawyer lays her empty palm to her chest and pushes.

Her father is behind all of it. The schemes to get rid of Lynell. The threats on her own life. Ellery's death.

Everything is his fault, yet he still sat across from her and lied through his teeth. He looked her in the eyes and played the part of a caring, worried father while secretly knowing he was in league with the people who wanted Sawyer out of the picture.

"What you do is dangerous enough . . . Look what happened to Ellery . . . You've been standing up. You're allowed to sit." She sees his words now for what they were. An attempt to take the leader of the rebellion off the board.

Maybe there was a hint of fatherly concern, but the majority of his motives have been selfish.

Through a visceral awareness, Sawyer knows she's on the bedroom floor, but she doesn't remember sitting. She sees Lynell kneeling, teeth digging into her bottom lip and hand hovering between them like it doesn't have a destination. They're outside of time, with no way to measure how long they sit before Lynell gives up, says something incomprehensible, and leaves the room. Reality is elastic. A distorted image plays in front of her like a movie flashback, pulling from her memories and her imagination. She sees Jude filling Lincoln's head with bitterness and kernels of an idea for revenge—Lincoln conspiring with oligarchs and committee chairs to regain what Gideon stole from his family seventy years ago—Bruce Macgill finding a group of men they can manipulate into being their own private militia by twisting their religious beliefs—Lincoln taking control over the Sin-Fighting Warriors by painting himself as some pure, wise Elder.

She remembers her father stressing that he doesn't care about Sawyer's sexuality, only that she's dangerously close to following in Paul's rebel footsteps, her father advising Sawyer to leave Ellery.

She sees her father convincing Thomas Johnson to Register Ellery—and Ellery dying at the hands of an egotistical need for dominance.

And she sees Sawyer and Lynell standing together against impossible odds.

Her surroundings disintegrate and Sawyer is back in her body, sitting on Lynell's bedroom floor, cheeks tight from dried tears. Her heart is in overdrive, as if compensating for the part of it that's decayed. She faces the bedroom door, knowing she should stand and join the others. Instead, she turns on her new phone and keys in the set of numbers that used to be a source of comfort.

She shouldn't use this phone to call one of *them*. The Elders. The enemies that personify everything in the world Sawyer is desperate to correct.

But she knows herself. She has to do this or she'll never be fully present tomorrow.

It rings four times. The pauses between each ring stretch into hours. Sawyer expects it to go to voicemail. She hopes it'll go to voicemail.

It doesn't.

"Yeah."

She closes her eyes. "Dad." Lincoln doesn't answer, probably trying to figure out which of his three daughters has called him from a random number. So, she helps him out by adding, "It's Sawyer."

"Are you okay? What number is this?" he asks with an edge of panic.

"When I graduated college, do you remember what you gave me?"

Lincoln gives a huff of a laugh that turns into a pause as he puzzles over the question.

"A key."

"I thought you got me a car or a house or something. But you didn't. You gave it to me, and said . . ." She trails off.

As expected, her dad finishes the story for her. "'Here's the key to the world, you'll be running it all in no time.'" She can hear his smile.

"I tried it in every lock I could find," Sawyer says. "It opens one of the drawers in your desk. There wasn't anything interesting in it."

She remembers being so disappointed that after spending weeks failing to unlock random doors, she found boring business documents, his old wedding ring, and a few antique pieces of jewelry and pocketknives. She figured her dad had grabbed a random key he never used to gift her in place of flowers or something *real*.

"I expected to find the jewelry gone, but you didn't take anything," Lincoln says. "Your brothers would have looted the entire drawer."

"Did you mean it then?" Sawyer asks, ignoring his attempt at levity. "That I would be a good leader."

"Of course."

"Being a leader is hard. People end up hating you, some enough to threaten you. Maybe even follow through on the threats. It's a dangerous, difficult job with little payout, unless you care about what you're leading."

"What's going on?" Lincoln asks.

"You're only a good leader to people who agree with you. If they don't, then it doesn't matter how good you actually are, they'll say you're bad. That you shouldn't run the world."

"Sawyer, honey . . ."

"I'm a good leader," Sawyer contends, ignoring him. "Maybe I wasn't at first, but I am now. I'm good at what I do. And what I do matters."

"I know you are, honey."

"I wish you trusted me the way I trusted you," Sawyer whispers. Then, before her dad can respond, she asks, "You love me, right?"

"More than anything."

Sawyer nods again, several tears dropping from her eyes. "I love you too."

"Sawyer."

She hangs up. He immediately calls back, so she blocks his number. She also blocks any thought of him in her mind. Her dad is gone. There will be time to mourn him later. For now, she must focus all her effort on destroying the Registration and those who protect it.

Like Lincoln D'Angelo.

CHAPTER 36

Telling Sawyer everything they know about Lincoln, and what it all probably means, was like dragging her heart through a nest of thorns. Lynell looks at her hands, half expecting to see them covered in blood. She lowers the splinted fingers and flexes her good ones until knuckles pop, then pushes them under her thighs so she can pay attention to the current conversation.

After leaving Sawyer in the bedroom, she joined the other four in the living room to share stories and plans. Hayes doesn't join in the discussions, but stands by the back door, arms at his side and earpiece secured. Malakai refuses to sit and looks back at the bedroom every few seconds. He clearly wants to check on Sawyer, but agreed to give her time. Harlow, rather than looking uncomfortable in the foreign house, is sitting in the armchair, legs crossed and hands folded over her knees.

Half an hour passes between Lynell leaving Sawyer and the bedroom door cracking open. Sawyer emerges, her eyes red and swollen.

Harlow jumps up. "Oh, Sawyer," she whispers.

"I'm okay," Sawyer says, voice stuffed. "Seriously. I don't want to talk about it."

So, they don't. They talk about everything *except* Sawyer's father. The moments someone has to mention Lincoln, they say, "one of the Elders" and expect the others to understand. With the Resurrection's existing plans, Ramsey's information from the convention's security, Harlow's suggestions, and their combined resources, it takes three hours for them to finalize a strategy Lynell is reasonably confident in.

Before their guests can leave, though, she pulls Harlow aside and the two women head upstairs to Lynell's office. Once alone, their shared history and family weighs heavy in the air. Lynell is searching for the right words to break the tension when Harlow does it for her.

"Are you okay?" she asks.

The words enter Lynell's ears and burrow into her throat, forming a hard knot she can't swallow around. She grinds her teeth and presses her lips together until the imminent threat of tears dissolves. "Yeah, of course."

Harlow's expression transforms into one of disbelief. With three steps, she's right in front of Lynell, placing her small hands on Lynell's shoulders. "You don't have to be okay."

Lynell's next inhale is strained, and jumps almost like a hiccup. She averts her eyes from Harlow's face, wondering if it's possible to surgically remove your tear ducts.

For as long as Lynell could remember, her biggest dream was to have a happy, stable family full of love. Her biggest fear was achieving that dream, then having it turn to ash around her. Harlow isn't family. She's a stranger. Yet, Lynell can't ignore the tug in her chest to the older woman, as if her deepest dreams and fears recognize potential in Harlow. In another life, she's Lynell's aunt and they've always known each other.

Harlow drops her hands from Lynell's shoulders. "My parents got divorced when I was nine years old."

It's so random that Lynell's eyes and throat are momentarily clear. She looks up at Harlow, who now stares at the office's window. "What?"

"It was several years before my dad joined the Registration committee, so it wasn't some big scandal. They separated on good terms, probably because they were never in love in the first place. They married because my mom got pregnant." Harlow shakes her head then looks back at Lynell. "That's one of the reasons I never even considered marrying Eric after I got pregnant. I knew, at least on some level, what kind of man he was. But mostly, I was afraid of being stuck in a loveless marriage the way my parents were for nearly a decade."

"Oh," is all Lynell can think to say.

"I know it's not the same thing, but I know what it's like to have your parents' failed relationship affect every decision."

Lynell's arms and legs are numb. She wonders why there isn't a couch in her office. The only seating is her desk chair, and the two chairs on the other side of the desk.

"I also know what it's like to have your entire life turned upside down because of the Elysian family," Harlow says.

"I . . ." her voice fails.

"You're not okay."

Lynell shakes her head. Harlow doesn't immediately reply, and the following pause gives Lynell time to piece together thoughts. She takes a deep breath.

"Are you?"

"What?"

"Are you okay?" Lynell clarifies.

Harlow seems to mull the question over. "Better than I used to be. But I'm not sure I'll ever be fully okay again."

Lynell is about to apologize for her loss or offer positive memories of Zach, but Harlow carefully steers the conversation away from her son.

"Tell me about them—all of them," Harlow says. "Your mom, your stepdad, your husband and daughter."

"Why?"

Harlow shrugs. "Because I want to know you and they're part of you."

The fact that she might truly care about Lynell and her history is shocking and unexpected. "You don't hate me?"

Sighing, Harlow gestures Lynell to the two stiff chairs in front of the desk where they sit, knees inches apart. "We just met. How can I hate you before I've even gotten to know you?"

Because I'm the reason your son is dead, she thinks.

But Harlow is giving her a chance she never thought she'd get, and Lynell isn't going to fuck it up. If anyone in the world will understand what it was like growing up in the earthly equivalent of hell out of fear of the Elysians, it's Harlow. She lost her child and Lynell lost her mother. No one else she knows has lost family because of Eric's blind, selfish desire for more power. No one else knows what it's like to love an Elysian and want to support them despite the Registration's faults.

No one else will understand the intricately complicated feelings Lynell has toward the family that both saved and destroyed their country.

So, Lynell talks. She tells Harlow about growing up with Alan as a stepfather and dreaming about her real father. She tells Harlow about her mother and watching Elizabeth slowly die under the pain, fear, abuse, and grief of a better life she never got. Lynell tells Harlow about attempting to build something better with Daniel but losing everything at the hands of her own fear. She tells her everything she learned about Eric through those torturous two weeks of fleeing the Registration. She tells her about refusing to give Eric what he needed for more power, then realizing now she's in his position and has no idea what to do because no one ever taught her what was good. They only taught her what *wasn't* good.

Lynell even tells Harlow about Zach and how he went from the stranger who Registered and tortured her to the cousin who sacrificed his life for her.

"He did what he did because Eric threatened you," Lynell says, tears streaming down her cheeks. She's surprised they haven't dried yet, with how long she's been talking. Her mouth is rough and dry, desperate for water, but now that she's started, she can't stop. Especially with the way Harlow listens with such open eyes and earnest concern. "He loved you so much that he was willing to do anything to keep you safe from his father."

A tear slips down the side of Harlow's nose. She hasn't been crying as hard as Lynell, but every once in a while, a tear falls and she sniffs. "He was a good man."

Lynell nods. "Yes, he was."

"He didn't have anyone to tell him what was good, either."

Knowing what Harlow means, Lynell drops her eyes and wipes her nose with her sleeve. Zach wasn't only taught what *wasn't* good, he was taught to be what was necessary for power and control. Yet, he was a good person.

"Zach was never in the position I'm in," Lynell says. "He never had to make the decisions I do. He didn't know what I do."

"Which is?"

Lynell's chest rattles with a shuddering breath. A glance at the window shows the moon high in the sky. Her body is wrung dry. She needs to go to sleep.

But she can't let go of this moment. Not yet.

She's never had this before. This feeling of talking to someone older and wiser than her who understands her struggles.

The feeling of talking about a problem with someone like a parent.

Elizabeth died when Lynell was fourteen, but she'd been fading for years. Lynell hasn't had someone she could talk to like this since long before she was a teenager.

And here Harlow is, ready, willing, and loving.

Zach trusted her, so why shouldn't Lynell? No one is made to carry such heavy burdens alone. Isn't that what parents are supposed to do? Help carry your burdens?

Harlow isn't her mom, but she's offering to ease the weight on Lynell's shoulders, and Lynell doesn't have enough strength to refuse the help.

CHAPTER 37

H arlow decided a long time ago she wouldn't pick sides.

Having a father on the Registration committee alienated her from her peers. It turned her into a symbol of the Registration to hate, or a stepping stone into a life of more power and riches. She vowed to be neither, instead living in the shadows. It turned out, the shadows were a great place to overhear important conversations and gather life-changing information.

Unfortunately, it wasn't information that changed her life. It was what she did. Agreeing to date Eric. Then refusing to flee when she became pregnant. Refusing to pick a side.

Now, twenty-nine years later, she's picking up the pieces of her mistakes to turn them into something better.

Harlow sits in the living room that doesn't fit the home's owner. It's warm, with thriving plants, family photos on the walls, and a small dog snorting from where it sleeps on its back, feet in the air and belly on full display. She thinks it's a pug judging from a squished, black snout and floppy black ears.

"Here you go," Lincoln D'Angelo says, passing Harlow a mug filled with steaming liquid and the string of a tea bag draped over the side. She thanks him and holds the mug close to her face, the steam gathering under her chin until there's a layer of liquid she has to wipe away.

They've been playing the roles of old friends, pretending their near-argument at his daughter's house never happened. When Lincoln pulled her aside to badger her with questions, Harlow was on the defensive.

She knows who Lincoln is, but she doesn't plan on letting him know who she is.

"You never told me where you've been," Lincoln says.

"It doesn't matter. I thought staying away was what was best for my son, but I was wrong." The tremor in her voice when she mentions Zachary is genuine. Lincoln studies her and Harlow feels like a teenager, forcing herself to remain small so none of the adults in the room take notice.

"I'm sorry for your loss," Lincoln finally says. "I should have said it yesterday, but I was stunned to see you and . . ."

Harlow gives him the smile-and-thanks that she's already perfected in the short time since her son died.

Her son died.

The thought has the same effect on her as coming face to face with Medusa would.

Breaking free from the curse of grief, she blinks and nods at him. She might not like the man, but she knows what it feels like to be terrified for your child's safety. "I'm sorry I thought for even a second that you'd put anything before your family."

Lincoln waves his hand in the air, brushing away her apology. She almost accused him of more yesterday, and she sends gratitude into the universe that she managed to hold her tongue.

"It's okay, I get it. I know how it looks, me not publicly announcing my support for anyone or any side in particular."

She doesn't want to talk about how it looks, and she definitely doesn't want Lincoln thinking about which side he's pledged loyalty to. She needs to put him in the past, when he saw her as an innocent, naive girl he could manipulate. Back then, his family was nothing but a reputation formed by secret whispers about Jude and speculation on what exactly happened between him and Gideon. Lincoln fought hard against that reputation, and if Lynell's theory is correct, he did a damn good job.

She and Lynell talked for hours last night, unearthing long-buried memories in Harlow's mind. Memories of eavesdropping on her father's secret meetings with Paul D'Angelo. Of meeting a woman a few years Harlow's senior who had the same look in her eyes that Harlow saw in the mirror. The look that she was waiting for something but didn't know what it was.

Elizabeth Crane asked Harlow about Paul, the D'Angelos, Harlow's family, the committee, the Registration. Her kin spirit silenced Harlow's internal alarms. As Harlow was in a better position to scrounge up information than Elizabeth, she began learning everything she could, spying on conversations, breaking into her dad's office, and allowing people like Lincoln to think he was manipulating her when, in reality, she was using him.

No one suspects the meek, young girl of having ulterior motives. The more arrogant someone is, the less likely they are to analyze the actions of their 'inferiors.'

"I'm not one to judge others on their lack of public stands," she says, grinning. She lifts her mug and looks into the murky brown water, letting the steam dampen her face. "Do you still keep in contact with my dad?"

"Your dad was never my biggest fan," Lincoln says. "Why would I keep in contact with him?"

"Oh, come on, Lincoln. Do you honestly think I don't know?" she asks, trying to sound teasing rather than accusatory.

Lincoln raises his eyebrows. But he clearly doesn't care about trying to appear innocent, because he smirks in amusement and says, "Know what?"

"What a pair we are," Harlow says, chuckling softly. "Can we put away the pretenses? I know family is important to you, like it is to me. But neither of us have the luxury of making decisions based on our family's opinions."

"What decisions are you referring to?"

"Before I left, I was nothing more than a committee member's child and Eric Elysian's object of desire. Then I got pregnant, and was reduced to an incubator for an illegitimate Elysian. You were a man with good ideas and ambitions who was rejected because an Elysian betrayed your father and ruined his name. But now? We have the chance to do something of value. With Eric out of the way, you have a nearly unobstructed path to retake what his family stole from yours."

"You think I'm trying to take control of the Registration." Lincoln says it as a statement, not a question.

It's exactly what she thinks, because she knows Lincoln and, for all his appearances of civility and willingness to step aside, he only wants one thing. To get justice for his father and reclaim what he believes he's owed as a D'Angelo.

"I think you should, and if you're the man I think you are, then you're not *trying*, you're in the process of *succeeding*."

"No offense, Harlow, but you were a kid back then and you've been gone a long time. How can you possibly know who I am?"

Harlow chews on her bottom lip, struggling to keep the perfect balance between submissive and knowledgeable. "You're right, I was young, and I've just returned. But does that matter? There's no way you gave up on what you wanted. Especially not with Eric being in control for nearly twenty years."

Lincoln studies her, as if searching for a crack in her exterior. "Where are you going with this?"

Harlow takes a deep, steadying breath. "I always knew that someone had vital information that Eric, the committee, and the oligarchs wanted, I just didn't know *who* had it." Harlow runs her finger along the rim of her mug. A lifetime of listening has made Harlow an expert at choosing the right words. "Recent events have changed that."

"I'm still not sure what you're referring to."

"Lincoln. Why do you think I disappeared? It sure as hell wasn't because I wanted to."

Knowing Eric was illegitimate was the least of Harlow's crimes. *"I'm not telling you shit, Eric. Dad trusted me with the code, not you,"* she once heard Eli say.

She wonders if she should've told Lynell the truth last night. Lynell shared so much with Harlow, and Harlow retaliated by keeping her secrets locked in a vault. Now, she contemplates the virtue of her silence. The secrets aren't hers to keep. They belong more to Lynell and Sawyer.

She can't change her decision then, so she commits entirely to her decision now.

"When no one thinks you're listening, you're bound to hear something dangerous," Harlow says. "I couldn't use the information I learned back then but now? Eric is gone and the girl who killed my son is in his place."

Genuine interest replaces amusement in Lincoln's eyes. "If you want to share your . . . information with the committee, why don't you approach your father?"

"I told you yesterday, I don't want to put him in harm's way. My father is an old man who remains on the committee out of pity. It didn't take long to learn that he'd lost any confidences he once had. I'm sure he's in the dark about possible *alternative* directions the oligarchs and committee may be planning to go."

Lincoln is unlike every other D'Angelo Harlow has known. His uncle appeared to wear his emotions on his sleeve while keeping everything important masterfully hidden behind a mask. His father lived so firmly in the past that he slowly faded from the present. His daughter struggles every day with demons both internal and external and somehow remains a soft, trusting, and hopeful human.

His young cousin, the lost D'Angelo, wanted love so desperately that she never learned how dangerous it could be.

Lincoln is all of them combined and none of them at the same time. He can be whoever he needs to be. Perhaps that's why he can be the loving father that Sawyer trusted with her entire self, and the brutal man the oligarchs want controlling the Registration.

"Were there such alternative directions, what makes you think I'd be privy to them?" He expertly keeps his face neutral, giving away no knowledge that he'd be privy to them because *he* is the alternate direction.

"Because Lynell told me. The brilliant thing about being gone for so long is that I can return as whoever I want to be. Do you know how easy it is to gain the confidence of a young woman in over her head who lost the family she recently found? I'm not sure what Eric tried with Lynell, but I'm not surprised he failed. He was never good at listening."

Lincoln frowns, and Harlow knows he's beginning to question whether he should believe her. "I thought you wanted revenge on Lynell. That's why you were at Sawyer's house."

"It's easier to get revenge on someone who trusts you," she says, which is true. And the best way to get someone to trust you is to tell them the truth.

At least, a version of the truth.

"No one wants Lynell in charge, but they can't get rid of her yet. Not until they know the code. And I'm close to getting it from her."

Lincoln's expression falters like a television losing reception. He didn't expect her to know anything about the code.

"So, why are you here?" Lincoln asks.

In deciding not to take sides, Harlow learned that all sides are flawed. They all have secrets and agendas. They also have a heart at the core that had, at some point, purely good intentions. Harlow lived in the spaces between until she overheard the wrong thing, poked the bear too hard, became a threat rather than a pest.

By the time she had a side she wanted to choose, she no longer had the choice. She had to hide.

As time passed, she began to forget who she used to be. She forgot the girl no one saw. She became no one. A ghost on the edges of society, surviving in secret.

Then Elizabeth showed up, pregnant and afraid. Harlow didn't need to ask to know that an Elysian was the father. She welcomed Elizabeth into her purgatory of a life, and began to hope for more.

Elizabeth's presence forced Harlow to be alive again. To be a real person. To be there for her and her baby.

It's only fitting that, once again, a D'Angelo child and an Elysian child have given Harlow a purpose in life.

"I'm here to pick a side."

CHAPTER **38**

LYNELL

Friday Morning

I t's five minutes before 7 a.m., but the convention center is already alive with preparations. People fill the main hall with various booths. Some advertise timeshares, insurance policies, business schools, and more. Others include interactive components like virtual reality goggles that walk guests through the history of the Registration. Most are vendors selling homemade souvenirs like shirts and keychains with pictures of Gideon Elysian's face. Lynell even sees a mug that says, *The Elysian Champion: Survivor, Conqueror, and Heir.*

Lynell and Daniel step onto the elevator, Hayes and three other guards flanking them. The security Ramsey spent so long increasing is incredibly inconvenient, but it would look far too suspicious if he tried changing it now.

Hayes swipes a key card over the elevator sensor and clicks the button for the top floor. The convention center is four stories and the public has access to the first two. Floors three and four require specific key cards to access, which only a handful of people have.

The elevator ride is silent. Daniel grips Lynell's good hand, her other feeling cold. She both wishes Ramsey was here and is happy that he's not. She can do this by herself, and Ramsey needs to be where he is.

The elevator doors open onto a much smaller, quieter floor than the first. There are two doors on either side of the hallway, one of which is open. Lynell heads to that one, Daniel half a step behind her, and enters a stereotypical hotel conference room with blue carpet and a long table. All eight committee members are already in attendance, sitting around the table in the same order as they did last Thursday.

Lynell studies each one, wondering who, in addition to Finnegan and Tamara, is secretly working with the oligarchs behind the scenes to manipulate the entire country. Which ones are to blame for every attempt at controlling Lynell, including kidnapping Anna?

"Good morning," Lynell says, making her way to the head of the table. Daniel sits next to her this time. He doesn't fidget, but in comparison to Ramsey's easy composure during the meeting last week, Daniel's nerves vibrate the air between them.

She knows the moment he recognizes Finnegan and Tamara, because he inhales a short breath and his legs tense. Thankfully, he's sitting to her right, so she can lay her hand on his thigh.

"Mrs. Carter, you made it," Finnegan says. Anyone else might have heard the words as a greeting, but Lynell easily recognizes the displeasure in his voice.

"Of course. This vote is incredibly important to me, my family, the entire country," she says, sure that those responsible for taking her child know exactly what she is referring to.

"Will Mr. Davenport be joining us?" Tilly asks.

Lynell tries to listen to the spaces between Tilly's words to decipher the woman's possible innocence or guilt. Is she asking out of authentic interest, or because she suspects the truth about where Ramsey is right now, and what he's doing?

"Not today," Lynell says.

"Alright, that's enough. We have one minute until seven and plenty to do today," Robin says. "I'll begin the voting and we'll continue clockwise. In the event of a tie, Mrs. Carter will cast the final vote. If the vote fails to pass, we will adjust tonight's speeches accordingly. If it passes, all will continue as planned."

The older woman runs through a few more housekeeping rules, but Lynell tunes her out. She lets her eyes travel around the table, looking at these people in a different light than the first time she faced them.

"Before we begin," Lynell says, "I want to remind the table, as a whole, to consider all options before voting. Trust me when I say killing this policy is what is best for everyone in the country, all of you included. Change isn't always a good thing."

She hopes it's enough without being too much. She could say outright that everything should stay the same because if they try to change it, then she'll make everything worse for them. But she knows that would do more harm than good, especially for Anna.

"You know what they say: the devil you know . . ." she continues, hoping they understand her subtext.

"Right, well, enough quoting old phrases. It's time for the vote," Robin says. "There will be no need for further discussion. A 'yea' in support of the policy change or 'nay' against it will suffice." She waits for everyone at the table to nod before she says, "I vote nay."

Tamara is next and Lynell knows what she's going to say, but that doesn't make the word feel any less like a blow. "Yea."

Tilly rolls her perfect heart-shaped, red-painted lips together. For her credit, she appears to consider her words before she says, "Yea."

Warner's confident "Nay," soothes Lynell's racing heart slightly.

Then it's Finnegan's turn and Lynell's pulse doubles in speed. He looks directly at her and gives a satisfied smirk. "Yea."

"Yea," Izrael says.

Junior pushes his glasses up his nose and says, "Nay."

All eyes turn to Verity. "Yea."

"The yea's have it. Five to three. Vote passes and . . ." Robin's voice trails off like someone had grabbed a remote and turned down the volume.

Lynell is no longer in her body.

She doesn't feel herself nod and pretend to concede defeat. She doesn't hear as Warner offers his condolences and encouragement that it will be okay because he's confident in her ability to do good. She doesn't process Finnegan's cocky smile or hear his taunting words. Lynell is not there as eight people casually gather their things to leave the room, where they just decided the fate for an entire country.

Lynell has already mentally moved on. She couldn't fight the vote without putting Anna in more danger. They didn't have time. But the actual voting is only one part of this policy change. Once she has the CCC, the vote won't matter.

The convention doors will open in three hours, giving plenty of time for thirty thousand guests to arrive and anticipation to rise for the evening's announcements. More time and money has been invested in this day than Lynell can comprehend, all meant to make her accession and speech the most important, most watched event of the year.

Except Lynell doesn't intend for that to happen. She won't let the corrupt oligarchs and committee move forward with their plan.

She will save the country from their greed.

CHAPTER **39**

LYNELL

Friday Morning

L ynell takes a private elevator to the second floor of the conference
building, to the back entrance for personnel. Two women younger
than Lynell walk past her without looking up. One wears an assortment
of clothing with random cutouts and silk material that clings to her every
curve, the other a baggy jumper cinched at her waist. The badges around
their necks say, *Digital Press,* which is code for social media influencers or
bloggers. Lynell thinks she recognizes the first as a girl she follows who explains news stories and political updates while doing makeup tutorials.

A month ago, she would've been excited to meet the girl. Today,
though, Lynell wishes the girls would walk faster so she can work without
being seen.

Once alone, Lynell rushes to the employee hallway door. Anyone can
access the hallway from outside the convention center but can't leave it to
enter the building without a key, because the doors automatically lock on
one side when shut. Since they're unlocked from inside the building, Lynell
is able to open the door without issue. She secures a large clasp on the top
of the door to keep it from closing. Then, in case someone takes the clasp
off, she stuffs a napkin into the strike plate hole and tapes over it. Next, she

tapes the deadbolt into the door to keep the automatic lock from kicking in. Daniel is doing the same on the other side of the building so rebels will have multiple ways inside without being seen.

As she returns to the third floor, she grabs her phone, checking for missed messages from Harlow or Ramsey. The plan can continue even if Harlow fails to get the CCC, but it will be much more difficult to convince Lincoln to share it with anyone after today.

If Ramsey fails, though, Lynell and Daniel will stop the plan in motion. They'll shut down the rebel's attempts to hijack the convention and allow the convention to continue as planned. They will not risk Anna.

Seeing an empty phone screen, Lynell blows out a breath, fear numbing the edges of her senses.

"Done?"

Lynell looks up at the sound of Daniel's voice and repockets her phone. "Yeah. Should we head to the surveillance room?"

He pats the chest pocket of his shirt. "Got the drive ready to go."

They walk together past several meeting rooms and lecture halls to a door tucked away in the back corner. Ramsey told her yesterday the door would be locked, so she doesn't try turning the knob. Instead, she knocks twice then steps back, waiting. A wiry man with thin lips and tan skin opens the door.

"Yes?"

Lynell puts on her best bitch face and pushes past him into the room. She ignores his shouts of protest and says, "I'm sure you recognize me," in a lofty tone.

A second man, this one twice the size as the first and so pale he might never have seen the sun, is sitting inside the security room, He spins in his chair, his back now to the wall of screens displaying every inch of the conference center.

"What is—" his words crumble to an end. He jumps up and starts to bend forward like he's going to bow then thinks better of it and straightens. "Mrs. Elysian."

"Oh," the skinny man gasps.

"What are you—how can we help?"

Lynell eyes both men with distaste. "I came to check on the convention's security," she says.

The room is so small that it takes merely four steps for her to be on the other side. Both men turn to watch her, their backs now to the door, while Daniel steps silently into the room, a USB drive in hand.

"What are your names?" Lynell asks.

They stutter out their names, still unsettled at the unscheduled appearance of Lynell Elysian.

Raising her voice to mask any sound Daniel makes, she says, "Good. And I hope you've both been trained well?"

They nod.

"It seems the cameras and videos are all working. Everything is recording and sent to cloud storage, right?"

They nod.

"And the speeches later tonight?"

"The cameras send their feed to us here and the computers project the video footage to the rest of the nation."

Lynell nods, relieved that Ramsey gave her correct information. Behind the men, Daniel raises two thumbs and slips from the room, unseen by anyone but her.

"Thank you. Everything seems in order. Keep up the good work."

She leaves while they stutter, "Thanks," in unison.

She and Daniel return to their personal greenroom behind the auditorium stage where Hayes is waiting, veins peaking from his neck and muscles tense.

"I'm going with you next time," Hayes says. "I don't care what you're planning."

Lynell smirks. "You're starting to remind me of Ramsey."

"I take that as a compliment." A modicum of tension leaves his body, but he stays at full attention, veins still popping under his skin.

"You'll be happy to know I don't have to leave this room again for the next couple of hours." Lynell crosses the space to sit in front of the vanity. She flips a switch, turning on the lights lining the mirror. Each cut, bruise, under-eye shadow, clogged pore, and pimple is illuminated, ready for scrutiny. "Are we sure I can't get a body double to go on for me tonight?" she mumbles.

Daniel steps up behind her, grabbing the back of the chair. "One, you're stunning, always. And two," he lowers his voice to a whisper she only hears because his mouth is inches from her ear, "you won't be on camera."

"If Ramsey . . ."

"He'll get her," Daniel says. He kisses the top of her head and meets her eyes in the mirror.

Still, Lynell can't help but think that he should have already gotten her. He left at the same time as they did this morning. They never had a real chance of saving Anna in enough time to find a way to stop the vote, but the success of the entire plan hinges on Ramsey saving her before the announcement this evening.

"I'm going to try to do something about this monstrosity anyway." She gestures to her face.

"Don't call my wife's face a monstrosity. I get very protective."

She smiles at his reflection then turns enough so they can kiss. Before they pull apart, she whispers, "We have to make sure Sawyer gets in okay."

"She'll text us. But if it makes you feel better, I can go to the check-in desk to verify your list of guests was added."

"Take Jeremy with you," Lynell says, referring to the guard stationed directly outside the greenroom. Jeremy was once friends with Zach and aided in their escapes from Eric's house, earning him more trust than most of the other guards.

"Yes, ma'am."

As Daniel leaves, Lynell clicks on her phone and opens the messaging app, staring at Ramsey, Harlow, and Sawyer's names as if willing them to text her. Then, before she can drive herself insane, she turns back to the mirror, wondering what sort of magic she'll need to perform to be presentable in a few hours. She wishes she had the skills of the influencer she saw earlier.

Phase one, done, she thinks, dabbing concealer under her eyes.

Now it's up to Ramsey to complete phase two.

CHAPTER **40**

Ramsey watches the house for an hour before he does anything, careful not to make a single mistake. Mrs. Elysian's plans for the evening are only possible if he succeeds.

The closest neighbor is a quarter of a mile away. Dozens of trees provide cover from aerial views. The natural protection provided by the home's remote location is one reason he suspects this to be the place where Anna and Catherine are being held. As evidence against Lincoln D'Angelo grew, Ramsey began looking into every piece of real estate the man owned. Street cameras caught a stolen van with tinted windows heading to one of Lincoln's rental properties on Sunday. Ramsey followed it through cameras as far as possible, which helped narrow the search.

He wasn't absolutely certain this was the house until this morning, when Jeremy returned from watching it and reported a guard change, during which the new guards brought bags with a box of Pull-Ups sticking out the top.

Now, Ramsey is hiding in a cluster of bushes in front of the house, observing. The security team has a lot to learn, currently acting more as a performance than an actual barrier of trained men and women. The seven guards are split, four inside and three following predictable patterns around the house.

Technology and time are more of an obstacle than the men. Ramsey counts at least three cameras, all of which are likely streaming live feeds. He must assume that Macgill, Reese, Nelson, D'Angelo, and anyone else has access to those feeds, as well as the guards inside the house. He can't interrupt the signal because the technology is too advanced, so he estimates he'll have three minutes after killing the first guard before reinforcements are sent out. Having a partner or a team with him would make the rescue mission safer and faster, but it would also be more noticeable, and create more variables. He can't risk trusting the wrong person or alerting the oligarchs and committee too soon.

It's a good thing that he works well alone.

As he has every seven minutes, a younger man approaches the bush that provides Ramsey's hiding spot.

With the other two out of sight, Ramsey crawls from behind his cover and steps up behind the guard, hooking one arm around the man's throat, pressing against his vocal cords to keep him from shouting, and leveraging another on his shoulder.

He then moves his hands to the guard's jaw and forehead and twists with all his strength, stretching the man's neck to its breaking point. It took him months to perfect the ability of snapping a neck, but now it happens in seconds, barely giving the man time to claw at Ramsey's arm.

He drags the body behind the bush and silently moves closer to the house, making it behind a thick tree right before the next guard turns around. The man pauses, probably realizing something is wrong before processing his colleague's absence.

Then he half whispers, half yells, "Will?"

Ramsey recognizes the following unclipping sound as a gun leaving its holster. The guard resumes walking, slower now that he's on alert, He passes Ramsey's tree. Before he can call out or warn the last guard outside, Ramsey is behind him, breaking his neck, too.

He doesn't bother hiding this body. The last guard will be dead before he has time to see it.

He's standing at the end of the driveway, watching the road. Ramsey crosses the front lawn, walking on the balls of his feet and keeping low to the ground so he makes as little noise as possible.

Then he accidentally kicks a pebble. The tiny rock rolls across the driveway and the sound grabs the final guard's attention. Ramsey is still two yards away when the guard turns.

His eyes widen. His hands go for his gun. His mouth opens to yell.

Ramsey leaps, and as they collide, he slams his elbow into the guard's head, momentarily stunning him. They both grunt and gasp as they fall to the ground, grappling. Ramsey can't get the necessary leverage to break the guard's neck, and too much time is passing. If he doesn't act soon, the guard will manage a yell, alerting everyone inside and anyone with access to the security video.

Rolling onto the lawn, Ramsey allows the guard to gain enough control to land on top. His accomplished smile lasts less than a second. Then his lips part with a gurgling gasp when Ramsey slams a knife into the guard's throat. His eyes widen in horror. Ramsey rips the blade free, pulling a waterfall of blood with it, and the warm liquid drenches Ramsey's face, neck, and chest.

"Fuck!" he exclaims, shoving the body off him. He springs to his feet, tucks the bloody knife into his belt, and retrieves his gun. He switches off the safety and raises the gun in front of him, rushing to the front door.

Without hesitation, Ramsey kicks the door with as much force as he can manage. It flies off the handle, wood splintering with magnified cracks. In one inhale, he takes in the house's interior layout, furniture, and most importantly, people. There are two guards in front of him, meaning the other two are somewhere else in the house.

Ramsey aims the gun at the closest guard's head and pulls the trigger.
BANG!

The bullet is lost in a cloud of red where the man's head was half a second earlier.

The body hasn't hit the floor when Ramsey turns to the next guard and squeezes the trigger. He miscalculated the man's height, so the aim is off and the bullet hits his collarbone.

Ramsey tilts the barrel of the gun up and shoots again, this time hitting straight between the guard's eyes.

Only then does Ramsey exhale. At the same time, a guard comes into view from a hallway, and Ramsey repositions the gun but he's a second too late because the guard manages to fire his weapon first.

White hot burning explodes from his leg. He tumbles and hits the ground, his vision spotting from the pain. He blinks, groans, and rolls onto his knees. The guard has lined up for a second shot but before he gets the chance, Ramsey raises his gun and pulls the trigger a fourth time.

The bullet rips straight through the man's throat, sending out a mushroom-like explosion of blood and pulp.

Back on his feet, Ramsey limps to the stairs leading into a basement. He's momentarily deaf from incessant ringing, so he doesn't recognize the shrill cries for what they are until he reaches the bottom of the staircase.

The seventh and final guard stands in the center of a concrete basement furnished with shelves of canned food and water bottles, a bed, a toilet, and a sink. The guard is holding a sobbing woman in front of his chest, the barrel of a gun pressed to her temple. Curled in the corner of the bed is a young child.

Catherine Imes and Anna Carter.

Anna is screaming and her face is bright red. Tears stream down both the hostages' faces.

"Take one step and I'll blow her brains out in front of the kid." The guard's words barely penetrate the monotone ringing from the gunshots in Ramsey's ears.

"I would advise against that," Ramsey says, his voice much calmer than the other man's. "The others are all dead. Reinforcements will take at least fifteen minutes to arrive, plenty of time for me to kill you."

"Before I shoot them?"

Ramsey's arms are steady, his aim never wavering from the sliver of the man's face.

He's using Catherine as a shield, but she's a small woman in comparison to his large stature. If she moved an inch, Ramsey would have a perfect shot.

"You're one of those Sin-Fighting Warriors, aren't you?" Ramsey says. The longer he studies the man, the more he recognizes him. Blonde hair, faded tattoos on his neck, scar from where he had surgery as an infant to fix a cleft lip. "Cameron, right?"

Cameron's long lashes brush his top lid when his eyes widen. "How did you . . ."

"I know all of you." Ramsey briefly glances to Anna, ensuring she's still safely on the bed. She's the reason Ramsey is here, not Catherine. He could shoot Cameron now and Anna would be okay. Catherine might be too, if she was lucky.

But Ramsey doesn't pull the trigger. Not yet. The child has been through so much trauma. She doesn't deserve to watch another family member be shot, even by accident.

"I also know that you're being manipulated. Your *Elders*," he spits the word out, "are exploiting your beliefs, turning you into a mindless soldier. You're replaceable."

Cameron shakes his head, jerking Catherine slightly. The woman yelps, and he presses the gun harder into her head. "Shut up!"

"Let the girl go, Cameron."

Catherine gives quiet, gasping cries. She stands frozen, too afraid to move, staring at Ramsey, her eyes stretched wide.

"No!" Cameron screams, causing renewed crying from Anna. "This is all a part of a bigger plan. The Elders have a plan!"

"The Elders are selfish humans who care about nothing and no one but themselves," Ramsey says, taking a small step forward. "As soon as you're no longer useful, they'll get rid of you."

"Don't move! I'll shoot her, I swear I will."

"The vote happened six hours ago, Cameron. It passed. You should know that. You can let Anna and Catherine go now."

"My orders are to hold them until an Elder comes tomorrow. The announcement must happen first," Cameron says.

Without warning, a wave of dizziness washes over Ramsey. Pain from the gunshot wound colonizes part of his body and he stumbles. Black dots fill his vision. He's losing too much blood.

Ramsey blinks, grips his gun, and steadies himself before Cameron can take advantage of his momentary distraction.

"It's too late, Cameron. I'm here, and I'm taking the kid. You've failed no matter what. The Elders will kill you for this. It's up to you whether Catherine dies, too. Tell me, does she deserve death? You believe in justice and holiness. Will shooting Catherine be justice? Will it make you holy?" The words wilt as they leave Ramsey's mouth, each second draining more energy.

"She's part of the problem."

Catherine closes her eyes and hiccups in broken breaths.

"She's an innocent young woman guilty of nothing except losing her sister to a madman and taking care of her orphaned niece."

"She is not an orphan!"

"Anna lost the only parents she ever knew."

"She's the product of the rotten Elysian line."

Cameron's replies grow increasingly desperate, and Ramsey is wavering where he stands. Too much time has passed. He has to end this now before reinforcements get here.

"It's up to you, Cameron. Do you face your death like a coward and take an innocent life with you, or do you face it with courage?" Ramsey asks.

The question seems to take Cameron by surprise. His hold on Catherine relaxes a fraction. She's too scared to make a run for it, but she's been leaning against Cameron, unable to hold herself up, so the slack moves her an inch to the left.

It's enough.

Ramsey pulls the trigger.

Blood sprays the side of Catherine's face. The bullet's force throws Cameron back, and he hits the shelf before falling to the floor. Anna is screaming, but Catherine has gone silent. She turns before Ramsey can tell her not to look. He follows her gaze and sees the corpse through the eyes of someone normal. Someone who hasn't killed and tortured dozens of people. Someone who doesn't intimately know what death looks like.

Half of Cameron's jaw is gone. The rest of his face, shoulder, and neck are drenched with his own blood, pieces of bone, teeth, tissue, and gray matter. The cartilage of his nose and broken white pieces of jawbone are visible. Even a section of his tongue has been blown away.

Then, Catherine screams. It's louder than Anna's screaming.

"We have to go, hurry!" Ramsey says, trying to cut through the sounds of terror. He heads to the bed and reaches for Anna, but the child cowers away from him. She's howling, and her wide eyes jump quickly around Ramsey. He remembers that he's covered in blood, and Anna just watched him shoot a man, so of course she's scared of him.

But Catherine is bloody too, and she doesn't have the presence of mind to carry Anna, so Ramsey mutters, "Fuck it," and grabs Anna's feet. The child screams and kicks as he drags her across the bed, then scoops her up. Her limbs flail, and he holds her tight with both arms.

"Catherine, we have to go!" Ramsey yells. He positions himself in front of her face, blocking her view of the mutilated corpse, and watches a thick, torn piece of Cameron's skin slide down her cheek. "Now! Others will be here soon."

Her eyes finally focus on him and a second passes before she nods.

"Good. Follow me." He hobbles up the stairs, the wound in his leg making every step excruciating. He's losing strength and has to apply everything he has left to keeping hold of Anna. By the time they make it to the car he parked down the road, Ramsey can no longer see straight.

Anna slips free from his grasp and falls to the ground. He groans and begins to bend down for the child, but Catherine is there first. The walk seems to have renewed her senses. She's not crying anymore. She picks up Anna and deposits her in the back seat of the car. Ramsey belatedly realizes he didn't bring a car seat.

Catherine's voice is strong when she says, "Give me the keys."

Ramsey shouldn't. He should drive them. He knows where to go and what to do. He's meant to be rescuing her, not the other way around.

A fresh throbbing pain destabilizes him, and he catches himself against the car. He fishes the keys out and hands them to Catherine, wondering if she's going to leave him here to die. She could, maybe even should. He's a stranger who killed seven men in a matter of minutes.

But Catherine bends over, wraps an arm around Ramsey's middle, and supports his weight as he stumbles to the passenger's door. Catherine opens it and he falls inside.

He's awake only until she turns on the car. Then he slips into unconsciousness.

CHAPTER **41**

T hree hours left before her succession.

The clock's short hand drags through the mud of time and stops at 6 p.m.

Four more hours, then the convention is over.

Lynell hasn't attended any of it, both for security reasons and because she has no desire to. She applies makeup, straightens her hair, and paints her nails. The dress specifically designed for tonight is hanging in a bag on the bathroom door, waiting for her to put it on. Ramsey had originally hired a team of beauticians and makeup artists to get her ready for the ceremony, but she had them fired. Having more people in the greenroom would complicate matters. Besides, she's been doing her own makeup and hair for a decade, and it takes her less than an hour to finish everything.

She paces the greenroom. Only an earlier text from Sawyer saying she successfully got in using the fake ID keeps Lynell's lungs from hanging themselves on her ribcage.

Neither Ramsey nor Harlow have texted. Her public succession is scheduled to begin in an hour. Unlike oligarch inauguration ceremonies, the previous two Elysian succession parties have been somewhat informal affairs that were more about celebrating them taking over the office. Lynell's has become a mix of those parties and the more formal inaugurations of oligarchs.

She's supposed to give a short speech before Finnegan Reese takes over to announce the policy change. Evidently, he's the country's golden boy committee chair, and everything sounds nicer coming from his mouth, even a genocidal death sentence.

Ramsey has until the end of her speech to text them with confirmation that he saved Anna. Less than two hours.

Lynell can't feel her fingertips.

"We should go check on . . . everything," she fails to come up with a real excuse for wanting to get out of the small greenroom.

"I don't think it's possible to check on *everything*," Daniel says.

"Then let's go check on Sawyer," she says.

"I don't think leaving is a good idea," Hayes says.

She throws her hands up in frustration. "This place is crawling with security. I'll be fine."

Hayes flexes his fingers and licks his lips as if considering her request against his better judgement.

"I'll wear a hat."

"Hats aren't disguises, babe," Daniel says.

"It was for that old superhero."

"You're not a superhero."

Lynell plucks a black cap off the coat rack and tucks her feet into slip on sneakers. "I'm going to check on Sawyer. Feel free to join me."

The two men share exasperated looks, but neither argues. She opens the door and nods at the two guards outside her room. Ramsey couldn't lessen the convention's security, but he could assign his most trustworthy, loyal, and obedient men and women to the job. He promised that they won't ask questions or disobey orders, even if those orders are, "Let any Resurrection rebel you see into the building," or, "Don't stop Sawyer D'Angelo from following Mrs. Elysian onto the auditorium stage."

"Stay at your post," Hayes says behind her. She hears the door shut, then Daniel rushes to her side and Hayes follows a few steps behind.

"Yeah, we're *super* inconspicuous," Lynell says, sliding into the comfortable voice of sarcasm. "Where do you think she is?"

The only thing she knows about the Resurrection's updated plans for the convention, in addition to Sawyer's speech, is that they've printed thousands of simple pamphlets with statistics against the Registration, possible alternatives, and ways people can get involved in the fight.

Rebels who got into the convention are slipping the pamphlets into bags and under seats, while those outside the building are leaving them on windshields of parked cars. She guesses there is more, but she doesn't know what, and she has no idea where Sawyer will be before the commencement ceremony.

"Text her," Daniel says.

Lynell momentarily forgot that she could use her phone while waiting for texts from Ramsey and Harlow. She stops in the middle of the hall, retrieves it from her pocket, and texts *Where are you?* to Sawyer. Seconds later, three dots appear on the screen. Then, *Room 110. Meeting room on the first floor.* She angles the phone for Daniel to see, then takes the back way out of the auditorium.

The cacophony of hundreds of voices makes Lynell feel claustrophobic, without having to be among the largest crowd. The stairs drop them at the back of the entrance hall, where most of the activity seems to originate. The auditorium doors are already open, but guests are taking advantage of the last hour to peruse the booths before Lynell's commencement.

Lynell and Daniel turn away from the crowd, heading to the meeting rooms on the East Wing. There are two hallways, the main one with a large mouth at the entry hall and a smaller one that is made up mostly of closets. The hallways meet at the end, creating a V. Room 110 is at the point of the V, and the door is already ajar on their arrival.

Hayes stands in the hallway while Lynell and Daniel enter, leaving the door cracked. Inside is an average-sized space with four round tables, several chairs, and a low stage at the back. Besides Sawyer and another woman, the room is empty.

"The candle will take about an hour to burn, so we should light it at five-thirty," Sawyer is saying to the other woman.

"I can't believe we're actually using one of Henry's ideas." The woman is a few inches shorter than Sawyer with more dramatic curves and dark skin. She has short sisterlocks that brush her shoulders, a long, round nose, and a perfectly pointed jawline. Lynell recognizes her but can't think of a name.

"Me either, but we need the distraction," Sawyer says. Then she sees Lynell, Daniel, and Hayes. "Hey, what's up?"

Lynell crosses the room, weaving between the tables to reach the other two women. "I couldn't stand waiting in that room. What are you doing?"

"Setting up a distraction to draw security away from the entrance hall before the speech." Sawyer stands from her crouch. "Lynell, this is the Resurrection CFO and Secretary, Dre—"

Daniel interrupts in a stunned, breathy voice, "Drea Chapman."

All three women look at him.

"Oh." He shuffles, a blush tinging his cheeks. "Sorry, I've just heard about you."

Lynell frowns. Daniel has heard of most prominent rebels, but he's never reacted to them like a fan before. She turns to Sawyer, who looks similarly confused.

Drea Chapman, however, smiles sadly. "You're Daniel, aren't you?"

"Yeah."

Lynell is about to ask what's going on when she remembers. Grant Woods, Daniel's old friend and Drea's ex. "It's nice to meet you, Drea," she says. "I'm Lynell."

"I know," she says, with a less welcoming voice than she'd used on Daniel.

"Right. Well . . . what is this distraction? Can we help?" Lynell asks.

Madison Lawson

"It's a small bomb," Sawyer says. At Lynell and Daniel's raised brows, she quickly adds, "Really small. More like a fire. Like, enough to blow up a chair and nothing else. This room will be empty, so it won't hurt anyone. It's barely enough to set off internal alarms and distract a few security guards. Not ours, they'll know better, but others who may cause problems. Like the oligarchs' or committee chairs' guards."

"It's not going to disrupt the speeches?"

Sawyer shakes her head. "Building-wide fire alarms are disabled, so only the security room will be notified of the fire. And we won't be able to hear the explosion in the auditorium."

"What's the candle for?" Lynell asks, gesturing to the tall taper sitting on the floor surrounded by newspapers.

"That's actually pretty cool," Drea answers with a grin. Apparently, her excitement about the bomb outweighs her dislike of Lynell. "The candle will take about an hour. Once it's low enough, it'll ignite the papers, which will spread over here."

Drea points to the line of papers and takes a few steps back, where a chair has been moved away from the tables. The newspapers stop under the table, and Lynell bends over, seeing something red hanging from the chair.

"The fire will pop open this balloon, which has a bit of gasoline inside. The gas will strengthen the fire and the chair will start burning. Once it reaches a certain temperature, this small bomb will go off." Drea points at what looks like a lump of trash in a plastic water bottle sitting on top of the chair.

"How does someone even think of that?" Daniel asks.

Lynell traces the fire back to the candle, her mind stuck on a carousel, running forward in a circle. The fire and bomb setup reminds her of the one at her house last week and she can't remember why. The bomb was accompanied by a fire, but there's something else. Something slamming against warning bells in her mind.

"Henry heard it from someone else," Drea says. "Can't remember who."

"You're sure it won't hurt anyone or cause too much damage?" Daniel asks.

⊣ 278 ⊢

"We made it as small as possible," Sawyer says. "I was just going to set a fire, but Henry said it'll have more of an effect if there's an explosion, even a tiny one."

"I'm assuming this isn't the only distraction you're setting up?" Daniel asks.

Someone responds. Lynell tunes them out, mentally chasing the carousel.

Then she catches it.

"This is what Johnson did at our house," she says. All three of the others abruptly fall quiet. "He used a fire to delay the bomb, which would set off at a certain temperature."

"How do you know that?" Drea asks.

"I read Ramsey's notes last week," Lynell says. She might've felt guilty if the old suspicion wasn't sparking to life again. "And I smelled fire before the explosion."

"I'm sure Johnson isn't the only one who knows how to create a delayed bomb like this," Daniel says, carefully masking any uncertainty. Or maybe she is imagining it, and he truly isn't worried.

"Henry definitely didn't learn it from a Registration employee," Drea says. "Someone in the Resurrection told him. Do you remember who, Sawyer? Sawyer?" She repeats the name when her eyes find Sawyer's face, which is etched with horrified realization.

"What's wrong?" Lynell asks.

"Harlow. He learned from Harlow," Sawyer whispers.

"Harlow and Ramsey . . ." Lynell quickly pulls her phone out of her pocket, an invisible hand ringing her lungs like wet rags and her heart a manic hummingbird. She opens a group text between Harlow and Ramsey. *Where are you?* she messages.

"Don't freak out. This doesn't mean anything," Daniel says.

"Danny, Harlow is Zach's mom. Grant thinks she might blame me for Zach's death, right? And she dated Ramsey, who until a few weeks ago was loyal to Eric."

"Because he was raised to be," Daniel says. Lynell doesn't know why he's arguing the fact. He didn't even trust Ramsey until a few days ago.

"And Harlow?"

"Even if Harlow did blame you for Zach, which I don't think she does, she'd never do anything as reckless as having your house blown up with dozens of other people inside," Sawyer says. "She ran away from that world for a reason."

"She ran in the same circles as Reese and Macgill and," Daniel pauses, glances at Sawyer, and finishes, "the others. It's not so crazy to think any of them have the same bomb knowledge."

Lynell rubs the back of her neck, unconvinced. Daniel steps between her and the other two women, gently pulls her hand away from her neck, and says, "We'll look into it tomorrow."

She searches his face for a sign that he's as worried as her. All she finds is steady assurance. He's always at his most composed when she's falling apart, like his first instinct is to shelter her from the storm.

"Fine," Lynell concedes.

"Let's get back to the greenroom. This isn't calming your nerves. You need to get ready anyway," Daniel says.

"I am ready." Still, she concedes with a nod. "Be careful," she tells Sawyer and Drea. "Remember, be backstage by six thirty."

"I know," Sawyer says.

"It'll be okay. You'll do great."

Sawyer smiles gratefully. "Thank you, Lynell."

Daniel grabs her hand, leading her out of the room and up the smaller hall with janitor's closets and utility rooms. Hayes glances at them when they exit, saying nothing as they start the walk back to the greenroom. At the end of the hallway, they head to the stairs, but pause when her phone rings.

She and Daniel look down at Harlow's name flashing on the screen. Her hands shake as she answers and asks Harlow to wait. They rush back to the greenroom and put the phone on speaker.

"Before you ask, no, I haven't gotten the cloak yet," Harlow says, referring to the CCC. "But I'm getting close. I don't think Lincoln knows exactly what he has. His dad told him it was important information that he'd know what to do with when he reclaimed the Registration and Gideon's half."

"There's no way he doesn't know," Daniel says.

"Maybe he thinks it's something important that will help him take back the Registration," Lynell says.

She knew it was a long shot that Lincoln would share the CCC with Harlow today, but Lynell couldn't help hoping. The deflating in her chest makes her think hope is a slow-working virus intent on killing her. She can't abandon it yet, though. Their plan can still work. After her speech tonight, Harlow will hopefully have more ammunition to convince Lincoln.

"I'll find out soon. He doesn't trust easily. He inherited Jude's fear of betrayal, I think," Harlow says. "Anyway, I called because I heard from Ramsey."

Terrifying hope cuts through Lynell's heart. "What? Really?"

"What did he say?" Next to her, Daniel leans closer to the phone, as if planning to climb inside and physically see the words coming from Harlow's mouth.

"He has her. It's okay."

The couch beneath them feels stitched together out of broken clouds and freshly fallen snow. Lynell is floating and falling and flying all at once, the rushing wind almost drowning out Harlow's next words.

"He was shot during the rescue and passed out. Catherine drove them to a hospital, and they rushed him to surgery, which is why he didn't call sooner. He just woke up, and the first thing he did was call me. His phone broke at some point, but he has my number memorized, so he told me to tell you that he got Anna."

"Are they safe at the hospital?" Daniel asks, before Lynell can request more information on Ramsey's condition.

"Yes. Catherine called the cops, but refused to tell them her name or Anna's, so they're being guarded as Jane and Janie Doe."

"Why did she refuse to tell them who she is?" Daniel asks.

"She's smart," Lynell answers. "She's already learning how dangerous it is to be an Elysian. She probably doesn't want anyone to know where she is until she knows who took them and if they'll come for her again."

"I agree," Harlow says. "Ramsey said he was going to call a few guards to come take over protection. He promised no one will know Anna is safe until after the conference."

"Where did he get shot?" Lynell asks.

"Outer thigh, it didn't hit bone or his femoral artery. He'll recover."

Lynell hears her own relief reflected in Harlow's voice, which reminds her that Harlow used to date Ramsey. She hasn't had time to sit and wonder about her COO's secret relationship with her cousin's mother, and the idea is still so unfamiliar that her mind tries to reject it.

"What about Anna and Catherine?" she asks.

"I don't have details on their condition, but Ramsey didn't notice any major injuries. He thinks they're shaken more than physically harmed."

Daniel sinks back into the couch of clouds, like the fear had kept him stiff for the last week and, now that it's gone, he can finally relax.

"I gave him your number, so he'll call with a more thorough report soon," Harlow continues. "It sounded like the doctors didn't want him on the phone."

Lynell grins, imagining a semi-conscious Ramsey still in the PACU demanding a phone before the doctors could even check his vitals.

"Thank you, Harlow," she says. She imagines saying the same to Ramsey, and never before have the words felt so inadequate. What can she possibly say to communicate how grateful she is that Ramsey risked his life to save her daughter?

"Of course. How are things there?"

"As scheduled," Lynell says. She considers asking about the bomb and Harlow's connection to teaching Henry how to make one, but knows now isn't the time. She'll have to wait to confront Harlow until after the convention, when Lynell is certain they're all safe.

"Tell her I'll be watching," Harlow says. She can't attend the conference because her return to Dallas is still somewhat of a secret, but she promised to watch from home.

"I will. Thank you again."

Harlow doesn't immediately answer, and the pause is so long that Lynell checks the call's connection. "Anytime, Lynell. You're family."

The words burn Lynell's eyes. She doesn't want to feel suspicious of Harlow, not after all Lynell told the woman yesterday and all she's done for her since. She wants to believe Harlow.

Something settles on Lynell's leg and she looks down to see Daniel's hand. The warm pressure on her thigh is more familiar than her own smile. Then he speaks, his voice more comforting than the best song in history.

"Stay safe, Harlow."

"You too."

The call ends, and Lynell closes her eyes, pushing two heavy tears free. Daniel's hand moves from her thigh to wipe the wetness off her face.

"You'll mess up your makeup," he whispers.

She laughs and opens her eyes to gaze upon Daniel. His face is a mosaic of the earth's wonders. Everything about this man makes her deliriously happy that she had his baby. The world is better with Daniel Carter in it.

"She's okay, Danny," Lynell whispers.

"I know." His smile is more her home than any house she's ever lived in. How she survived two years without him is beyond her.

In that moment, sitting next to Daniel, revived from the news that their daughter is safe, Lynell silently makes a promise to the universe and every god that exists.

She promises to do whatever it takes to give Daniel and Anna a life they deserve.

She will demolish empires for them.

She will happily set the world on fire.

She will build them a new world from the ashes.

CHAPTER 42

T J could be guarding the Elysian bitch's offspring or protecting the Elders. He could be doing anything else but following Sawyer D'Angelo all day. But he has his orders, and it was very clear that if he failed and Sawyer D'Angelo fucked up the policy change announcement, he would be dismissed. Tonight is important to the Elders and the entire country.

Therefore, TJ is here, watching the rebel walk around the convention with a sneer that makes him want to put a bullet in her mouth.

He should shoot her. She deserves to die more than most people. She's a snake in the grass, and someone must chop off her head before she damns anyone with the seduction of an apple filled with false knowledge.

She and the Elysian bitch have pushed the plan off the rails too often to keep living. They're standing on two of the tallest peaks in the country, guiding the American people further from who they were created to be. TJ expected them to have jumped or fallen off the cliffs already. But they're helping each other climb even higher.

He *thought* the Elders would order their deaths after what he overheard on Wednesday, but they didn't. In fact, they said by any means necessary, Lynell Elysian has to stay alive. None of them except Elder D'Angelo cared about Sawyer. Elder D'Angelo has been giving TJ orders concerning his daughter for six years. Each has been coated with a reason the other Elders agree with, but the center is something more. Something only TJ knows.

First, kill Ellery. Because she was going to give a speech that could ruin everything and because she was dragging D'Angelo's daughter into a life of sin.

Next, plant a mole in the Resurrection to keep an eye on the rebels but also to lead Sawyer away from dangerous activities during her angry rebel phase.

Then, follow her, because the Resurrection was getting too big but also because D'Angelo was worried she was getting too deeply attached to the rebellion independent of Ellery. When it became clear that was happening, threaten her. On the surface, to take the Resurrection leader off the board. To D'Angelo, to scare his daughter into safety.

Now, do whatever it takes to make sure Sawyer doesn't do anything reckless with Lynell. The Elders don't want them working together. Elder D'Angelo doesn't want Sawyer becoming such a problem that she has to be killed.

TJ has studied each rebellion, each religiously driven crusade, each man or group who has attempted to cleanse history, establish a new ruling order, or do God's will as closely as possible. They all failed. One main reason is that emotion plays too much a part in their actions. They selfishly crave control through violence and chaos. They act out of anger.

Or, worse, they don't act because of some perverted sense of love and justice. Weaker men see it as morality, but TJ sees it for what it is: a refusal to make sacrifices for the greater good.

He doesn't want to admit it, but TJ is beginning to worry that Elder D'Angelo might be one of those weaker men. His refusal to sacrifice his sinful, broken, selfish daughter could ruin everything. The possibility is dynamite stuffed between TJ's ribs.

Elder D'Angelo is the reason he and the others were brought together to become the Sin-Fighting Warriors. He gave them a direction and a purpose. Those early years were full of small yet powerful acts. Then, they managed to make a real statement. To silence twelve voices that were misleading the entire country was an honor. The purpose and direction grew to bigger, better things. The other Elders joined, and TJ saw hope for a new future. He gladly surrendered his independence and autonomy to wiser men for the good of the country. He willingly sacrificed anything and everything for the future the Elders promised. Sacrifices are necessary.

But at a certain point, it's no longer sacrificing. It's surrendering.

TJ does not surrender.

CHAPTER 43

P hase two successful. Phase three is a go.

Sawyer reads Lynell's text again, her heart a gallop of nerves and excitement. This is what she's wanted since before meeting Lynell. She's wanted to give Ellery's speech, to finish her wife's last project. She still wants that, but she wants so much more now.

The Resurrection was once an extension of Ellery's work, but it's gone through a metamorphosis. It's not Ellery's or Lynell's. It's not even Sawyer's, really.

The Resurrection stopped being a group of rebels or a desperate attempt at keeping her wife alive long ago. It became hope. A possible future. A life.

That's what Sawyer thinks about as she splits from the crowd heading in the direction of the auditorium and slips into a small hallway leading backstage. Chuck Wright, the Resurrection's Head of Defense, dressed in a security guard's outfit, stands at the end of the hallway. At her approach, he covertly opens the door he's been guarding and escorts her through.

"The succession ceremony starts in ten minutes," he whispers.

"You have the jammer?" Sawyer asks.

Chuck nods, gesturing to his chest pocket. Once turned on, the device will jam all phone and radio signals in the building. "The others are in place, too. I must say, working with the Elysians makes our lives much easier."

"Yes, it does," Sawyer says with a smile. Before Lynell, their plan was to record Sawyer in another part of the convention center and rely on their tech expert to interrupt the broadcast with their video. Now, they're able to infiltrate the convention with dozens of their people, replace business cards with their own, plant listening devices, and replace Lynell on the actual stage with Sawyer, proving to the world that the leaders of the Resurrection and Registration are working together. None of that would've been possible without Lynell's help.

"I've got it from here," Sawyer says, stopping in front of a locked door.

"Good luck. You'll do great." With that, Chuck turns around, heading back to his post.

Sawyer knocks three times, pauses for five seconds, and knocks three more times. A second passes, then the door opens, revealing Daniel.

"That was fast," he says, stepping aside to let her through.

Lynell is standing in the center of the room wearing a sleeveless black dress with gold buttons that enhances her natural beauty and simultaneously makes her look ten years older. The three individual finger splints have been replaced with a single sleek black one holding all three fingers. Anxiety sweeps over her face. Sawyer realizes this is the most nervous she's ever seen Lynell.

"Are we positive that you can't take over right away?" Lynell asks. She's wearing a wireless microphone tucked behind her ear and resting against her cheek.

Sawyer chuckles. She doesn't much care about some pointless ceremony declaring Lynell the Elysian owner of the Registration, but Ramsey and Harlow both stressed how important it was. Lynell has to be legitimized publicly before handing her stage to a rebel.

"We're positive, Lyn," Daniel says. He runs a hand down her arm and lifts her chin. "It'll be quick, and you'll do great."

Before Sawyer can offer encouragement of her own, someone knocks at the door. She presses herself to the wall next to the door, so she's out of view when Hayes opens it.

An unfamiliar voice says, "Are you ready, Mrs. Elysian?"

Lynell nods. She gives Sawyer a quick glance and faint smile, then follows the other two out of the room.

CHAPTER 44

LYNELL

Friday Evening

A ny other day, this dress would've been one of the most comfortable, gorgeous things Lynell has ever worn. Today, though, it's sandpaper against her skin. She wants to rip it off, scrub her face clean, and run away.

She follows a woman several decades her senior across the backstage floor, to the side of the stage. A sliver of the audience is visible, and all of Lynell's vital organs drop to the soles of her feet. Every single chair is occupied. The auditorium itself holds over fifteen thousand people, and the rest are in overflow rooms throughout the convention center. All thirty thousand guests, plus the several million in the country, are about to watch her.

The biggest crowd Lynell has ever been in front of was maybe a thousand parents at a high school Christmas performance. And she'd been one of dozens of kids then, basically invisible. Now, she'll be the center of attention.

She swallows burning saliva. In the center of the stage is a podium. Two older men she recognizes as the most well-known oligarchs, Bruce Macgill and Oswald VandeBerg, stand in front of the podium. They appear to have been talking to the crowd for a few minutes already, like openers at a concert. They're both wearing hands-free microphones to amplify their voices, like the one attached to Lynell.

Macgill says, "I'm sure we don't have to tell you who is about to join us on stage, but let me refresh your collective memory." He takes a few steps to the side. "She is the youngest person ever to hold this office or even to have a seat on the Registration committee. Until recently, she lived like any normal citizen, earning her living and giving back to the community. She is a mother, wife, daughter, and friend. She has supported the Registration since long before any of us knew who she was. And she is ready and eager to continue her family's legacy!" Macgill pauses, then, louder than before, shouts, "It is my sincere pleasure to welcome to the stage, Mrs. Lynell Elysian!"

The cheer following his words is so loud that she only hears a second of it before her ears shut down, and all that remains is a monotone roar deep in her gut.

Daniel touches the small of her back, giving her a flare of confidence. But he stands still, and she walks onto the stage without him. Her legs miraculously don't shake. She keeps her attention on Macgill, whose smile is wide and brilliant but vanishes before reaching his eyes.

When she's close enough, Macgill wraps his arm around her waist and pulls her in close. He smells like peaches and cinnamon.

"Mrs. Elysian, everyone!" Macgill shouts, turning them both to face the crowd. Her ears decide to work again, and she's slammed with thunder made of clapping hands and whooping voices. This time, though, she catches booing mixed with the cheers.

Lynell remembers a beat late to raise her hand and wave. She plasters on a smile that everyone surely will notice is fake and looks around the room, though she can't make anything out beyond the lights. She knows there are cameras hanging from the ceiling, on either side of the room, at the back of the crowd, and directly in front of them.

What must be several hours later, Macgill drops his arm from her waist and the applause slowly tapers off.

"Thank you so much," Lynell says. She doesn't recognize her own voice.

"Murderer!" someone shouts from the audience. Lynell blinks. Before she can process the word, the man on her other side, Oswald Vanderberg, starts speaking. Either security is controlling the crowd or the oligarchs command too much respect, because she doesn't hear another insult or boo.

"Yes, what a fantastic crowd!" Vanderberg shouts. "It's always a pleasure to address the American people." He's decades older than Macgill but must be on drugs or incredibly healthy, because he has the energy of a much younger man.

She wonders if she's expected to make small talk with them. That wasn't in the notes or mentioned at the pre-rehearsal. Maybe they would've told her at the rehearsal, but she missed it thanks to being shot at and confined to a safe house.

"Mrs. Elysian, or Lynell?" Vanderberg pauses, giving her an expectant look.

"Lynell," she says, without thinking.

"Lynell it is," Vanderberg says, seamlessly taking her expressionless response and turning it into something worthy of a show. "How are you feeling right now?"

She catches her frown before it can fall. A question-and-answer portion definitely wasn't discussed. "Honestly? A bit nervous."

Vanderberg chuckles. "Understandable. You've never done anything like this before? Addressed such a large crowd?"

Lynell understands then. She hasn't done any public interviews or speeches or anything since taking over. The oligarchs are taking advantage of being the first to offer the world insight on who she is. "Never," she says. "I've never had the opportunity before."

"Of course not," says Macgill. "But it's in your blood, isn't it? What was it like to learn of your true heritage?"

"There's not a sufficient way to describe it," she says. The further into the conversation they get, the more she relaxes. She's forgetting about the crowd and lights and cameras, focusing entirely on this conversation with a thirty-year-old man stuck in a seventy-year-old's body. "I didn't have the easiest or most comfortable childhood. I never knew who my dad was. So, it was a culture shock when I found out the truth."

"I'm sure it felt right, though," Vanderberg adds. "You're an Elysian to your core, aren't you?"

Lynell wants to say, 'only technically,' but she knows better. "Yes, I am. I always knew there was something missing about me and my family. Learning who I am was like becoming a full person for the first time in my life." She hopes it's enough to make Ramsey proud, because she can't stomach thinking of anything else to say.

"Did you learn the truth when Zachary Elysian Registered you last quarter?" Macgill asks.

Her brain stumbles to a stop, refusing to send a speech command to her mouth. She's looking at Macgill's sculpted face in stupidity. He looks like a mold of someone meant to be attractive but who had very little to work with. He's a middle-aged, conventionally unattractive man who has plenty of money to spare in the quest of beauty. Audience members take the question as their opportunity to boo and shout words like "murderer," again, and "fraud," and "rebel sympathizer." They manage a couple of seconds before being silenced again, likely both by guards and Vanderberg's voice.

"Now, Bruce," Vanderberg says. "Now isn't time to recall the past, it's time to look ahead!" He smiles, showing yellow-tinged teeth. "Have you considered the future, Lynell?"

This, she can answer with complete honesty. "I've done little else but consider the future. I have complete respect for the Registration, and I can't wait to serve the country the way my grandfather and father did. I am blessed to have this birthright that has changed and saved our country, and I promise we will continue to work for the good of all people."

"That sounds like part of your succession address!" Macgill says, false laughter painting the curves of his words. "We don't want to step on your moment."

"No, we don't," Vanderberg says. "So, before we get carried away, are you ready to officially take your rightful place as the Elysian Heir and owner of the Registration?"

Lynell nods. The ground is becoming steadier as they return to the scheduled events. She sees Macgill walk away from the corner of her vision.

"Perfect. Lynell Elizabeth Elysian, do you swear that you are Gideon Elysian's legitimate heir?"

While Vanderberg speaks, Macgill returns holding something indistinguishable. It must have been stored in the podium behind them, because there wasn't enough time for him to leave the stage completely and return.

"I do swear," Lynell says.

"Do you swear to lead to the best of your ability, prepared to support the country and work with the oligarchs and committee chairs to faithfully uphold the Registration?" Vanderberg asks.

Neither Eli nor Eric were asked to make this oath. After they swore they were Gideon's legitimate sons, they moved right into giving a short address, then partying.

Lynell has never had trouble lying, though. She says so truthfully that she'd probably pass a lie detector test, "I do swear."

"Do you swear to protect the Registration from rebels who would seek to destroy your grandfather's work?"

"I do swear."

"Then, without further ado, it is my honor to present you with the ceremonial keys to the Registration, your rightful inheritance and the country's saving grace." Vanderberg accepts a small silk bag from Macgill, then passes it to Lynell.

She takes it, uses her left pinky to open the cinched top, then dumps the contents into her right hand. A shiny gold key on an equally polished chain falls into her palm. It's a small, unremarkable thing that probably doesn't unlock anything, but Lynell has rarely felt so happy to hold an object. The moment is comparable to when Daniel slid her wedding ring on her finger.

She hooks her pinky around the chain and grabs it, holding it out for the audience to see, imagining cameras zooming in on the likely useless yet life-changing key.

Lynell looks up at Vanderberg. Her heart twists and heat she doesn't want to consider fills her eyes. "Thank you, Mr. Vanderberg." Lynell is horrified to hear the wobble in her voice, and a far too positive emotion wells under her skin.

"It's my pleasure," Vanderberg says. "Welcome to your future, Mrs. Elysian."

Macgill says something similar that Lynell fails to interpret. The crowd is screaming and clapping again. This is the first applause that's not broken up by boos. It goes on for several minutes, giving Lynell time to reach the podium. She grips the edges, wishing her traitorous body would stop being so damn *happy* about inheriting a business built on death.

She takes a deep breath and waits for a pause in the cheers. Then she begins.

CHAPTER 45

S awyer is alone. She wants to crack open the door and watch the commencement but knows it's too risky. Daniel will come get her when it's time. Until then, she must wait out the next thirty minutes alone, trying not to slip into a desert storm filled with fear and uncertainty. Malakai offered to wait with her, but he's more needed outside. She's safe in this locked room and Malakai can help with crowd control.

For the first ten minutes, she attaches the wireless mic left on the coffee table and attempts to practice her speech.

When that fails, she pulls out her phone, reading through texts. But the words are sand slipping from her mind.

Finally, she sits on the edge of the couch and imagines what will come next. Will the country actually watch and listen to what she's saying? Will the Resurrection grow with new members? She hopes for a peaceful solution that's better for everyone.

She expects war. She imagines who will be watching. Strangers and acquaintances who will form their own opinion of her. Committee chairs and oligarchs who will want her dead. Friends and family who will either be proud of her or ashamed.

Her father. Her sweet, loving father who has been lying to her for so long that she's unsure if she ever really knew him.

"Lincoln has been working with them for years. I think he wants to take over the Registration. He's known about all of it. He's been a part of all of it. Even Ellery's death." Lynell's words from the day before cut through her mind. For a moment, she didn't believe any of it. She wanted proof. She thought Lynell might be tricking her.

Then Harlow found her, and her face broadcast the truth. She opened her mouth, and Sawyer couldn't run from the facts. Before yesterday, any time Sawyer asked Harlow questions about her past, Sawyer's family, or her friendship with Elizabeth Crane, Harlow would say, *"It's not my story to tell."*

Maybe it wasn't Harlow's story, but it's Sawyer's. It's Lynell's. And they will tell it.

A soft knock.

A turn of the doorknob.

Daniel peeking inside.

It's time.

CHAPTER 46

LYNELL

Friday Evening

"Thank you, everyone," Lynell says, smiling wide. "This is surreal." She holds the key up again, watching it turn and catch the spotlight. "I've never felt closer to my father, Eli Elysian." The truth in the sentence is a hook at the back of her throat, choking her with denied tears. "I don't take this position lightly. I know it is more than a name or a job. It's a responsibility that requires respect."

She and Ramsey prepared a full speech in case Sawyer can't take over, but she won't have to give it. She's not sure she could if she had to. Thankfully, she doesn't.

All she has to do is talk for a few minutes, giving the others time to secure the backstage so Sawyer won't be interrupted. Ten minutes, at most. At least three of those have passed already since Macgill and Vanderberg left the stage.

Lynell can't imagine how long the next seven will stretch.

"As honored and humbled as I am to be here, I wish I wasn't. I want to serve the country and lead the Registration, but I wish I didn't have to yet. I wish my dad was still here. And I wish my cousin, Zachary, was here." She should probably mention Eric, too, but she doesn't.

The country will soon have more to talk about than her omitting Eric's name, anyway.

"I only knew one of them, but both were amazing men. My mother used to tell me stories about my dad, the king of a distant land. A good man and great ruler who would sacrifice his life for his people. I dreamt of joining him one day on a throne of my own. I never knew how literal that would become."

She pauses, unable to swallow around the rock in her throat, and closes her eyes, inhaling as much oxygen as possible. The crowd begins muttering at her silence.

She exhales and opens her eyes, forcing her voice to fill with confidence. "He's gone, as are Zachary and Eric. But I'm still here. The Registration is my birthright. It saved our country once, but too many people have turned it into something it was never meant to be. It's my job to uphold the good parts of the Elysian legacy and change the bad parts. I intend to do just that. To make necessary changes that my father only dreamt of.

"Eli Elysian left me, his heir, the key needed to stop those who want to corrupt the Registration. I will use the gift he gave me to turn the Registration into what it was meant to be. An agent of good, for all of us. For my family and yours." She pauses, knowing that only people aware of the code will hear the hidden meaning and know that by 'gift' and 'key' she means the code.

With a small turn of her head, she glimpses Daniel and Sawyer in the corner, offstage.

She smiles. "What I've learned already is that no one can do good alone. Too often, pride keeps you from asking for help. To ask for a *companion*. That is the downfall of many. Because no one can survive alone. No one can lead alone. More importantly, no one can cause change on their own. My father and grandfather were not alone, and neither am I." More muttering fills the room, but Lynell feels more confident than she has all day. "I'm sure you will all give her the same respect you've given me, and I think you will be incredibly interested to hear what she has to say."

She lets go of the podium, raising one hand in the direction of Sawyer. "Allow me to introduce you to my friend and partner, the leader of the Resurrection, Sawyer D'Angelo."

The crowd reaction makes the previous mutters sound like a single cat's purr. A thousand voices like instruments play in different notes. Gasping, shouts, boos, and just as loud, cheers. Sawyer walks on stage, elegant and tall and poised. She reaches Lynell and pulls her into a hug. Sawyer's breathing is shallow, but she expertly hides her nerves.

"Thank you, Lynell," she says, not swayed by the continuing chaos of sounds. Her mic is on, but Lynell doubts anyone can hear her over the shouting.

"Thank you," Lynell responds. She turns to the crowd and says, "That's enough. I think we all need to hear what Ms. D'Angelo has to say." She waits next to Sawyer until the other woman nods in acknowledgement that she's okay.

Then Lynell takes a step back, making space for Sawyer to take over at the podium. With nothing to hold onto, Lynell forces strength into her legs to keep her standing next to Sawyer while she gives the speech Ellery was killed for.

CHAPTER 47

O ne of the side walls backstage is filled with monitors portraying feeds
from the many cameras facing the stage, audience, and exits. Daniel
stands in the middle of the screens, watching his wife swear to protect the
Registration then accept those stupid keys. To a stranger, Lynell probably
appears confident and comfortable, but Daniel sees the strain in her smile
and the way she locks her joints to keep from shaking. When she lifts the key
up, Daniel turns his attention to screens filming the audience.

The majority of people are sitting fairly still, eyes glued to the stage in
front of them, but some are already murmuring, frowning, and shifting in
their seats. Then, Macgill says, "Our fourth Elysian leader, ladies and gentlemen. Here's to a stronger Registration and a more united country!"

The entire crowd erupts in applause. While they're cheering, Lynell
walks to the podium and the two oligarchs walk off the stage.

Daniel practically feels the timer start. He turns away from the monitors and joins Hayes at the left wing offstage. He stops about a foot in front
of the other man.

"Mr. Vanderberg and Mr. Macgill," Daniel says, holding his hand out
to the oligarchs.

Macgill's eyebrows lower and he looks incredulously down at Daniel's hand. Vanderberg covers the awkward moment and accepts the handshake for half a second.

They know Daniel's history, and probably think having an ex-rebel as the ruling Elysian's spouse is worse than a rat leading their nation.

He gives them a dramatic smile. "I'm Daniel Carter. I'd love to speak to you about my responsibilities as Lynell's husband. We can head upstairs or use one of the free greenrooms."

"Now is not the time," Macgill says. "Schedule a meeting with our assistants and we can . . . talk later." He gives an unnaturally long pause before the last two words, as if having to gather the strength to finish the sentence.

"Besides, shouldn't you stay and watch your wife give her speech?" Vanderberg says, looking back at the stage.

Daniel follows the direction of his gaze and sees Lynell's grip on the podium loosen slightly as she relaxes into the speech. Pride glows in his chest, and his flesh seems to vibrate as the timer ticks closer to zero.

"I've heard this speech several times before," Daniel says, which is only half true. Lynell practiced a version of it on him twice, but neither one of them could focus for long with everything else going on. "Besides, I'd really love to get to know the people my wife will be working so closely with."

Lying has never been his strong suit, but something about these two men makes it easier than walking.

Before either oligarch can respond, Hayes steps forward and says in a loud whisper, "Sir, we have a problem at the west entrance."

"Not now," Daniel says, clipping the words to sound annoyed and authoritative.

"Your . . . old friends need your help," Hayes adds. Daniel privately thinks the man could have a career as an actor if he wanted.

"Fuck." Daniel pauses, pretending to consider the situation before looking back at the oligarchs. He's pleased to see a note of shock and curiosity on both of their faces. "I'm sorry, gentleman. I will have to schedule a meeting after all. Enjoy the rest of the conference and maybe I'll see you later this evening." He turns away and follows Hayes towards the back exit. He wants to ask if the oligarchs took the bait but refrains.

They pass the monitors and he hears Lyn say, "The Registration is my birthright," which means they don't have much time left.

Hayes opens the back door and lets it fall shut after Daniel steps through. "Wait," Hayes says, holding up a hand. His eyes are shut and he has a finger pressed to one ear.

Daniel stops walking. "Did they go?"

There's a beat of silence, then Hayes opens his eyes and nods. "They left through the south entrance, like Ramsey said they would. Malakai just gave the all clear."

Without waiting, Daniel turns around and opens the door again. Ramsey promised the oligarchs would attempt to catch Daniel with a group of rebels by intercepting them from the southwest. Once they left backstage, Malakai would lock them out.

Daniel rushes to their greenroom, knocks, and pushes the door open. Sawyer looks up, her face so pale he might think she had the flu.

"It's time," he says.

She nods. Her steps are shaky, but when he reaches out to steady her, she dodges his hand. "I'm okay," she says.

They don't have time to debate the issue. Lynell is saying she'll use the gift Eli gave her and Sawyer will be going on stage any minute. Daniel speeds up, his heart faster than his feet. They arrive in view of Lynell a millisecond before she glances in their direction. Her answering smile helps push some tension out of Daniel's body. It doesn't seem to go far, though, because Sawyer stiffens as Lynell continues.

"You'll do great," Daniel whispers. "This is who you are."

Sawyer looks at him, something indiscernible flashing in her eyes. Then she stands straighter and by the time she leaves his side to walk onstage, her face has started regaining color.

Daniel's attention is quickly pulled away by the sound of several quick footsteps. A group of people are running in through a back door, heading for the stage, like they're going to tackle Sawyer and Lynell in front of the entire country. They don't get two feet before they're stopped by Malakai and a group of rebels. Daniel runs to help the rebels with the fight.

"Carter!"

Daniel stops and spins at the yell.

Bruce Macgill.

He got back in. How did he get back in?

A huge part of their plan was to make sure no guards, committee members, oligarchs, or Registration loyalists were still backstage when Sawyer was announced. It's easier getting them out of the way beforehand than to try and contain them after.

Clearly, that part of the plan didn't go perfectly.

"You fucking traitorous piece of shit," Macgill says. He's getting closer, unobstructed thanks to most of their guards, rebels, and Regulators working to contain the audience. Daniel doesn't see a weapon on him, but that doesn't mean there isn't one.

"You're not stopping this," Daniel says, changing directions to block Macgill from getting to the stage.

"Did you really think your little plan was going to work?" Macgill says, meeting Daniel halfway. "I've dealt with rebels far older and smarter than you before." He sounds collected, but the violence in his eyes tells a different story.

Macgill's fingers twitch and Daniel moves without thinking. He jabs the palm of his hand out, feeling it connect with Macgill's upper arm. The oligarch reaches up with his other hand and Daniel dodges, a needle missing his neck by less than an inch. He kicks, but Macgill blocks the move then elbows Daniel in the face. Sharp copper fills his mouth when his teeth sink into his cheek.

For a moment, he's shocked at how good of a fighter the older man is. Daniel assumed Macgill would be weak and incapable of fighting his own battles, but he was clearly wrong. Macgill's strength and training is obvious when he circles Daniel and manages to get him in a choke hold. He presses down on Daniel's windpipe and pushes a hand into his shoulder, near the gunshot wound. Daniel would've screamed from the pain, had the pressure on his throat not blocked sound from escaping.

"The time for Elysians is over," Macgill says, his mouth right next to Daniel's ear. "Your bitch wife and daughter have no place in our world."

Rage blinds Daniel. He struggles, trying to stomp Macgill's feet or rip his arm free, but each attempt is weaker than the last. Anger fills every corner of Daniel's consciousness and will soon be the only thing remaining.

Then he's free and gasping for air. His vision kaleidoscopes with color and he doubles forward, wheezing in painful breaths. Once he can see semi-clearly, he looks back for Macgill. The man is on the floor, eyes shut and arms pulled behind his back. Malakai squats behind him, tying his hands and feet together.

"Did you . . ." Daniel breathes.

Malakai nods.

"Thank you."

"Go help the others with the audience," Malakai says.

Daniel obeys, taking off-kilter steps toward the door between the house and backstage. He passes the monitors on the way and pauses.

In the center screen is Sawyer and Lynell on stage, both standing tall, their poised composure in sharp contrast to what the surrounding screens show.

Chaos. People standing on their chairs, screaming and waving fists in the air. Others throwing shoes, phones, and loose belongings. Regulators, guards, and rebels are working to keep them contained and have formed a line in front of the crowd, stopping some of the bolder audience members from storming the stage.

Then Daniel notices that the anarchy is only happening among half the crowd. They're so loud and wild that they demand all attention at first, but closer inspection shows plenty of guests still sitting, frozen, listening, or talking quietly to their neighbors. There are even some attempting to pull neighbors back into their seats.

Daniel moves his attention to the head of the crowd. Most of the front row was reserved for committee members, oligarchs, and other important guests. Several seats are empty, having never been filled. Finnegan Reese and Tamara Nelson are likely still locked in their own office on the third floor, their guards knocked out with some tranquilizers. It appears that only two committee members and three oligarchs made it to the convention.

Junior Booker, with his thin glasses and even thinner nose, sits as calmly as ever, looking completely unbothered as he watches Sawyer give her speech. Two seats down is Verity McGowan with her platinum hair and sagging skin, also sitting still without a struggle. Their unflinching acceptance of the situation is unsettling, but Daniel will let Lynell and Ramsey figure out what it means later.

Of the three oligarchs, Daniel recognizes only one: Michaels Sutton. Of course, he isn't fighting, but he is frowning at Sawyer. His two *brothers* have both been contained with their hands and feet tied together. Daniel argued that any oligarchs and committee members who made it to the audience should be removed or knocked out, but he was overruled. Apparently, it's so important they hear Lynell and Sawyer that the consequences of such obvious insurgency against their country's rulers will be worth it.

Still, the sight of two oligarchs tied up, forced to listen to the leader of the rebellion talk about ending the Registration makes Daniel's entire body feel stuck in the Antarctic. They will surely want revenge for such treatment.

He tears his eyes from the screens and runs for the door to help calm the rest of the audience. He opens the door and, in two steps, zeroes in on one man walking towards the stage. No one has stopped him yet because he's walking slowly and silently, showing no signs of attacking or disrupting the speech.

Even if he doesn't try to assault the women on stage, he's more of a threat to their plan than anyone else in the building. One look at him could break Sawyer.

Daniel sprints toward Lincoln D'Angelo.

CHAPTER 48

T *his is who you are.* Daniel was right, Sawyer thinks. This is who *she* is. Not her father or uncle or wife. And she's not going to fear herself. Not with so much counting on her.

Her back is straight, and her voice is strong as she begins.

"Perhaps no one can understand the pressure of family legacy Lynell Elysian lives under better than myself. Our families have been defined by the Registration for decades. We live on the same coin but spent most of our lives never meeting. It would've been the easiest thing in the world to hate each other. After all, our grandfathers shared a partnership that ended in betrayal. But I'm tired of living in a world where hatred calls the shots.

"Lynell's life has been defined by death just as mine has. Just as many of yours have. Our children are desensitized to violence and murder. Do they not deserve better? Do we not all deserve a world where death is a terrible inevitability, not an acceptable currency?"

She pauses for a breath and looks down at the paper she'd carried onto the stage with her. The commotion from the crowd is deafening even as she refuses to hear it.

"My wife was killed by a puppet of those who hold our country by a choke hold. Her life was taken because she was going to speak her mind. I'll never get her back. But I don't intend to allow her killers to win. Ellery's words are worthy of being spoken. You all need to hear them. So, six years late but still as applicable as ever, here is the speech you were all robbed of.

"Ellery's favorite flower was a peony. They are big and fluffy and colorful. They smell amazing and, most importantly, they're resilient, which was important in our house because I kill every plant I touch. But peonies can live for more than a century, practically dying in the winter but returning as beautiful as ever. They're not defeated by death.

"We are alive. Every single one of us is alive today and we have the right to take advantage of every breath we take. It is your right to live without the fear of death. But who here has never considered the moment they take their last breath? Who has not felt death's proximity growing closer every quarter?

"Nearly seventy years ago, this country invited death to coexist with life. We were destroying ourselves. We killed each other over disagreements on the composition of human life. The value of life. The worth of one life over another. I can't begin to understand what the world was like then, but I can imagine the fear because we are still feeling that today. The Registration ended the war. It was a sufficient Band-Aid over our country's bleeding wounds. But it never stopped the killing. It redirected it. It has made death—"

The rest of her sentence disappears into a distant BOOM that shakes the building. Sawyer's balance is kicked out from under her feet, and she hits the floor, lungs collapsing with a violent expulsion of air. Before she can pull in more breath or regain her senses, something heavy collides with her. She doesn't realize it's a person until large hands encircle her throat.

CHAPTER 49

Daniel lurches forward, the explosion using his momentum against him. He barely manages to not fall and has to dodge several people falling, fighting, and struggling to stand after the entire building shook from what must've been a bomb.

He doesn't care about any of them. His focus is still firmly latched on Lincoln D'Angelo, now pushing to his knees. He's in the process of standing when Daniel reaches him.

"Hey, asshole," Daniel says.

Lincoln turns, eyes wide and face blank. His lips part, but he never gets to reply. Daniel pulls his arm back and puts all his strength into the punch that lands in the center of Lincoln's face. The man drops onto his back, letting out a pained, "Oof."

Daniel drops to his knees on top of Lincoln and punches again. Blood flies from Lincoln's face and Daniel's ears roar, whether from the explosion or his own overwhelming anger, he's not sure.

The tiny section of his brain still holding onto clarity and sanity screams at him to stop and think. Lincoln isn't the only man behind Anna's kidnapping. And he's not *Daniel's* dad. He didn't do to Daniel or Lynell what he did to Sawyer. But the rest of Daniel's brain doesn't care. All he sees is the man responsible for so much pain. The man who stole Daniel's daughter and betrayed his own child. Daniel sees every man, every father, that has fucked up their kid's lives.

He sees Eli abandoning Lynell. Alan abusing her every day of her life under his roof. Eric beating Zach and threatening Harlow's life. Daniel's own father fleeing to England, leaving him and his sister and mother to face this dangerous life alone. Daniel even sees himself, failing Lynell and Anna. He sees them all in Lincoln's face and is filled with the desire to punch until there's no face left to see.

"Stop!" Lincoln shouts.

Daniel doesn't want to stop. He punches again.

"Please!"

Another blow.

"Wait!"

This time, Lincoln manages to block the punch and the break between blows gives Daniel's mind time to catch up to his actions. His hands stay fisted but his arms freeze. His shoulder throbs and his bile pushes up his throat when he sees the damage already done to Lincoln's face.

"I didn't want this," Lincoln moans.

Daniel isn't sure what he means by 'this.' Daniel beating him? The bomb? Sawyer being a rebel leader?

"You tried to kill your daughter," Daniel spits.

Lincoln shakes his head. He might be crying, but it's difficult to tell through the blood. "No, no. Just show her that she's better than this. She has to be."

Daniel still has no idea what the man is saying but he doesn't care. The rage is receding, replaced by fear. He leans away from Lincoln and is pushing to his feet when someone grabs his arm and forces him around.

"We have to go," Hayes says. "Now."

Daniel gives Lincoln one more disgusted look before following Hayes, hoping desperately that the last few minutes haven't ruined everything.

CHAPTER 50

Lynell's ears ring. Black dots pepper her vision. She groans, belatedly realizing what happened. Blinking away the shock of the explosion, she rolls onto her stomach, and looks for Sawyer.

Someone has climbed onto the stage and tackled her. A man is holding her down, yelling something into her face.

Thomas Johnson.

"Sawyer!" Lynell screams, struggling to stand.

By the time she's back on her feet, Malakai has already started running. She watches as he leaps through the air, catches Johnson around the middle, and yanks him off Sawyer. The men roll together for several feet, throwing elbows and punches.

"Are you okay?" Lynell asks, reaching Sawyer's side. She grabs Sawyer's arm, helping to pull her up.

"Yeah." Directly after saying it, Sawyer coughs and spits out a glob of red saliva. She groans, holding a hand over her midsection.

"We have to go," Lynell says. "Malakai!"

It takes a few moments for Malakai to extract himself from Johnson, who looks crazed and bloody from the fight. He starts to lunge again, but other guards have already arrived. Lynell doesn't stay to watch them subdue Johnson. She and Malakai run the other way, pulling Sawyer along. Once backstage, Lynell frantically looks around for Daniel.

The door between the audience and backstage swings open and her heart stutters from hope to disappointment to a modicum of relief when Hayes steps through.

She catches his eyes and mouths, "Danny?"

Without hesitation, Hayes turns around and rips open the door again.

Lynell lets go of Sawyer. "Take her to the greenroom," she tells Malakai. He nods and she takes off to follow Hayes. The absolute chaos of the auditorium overwhelms her senses and it takes a few blinks before she's focused enough to search for Hayes and Daniel. She finds them not far away, Hayes dragging Daniel in her direction away from a beaten and bloody man on the ground.

"Danny!" she yells.

At her voice, Daniel looks up and walks faster, meeting her a second later with a concerned expression.

"I'm okay," she says. She grabs his hand and notices his red knuckles.

"It's fine. Later," Daniel says before she can ask.

Screaming erupts from the crowd. The three of them run through backstage to the greenroom, Hayes shouting orders as they go. Once safely inside the room, Lynell lets go of Daniel's hand and drops to Sawyer's side. They wait for too long until Hayes is certain the way outside is clear.

"What happened?" Lynell finally asks, sitting between Daniel and Sawyer in the back of a car.

"Someone must have tampered with that bomb Drea and Sawyer set up, because it was five times the size," Malakai explains. "And it went off too late."

"How did Johnson get in?"

"We don't know yet."

"Are you okay?" Lynell asks Sawyer.

"Yeah, just bruised."

"We're headed to the hospital," Hayes says. "Ramsey had the whole floor cleared out."

"Is Anna still there?" Lynell asks.

"Yes," Hayes says, and blissful relief and anxiety replace Lynell's blood. "Harlow is going to meet us. Everyone will be there."

That should calm Lynell down, but it's as if there's a block between any possible relief and the chaotic hurricane of confusion and fear. She leans into Daniel and watches Sawyer the entire drive, waiting for the other woman to crumple or explode or disappear.

But she stays there, corporeal and alive next to Lynell, the entire drive. Sawyer is there, following them into the hospital, up the elevator, and onto the quiet floor devoid of visitors or more than a handful of nurses and doctors.

Any awareness of Sawyer evaporates when Lynell hears a soft female voice talking and a reply that sounds like a child's murmurs. She and Daniel rush to the patient room where the sounds are coming from. The door is half open and Lynell almost barrels inside but Daniel's fingertips on her wrist stop her. He taps his knuckles on the door.

"Yes?" someone says.

Lynell and Daniel step quickly inside.

The room has one bed with two occupants.

Anna. Her beautiful daughter. She's sucking her thumb. Her large blue eyes, as wet as the ocean they're made of, watch Lynell and Daniel closely. She's in the arms of a woman who must be Catherine Imes, Zoe's sister. Catherine looks older than Lynell thought, but that's likely because of the stress she's been dragged through these last two weeks.

There's a bruise surrounding her right eye, and on her jaw. Her right eyebrow is cut in half by a scab and her bottom lip is freshly split. Her right arm is in a sling but there's no cast or splint, so Lynell guesses it's due to a sprain or maybe a dislocation. Other than that, there are no obvious signs of abuse. She has an IV in the crook of her arm and a monitor attached to her chest. A smaller monitor is stuck to Anna, though there's no sign of an IV.

It's been two weeks since they've seen Anna, but she looks bigger already. Lynell was bracing herself for Anna to look tiny, underfed, and broken. But for the shining eyes welled with tears, she looks completely fine. Catherine clearly took all the beating for them both.

Lynell doesn't think she'll ever sufficiently express her gratitude or remorse to Catherine. Not even dying would be enough to thank her for protecting Anna.

They couldn't have asked for a better family to have taken her daughter in.

"Catherine?" Daniel asks. He takes a step closer to her but stops when Catherine tightens her hold on Anna and pushes her back further into the hospital bed. "I'm Daniel and–"

"I know who you are," Catherine says, her voice harder and lower than Zoe's.

"Are you okay?" Lynell asks, wincing at the futility of the question. She might as well sew her lips shut.

"I've been better." Catherine's steely glare softens a little and she adds, "But I'm alive." She rests her chin on top of Anna's head. "We both are."

Lynell's eyes drop back to her daughter, and any control over her tears becomes nonexistent. They fall with earnest, desperate to be liberated. She feels her lips moving and hears the words and knows she should slow down, say less, calm down, but she can't. If she could fix this, fix everything for all of them, by simply talking, then she would never take a breath.

"I'm sorry. I'm *so* sorry. Honestly. I wish more than anything that you and Anna were never caught up in this. I wish I could take it away or change it all. I wish I could erase myself from your life. Both of yours. I can't begin to say how sorry I am for what you've been through and who you've lost. I'd trade places with Zoe in a second. All of you deserved so much better. But I'm so beyond grateful for all of you. You've taken care of m—Anna when she didn't have anyone else because of me." She almost said 'my daughter' but managed to grapple the words into submission before they passed her lips.

She doesn't yet have the right to claim Anna. Not in front of the woman who lost her sister, lost her safety, lost her innocence, and has been more of a mother to Anna then Lynell has ever been. She's going to tell Catherine that, to tell her how kind and brave Zoe was and all her plans to make up for it all, but the pause gives Lynell necessary space to shut up. She inhales sharply, the breath wobbling over sobs, and steps back, as if the distance will keep her from breaking further.

Catherine is going to yell at her, tell her to leave the room, promise to keep Anna away from them forever. Catherine has the right to do any of that to Lynell.

But Catherine doesn't do it. Instead, she sets her jaw, looks down at Anna, and says, "Anna is okay. That's the only thing that matters."

This time, Lynell can't hold herself up. She manages three steps to the chair next to the wall before her muscles stop working. She folds herself into the chair, unable to see through the onslaught of tears. Her brain screams at her heart to *pull itself together, this isn't the time for theatrics*, but her heart doesn't have ears and she's not strong enough to hold everything back now that it's broken free.

Her sobs are gongs in her ears, but she thinks she hears Catherine speak.

"That man, Ramsey. He works for you, doesn't he?"

"For Lyn, yeah. Is he okay?" That's Daniel's voice. Lynell would know it in any state.

"Yes. He's in the room across the hall. He saved our lives."

"He saved ours, too."

Lynell has no concept of time. By the time the tears slow down, her body barely has energy to breathe. Then she looks up and sees something that could stop even that.

Daniel, standing next to Catherine's bed, holding Anna. His knuckles are still red, but the blood has dried. Anna is perched on his side, tiny hands pressing against his jaw as she explores his growing stubble. He blows out his cheeks, then she slaps her hands to them and he lets out what must be all the air in his lungs.

Anna laughs.

Lynell could listen to that sound on repeat for the rest of her life.

She keeps watching them, the tears now silent as they slide down her cheeks. The love and hope alive in her scatters every dark thought to the shadows. Her mind goes blissfully quiet for a moment, then, motion in her peripheral vision has her head snapping to the side.

It's only Hayes, repositioning his stance. Seeing him makes her think of Ramsey. The man who risked his life to save every member of her small family. She should go to his room to check on him, thank him, and update him.

She'll do that. But not yet. Right now, she wants to soak up every peaceful moment with her daughter and husband that she can. She returns her attention to them and meets Daniel's eyes.

"Want to go see Lynell?" Daniel asks Anna in a quiet voice. The child looks slightly nervous but still nods. He walks over and asks Lynell, "You good?"

For a response, she nods and holds out her arms.

Daniel sets Anna into her lap.

It's not the first time Lynell has held Anna, but it very well could be. Anna squirms and looks back at Catherine, who doesn't smile but also doesn't demand to have the child returned.

"Hi," Lynell whispers.

Anna turns to her. She reaches up and touches Lynell's wet cheeks. Maybe she's imagining it, but she thinks there's a hint of recognition in Anna's eyes.

"Want to tell me your name?" Lynell asks.

A beat of uncertainty before, "Anna."

The word melts everything in Lynell.

"I'm Lynell," she says.

Anna smiles.

There's still so much to do. Harlow has to get the CCC from Lincoln, who will hopefully take the bait and believe Sawyer already has the information. They have to stir rebellion in the people. Ramsey has to use the information he found from something called the *Midnight Files* to postpone any announcement, or implementation of the policy change.

Lynell has to use the code.

It will all happen, she's certain of it. But it can start tomorrow, after one night where they're all together, safe from bombs, bullets, family betrayal, or anything else. Lynell will grant herself one night before everything changes.

Then she'll do anything necessary to create a better world for the perfect child sitting in her arms. She will not be stopped. She's the Elysian heir. It's not a role she's forced to play anymore. The identity, and everything that comes with it, is woven into the very strands of her DNA.

Her life has been written in blood. Her inheritance and legacy were carved into history using the lives of nameless strangers. She will never escape the permanent stain of death.

But she can transform it. She can take the blood of death and make it a thing of life instead. She can leave her daughter a better legacy than the one she received.

She already did the impossible and survived the Registration. Now she'll do what has never been done.

She'll conquer the Registration. Rewrite it into something good— using her own blood.

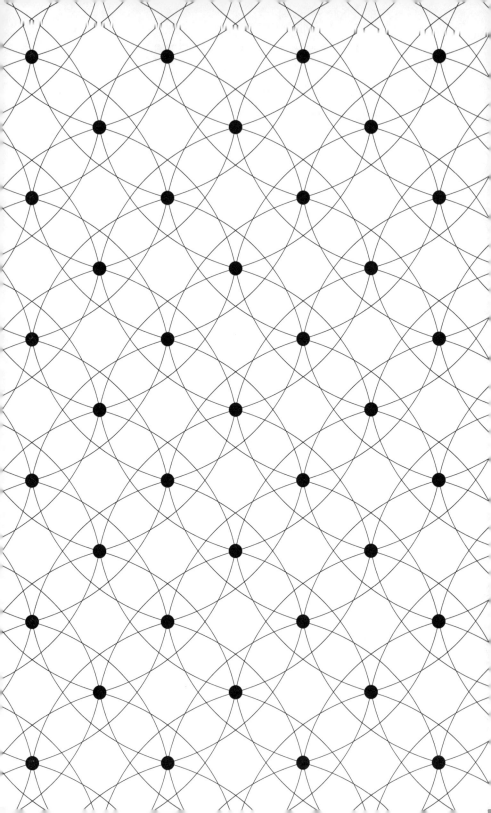

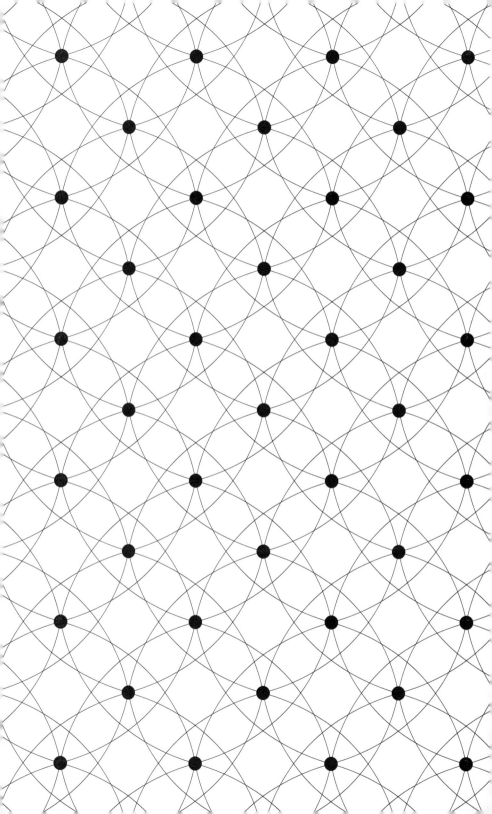

ACKNOWLEDGMENTS

Thank you to Helga Schier, my wonderful editor and hardworking member of the CamCat family. You make every project you touch so much better, and this book wouldn't be what it is without you. Your dedication to supporting me and other authors is nothing short of incredible, and I'm forever grateful for your editorial eye and encouragement.

I equally owe my amazing agent, Julie Gwinn, for all I've accomplished thus far as an author. It doesn't matter what project I throw your way; you always receive it with joy and help me polish my work. Any author would be lucky to have you on their team, and I can't wait for what the future holds!

Talking about this book being what it is, there are several others I must thank. First, Lo. No matter how busy you are, I know I can count on you to jump into whatever Google Doc I'm working in and read through my earliest drafts. Your comments and suggestions are essential to my ideas turning into books. Thank you for always being willing to brainstorm with me, talk through the story, come up with what cars my characters would drive, and everything else you do during the writing process.

Next, thank you, LJ. You are one of the most consistent and loyal friends I've ever had, and I cherish our weekly writing dates. You have not only one of the wisest minds I know but also one of the kindest hearts. Thank you for being among the first readers of *The Registration Rewritten* and offering your critical eye. Never doubt your value, worth, or voice.

Finally, Mollee, thank you for jumping in last minute to help edit this book. Your feedback is always exceptionally helpful. I feel honored to know you and call you one of my best friends. Remember how brilliant, loving, supportive, and creative you are, and don't sell yourself short. Keep writing—you have stories that deserve to be told.

Unlike many other creatives, I never had to pursue my dream without support. Since the beginning, my parents have been on my side, full of confidence in my abilities. The words needed to express my love and gratitude for them have not yet been invented. Mother, I dedicated this book to you for a reason. It's not an exaggeration to say you are the *best* mom anyone could ever hope for. You are kind and genuine and humble and stronger than you'll ever know. You are my best friend and my hero. Daddy, I still miss you every day and love you more than ever. Thank you for teaching me to be the best version of myself. You always had time for me, and I'd do anything for a little more time with you.

My incredible family doesn't stop there. Meg, thank you for being my biggest fan and never making me doubt that you'll always be on my side. I love growing with you and enjoying life, whether in New York, through books and TV shows, singing in the car, or just talking. Haley, thank you for being such a fantastic big sister who is always there to protect us. You are one of the bravest, strongest, most loyal, and hard-working people I know. If I'm half the person you are, then I'm happy with who I've become. CJ and Aaron, thank you for not only being near-perfect husbands to my sisters but also my brothers. You are both so patient and loving, something us Lawson girls desperately need. You are blessings to our lives.

Dog parents will understand when I say I have to thank my dog, Teddy Lupin. I wish you could read or understand when I say I love you more than I probably should. You saved my life, gave me purpose when everything felt hopeless, and made me smile when I didn't think I had any reason to.

I wouldn't be who I am, and this book wouldn't even exist if I didn't have an entire team of wonderful friends who I definitely don't deserve. Zoe, you are the evergreen friend everyone dreams of, but so few are lucky enough to have. Thank you for always being my person. Cat, you're the type of rare steadfast friend that I long to be with on my best days and my worst days. Thank you for being my J for life.

Alex, I never expected you to be in my life, and every day, I'm grateful that you are. I admire your strength, resiliency, faithfulness, and humor more than you know. I love you today and always.

Cate, you're a twin flame, and you deserve to burn as bright and hot as you can. Thor, there's no one else I'd rather call and watch amazing shows that rip our hearts from our chests with. Both of you are some of the most inspiring people I know. Thank you for sticking with me through it all.

I can't name everyone, but all of you, my friends and family, have given me priceless love and encouragement, for which I'm beyond grateful. Thank you to everyone at CamCat and Seymour for partnering with me on this dream-fulfilling journey.

And finally, thank you to every reader who decided to take a chance on me and pick up this book. As cliche as it sounds, your support is what makes this possible. Don't ever stop reading because there are endless deserving stories waiting to change your life.

ABOUT THE AUTHOR

M adison Lawson writes sci-fi and fantasy novels full of suspense, social commentary, diverse characters, and complex relationships. She received her B.A. in English with a focus on Creative Writing from Texas A&M University and her M.A. in Literature from North Carolina State University. Madison is an award-winning short story author, and her debut sci-fi thriller, *The Registration*, was picked up for a film adaptation by Sony Pictures. Madison is represented by Julie Gwinn at the Seymour Agency.

Growing up in a small Texas town, Madison began exploring the world through the page so much that she often lost sleep to finish a book, got detention for writing a story in class, and convinced herself it was okay to read Harry Potter one more time. As her curiosity expanded, she began writing, reading, and traveling to discover the world, make new ones, and understand her own a bit better.

Madison currently resides in Texas with her dog, Teddy Lupin.

To learn more and stay updated, visit Madison's website, madisonlawson.com, and follow her on Instagram (@madisonlawson) or Twitter (@madisonlawson96)

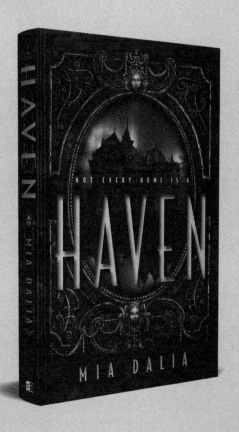

JEFF

DRIVE, DRIVE, DRIVE until the road is done with you. Until it spits out the final destination at you like some kind of begrudging reward. Until you're through. That's the deal.

The summer morning is unseasonably autumnal, as crisp as a freshly starched shirt. The leaves are looking festive, though it is much too early for them to change colors. Maybe they are gearing up for the months to come, putting on a dress rehearsal. In theory, at least, the leaves are meant to make up for the miserable New England winter that inevitably follows their departure.

Jeff Baker tries to enjoy nature, and when that fails, he focuses on the road itself—the way it disappears beneath the wheels of their five-year-old forest-green Subaru. It's soothing in a way, the certainty of the motion, the steady progress forward. North.

There used to be a time when Jeff loved driving; a time that by now is but a vague, faded memory. His first car was a beat-up '87 Mustang, produced decades after that pony was at its prime, and the two of them were inseparable. The AC never worked, so the windows were rolled down for as long as the weather permitted, the wind blowing through his hair like freedom, like youth itself. It seems that ever since then, his vehicle selections have been increasingly less exciting, more sedate, staid. Practical. Now here he is, behind the wheel of a car that positively announces to the world that a liberal-minded, environmentally conscious family is inside it. A cliché if there was ever one.

Jeff knows that it suits the man he is today: a husband, a father, someone with a stalled but reasonably lucrative middle management job; a man with a softening gut and receding hairline, wading knee-deep into the still, murky waters of middle age. He sighs, adjusts the rearview mirror, and tries valiantly to ignore the kicking at the back of his seat. When that doesn't work, he snaps, abruptly and frustratedly.

"JJ, how many times have I told you not to do that?"

Jeff can feel his son's insolent shrug without turning around to see it. It's one of JJ's signature moves—the kid is the personification of a sullen, surly teen. Although they share a name and Jeff loves the kid, he recognizes nothing of himself in Jeff Jr.

His son is lazy, aimless, slovenly in a way that physically upsets fastidious Jeff. What's worse is that the kid doesn't seem to be clever or interesting or even funny. He gets by in school with barely passing grades, participates in no sports or extracurriculars, and spends most of his free time glued to one screen or another. The video games he plays seem too violent to Jeff, but he can't figure out a way to ban them outright, because: (a) he doesn't want to be that dad, and (b) he doesn't necessarily believe in the connection between on-screen and real-life violence. After all, violence has been around long before video games were even invented.

Still, it's difficult to think of a bigger waste of time than these stupid games. At least the kid wears headphones to play them. The constant *rat-tat-tat* of guns in the background would have driven Jeff crazy by now.

Jessie is sitting next to her brother, occupying, it seems, only half of her seat. Wherein her brother's girth is forever expanding, Jessie appears to be shrinking. It makes her brittle, Jeff thinks, in appearance and temperament. So much like her mother.

The two kids are only a couple of years apart, but you'd never guess they were related. Never guess they came from the same house, the same people. There is a lot of nature vs. nurture baggage there that Jeff doesn't care to unpack.

His daughter is unfathomable to him; the way she talks in text message abbreviations, the eager manner in which she subscribes to the latest trends without ever taking a moment to examine them for herself, how appearance-conscious she is.

This isn't a great time to be a kid. There's a steady bombardment of social media disseminating shallow values, unchecked materialism, and flat-out lies.

He doesn't even know what wave of feminism everyone's supposed to be riding now. Jenna might, but he loathes to ask. She wouldn't just answer, there'd be a lecture. Jeff despises being lectured and tends to avoid long-winded debates. He likes simple things, short, clear-cut explanations, yes-or-no answers whenever applicable.

Jenna is doing her nails next to him; *screech-screech* goes the thin emery board—a sound Jeff can feel in his vertebrae. He hates it, hates the way he has to just sit next to her and inhale the dead nail particles she's sending into the air, but asking her to stop would be as futile as expecting JJ to stop kicking the freaking seat.

Jeff likes to think of himself as a man who picks his battles. And there have been some. Over the years, that number has dwindled. Lately, he doesn't know if it's just something he tells himself to cover the fact that he has, slowly and inexorably, become a pushover.

Jenna is thin like their daughter, all gym-tight muscles and yoga-flexible tendons. She has been dying her hair the same shade of blond for so long that sometimes Jeff is surprised to see her natural light brown color in the old photos. She looks good, younger than her years, certainly younger than Jeff.

If he doesn't tell her that enough, it's only because they don't talk that much anymore in general. Or maybe it's because her undeniable physical attractiveness appears to have lost the sunny warmth, easy charm, and shy sexiness of the Jenna he fell in love with so long ago. It's almost like his wife has Stepforded herself, trading in all the delightful aspects of her character, all of her fun quirky self for a perfect surface appeal.

Is that what two decades of marriage do? Or living in a society obsessed with youth and beauty? Or being a mother? Or—a more somberly horrifying thought—is that what living with Jeff for twenty years does?

Jeff wants to hit the rewind button and watch their lives again, in slow motion, noting every salient plot point, every crucial twist and turn, to understand how they got here. But it doesn't work that way, does it?

From one of his more interesting but ultimately useless college courses, Jeff remembers a quote: "Life can only be understood backward, but it must be lived forward." It's one of those sayings that sounds smart unless you really think about it, because once you do, you'll see that the former part of it is ultimately useless, while the latter is simply unavoidable.

Jeff had a good time in college. He did well in high school too: just smart enough, just fun enough, just inoffensive enough to ensure certain easy popularity that enabled smooth sailing amid the various social cliques and characters. After graduating, out in the real world, his stock began to slowly but definitively tank. He could never quite figure out why; perhaps, something about the absence of predetermined social structure, or increased expectations.

Either way, by the time Jenna came along, he grabbed onto her like a life preserver and held on steadily and faithfully ever since.

He had never done well on his own when he was young, found solitude oppressive. Depressing, even. Now, of course, he'd kill for some, but it is much too late. Even his man cave occupies only a corner of the basement at home, sharing the rest of the space with laundry and storage and the moody boiler, and thus is perpetually loud and nowhere near private.

He likely isn't going to get much peace and quiet for the next month either, but he agreed to go anyway.

After all, one simply doesn't say no to a free vacation.

And sure, as he pointed out to Jenna while they were making plans, it wasn't entirely free: there was the cost of gas, tolls, food, etc., but the main expense, the house, was taken care of, and so here they are now, driving, driving north.

"Are we there yet?" JJ pipes up from the back seat, too loudly because of the headphones he rarely takes off.

It was funny the first few times—no, not really—but now it grates on Jeff. He forces a smile. "Almost," he replies with false cheer.

The truth is, everything around here looks exactly the same to him: the same tall trees, the same tiny weather-beaten towns, the same road signs. If not for the chatty GPS, he would be hopelessly lost. He wants to thank his digital navigator every time she points out a turn amid a number of interchangeable ones; she seems to be the only helpful person around. Though, of course, she isn't even a person.

Jenna is listening to an audiobook. Without even asking, Jeff knows it's one of those domestic thrillers she loves that really ought to be shelved under women's fiction. Something about scrappy heroines untangling their husbands' dark secrets. He tried a couple out of curiosity some time ago at Jenna's prompting and found them unoriginal, uninteresting, and blandly indistinguishable from one another. When Jenna asked for his honest opinion, he gave it to her, like a fool. They never spoke of books again. He shouldn't have said anything; he certainly shouldn't have added that it was still a step up from her normal self-help fare.

Jeff returned to his historical tomes, fictional and otherwise, spicing it up occasionally with a science fiction novel. Though lately, the sci-fi has been garbage; he hates all the space operas, all the sociopolitical messages overriding the plots. To him, the genre has always been progressive, subversive, and thought-provoking. He doesn't know why it needs to try so hard now.

He tried giving some of his old books to his son, only to find them unread, languishing amid the piles of trash obscuring the floor of JJ's room. Watching movies together proved equally futile. Jeff cannot force himself to sit through the mindless violent crap his kid enjoys. And if he has to see another freaking superhero movie . . .

Jeff doesn't know what his daughter is listening to, but it's likely the latest in pop music. Of all his family, Jessie is the most mysterious one to him. Almost a complete stranger, with his wife's features and his surname. He loves her just as he loves JJ, but the kids remain baffling.

They are supposed to be a team. That was presumably the grand idea about the obnoxious cutesiness of giving their kids J names.

"We'll all be a J. Baker," Jenna told him at the time, back when he still found her enthusiasm, if not all of her ideas, adorable, and here they were. A family with interchangeable initials. Like they were the sort to embroider them on sheets and towels. Like it mattered.

Jeff is the only one listening to the radio. Never politics—after the last election, he had stopped following them entirely. Now that there is another one coming up, it's difficult to care or remain hopeful. A new decade is looming ahead.

The 2020s have an apocalyptic feel to Jeff. He sticks with music. The station he played while driving out of the city had faded into static miles ago, and now he's stuck with some local DJ inexpertly mixing '80s and '90s hits, plying the nostalgia factor.

And hey, it's working. Jeff remembers these songs. Remembers singing along to them, driving to them, drinking to them, making out to them. Sometimes he even sings along, but quietly. If his voice gets louder, he gets a kick in his seat, which may be unintentional but feels like an unspoken criticism. He wishes he didn't save up his vacation days so diligently. He wishes they weren't set to expire due to the new company policy so that splurging them all on a month-long vacation was his best option. He wishes Jenna didn't have to inherit access to this supposedly amazing lake house within driving distance that's simply too good to pass up.

The house was never mentioned to him before, but then again, neither was Jenna's aunt, Gussie. Or maybe she was, and Jeff forgot? Would he forget a name like Gussie?

From what he gathers, the childless, eccentric aunt left the house to her entire extended family to delight in on a timeshare basis, and Jenna finagled a month just for them.

They haven't had a vacation in a while, and never one this long. Jeff faked excitement at the idea the way he felt he was supposed to, but his actual reaction was closer to the eye rolling the kids gave when Jenna made the announcement. At the time, he thought it was going to be trying and likely tedious. He still thinks so, but he went along with every step of the plan, and now they are almost there and it's much too late to change a thing.

Maybe it will be relaxing, he tells himself without much conviction. Maybe the house will be larger than their small townhouse or have better soundproofing. Maybe he'll finally be able to finish the Nero biography he started months ago.

The voice of experience pipes through, laughing at the tentative hopefulness of Jeff's maybes. Jeff sighs and focuses on driving. "Sunglasses at Night" plays on the radio, and he sings along under his breath. "Don't switch a blade on a guy in shades, oh no . . ."

A kick in the back of his seat follows as swiftly as a slap.

CamCat Books

VISIT US ONLINE FOR MORE BOOKS TO LIVE IN:
CAMCATBOOKS.COM

SIGN UP FOR CAMCAT'S FICTION NEWSLETTER FOR
COVER REVEALS, EBOOK DEALS, AND MORE EXCLUSIVE CONTENT.

CamCatBooks   @CamCatBooks   @CamCat_Books   @CamCatBooks